LUCILLE GUARINO

ELIZABETH'S
MOUNTAIN

A NOVEL

Black Rose Writing | Texas

First printing

This is a work of fiction. Names, characters, businesses, places, events, and incidents are either the products of the author's imagination or used in a fictitious manner. Any resemblance to actual persons, living or dead, or actual events is purely coincidental.

ISBN: 978-1-68513-392-4
LIBRARY OF CONGRESS CONTROL NUMBER: 2023948130
PUBLISHED BY BLACK ROSE WRITING
www.blackrosewriting.com

Printed in the United States of America
Suggested Retail Price (SRP) $21.95

Elizabeth's Mountain is printed in Garamond Premier Pro

*As a planet-friendly publisher, Black Rose Writing does its best to eliminate unnecessary waste to reduce paper usage and energy costs, while never compromising the reading experience. As a result, the final word count vs. page count may not meet common expectations.

For *Michele, Marissa, Olivia* and *Sofia* – two generations of tales

"The mountains are calling and I must go."
–John Muir

PRAISE FOR ELIZABETH'S MOUNTAIN

"Guarino's exploration of enduring relationships through a lens of historical and contemporary romance, coupled with her well-developed characters, makes this book a noteworthy read for those who are drawn to stories that span different periods and showcase the complexities of life and love."

–Literary Titan *****

"*Elizabeth's Mountain* by Lucille Guarino is a thoughtful and poignant novel that fulfills the reader's expectations of women's literature. I liked that the story had two heroines from different generations. Elizabeth's memories evoked the glamour and nostalgia of historical literature, while Amanda's life contained the sparkle of contemporary romance."

–Reader's Favorite *****

"An engaging and charmingly written story that has an absorbing and life-affirming quality. *Elizabeth's Mountain* is a novel that will have its readers lingering on its pages and reflecting on the happenstance of life. ...When you turn the last page, you're not thinking, "My what a lovely story!" When you turn the last page of *Elizabeth's Mountain*, you think, "I'm really going to miss these folks," because they feel so authentic."

–BookViral *****

ACKNOWLEDGMENTS

A huge thanks for those who encouraged me with words like *engaging, lyrical,* and *lovely voice.* And my favorite – *Please, write more!* I keep those words on a wall by my desk so that whenever doubt sets in, they remind me to press on. In no particular order, these people deserve to be acknowledged during my writing process.

Ann Leslie Tuttle and Pamela Taylor for their proficient freelance editorial services, and my dependable beta readers: Erica Haraldsen, Katherine D. Caldwell, Laura Ashley Barrow, Barbara A. Luker, Marie W. Watts, and Iris Glatzner Leigh. Also, to Jeannie Neufeld, who was there from the very beginning of this novel and in my writing journey.

To Black Rose Writing's acquisition team and its creator, Reagan Rothe, thank you for your excitement for *Elizabeth's Mountain* and for bringing me into your writing family.

And finally, to my husband, Peter. Thank you for getting equally excited for me in all aspects of my book journey and for inspiring some of its wonderful mini-plots.

ELIZABETH'S
MOUNTAIN

PROLOGUE

Ninety is older than I ever saw myself - nearly two decades longer than my parents lived. But here I am. I still go on . . .

I can hear the hullabaloo coming from my kitchen, my hearing aid picks up a word or two – cake . . . candles . . . the shushing of little ones. Squinting in the bathroom mirror, I push a wisp of hair off my forehead exposing an old scar under a thin white hairline. The face that looks back at me is etched with little creases and lines. Every one of them could tell a story. I wince. *I know you're still in there somewhere, Elizabeth.*

"Nana, do you need any help?" Amanda raps on the door as I smear balm over my dry lips. Amanda is my daughter Caroline's youngest. At thirty-four and unmarried, she's a nurturer by nature and in her profession as a nurse practitioner. Also my loving caregiver and companion. I've always been independent and self-sufficient - a doer and a go-getter. I'm the driver, the navigator, the planner. Or I was. Old age is humbling. "Coming, dear," I say as I reach for my cane.

Amanda and I walk toward my kitchen as lights are dimmed and singing erupts. It's a miracle of sorts that we got the whole family together. The resounding voices of my great-grandchildren make me smile as the words "Make a wish" travel to my ears. How many wishes is a person afforded in their lifetime? Surely, I've used mine up.

I have but one wish left now. Ever since I received a query letter from developers interested in purchasing my house and the two acres of land it sits on, I haven't been able to think about anything else. I haven't spoken of it to my children. Not yet. The initial purchase price offer would make their heads spin. *Oh Lord, help me to know what to do while there's still time.* I puff out the candles on an elaborate sheet cake iced with pink roses.

Caroline and Amanda have taken care of everything, from the colossal family-photo collage to the beautiful bouquet of long-stemmed pink roses. For today I can relish all these niceties and put my dilemma aside.

I wobble over to my wingback chair dressed with lace doilies in my favorite part of the house – the sunroom off the kitchen. Looking out over my deck, I'm struck as if for the first time by the mesmerizing colors and forms on display. To think my children had wanted to celebrate out in a fancy hall when you can see beautiful mountains and streams right in my backyard. Good thing I quashed that idea, just as I did when they suggested an assisted living facility to me a few years back.

"I never tire of this view," says my son, Joseph, inserting his hands inside his pants pockets while gazing outside. An explosion of wildflowers extending as far as the Appalachian Mountains waves to us. I've always believed the New Year starts with spring, the old supplanted with the new.

Joseph plops himself down in the chair closest to me while some of the others trickle in. He reaches for my hand and leans in. "You were right, Mom . . . about having the party here."

"I wouldn't have it any other way," I say.

"Well, it's official. You're a nonagenarian." It's striking how my son's sixty-five-year-old face resembles his father's - the way he smiles with the right side of his mouth tilting up, his warm, intelligent brown eyes, silvery hairs framing his temples, his casual, approachable demeanor. It dazzles me.

"Nonagenarian . . . my foot." His oldest daughter, Kathy, walks over to us. "I only know that ninety is amazing," she says right before she snatches her youngest, high-spirited son, Tommy, in mid-fall, knocking into and upsetting a table display of some of my mementos. Raising two young kids after her recent divorce observably challenges her. "All that you've seen and lived through . . . it's extraordinary when you think about it."

"Every day's a blessing," I say.

"Ninety looks good on you, Nana," Kathy says, while she rights some of the framed photos that had fallen over onto my lace-covered table. Among special photos are treasured keepsakes of some of the high points of my life, including a plaque of recognition for my twenty-five years of dedicated service as a nurse.

Amanda enters the sunroom and opens another window to give us a cross breeze. I take in a deep, measured breath, the whiff of fresh mountain air, honeysuckle, and azalea filling my nostrils. It greets me like an old friend.

Amanda moved in with me several months ago. She was in a relationship for three long, stagnant years before they mutually broke it off. I daresay, Amanda's boyfriend was about as exciting as a yawn. Biased as I am, I know Amanda is a special person, giving and unselfish to the detriment sometimes of her own happiness. Is it wrong for me to want her to experience love? Not the half-hearted, tolerant kind, but real, true love in its most fervent form. I think not.

They were living together before Amanda moved in with me. I don't like to judge, but I never understood the living-together-with-no-commitment mentality. Not one to hold back, I told her, several times, but Amanda would just heave a sigh and shake her head. Not in a dismissive, rude way, because Amanda was never unkind. Traits missing in her mother, who sapped the lot of us on many occasions.

My grandson, Joey, walks over to me with his wide-eyed fiancé, Olivia, his arm wrapped casually around her petite waist. There is nothing more joyous than watching two young people in love. You can see it in their eyes and in their smiles.

"I love your home," Olivia says. "It's so beautiful here."

"Thank you. I'm glad we were all able to come together and celebrate your engagement to my grandson as well. It was such wonderful news to me. I haven't seen my Joey in – well, it's been too long." I motion for her to come closer to my lips and whisper into her ear. "He was always my favorite."

"Nana," Joey overhears, shaking his head. "You say that to all of us."

It's true, but we do have our favorites, even if we don't like to admit it. Joey's approachable nature is so like his father's and grandfather's. It touches me.

"Say, you know those comic books you gave me when you and Amanda cleaned out your attic? I had a chance to look them up," Joey says. "The 1952

Good Girl Art issue from GI in Battle is a real gem, but the one Superman first appeared in is even rarer. It dates back to 1938."

"Are they valuable?" Amanda asks while she gathers up discarded cake plates.

"To a collector they are. And they're in pretty decent shape too."

"And to think we almost tossed them out," Amanda lets slip.

"We do need to be on our way," Joey says, his long-fingered hands clasping mine. He's got his father's and grandfather's hands. "Olivia and I have to be at work tomorrow." He gives me a careful hug, the new normal since the pandemic. But it's still a really good hug. "I love you, Nana."

My son and I exchange a secretive look. Joey and Olivia plan to wed sometime next spring. I'm giving Joey the keys to my husband's '53 Chevy Corvette, still sitting in my three-car garage, as a surprise wedding gift.

Amanda rushes over with her phone camera. "One more picture of everyone before you go."

Another memento for my overflowing table.

Evening falls and I look out through the trees of the Blue Ridge Mountains. Caroline and Amanda are in the kitchen straightening up. The others left in a string of tender hugs and goodbyes, leaving me alone and retrospective in the sunroom.

I talk to my husband in my mind as I often do in my dreams.

"I felt your presence at my party today - the essence of you. Look at how our family continues to grow, flourishing in ways we never could have foreseen. Amanda is our nurse practitioner, more than four years now. Joey is finishing medical school. He wants to be an orthopedic surgeon. Might you and I have had some influence on them perhaps?"

"Are you ready to retire for the night?" Amanda asks, coming into the sunroom and gazing out the windows at the festive lights strung over the deck for my party. "Mom's almost through in the kitchen. There's so much food left over; I told her to take most of it. You and I could never eat it all." She turns to face me. "Did you enjoy your special day?"

"Oh, yes. Having everyone together again like old times - that was the best part."

"It was really nice seeing everybody," Amanda says. "Joey and Olivia's wedding next spring will be the next time, I suppose."

"I'm almost done in here," Caroline shouts from the kitchen.

"I'll finish the rest," Amanda says.

Caroline joins us in the sunroom. "We're heading out now."

"Sure you and Dad don't want to spend the night?" Amanda asks her. "You can leave tomorrow morning."

"Dad says he's fine to drive home tonight. Besides, he has some things he wants to do tomorrow."

Things to do. I haven't uttered those words in a long while. A lifetime ago, when my days were filled with so many things to do it seemed like I never had enough time for it all. *And now, I'm forced to make some very hard decisions that will impact my family. Decisions filling up every part of my mind. If only this were easy.*

Caroline flurries over to Amanda and gives her a parting hug. "Dad's waiting." Then she comes over to me and pecks me on the cheek. "You looked really nice today, Mom. Blue is your color." Caroline's energy from today is unwavering. I imagine her collapsing as soon as her car rolls out of Asheville. Stopping short of the doorway, she turns around and walks back toward the vase of pink roses on my portraits table. "This would make a lovely centerpiece on your dining room table," she says, snatching it up as she heads out of the room with it.

"But Nana rarely goes into the dining room," Amanda calls after her.

Amanda meets my eyes. "For goodness sake," she says once Caroline is out of earshot. "What good are the roses going to do you in the dining room where you won't even see them?" She comes over to help me out of my chair. "Soon as the coast is clear I'm moving them back in here, where you can at least appreciate them."

I chuckle. Caroline has my mother-in-law's traits – possessive and interfering. Now, in her late sixties, she could be her grandmother's clone. The power of genetics is an amazing thing to watch.

"She wouldn't be my daughter and your mother if she didn't have a say in things," I say. "Can't blame her for trying."

Steadying my arm with one hand, Amanda passes my cane over to me with her other. "Sure I can."

Amanda assists me with getting ready for bed.

"Besides the roses, I think maybe my bed should also be moved into the sunroom since that's where I always want to be," I say, reclining into my pillow.

"Nana, if I didn't know you so well, I'd think you were kidding."

I give her an affectionate gaze, ever more grateful for our shared living arrangement. The dispirited loneliness I felt during the Coronavirus lockdown is still too recent in my memory, lingering like the dreams that transported me back to when I was eighteen years old, the persistent threat of polio on everyone's mind, triggering genuine fear and worry.

"Night, Nana," Amanda says, turning to leave.

"Good night, dear."

In the hodgepodge of my memories, it astounds me that seventy years ago can seem like only yesterday, but as I reminisce about my past I don't focus on the hardships anymore. It wasn't always that way.

I was young during the worst years of the Great Depression, where my story begins, at a time when despair and gloom were strongly felt and unconsciously passed down to the children. Back then, I didn't know there were other ways to feel . . . until I did.

CHAPTER 1

Elizabeth
1932 to 1951

Two miscarriages had preceded my birth in 1932. My mother would later tell me why she believed I made it to full-term. She remembers how I cried, loud and defiant, my tiny fingers curling into tight little fighting fists. "You were my strong girl," she'd say, and then roll her eyes. "And quite lively."

Mom had to cut up some of her few dresses to make baby clothes for me. She and my father lived off beans and potatoes, spaghetti or rice, and anything else they could use to make some kind of soup.

In my youth, Dad was either looking for work or working short-term manual jobs. His large hands were dry and chapped whenever he held mine. He learned roofing, plumbing, and auto mechanics, which later became his most skillful and productive line of work. When work was busiest, Dad would put in as many hours as he could. It seemed he was hardly ever around in those years. Late one night, when I heard the creak of the front door, I climbed out of bed and peered into the kitchen.

"Why are you still awake?" Dad asked. I could barely make out his face in the semi-darkness. "It's very late."

"I wanted to see you."

Dad took the plate of food Mom had left on the stove for him and brought it over to the table. Glancing at me through tired, glassy eyes, he gave me a slight smile. "You're a good girl, Lizzie," he said, putting forkfuls of food into his mouth.

Wanting to engage him longer, I asked, "Can I get you something?"

"You should go back to sleep. You have school tomorrow."

Although the words "I love you" were never spoken, I felt my dad's love in little ways – a wink, a piggyback ride on Sundays before bedtime that concluded with tucking me into my bed. On some mornings, after he had left for work, I'd find a nickel on my dresser that I would spend on candy at the store just around the corner from our home in Maplewood, New Jersey.

My mother, with short wavy chestnut hair in her earlier years, often stood in front of the stove wearing a beige-printed, cotton dress that hung to her midcalf - one of two dresses she often swapped - stirring a pot of stew or sauce for spaghetti. If she wasn't cooking, she was either hand sewing or leaning over her black Singer sewing machine.

We were a symbiotic threesome – our roles clear and assured. My paternal grandparents and uncles lived in Italy, and my maternal grandparents passed away before I was born. My mother's only sibling, a brother, lived in New York, but we hardly ever saw him. So, it was just us three, making our way, doing our best.

When my mother discovered she was four months pregnant at the age of forty, she was dazed and anxious. She had, after all, miscarried twice, and the thought of becoming pregnant again after seven infertile years seemed unlikely. It explained the general malaise she'd been feeling for the past few months. But as the time moved closer to her giving birth, we all delighted in the prospect of a new addition to our family, even welcoming the unexpected disruption, and I was eager to fill the important role of becoming a big sister.

Rosemary came into this world in 1939. Though America was on the precipice of a world war, the struggling economy was somewhat easing. With healing came hope, and in the small world that was my family, Rosemary's birth was celebrated with the utmost joy.

Although I was only seven when she was born, I spoiled her. We all did. I called her Posey and took on the role of mini-mother, running to her aid and soothing her when our mother was too busy. We shared a bedroom, and often I tended to her when she stirred or woke up during the night. I'd lean over her crib, and as soon as she saw my face, she would smile with delight. I taught her the alphabet, nursery rhymes, and later, how to read.

Posey was cheery and innately playful, her silly moods in complete contrast to my more serious disposition. On many occasions, her frivolities and nonsensical activities made us laugh in spite of ourselves.

Once, Posey squeezed her little body into a bucket. "Posey," I said, "now how do you plan to get yourself out of there?" Her arms were plastered to her sides so that she became utterly stuck. Posey didn't cry or plead for help. Instead, she rolled around in the bucket in our yard, laughing as if she had invented a new game.

One of the last fond memories of my little sister was on her tenth birthday – a dark-blue plaid party dress, a cone party hat, long hair falling in ringlets, a toy piano, small bowls filled with M&M's, a lopsided, chocolate-iced birthday cake. She was happy in the moment, carefree, her dreams just beginning to bud in her garden of life.

***

The sounds and images happened in quick, harried flashes – Posey shuddering and vomiting, curly locks sticking to sweat on her feverish forehead, my mother's panicked wails, sirens, neighbors coming outside, a door slamming behind my mother after she grabbed her purse and raced to get into the ambulance taking my sister to the hospital. Before she hurried out the door, she looked at me for a split second with palpable fear in her eyes. "Tell your father!" And then they were gone, carried away by flashing lights and sirens. My eighteen-year-old self was left standing there, alone and terrified. How I wished that my boyfriend, Robbie, were there with me instead of fighting a war somewhere in South Korea. If only I could call him. He'd come over right away.

I went over to my front porch and sat in the rocking chair with the red plaid cushions. Robbie always liked to sit in that chair. My father was at work at the time. I rocked and rocked, running through what I had observed in my mind. Posey had complained of her ear hurting her, she was weak and confused, and she couldn't move her neck. The onset of her symptoms had been swift. "She's going to be okay." I repeated over and over again, and then I prayed to God.

Hours later, my sister died in the hospital. That she could have become so critically ill in only a matter of hours stymied us. It was a brain herniation that took my young sister's life; her diagnosis was bacterial meningitis. She would have turned eleven the following month.

I was in shock, and for the next couple of days, I moved around on autopilot, afraid of what it would feel like when the shock wore off.

The unbearable grief did come, as it inevitably always does. It slammed its thorny jabs right into my heart so there were moments when I thought I would also die. I might have even wanted to. But there was my mother - or the hollowed-out version of her - unresponsive and unable to move or get out of bed. She was so consumed with grief, it was as if I lost her, too.

"Mom . . . Mom, you have to eat. Let me fix you something. Please, Mom." I rubbed her back and shoulders. I brushed her hair. I brought her water and made her sip it. I lay next to her with my arm around her, talking only to her back. "Mom, open your eyes. Please. Look at me." There was a dullness behind her eyes now, the manifestation of grief.

Family, friends, a priest from our church . . . all came over to console us. But as the days and weeks moved inevitably forward, my mother retreated further into the abyss that is mourning.

Feeling helpless and lost, my father sat me across from him at our kitchen table one day. His eyes were bloodshot from crying, and it broke my heart. I had never seen him like this. "Lizzie." He put his hand on my shoulder and squeezed it. "Listen to me. You need to take care of your mother." Dad's eyes closed for a moment and then he looked me in the eyes. "She needs you." But what I heard was, "I can't do it. I don't know how."

***

"Keep a watch on her," the doctor said, his house visit confirming what we already knew. My mother suffered from reactive depression. "Just continue to give her encouragement and support, and above all, time."

My parents were equally afflicted with grief, but each mourned in their own way. While my mother shut off from everything and everyone, my father sought diversion and did the only thing he knew how to do – working night and day.

In between working a few hours a day at Angelo's, a produce market run by second-generation Italians, I took over all the household chores, the cooking, and the coaxing of my mother to eat to survive. Working at the market gave me a reprieve since laughter or music - or even a simple smile - became void in our home, extinguished by devastating sorrow and loss. When my head would finally hit the pillow at night, I talked to Robbie. "Please, be safe and come home soon. I love you, and I miss you so much." Thankfully, within minutes, I would succumb to sleep from exhaustion.

While my mother still struggled to continue her activities, she did resume some of the cooking and sewing with my help, and her former passion and pace gradually returned. I knew this because I had purchased a blouse on impulse from a mail-order catalog one day. "It's nothing like the picture," I said. "I hate it! I don't know what I was thinking." I tossed it over the back of a chair. The next day when I returned from work, the same blouse hung on the back of my bedroom door, refashioned. Tears filled the corners of my eyes when I noticed that the buttons had been removed and replaced with more ornamental ones, the cuffs were now edged with lace, and the collar had a simple embroidery motif. My mother's handiwork. This was a huge first step for her. I went over to her and kissed her cheek. She only shook her head, but I saw a glint of light come from her eyes.

My mother was never the same again after losing her child, a shell of the person she once was, but any and every sign, no matter how small, gave me hope. I needed to feel hope again. While caring for my mother, I had neglected myself, my own needs. I never really had the chance to mourn my sister's passing.

The only distraction that saved me from total despair in those days was the letters that arrived from my fiancé in Korea. It was the future Robbie described in his letters to me that gave me reason to go on.

For every letter Robbie wrote me, I wrote him back three. I wrote to him about my sister's passing, the most difficult letter I've ever had to write.

Robbie took the news hard. He and my younger sister shared a mutual fondness. He was like a big brother to Posey.

I was counting the days and hours until I could be with Robbie again, saving up to buy my very own set of china, on the path to marriage when he came home. Most girls in those days were married by the time they were twenty. Robbie had been my high school sweetheart. We'd played in the same neighborhood growing up, and we were both from Italian Catholic families. I think we always had an eye for each other, but the day that settled it was after I hadn't seen him for a few weeks one summer in 1948 since he had been away at a baseball camp. Besides singing, baseball was the other thing Robbie loved.

When we both returned to high school after that summer, I saw him standing over by his locker – a man suddenly, not a boy, his back and shoulders more muscular, his voice somehow deeper. A rush of attraction swooped in on me when I heard his full-throated laughter while talking with one of his friends.

When he turned around, he spotted me down the hall in my blue Catholic-school uniform skirt, my young curves and slender legs, and wearing my long, wavy hair down with one small barrette holding back bangs. Our eyes met and the pull was undeniable. By the time the leaves were turning colors, we were going steady.

We'd share a soda in front of a soda fountain. Once, Robbie, who often talked with his hands, knocked his soda over, spilling it onto his pants and making me laugh. He was not amused. The conversation had started lightly enough – the upcoming church dance, the home high school football game on Saturday. They were our greatest quandaries in those days. Up until then, I was untouched by war. Only the adults seemed to ruminate and talk about it. But there was Robbie talking about stopping communism from taking over the world, the draft, and service to our country. I just wanted to think about the dress my mother was making me for the dance.

His boyish side grin, the way he swept his dark hair to one side, and the smell of his tobacco and spicy cologne all attracted me. He liked to sing along with songs on the jukebox. He had a smooth baritone voice that made me giddy every time he sang. We were so young, but we were crazy in love with each other. I used to practice saying his surname with my first. I liked the way it sounded. From Elizabeth Moretti to Elizabeth Bianchi. It was pleasing to my ear.

We attended our last dance together at St. Joseph's Church a couple of weeks before Robbie had to leave to serve our country – me in my navy-and-white polka dot A-line dress with short, ruffled sleeves, Robbie wearing his nicest high-waisted trousers and button-down shirt with his favorite red-striped tie. I felt really pretty, wearing a touch of lipstick and rouge, a thick matching headband accessorizing my long, wavy hair. The hairband had been my mother's idea; she wanted to use up the dress's spare fabric.

Robbie couldn't stop looking at me and beaming. "Your eyes look more gold right now," he said. "It's amazing how they can change from green to brown to gold."

"It's called hazel," I said.

"Well, you know what, Hazel-Eyes? We're getting married ... soon as I come home to you," he declared, and then he put a toy ring inside my hand. "You're my girl," he winked. "I love you."

I threw my arms around his neck. You would've thought he had given me a real diamond the way I acted, but I was truly enamored and remained so for several weeks, my happiness ebbing as each day drew closer to Robbie's departure.

Standing on my screened-in front porch in the summer of 1950, Robbie held me tight, my face pressed inside his chest as he crooned out Frank Sinatra's song, "Bye Bye Baby." I told him I would never take his ring off, and I stayed true to my word. I wore it for over a year, a black ring mark portending an ominous sign.

***

It was a dreary day in late October of 1951 when Robbie's mother and younger brother walked down the street in the drizzling rain toward my house. Robbie's brother held an umbrella over his mother while she leaned into him. Tightness started in my chest at the sight of them, but I quickly dispelled it. The brain has a strange way of protecting us when our instincts race ahead. Even though Robbie's mother had never stopped over at my house before, I rationalized that maybe she just wanted to say hello, or perhaps she was bringing over a cake she had baked. But one of Robbie's mother's arms was tucked inside her son's. Her hands held nothing in them.

I watched through my window as they turned onto my front walk. Robbie's mother stopped all of a sudden, shaking her head as if she couldn't go on. Robbie's brother was talking to her, gently coaxing her forward. I shuddered, swallowing hard as panic rose up in me. The doorbell rang. A feeling of dread whooshed through me as I walked slowly onto the porch, but not before I cried out, "Mom!"

I wanted to ask her why she had come, but I also didn't want to know the answer. Robbie's mother moved toward me inside my porch, opening her mouth to speak, but the only sound that escaped was a wail. She immediately started to cry, her son supporting her with his arm.

"No. No," I gasped, shaking my head, struggling to breathe. Robbie. My Robbie. I turned around. My mother had come up behind me and put her hand on my shoulder as if to say, "I'm right here."

Robbie's brother spoke first. "I'm sorry," he said. "I'm really, really sorry. We have bad news."

I looked at my mother. Her face had gone pale, mirroring my own.

Robbie's mother was sobbing and trying to talk, but it was hopeless. Words were useless. We held each other in the way two people who share their grief do – tight and clinging.

Robbie had died in battle. Two Casualty Assistance Officers had come to his parents' house the day before to give them the news. For that one whole day, I'd gone about my life as if Robbie was still alive, still full of hope for the two of us. One meaningless day. It made me strangely cross. Why did they wait to tell me?

Would it have made any difference if I had learned yesterday instead of today? Would it have changed anything? I knew it wouldn't. But being rational was the last thing I cared about. I hurt so bad, it made me physically ill.

Robbie's brother met my stricken eyes. His mouth was moving, filling in some of the details. I heard "captured terrain that bordered the North and South"... "my brother died a hero."

I half-listened; one detail was all that mattered to me then. Robbie was dead. He hadn't even turned twenty.

After Robbie's mother and brother left my house, I needed my mother. But when I looked around for her, she had retreated to my bedroom. I went to her seeking comfort. She was tucked tightly under a blanket on Posey's bed, whimpering and moaning like a wounded animal. In that instant I knew – my mother could not be my strength. I just had me. I didn't know my whole soul could hurt so much.

A dark gloom cloaked me following Robbie's passing - the flag-draped casket, the black-and-white photograph of Robbie and me at our last church dance, his last letter to me that I received two weeks before his death.

Lizzie, my girl,

I'm sorry if I can't match your letter writing. It's hard to see to write sometimes. The rainy weather, the nighttime. It can be very tough. Even though I cannot be there with you, I am with you in my thoughts. I dream of us all the time. The photograph taken of us at the dance is with me always. It's what keeps me going. I know I have to get back to you, to the way things were. I have every intention of making it back to you, Lizzie. The first thing we are going to do is go dancing. Well, maybe the second. First, I'm going to kiss you and kiss you and kiss you!

Don't worry about me. Just be proud. As proud as I will be one day to call you my wife.

I miss you and I love you so much.

Yours,

Robbie

It was the bleakest time of my life.

CHAPTER 2

Amanda
Nine months ago

I didn't anticipate ending it when I did. There was no plan. The moment just presented itself the way life's crossroads happen sometimes.

"Have you seen the TV remote?" I asked in a routine moment. Tom's eyes were leveled on his cell phone as he shook his head. I surveyed the couch where I spotted it stuck between two seats. A fleeting image flashed in my mind from three years ago when we first sat on the cushy couch inside the furniture showroom.

"What do you think?" Tom had asked, and I joked that we could lose a lot of things in those detached cushions and Tom said, "I think we should buy it." He leaned in to kiss me, smiling with all the anticipation of our moving in together, and our first joint purchase was made.

Disappearing items had since proved me right, but in the scheme of a few lost coins or pens, it didn't even come close to a greater loss - the loss of hope.

I sat opposite Tom and dropped the remote on the table. I had just finished eating Chinese takeout after another long workday. It was a day like most others, Tom in his digital world, me in my head. And then I dropped it out.

"I think we should quit us."

As he took his eyes off his cell phone for a millisecond, his downward glance told me everything I needed to know. His response was as lukewarm as our relationship had become. "Quit or take a break?" he asked, his demeanor unchanged.

"I'm going to move out," I said. "You can put that in whatever category you want."

With a typical show of resignation, Tom placed his phone face down on the couch's arm and took in one long, weary breath. For the first time that evening, he forced himself to look at me. "So, we're having this conversation now, are we?" The tedium in his voice was dispiriting, but I pretended not to notice.

"We're having this conversation," I said. "It's time, don't you think?"

"Is this really what you want?" He could have faked some kind of emotion – hurt, outrage, disappointment - but he didn't. And that, right there, was the sum of our relationship – tired and disconnected.

"I think if we're being honest, it's what we both want," I said.

It was true. We had stopped giving us attention a year or more ago, focusing on our careers and not on each other. We went from adequately interested to mostly platonic in the four years we knew each other. I tried to remember what had attracted me to Tom in the first place. He was intelligent in an unexpected way, composed and eternally boyish. He had a head of loose curly hair that was a little too long and had a tousled look, even when he combed it. I used to play with it sometimes when he would let me, running my fingers through its thick locks or ruffling the hairs on top of his head. I hadn't done that in a long while.

While Tom was busy working as a technical support analyst, balancing working from home and out in the field all over the Carolinas, I was getting my Masters of Science in nursing and then putting in hours at the hospital during the height of the Covid pandemic. The one prerequisite we hadn't considered when we moved in together was that we were not in love with one another. Our moving in together was a matter of convenience and perhaps maybe we pretended at love for a while, but there was no forward-moving progress, no intentions. We were in a stale rut and one of us had to make a move.

When Dawn, a coworker and nurse friend of mine became engaged, she glided into the hospital during our common shift as if on air, gleaming with excitement. In that girlfriend confiding moment, I told Dawn how happy I was for her and it made me realize what I was missing in my relationship with Tom – desire. I knew that I would neither feel nor look the same as Dawn if Tom had proposed to me. Hearing me say it startled me, but the honesty gave me courage. I had to accept the truth if I ever wanted to experience that feeling. I wasn't ready to give up on love. The words 'relationship' and 'lonely' should never be in the same context, and yet I was loneliest when I was at home with Tom, the frequency of his low leaning head, his distracted eyes, his back when lying in bed together. Intimacy had been replaced with artificial enactments; we both became good at play-acting.

It only took Tom a few minutes before he asked what I planned to take with me.

"Not very much," I reassured him, "and don't worry . . . you can keep the couch."

***

Much to my almost ninety-year-old grandmother's gladness, I moved in with her in the big farmhouse on the mountain. It was an easy choice since it was also close to the hospital and doctor's office where I worked in Asheville. When I first pulled into her long winding driveway, my car packed with my choice possessions, I let out a long sigh, a final respite from my recent unhappiness. I stepped outside my car, the surrounding mountains in all their serenity welcoming and comforting me, and I knew then that I was in the perfect place to begin my fresh start.

Nana is one of my favorite people in the whole world and she still demonstrates a certain level of independence despite the increasing challenges of turning ninety. But as proven during the isolating months of the pandemic, I provide her with sorely needed companionship and helpfulness. For me, she is a beacon of light, her positivity always uplifting.

Nana once told me that sometimes things happen for reasons we can't understand while we are living it. Only time can give us perspective. I guess my nana is qualified to say that. My understanding of time is how much of it I have already wasted on a relationship that was going nowhere fast. To pour salt in the wound, I learned that Tom got engaged to one of his co-workers three months after I moved out. Was she the reason for his increased disinterest? Were there signs? I was too busy in my own world to notice.

When two people drift apart, must blame be at its core? I don't think so. I was just as disheartened and unfulfilled as he was.

"Have faith," I hear Nana say. "One day someone will come along and sweep you off your feet. Just like your grandfather did to me."

To which I grumble, "Maybe that's how things were in your day, but guys like Grampa don't exist anymore." I sounded the way I felt - particularly disparaging. "Chivalry is most assuredly dead." Sometimes I think I was born in the wrong era. An old soul in a progressive age.

Nana tsk-tsked. Forever the romantic optimist, she maintains that my person is out there somewhere. I just haven't found him yet.

Since I was twelve, I loved spending time at my grandparents' house, where I felt warm and safe. It's uncanny that I should find myself back there again, unmarried at the age of thirty-four. Life is as unpredictable as it is serendipitous.

Sitting outside on Nana's deck, I'm surprised when a memory burst pops into my mind of a time when my older sister, Cecily, and I were playing in the backyard. It was in the early days when they had just moved into the farmhouse after retiring. A black bear had suddenly appeared, and Grampa ran over waving his arms and shouting while my sister and I slinked back inside the house. When Nana caught wind of what was happening she took off outside carrying two pots with her, joining Grampa and jumping up and down while slamming the pots together. After the bear had been scared off, Grampa gripped my nana's shoulder and said, more worried than angry, "You should have stayed inside, Beth." And my nana answered, "And leave you out here alone? Not a chance." They argued for a minute longer and the next thing my sister and I knew, they were holding each other in a tight squeeze, shaking their heads and laughing.

"Your stubbornness never ceases to amaze me," Grampa said.

"And I'm amazed that you're still amazed," Nana had replied.

I remember how they looked at each other, after the fear passed, their loving eyes locking, as I had seen on so many occasions.

I think, maybe, they set the bar too high.

CHAPTER 3

Elizabeth
Spring 1952 to Spring 1953

One day several months after Robbie's funeral, I slouched into my kitchen. Dad was dunking his buttered roll into his morning coffee, reading the newspaper. "Good morning," he said, looking up.

"Is it?" I muttered.

Dad let out a sigh with a look that was part frustrated and part concerned. "You know, Lizzie," he said. "We have to go on."

I wanted to scream! *That's your fatherly advice?* I felt like saying. *And what if I don't want to go on? Hmmm? Maybe I don't want to live anymore. What's the point?* I grabbed my purse and started for the door. "I have to catch the bus for work," I fumed, shutting the door behind me, and shutting out his words.

Part of me hated what I was becoming. Part of me liked the power of entitlement it gave me. No one was going to fault the grieving fiancé for her right to be distraught or indignant. A new emotion had settled in me. Anger. I was angry at the world, at God. I became spiritually disheartened and detached and was experiencing headaches every day. The isolation was abysmal.

It wasn't a feeling I wanted to have, but there it was, in all its lowliness and cynicism. I had been standing on lava for so long, gasping for air and trying not to get burned. I needed to feel in control again, to have some power over my life. Being casually cruel, not worrying about consequences. I could protect myself from getting hurt again if I stopped caring.

It made the next stage of my life easier. When summer came, I started seeing Jim Madigan, one of Robbie's friends from high school. Jim returned from Korea on a medical discharge due to shrapnel wounds to his shoulder and arm. After being medevac'd to a MASH unit where they stabilized him, Jim had to be airlifted to a hospital in Japan because of the seriousness of his injury. There, he spent the longest month of his life. Two surgeries behind him, Jim, like so many, was moving on with his life - one not comprised of war and combat and hospitals. I realized we weren't that much different, both of us trying to endure.

He came over on one of my particularly low-patch days. We sat on my front porch, talking. Mostly about Robbie, honoring his memory with funny stories of him. And then we moved on to talking about people we knew.

I remember how I first felt when Jim took the rocking chair with the red plaid cushions that had been Robbie's favorite resting spot. It startled me at first. Still wearing a close buzz cut, except for a longer mane of hair growing over his forehead, Jim leaned his head back to get more comfortable. "Nice chair," he said, putting his hands on his knees and rocking. I felt a pang of resentment. How does God decide who lives and who dies? Why did Robbie and my little sister have to die? It was going to be another dark day; I could feel it creeping its way inside my head, dragging me down. I didn't like where my feelings were headed. I wanted Jim to leave. Soon.

Jim said something then, breaking through my heated thoughts. "I'd like to visit you again, if that's okay. I missed this. I miss Robbie. He was my friend, too. Tommy...Billy...I miss everyone."

I put my head in my hand, feeling another dull headache coming. My thoughts were all over the place, muddled by heartache tinged with gloom and guilt. Internally, I said, I don't know if I can do this. I can't do this. I'm not ready. It still hurt so much. Nevertheless, I nodded. A survival instinct took over.

Jim's visits became more regular and frequent, and I welcomed the camaraderie. Jim shared in my grief, making my journey easier. I was coping better, and I wasn't experiencing as many headaches. We became convenient friends - two lonely people offering emotional comfort, passing time together. No expectations, no commitments, no risk of getting hurt.

One day when Jim came over, he surprised me. "How about taking in a movie? I haven't been to the movies in a really long time." Jim stood in my doorway, his damaged shoulder slightly lower than the other, smoking a cigarette and smiling with self-confidence.

"Right now?" I asked.

"Yeah. Why not? It's a Charlie Chaplin movie called *Limelight*. What do you say?"

I was ready to decline his invitation. I think I even said so in my mind. Then, the idea of going to the movies - something I used to enjoy very much - took control.

Walking side-by-side with Jim on a beautiful autumn day after a string of mechanical-living months was like an awakening. I felt alive again. I took in the colored leaves under my feet, the warmth of the sun on my face on the way to the theater, and the crisp air when Jim and I headed back home afterward. In the dark theater, Jim had reached for my hand and held it in his. I didn't pull away, though I knew I should have. Our friendship had grown closer, more comfortable in the way two people who've confided so much in each other become, but I didn't want to encourage romance. Or at least I didn't think I did.

Walking under a full moon that chilly evening, Jim put his good arm around me. I glanced up at the moon, defined and illuminating, and for a brief moment, I wondered if it was a sign of a new beginning. It could be a sign, I supposed. Why then did I still feel so guilty?

When we arrived at my house, Jim tilted my chin up before kissing me on my lips, sweetly and gently. We stared into each other's eyes; neither one of us spoke a word. I looked away first, sensing his anticipation for an invitation to follow me inside. I knew he didn't want the night to end. Our friendship had taken a pivotal turn, and I needed to be by myself, to think and clear my head.

I wanted to tell him that things were moving too fast but instead, heard myself say, "Today was a pleasant surprise, but I'm rather tired and have to get up early tomorrow." I'm not sure what Jim thought, but to my ears it sounded nervous and tinny. I bit my lip. "Thanks for a nice evening," I added, turning to leave. "Good night, Jim."

"Well, good night then," Jim said, sounding a little dejected. And then, without missing a beat and using his best Humphrey Bogart accent, he said, "See you again, kid."

I had to smile and nod. When I got to my doorway, Jim was shouting something at me from the sidewalk. "Hey!"

I spun around. "What?"

"I almost forgot. My dad and I are looking at some new Chevys. Maybe next time we won't have to walk," he said, unshakeable. "I'll be picking you up in the new car."

My mother and father were sitting at the kitchen table when I walked in, looking expectant, hopeful even. "Where's Jimmy?" my mother asked, flirting with his name. "I saved him a slice of apple pie."

You too? Things were so much less stressful when Jim and I were just plain friends. Why did I have to explain myself? Why must there be expectations? Hadn't I wanted to avoid all that? "He had to get home. He has an early day tomorrow." I lied.

I went to my bedroom to lie down. I could be alone in my anguish in my room, the room I shared with my sister's ghost, where sadness lay in wait for me.

What right did I have to be happy? The first anniversary of Robbie's death was coming up. I turned on my side and faced Posey's bed, still made up in that tidy way before the covers got turned down. I visualized her pulling down the cover and tucking herself in.

"Are you sleeping, Lizzie?" she would ask.

"No, Posey," I would answer. "I'm reading."

"Can you read to me?" she would then say. "Please, Lizzie. Please read to me."

"It's late. You should go to sleep."

"Just for a little, Lizzie. Please."

Reading was a special time we shared. I pulled out C.S. Lewis' newest book, *The Lion, the Witch and the Wardrobe*. Posey would have enjoyed it. I never got the chance to read it to her.

"People who have not been in Narnia sometimes think that a thing cannot be good and terrible at the same time," Lewis wrote.

Good and terrible. Only this wasn't Narnia. This was my life. I did what I did on so many nights. I cried myself to sleep.

***

The hustle and bustle of the Christmas season was a satisfying diversion. I even allowed myself some holiday merriments – decorating, listening to songs, baking cookies. And I secured a temporary, part-time job as a cosmetic counter assistant at Bamberger's in downtown Newark, New Jersey. The department store had eight floors, and its white-gloved elevator operators designated it the ultimate shopping experience, covering an entire city block. I still kept my part-time hours at the market too, which had more flexibility. I welcomed the longer, steadier workdays. Keeping busy meant there was no room for anything else.

Jim was busy too. Besides lots of physical therapy for his damaged arm, he was working alongside his dad learning the plumbing business. Occasionally, on a Sunday, Jim would join my family and me for dinner. I could hold off my mother's persistent invitations only so much. It was good to see her get excited about something again, engaging in life. She would make meat lasagna, knowing how much Jim liked hers, or some other kind of pasta dish with meatballs. Sundays were usually pasta days.

It was the day before Christmas - a day that should have been uneventful but, in the end, turned prophetic. I was standing at my bus stop outside Bamberger's after a frenzied last-minute shoppers' work shift. A Salvation Army volunteer was ringing a bell nonstop near a bright red kettle. I walked over and dropped a few coins into his donation bucket. On my way back, I passed a street preacher on the corner handing out prayer cards to anyone who would take one. I accepted the religious card from his outstretched hand. He smiled, thanking me.

My bus pulled up, so I started toward it. "Peace be with you," he called after me. I turned, and gave him a polite smile before boarding.

Once seated, I read the prayer card.

For I know the plans I have for you, Declares the Lord, plans to prosper you and not to harm you, plans to give you hope and a future. - Jeremiah 29:11

I slipped it inside my purse and rested my shopping bag containing Jim's new shirt on my lap. Riding the bus, I thought about the new president who was going to take office in January. Dwight Eisenhower's number one campaign promise would hopefully put an end to the war.

The new year rolled in, and instead of being laid off from my holiday position at Bamberger's, management told me I could stay on part-time until a permanent, full-time position opened up, which could be sometime in the spring. In the meantime, I considered having a talk with my parents about a new kind of motivation that was beginning to grow inside me. At first, I dismissed it, thinking it was just a response to what I'd lived through – my sister's illness and death, my boyfriend dying from battle wounds. I understood that the course my life had taken was leading me there. But the goal of becoming a nurse continued to bubble inside me, and I started looking seriously into programs. I'd need to apply by late spring if I wanted to start in the fall.

On a cold, rainy day in late March, I'd started toward the Market Street bus after work when the freezing rain on my face reminded me I'd left my umbrella in the store. I rushed back to get it and returned in time to board the bus, finding a seat in the back.

The sights outside the rear window that day were familiar - winter not letting up, a gray overcast, people on foot all bundled up and clutching their scarves and hats against the icy, cold rain. I was grateful to be seated inside the warm, dry bus while the restless sound of sleet pattered around us. I was looking forward to spring. It meant I was getting closer to starting my new full-time position in beauty sales, and I'd soon be filling out the necessary application forms for nurse's training. I wanted to keep all my options open.

A skid, a spin-out, a violent shake. Then screams echoed throughout the bus, some coming from inside my head. The bus lurched forward, and I was launched out of my seat. A tangle of flailing limbs and passengers being tossed like dolls flashed in my vision before my body was hurled into another's. The noise was earsplitting and screeching, exploding in my head before everything went dark.

CHAPTER 4

Amanda

I start up the stairs to my bedroom after seeing Nana to hers. Snippets of her party replay in my mind.

The weather had turned out for Nana. When I awoke to my alarm and pulled open the drapes and sliding doors to my small private balcony, I was elated to see what a crystal-clear day it was starting out to be, the blues of the mountains more brilliant than the sky, the tingling air cool and comfortable. The sweet, soft aroma of late springtime could already be felt, and I sighed. I love how each season dresses up the mountains in its distinct splendor – vibrant wildflowers, lavish greens, autumn golds and crimson, the whiteness of snow against a sapphire blue sky. It shouldn't have surprised me that Nana would have put in her special wishes to the mountain god. It made me smile.

By late afternoon everyone at Nana's party had dispersed throughout the house and outdoors, eating and drinking and chatting away. I moved to the sunroom to join my cousin, Kathy, Uncle Joe's oldest daughter, so I could talk to her in private and ask how she was coming along. A recent divorcee with two young children, single-parenting except for every other weekend. I learned that she and the children were able to stay in her house, the one redeeming quality of her ex-husband.

While we talked we watched her active six-year-old son, Tommy, line up his little plastic dinosaurs on the ledge of one of the sunroom's windows.

"I know I'm blessed," Kathy said. "I have two beautiful children. But it can get hard sometimes."

"You're doing great," I said.

"Don't get me wrong. I would never want to go back to the way things were while I was married. The fighting . . . the noise . . . the cheating - I don't miss any of that. It's just hard being a single mom – even just being single again."

"It will get better, Kat." Neither one of us is currently in a serious relationship so I identified. "Never, ever lose hope." I hugged her tight. "You deserve better," I said over her shoulder, the meaning behind my words restoring us both.

When I turned around, Tommy was throwing a tiny ball against the window, trying to knock over the dinosaurs he'd lined up. His mother rushed over. "Tommy, no!"

I went over to him and squatted down so I was level with his eyes. "Do you suppose the dinosaurs like the view of the mountains too?"

"Yep," Tommy said. "Too bad they're extinct."

I looked up at his mother, impressed. "Well, maybe we can pretend for now that they aren't, and we're all living in prehistoric times."

"That was a really long time ago," Tommy exclaimed.

"Sure was," I said. "I think your dinosaur friends like it here. Do you know how I know?" I said, stoking Tommy's precociousness. "See all those mountains and trees way out there? Well...parts of all of that are a billion years old."

"A billion?!" Tommy set the dinosaurs back up again on the sill, turning each one around so they faced the window, a calmer renewed interest in his activity.

"Thanks," Kathy said while I stood up. "That should keep him occupied for . . . oh, I don't know . . . maybe five or so minutes."

"Kat, if you ever need me for anything, please call. You don't live too far."

"Thanks," she said. "Perhaps we can do a single girls' weekend sometime."

"I'd like that," I said.

Tommy raced past us, his five-minute attention span ended. "Let me go see what other mischief he's gonna get himself into," Kathy said and then followed after him.

My cousin, Joey and his fiancé were getting ready to go back home to Jacksonville. I held them up for one more picture of everyone before they left. I set my phone up on a tabletop tripod before calling everyone together and grouping them around Nana. Leaving a spot for myself, I'd just sprinted over in time to be in the picture when my sister, Cecily's three-year-old daughter, strayed from the group.

"Come back over here, Posey," Nana said.

"Mom," my mother said a little too loudly, startling us all. "That's Lauren."

Confusion spread across Nana's face as knowing looks passed from one to the other. It's astonishing what the brain remembers. Some days, Nana's as sharp as a tack; others, not so much.

I pulled little Lauren back into the group before the auto setting snapped the picture, procuring another picture for Nana's collage.

***

I slip on my nightshirt and head to the bathroom to brush my teeth. I'm grateful Nana's ninetieth birthday party went off without a hitch, mostly thanks to my mother. She took care of everything, which in essence means no detail was left to chance. From the caterers to food selections, she handled it all. I love my mother. The eldest child of my grandparents, she is strong and self-confident, a force to be reckoned with. She is also controlling, inflexible and painfully direct. No matter how old I am, she still elicits anxiety in me.

Mom had given me instructions for today's celebration - an e-mailed list of things I needed to take care of before she arrived at the house. With my upcoming four-day trip to Nashville a couple of days away, I was grateful that the list was just simple things. *Help Nana get ready. Talk her into wearing that pretty blue-print blouse with the tie sleeves (you know the one). It'll look good in pictures. Her white pearls would go nice with it too. Florist should arrive by noon - the pink roses should go in the dining room. Caterers will be there by noon too.*

Good grief. I sigh. At least it's over now.

I plop into bed and my head sinks into the pillow, my mind still swimming with conversations and activities from the day. It was good seeing everyone and getting back to family gatherings and celebrations of milestones.

I roll onto my side and see the suitcase I've begun to pack for the upcoming American Hospital Association summit in Nashville. I leave in two days. This leadership workshop is the first since the pandemic that will be in-person, and I hope to be able to mix business with pleasure.

Being in a relationship, even a mundane one, did have its benefits. I'm aware that the homebody in me has been forced out of her comfort zone. I'm also aware that the caregiver in me often puts others before me, but I've been spending a lot more time with myself these past few months, and while I have to admit it's a bit uncomfortable, I'm going to take my own advice and remember how to have fun again.

My phone dings.

Dawn
Hope it's not too late. Are you still awake? How did your grandmother's party go?
How many dresses do you plan on taking on the trip? Countdown begins to the Music City . . . !!

And . . . I have the perfect wing girl to do it with.

CHAPTER 5

Elizabeth
March 1953

White lights, bright and blinding, hung from the ceiling over me. I heard voices - several. Someone was wiping my forehead, my eyes. A woman in a white cap with a fringe of gray curls. "Doctor, she's waking up," the woman called out.

Through my wet, blurry vision, a man's face appeared. He was pulling down on my lower lids, shining a light into my eyes. "Pupils are dilated," he said to the woman wearing white.

The room spun around me. From just outside it, I could hear a loud commotion, scuffling of feet and jumbled, urgent voices all talking at once. I tried to ask where I was, but my tongue felt like cardboard.

"You're in a hospital emergency room," divulged the man, warm brown eyes gazing into mine. "You were in a bus accident. I need you to lie still now. You have a nasty cut on your head. I'm going to stitch it up for you." He took a cloth with bright red splotches covering it to dab my forehead and must have seen fear in my eyes. "We're just cleaning you up some more."

The terrible bus scene came back to me in photoflash clips. I remembered I was due at work, so I tried to lift my head off the table, but my heart and head pounded and I felt like I was going to throw up. I managed to catch a glimpse of the front of my blood-splattered blouse and my blood-stained coat thrown over a chair. *Oh my god!* I was frantic. "I have to get to work." Angelo would be wondering where I was.

"You aren't going anywhere, honey," the woman said from somewhere in the room.

The man placed his hands gently on my shoulders. "Now, now, I need you to try and stay still for me. Okay? Can you do that for me?"

"Haftogo." I muttered. "My parents."

"We can call your parents as soon as I get you stitched up."

The thought of my parents receiving this phone call sent a jolt through me. "No! You can't call them. You can't."

"I'm sorry, honey, but don't you think we should? They might wonder where you are." The woman was talking again. She came up alongside the man. "We should let them know."

"No," I insisted again. "You don't understand . . . it'll kill them."

The man and woman looked at each other. "Tell you what," the man said. "If you lie perfectly still and let me take care of that gash on your forehead, I'll have the phone brought closer so you can call them yourself. That way they can hear your voice. Would that be better?"

My head was killing me - a headache like I had never known, worse than a migraine. I squeezed my eyes closed and took a small breath. "Okay." I acquiesced. What choice did I have? Achiness pulsed in my right arm. I tried to lift it, but the pain became excruciating. "My arm," I cried.

The man saw the panic and questions in my eyes. "Relax now," he said. "Your arm is broken. We're going to fix that too, but first thing's first." He looked over at the woman in white. "Hook her up."

"What're you doin'?"

"We're going to give you something for the pain."

I turned just in time to see an IV needle inserted into my hand. *God, this isn't happening. How did I get here? In an emergency room.*

"My name's Dr. Paterson," the man said, engaging me in something of a conversation as a distraction. "And this is Nurse Agnes." He nodded toward the woman. "What's yours?"

"Elizabeth."

"Can you tell me if you're feeling any pain in your neck or shoulder, Elizabeth?" I shook my head. "You got pretty banged up," Dr. Paterson said, matter-of-factly. "But you're going to be okay," he reassured. "You were lucky."

I closed my eyes in dizzying pain and confusion. *Lucky? Is that what you call it when you're lying on an operating table in the ER?* I didn't quite see it that way.

***

The first couple of days in the hospital were a blur. My fatigued body didn't feel like it belonged to me. Everything hurt and I slept continuously, days melding together without any distinction.

"How are you feeling, Elizabeth?"

I willed my eyes to open. "Tired," I slurred. "So very tired." I focused weakly on the kind face leaning over me in the dim hospital room, recognizing the face of the doctor who was with me in the ER.

"Rest is good. It's your body's way of trying to heal," he said, before my eyelids fluttered shut again, transporting me to dreamland, playing ball on the sidewalk with Posey or dancing with Robbie while he whispered sweet words in my ear.

One early morning I felt a wet coolness on my skin, heard clanging dishes and trays, and my eyes sprang wide open. "Well, hello there," a young nurse said as she finished sponging me down. "You're just in time for breakfast." I inhaled the scent of cooked eggs and toast sparking a healthy hunger, and she helped me sit up. I ate like I'd never eaten before, my stomach gurgling back to normal. The nurse nodded, evidently pleased. "Be back later."

In the following wide-awake days, I learned the harrowing details of the bus accident and why Dr. Paterson had used the word "lucky" to describe my condition. In comparison to others who were on that bus, my injuries were not life-threatening. Apparently, the driver had lost control due to icy road conditions and hit black ice too fast. The bus spun out and toppled on its side before colliding with a tree. Six people who were sitting up front died, including the driver. Eight others were seriously or critically injured.

I was filled with an eerie sense of contrition and humility and gratitude. That I may have only escaped mortality by seconds lurked in the back of my mind like an omen. Was it just a fluke? Or was it the plan all along? A sense of purpose and meaning began to emerge, feelings that had lain dormant for such a long time. The truth reared up in my heart - I didn't want to die. I had been granted a second chance at life and I wanted to get back to it . . . just as soon as I could go home.

My parents visited with me for hours on end, especially my mother who couldn't do enough for me and wouldn't leave, falling asleep in the chair by my bed. I never wanted her to see me sad or frustrated, and it put a lot of pressure on me. I realized I was still trying to protect her.

After a nurse assisted with my first real shower and shampooing dried bloody flecks out of my hair, my mother brought over some of my favorite beauty products and my long, white eyelet nightgown so I didn't have to remain in the hospital's gown.

I had recently gotten my plaster cast on when Peggy, a girlfriend of mine from high school, came to see me. She was the fourth person to sign my cast after my mother, my father and Jim. I saw it as an opportunity to relieve my mother, telling her we wanted to have some private girl time. And I even convinced her I was doing much better and didn't need her to come every day. Then I told her I wanted some new clothes for when I hopefully started my new position at Bamberger's, and she got right to work on sewing outfits for me.

"When does the new position start?" Peggy asked.

"It could happen sometime next month," I said. I'd missed the deadline to apply for the nursing program, so I decided to take the full-time position Bamberger's offered me. Plus, I'd need the money I had saved to go toward a car now, and not for nurse training.

"Will you be able to start on time?"

"I hope so. I'll get my own counter."

"I'll be sure and look for you," Peggy said. "I shop there all the time. We can have lunch together in the upstairs restaurant."

It all sounded so wonderfully normal. "Yes. I'd love that."

Jim brought me candy and flowers and magazines daily and promised me a ride in his brand-new Bel-Air as soon as we got the chance. Before parting, he leaned down and kissed me on the lips. "See ya' tomorrow," he said. Even though I protested and told him he was too busy to come every day, he just shook his head at me. "Let me worry about that. Just work on getting better." If there was one thing I liked about Jim, it was that he was so darn nice; but at the same time, it was also the one thing I found annoying about him. It frustrated me and I couldn't understand why.

One morning, an older nurse came in to check my vitals. "Dr. Paterson will be in to see you again later today."

"Again?" I asked.

"He last looked in on you during one of his night shifts, while you were asleep. He's been working around the clock, tending to some of the others hurt in the bus accident. You're very fortunate."

"I know," I said. "I heard how bad some of the injuries were."

"Oh, yes, well that. But also because you were lucky he happened to be on call that day. He's kinda new here, but we've been hearing good things about him. He was a trauma surgeon in the Army. I'd say you're in pretty good hands."

"You said he was in the Army?"

"Yep. A surgeon. And a very good one, which I can attest to." She came over to my bedside and studied the sutures under my hairline. "Ah, yes," she said. "This is going to heal quite nicely. In time, the scar won't even be noticeable on that pretty, young face of yours."

I sighed. "I'm very grateful. So, Dr. Paterson was in Korea then?" I asked, continuing my train of thought.

The nurse peered into my eyes with her steely blue ones. "That's right, hon'. They tell me his MASH unit wasn't far behind the front lines." She gave me a tight-lipped smile before she stood up to her full height, which appeared petite in stature.

"It's you," I remarked, remembering the sound of her voice, the curly gray spirals poking outside of her nurse's cap. "You were in the emergency room with me." I read "Agnes" on the name tag pinned to her lapel.

"That was me all right. And I must say . . . you look a helluva lot better than you did that day."

I winced. "Explains why no one would lend me a mirror."

Later that day, as promised, Dr. Paterson stopped in to check on me, wearing a white lab coat, open to reveal a blue tie partially hidden under a stethoscope, and carrying a clipboard. He looked right into my eyes, a genial smile broadening on his face. "Hello, Elizabeth," he said, drawing the curtain between me and the other patient in the semi-private room, making my space seem even smaller. "You look bright and alert today."

I put down the comic book Jim had brought me – *Adventures of Dean Martin and Jerry Lewis*.

"So, how are we doing?" he asked, considering the cast on my broken arm. He placed the clipboard at the foot of my bed and came closer. Leaning over me, he gently touched my shoulder and neck area.

I remembered his face from when I was in the ER, the one I glimpsed through my haziness in those first couple of days when all I wanted to do was sleep. I hadn't realized how young Dr. Paterson was, his tender brown eyes and presence surprising me. A moment of self-consciousness stilled me.

"Are you feeling any pain in these areas?" he continued. He looked candidly into my eyes. "Can you move your neck a little for me?"

I did what he asked. "Feels okay."

Dr. Paterson stood up, pulling a pen from his coat pocket so he could write something on my chart.

I couldn't stop thinking about what Nurse Agnes had told me earlier about him. Contemplating how to broach the subject, I acted on impulse and forced it out quickly. "I heard you were an Army surgeon in Korea."

Dr. Paterson remained unfazed. "That's right," he nodded, still perusing his notes.

"My fiancé died over there." It just spilled out of me. "It was over a year ago."

His gaze lifted from his clipboard. "I'm really sorry to hear that."

"His name was Robbie. Robert Bianchi." I paused, waiting for any sign of a reaction. *What if Robbie hadn't died right away? What if he had a chance to say some final words?* It couldn't hurt to ask. I ventured on. "He was only nineteen. You didn't by any chance . . ."

Dr. Paterson answered before I could finish. "There were so many," he said with compassion. "Too many to tell apart. I saw a lot of young people - so many very young ones - eighteen, nineteen-year-olds who were brought to us right from the front lines." He took a seat in the chair next to my hospital bed, his clipboard resting on his lap, and looked away for a moment.

Once again, I was startled as I saw his handsome, youthful face, his downcast meditative eyes. "I'm sorry," I said, giving him a sheepish smile. "I just thought, maybe..."

"It's okay. I understand."

"It must be hard to talk about. I mean, what you've seen."

"It was very sad, very hard."

"Robbie was fighting somewhere along the line that divides the North and South," I said.

"Yes. A lot of heavy fighting went on there. So many brave young men. I'll never forget them."

"I know so little. I don't know if he died right away, or if he . . ." My voice cracked and a sting of tears came to my eyes. Dr. Paterson patted my shoulder. "It's just that I haven't had a chance to talk to anyone about it, no one who will listen to me anyway. My parents . . . well, it's too much for them. Ever since my younger sister passed away. My friend, Jim . . . he was wounded over there; he doesn't like to talk about it. He'd rather talk about cars and comics and...." I rambled on. "I don't blame him, of course. So many feelings are bottled up inside of me; sometimes I feel like I'm going to burst."

Dr. Paterson glanced at his watch. "I still have a few more minutes. I'm listening."

I smiled.

"You know, that's the first time I've seen you smile." He smiled in return.

A shy feeling came over me and I looked away for a moment. "Do you think it's strange? You know... that I feel the need to talk about it?"

"Not at all. Talking and healing go hand in hand. Keeping everything inside can stunt the healing process. You have to go through it to experience the truth before you can move on. There's no easier way. I understand how you're feeling," Dr. Paterson said. He sighed. "My time there . . . what I saw . . . well, it was beyond my worst expectations. That's my struggle."

"I'm sorry," I said again, placing my good hand over my heart, the other dangling outside my plaster cast. "It's hard to even imagine the horrors of war. You were there. You saw it firsthand. Forgive me."

"No. We're doing what we need to do, as hard as it is. Talking about it."

"Were you over there long?"

"I put in my two years' service. I received my doctor's draft notice as soon as I finished medical school. Then I was shipped off to Korea."

I shook my head in disbelief. Could anything be more challenging than hands-on training treating victims of battle wounds? "I don't know what to say."

"Well then, perhaps we can change the subject back to *you* and how you're feeling," Dr. Paterson said, smiling and resuming his doctor role. "Do you have any health questions for me?"

"Well, my headaches are better. But my arm not so much."

Dr. Paterson got up out of the chair and checked the elevation of my bed. "How have you been sleeping?" He asked.

"Ok, I guess."

"When you lie back, I want you to elevate your broken arm, keeping it above your heart. Like this," he said, stacking two pillows under it. "This will help prevent swelling. I'll see to it you get more pillows."

I fell back against the mattress and briefly closed my eyes, feeling both rested and tired. Mentally and physically.

"Lucky for you, your break didn't require surgery since the bone fragments didn't shift out of position," Dr. Paterson said. "Depending on how fast you heal, the plaster cast can probably come off in three weeks. Then we can put your arm in a brace, which should be more comfortable for you."

"I'm not in as much pain anymore. It's more like a stiff feeling."

"That's expected," he said, "as you continue to heal."

He glanced at the comic book I had tossed on my bed when he walked in. "Highly recommended reading," he teased.

I picked up the soft, thin-papered book and grinned. "From my friend I told you about."

"The one who likes comics," he said.

"I know you're busy and I've kept you. I'm sorry."

"That's a whole lot of sorry's," Dr. Paterson said. "No need to be sorry."

Nurse Agnes poked her head into my room. "Dr. Paterson, can I talk to you for a moment? Sorry."

He looked at her and then back at me. We both chuckled. He picked up his clipboard and walked over to her. "No need to be sorry."

Dr. Paterson wasn't what I had expected, although I didn't know what I expected. The doctors I had ever known . . . well, they were different somehow - older, more reserved. It was touching how Dr. Paterson's face could shift so naturally from serious to warm and friendly. I was still smiling, even long after he had left.

CHAPTER 6

Amanda

I throw myself onto one of the hotel room's queen-sized beds and kick off my low-heeled pumps, staring out the floor-to-ceiling windows as if in a trance. The panoramic view of downtown Nashville is magnificent. The sun has already set, and the city's lights have begun to flicker on.

"I'm so glad you were able to book the corner room," Dawn says, standing in front of the windows with her arms crossed. "What an amazing view up here." Dawn and I preferred sharing a room rather than getting a connecting one so we could spend more down time together.

"Yes, it is, isn't it?" I murmur.

Mesmerizing minutes later, Dawn goes over to the other queen-sized bed and sits on its edge. "Sure you don't want to grab something to eat?"

It's 8:15 already and, although I missed dinner, my short flight from Asheville to Nashville has made me tired. "I'm not hungry," I say, rolling over onto my side, facing her. "You?"

"I'm going to get some peanuts or something from the vending machine," Dawn says. "Do you want anything?"

"No, thanks. A shower and a good night's sleep are what I need most right now."

"Remind me when this thing starts tomorrow."

"Eight-thirty sharp."

"I'm ready for it," Dawn says. "Especially the part that comes during and after our spa treatments. If this is anything like last year's virtual, we're going to need some play time."

I nod. Where these workshops are typically long on information and statistics, they fall short on excitement. We'll need to be rested if we want to stay awake during the training.

While Dawn leaves to find the vending machines, I pull my iPad out of my attaché, scanning the conference program once more. The first two days will be led by healthcare attorneys, the last two by renowned doctors. Tomorrow's format will focus on medical malpractice and minimizing losses. I sign out, already dreading those lectures.

A new message appears on my cell phone. It's from Dorothy, Nana's part-time caregiver. She had dinner with Nana before heading out. Dorothy has been with us for two years, aiding Nana in every aspect of her daily activities. I know I can count on her while I'm away. I make a mental note to be sure to call my nana after tomorrow's sessions, before she goes to bed.

I hang up the clothes I'd packed – suit jackets, skirts, and pantsuits for the days, summer dresses for nights. The sleeveless, rainbow-striped metallic dress is my most provocative, I think, observing it on the hanger - chic with a deep V neck and much shorter length. It will show a lot more skin than the other dresses I brought. I threw it in at the last minute, arguing with myself over whether or not I'd even wear it.

Dawn returns with a handful of snacks. "Things are beginning to get interesting." Her eyebrows shoot up. "A swarm of drop-dead-gorgeous lawyers just entered the lobby."

I shake my head and grin. Dawn has a way of overstating everything. It's her mojo, which is why I like her so much. "You had to go all the way down to the lobby to find a vending machine?"

"I went on a quick tour. Wait'll you see the rooftop terrace!"

"So, the men in the lobby - how do you even know they're lawyers?" I ask, more interested in how she concluded they're lawyers than in the drop-dead-gorgeous part which, of course, is subjective.

"I overheard them talking about the healthcare conference. They had that lawyerly look."

"What is the lawyerly look exactly?" Dawn has once again pulled me into her web of intrigue.

"Open-mindedness, outgoingness . . . it shows in how they carry themselves. You know, the defenders-of-freedom and negotiators-for-peace type. Trust me, they were lawyers. Not as narcissistic as our hero doctors."

"Wow," I say, shaking my head. She's done it again. Overplaying, overstressing, and overgeneralizing. What's even stranger is that I actually believe her. "I suppose we'll find out tomorrow, won't we?"

Dawn passes me an open bag of M&M's. "No thanks," I say, returning my attention to the closet.

"They all looked rather young, too." Dawn continues. "Thirty-, maybe forty-somethings."

"Hmmm," I say, glancing down at the diamond ring on her finger. "Too bad you've joined the Unavailable Club now."

"Yeah, but you haven't," she's quick to point out. The sound of it stings a little but I know she didn't mean it the way I felt it. "Hey, you never know who you could meet."

"By chance," I say, "in those ten or so seconds of evaluating everyone, did you also happen to notice if any of them were married?"

Dawn lets out a groan. "Okay, so I didn't get that far. Yet. Besides, like I've been telling you, my cousin is really interested in meeting you. He'll be an usher at my wedding, and you'll be partnered with him. He keeps asking about you."

"He doesn't even know me."

"Well, through me he does," Dawn says. "And . . . I might have shown him a few photos of you on my phone, so there's that."

"Ouch," I say.

"Look, it can't hurt to just meet him. All you have to do is say the word."

"The word?"

"That you're *ready* to put yourself out there again."

"Oh. That word." I shake my head. "I love you for trying. You and my nana would get along great."

Dawn laughs just before her eyes fall onto my figure-hugging striped dress, still with its price tag, now hanging in the closet.

"We-ell," she says, tacking on an extra syllable to the word. She lets out a soft whistle and runs her fingers over the metallic fibers. "Someone's pulling out all the stops." She reads the price tag and whistles louder.

I shake my head. "I don't even know why I brought it," I confess. "It's just taking up space."

***

"Only eight more hours to go," Dawn says as we arrive at one of the Marriott's three restaurants for breakfast. It's crowded with the convention's attendees. "We can do this."

"I have to do this," I say, setting down my plate of egg white omelet and fruit. "I promised Dr. Cullen a detailed report on my return." Dawn and I take two seats together at a small table.

"Look over there," Dawn says, eyeing some suits that have just entered the room. "That's them."

I try to follow her gaze. Three men, dressed sharply in two-piece suits, clear camaraderie between them, amble over to the breakfast buffet.

"Now tell me those aren't lawyers," Dawn says.

I pull out the program from my conference bag, looking at photos of the lecturing attorneys on the schedule for today and tomorrow. "This one right here," I say, pointing at the headshot, "looks like he could be one of them." Dark ash-blonde hair, short on the sides, longer on top with no part, a short, uniform-style beard and mustache, pensive gray eyes. I look back up from the photo to the men assembled at the buffet. "Yep, that's him. He's the speaker for the afternoon session." I read his short bio aloud. "Jesse Taylor, Esq., a 2007 graduate of Duke University School of Law, practicing healthcare attorney since 2012 with special expertise in medical malpractice defense."

"Did I call it or did I call it?" Dawn says, patting herself on the back. "Well . . . was I right?" she asks, looking over at them and then at me.

"About them being lawyers?"

"No. Well, that, too, but about the good-looking part?"

"I guess," I say in a non-committal way, rising from my chair. "I'm going to get some coffee before this thing starts."

I'm at the coffee bar fixing myself a cup when a hand reaches over mine for a creamer. "Excuse me," a deep voice says as I turn from the table.

"Certainly," I say, stepping aside to make more room. I look up after securing a lid on my hot cup of coffee. It's him. Jesse Taylor. He's no more than two feet away from me. Our eyes lock reflexively, independent of our wills. We gaze into each other's eyes long enough to border on awkward, but neither of us turns away. I can't help thinking there's a down-home boy hidden beneath the guise of impeccable grooming and an expensive-looking suit. "Hello," I say finally, offering him a handshake while maintaining eye contact. "I'm Amanda."

"Hello, Amanda. I'm..."

"Jesse Taylor," I say. I must be blushing. His smooth hand has a firm grip. I make a mental note - reasonably self-assured and confident. No wedding ring. "I recognize you from your photo in the program. You're one of today's speakers, isn't that right?"

"Yes. That would be me," Jesse says, releasing my hand. "I go on after lunch break." He resumes adding creamer to his coffee, stirring it. "Promise you'll hang in there 'til then," he says, cracking a warm smile that lights up his face. I detect a slight genteel drawl in his voice, an accent adopted perhaps in recent years.

I nod and smile back, switching the hot coffee cup to my other hand. "Well, I'm usually a morning person, but I'll give it my best."

"You know, you look familiar to me," Jesse says. "Perhaps we've crossed paths somewhere before?"

Someone from Jesse's group walks over to us. "They want us to get started," he says.

"Matt," Jesse says, "this is Amanda. Amanda . . . Matt." We shake hands, exchanging glances.

"Nice to meet you, Matt," I say. Matt looks around the same age as Jesse, but I notice he's wearing a wedding band.

"Where are you from?" Matt asks.

"Asheville," I say. "I work with Dr. Cullen, a cardiologist in the area. I'm an NP."

"So that's where I probably saw you . . ." Jesse muses. "Over at the hospital in Asheville."

"Could be," I say. "I'm at the hospital a lot doing rounds."

"Did you say you work with Dr. Cullen?" Matt asks. "I've heard of him. Doesn't he work with the Cardiothoracic Surgeons Group in Charlotte?"

"Yes," I say. "He does."

Matt and Jesse exchange a look. It becomes abruptly quiet all of a sudden.

"An esteemed group of heart specialists," Matt says. "Their innovations in heart transplantations are well known in the medical and legal community."

"That would be them," I say, looking over at both men. Something has put Jesse off. I'm picking up on something, but I'm not sure what it is. Sensing a change in mood, I tuck a strand of my hair behind one ear, feeling self-conscious. "Well," I say, "I'll see you both inside then."

"Maybe we can all catch up later," Matt says. "We'd appreciate your feedback."

I nod. "Okay, I guess. If you'd like. Matt . . . Jesse . . . it was nice meeting you both." I turn to leave.

"Amanda," Jesse says, as if being jolted back and not wanting me to leave yet. "Can you do us a favor?" I look at him with curiosity. "Sit near the front where we can see you. If, when either one of us is speaking, you start to lose interest, give us some kind of a signal." Jesse and Matt share a laugh.

"A signal? I don't think I could . . ."

"Tuck your hair behind your ear like you just did," he says, catching me off guard. I didn't even realize I had. "That would work," Jesse says.

"Honestly . . . I don't think I should speak for the others."

"You won't be," he says with a grin. "You'll be speaking from honesty."

Everyone is starting to file out of the dining room. We follow them down the black and white marble floors to the expansive convention room. Dawn is looking for me, then finally spies me, talking with Jesse and Matt. I wave her over and make hasty introductions.

Turning toward Jesse and Matt I say, "Well, we should go find our seats. Good luck today."

"See you later," Matt says, giving us a well-rehearsed, lawyer's smile.

"Now don't forget," Jesse says. "We're counting on you." He's fully back from his reverie - or whatever it was.

"Sure thing," I say, half-pretending to go along.

***

The morning program over, it's time for lunch. Dawn and I have returned to the dining room and are surveying our lunch options, when she pulls her cell phone out of her purse. Her fiancé, Greg, had called and left a voicemail. "I'm going to go outside to make a call," she says. "Save me a seat."

"Will do," I say, drifting over to the salads table. I find a seat at a large round table near the atrium windows, looking out at downtown Nashville, Honkey Tonk highway only a three minute Uber ride from here.

Dawn finds me and takes the seat I saved for her. "Everything okay?" I murmur to her. "Yes," she says. "Greg called to say he misses me already."

Moved by the cuteness of it, I say, "Awww."

"I know. It's weird. We'll just be away from each other for four days."

"Not weird," I say. "He loves you."

"We've never really been apart, not since we started dating."

I emit a long, generous sigh and smile at her. "I could remind you that 'absence makes the heart grow fonder', but I think you two are way past that. You couldn't get any more fonder."

Dawn smiles, the dimple in her right cheek deepening. Her look is wistful as she drops her eyes to the table. She doesn't say it, but I can tell she misses him, too. I've forgotten what that feeling is like. My relationship with Tom was more in the vein of "out-of-sight, out-of-mind". It still hurts a little. I can't lie. Not because I miss Tom. I don't. I miss those feelings.

Conversations around our lunch table are in full. The person sitting on Dawn's other side is chirping in her ear. I can overhear pieces of it. Shop talk mostly. Dawn gives me her "I'm gonna need a drink" stare.

I scan the dining room and find Jesse. He's with Matt and some others over by the bar, a drink in his hand. He looks in my direction. I didn't just imagine it - he gives me a slight nod from across the room. I nod back and smile. I feel like someone who's just made a new friend but resist every compulsion to get up and walk over to him. Instead, I excuse myself to go to the ladies' room while Dawn works on the food still heaped on her plate.

On my return to the dining room, a man stops me – close-cropped hair, thick brows, dark-rimmed eyeglasses. He introduces himself as Eddie, a dermatologist from Alabama. "Hello, Eddie from Alabama," I say, in the kindest tone I can manage, my eyes peering around and past him, all the way over to the bar. Jesse is leaning on it, facing out into the room, watching me.

"I've been meaning to make your acquaintance," Eddie says, his southern accent unmistakable. "I saw you earlier at breakfast."

"Is that right?" I say. "Name's Amanda."

"So, where ya from, Amanda?" he asks in a friendly drawl.

"North Carolina."

"You have very beautiful skin," Eddie says. A fitting yet unoriginal pickup line from a dermatologist, I think.

"Thank you," I say. Eddie refuses to be deterred by the signs I'm giving off: distracted eyes, shifting feet, short responses. I look over at Jesse, watching him watching me. I plan my escape.

"Well," I say, "I have to get back to my friend. Nice meeting you."

"I'm gonna be at the Bourbon Steakhouse Restaurant for dinner this evening. Perhaps we'll see one another there," Eddie says, pushing his glasses up higher on his nose.

"Uh-huh. I'm sure we'll run into one another," I say. Tactful, yet noncommittal.

My eyes travel back to the bar. Jesse's no longer there. His empty tumbler is all that remains. He's the speaker for the afternoon portion, which will be starting shortly. I'm ever more interested to hear him speak, my curiosity in him piqued.

Dawn and I meet up and return to our seats in the convention hall amid the din of murmuring voices. When Jesse walks up to the podium, the chatter subsides.

"Good afternoon." His greeting allows everyone a moment longer to settle in.

"A doctor and a lawyer see this beautiful girl," Jesse says. The room falls quiet. "They both try to woo her. Every day the doctor gives the girl a rose. The lawyer gives her an apple. This goes on for a week before the girl finally asks the lawyer, 'I understand the meaning behind the rose, but why an apple?' The lawyer replies, 'Haven't you ever heard that an apple a day keeps the doctor away?'"

The audience erupts in laughter. Despite the fact that two-thirds of Jesse's listeners are doctors, he's immediately drawn them in with a joke. Smart. Jesse eases into the subject of medical malpractice, clearly a skilled and knowledgeable speaker. His manner and movements are synced with his words, actively and expressively emphasizing their meaning. Every now and then he moves away from the podium, and goes to one side or the other of the room, looking directly at individual members of the audience. I pull my eyes away from him for the first time and glance around the silent room of riveted spectators. Some take notes, others choose active listening. I, myself, have not jotted down a single word, unlike in the morning's lecture. Jesse has won the group over. He's made us feel like he's not only our advocate, he's our friend.

"He's good." Dawn whispers over to me. "And not hard to look at either."

I simply nod, not sure if she's noticed that I haven't been able to take my eyes off him.

Forty-five minutes into Jesse's speech, he lays out five main causes that put healthcare workers at risk of being sued. I want to be sure I remember them all, so I open my notebook and start listing them in the order of most and least likely.

"Physicians are not the only ones who get sued for malpractice," Jesse says.

I look up from my notebook, tuck a strand of hair behind one ear. Jesse is standing in front of my side of the room, not too far from where Dawn and I are sitting. He looks right at me, his eyes like magnets to my own. Then I remember something. The signal. Did he just see me tuck my hair behind my ear? Does he think I was sending the signal that I was becoming bored? Was he even serious about that?

"Ma'am," he says, "what's your first name, may I ask?" He's looking straight at me.

For a few alarming seconds I can't find my voice. "Amanda," I finally say.

"Nice to meet you, Amanda," Jesse says for the purpose of the others. "And what, Amanda, is your profession?"

I know he knows my profession, but I go along. "I'm a nurse practitioner."

"Would you say, Amanda, that many patients see nurse practitioners before ever seeing the doctor?"

"Well, yes, that's true." I'm strongly aware now that Jesse has brought me into his lesson plan.

"How many in here can say the same?" Jesse asks, turning to the audience. Hands go up. "Take a look around," Jesse says to all. "One-third of the room has their hands up. The increased scope of one's job description," Jesse points out, "whether a nurse practitioner or a physician's assistant – puts you at a greater risk. This applies to all those who provide a substantial amount of care in a patient's daily living." Jesse walks to the center of the room and looks over at me. "Thank you, Amanda."

He looks toward his audience and relays a true case scenario in which an NP evaluated a fifty-year-old woman complaining only of feeling weak. The NP sent her home after the blood work showed no elevated white blood cell count, and a few months later the woman died of an aneurysm.

Midway through his presentation about the malpractice suit that followed, Jesse steps back behind the podium and takes a purposeful pause for effect, the audience waiting to hear what happened next. "The jury deliberated for a couple of hours before coming back with a verdict. The nurse practitioner was found not liable for the woman's death." The audience erupts in one collective exhalation.

"There are two takeaways from this story," Jesse points out. "Don't lose faith in your knowledge. You can only do the best you can with the information you have. But in those times when you feel like you're losing faith, when you want to get it over with and simply settle, that's where we come in. We will fight for you even when you aren't so sure." He turns to look at me again. "We'll have your back." Jesse turns to leave, signaling he is done. "Thank you," he says, walking off to a round of applause.

And thank you, I say to myself, for setting me up.

CHAPTER 7

Elizabeth
March 1953

"Do you have enough to keep yourself busy?" Dr. Paterson glanced at the pile of comic books on a cart near my bed.

"More than enough of what I don't want," I said.

"Have any of our volunteers been to your room yet with a variety of reading materials for you to pick from?"

I shook my head. "Not unless I was asleep."

"Just a moment." Dr. Paterson stepped out for a while. He'd been continuing to visit with me during his rounds or breaks, setting aside extra time for our follow-up talks, which I think he enjoyed as much as I did. I found myself looking forward to them each day. When he returned, he assured me that more reading selections were on their way.

"Thank you. I need a good read."

"What do you like?" he asked. "Crime novels, action and adventure, fantasy maybe?"

"I like books by Agatha Christie and short stories. The last book I read was *The Lion, the Witch and the Wardrobe*, so I guess my taste varies. I can't put myself in one box."

"No," Dr. Paterson agreed, studying my face and smiling. "I can see that."

"How about you? Do you get much time to read?"

"When I can. *The Invisible Man* was the last book I read. It was good. When I'm not reading, I'm catching up with family, seeing my two nephews every chance I get. I missed a big portion of their growing up. I missed a lot." He looked up at the ceiling and sighed. "I'm slowly getting back to some of the things I used to enjoy."

"What was it like? Korea. If you don't mind my asking," I said. And then, "You don't have to talk about it if you don't want to."

He came around to the side of my bed and pulled over a chair, a sign that he wasn't ready for our conversation to end either. "Well," he began, "certainly nothing like this. Surgeries were performed in mobile hospitals."

"Mobile hospitals?"

"That's a fancy way of saying plain brown tents. The sides would be tied down, one naked bulb hanging over the operating table. That was it. We never knew if it was daytime or nighttime, but then it didn't make any difference."

An image of Robbie lying on a table inside one of those tents flashed before me and I closed my eyes briefly, realizing he may never have even made it there. I pressed on, listening intently, asking follow-up questions, captivated. Dr. Paterson didn't seem to mind sharing a little with me about his experiences there, although I knew he was being careful not to overdo it.

"When did you sleep? Weren't there shifts?"

"There were no shifts. There was a shortage of doctors, so we didn't sleep until the wounded stopped coming through the tent flaps. I drank gallons and gallons of black coffee. Sleep was a luxury we couldn't afford."

Listening to Dr. Paterson talk about what he had lived through put some perspective on my own hardships. "I haven't gotten a good night's sleep in a long time," I shared. "Not since my sister died."

Dr. Paterson nodded. "I still hear the medevac helicopters coming in my sleep." A look of surprise came over his face in all its vulnerability. He had gone deep and instantly looked like he wished he hadn't. He cleared his throat and resumed his caretaker role. "Elizabeth, if you need help with sleep . . ."

A young man entered my room pushing a rolling book cart. "Can I interest you in any books?" he asked me.

"Ah," Dr. Paterson said, rising. "Just in time. I think she may be quite ready for some new reading material." We swapped a smile and with that, he headed for the doorway. "I'll leave you to it." He turned to look at me. "Reading relaxes the mind. Tonight, you'll get a good night's sleep." I watched him leave, already yearning for tomorrow's visit.

I perused the selection of books on the cart, settling on *The Glass Menagerie*. I must have dosed off while reading because when I stirred from my sleep, it was nighttime. Nurse Agnes was in my room talking with another nurse.

"Well, you're out of luck," Nurse Agnes said to the younger nurse. "Dr. Paterson is off tonight."

"I'd hoped to be able to meet him," the cute, young blonde nurse said, talking in a low voice as she went over to tend to my roommate. "Our shifts haven't matched up yet. I hear he's quite handsome. And eligible." She looked over at Agnes, her light curls springing like shaky coils around her cap. "Why do you think that is?"

Nurse Agnes put a blood pressure cuff on my arm. "Might have something to do with the fact that he was preoccupied with trying to save lives in a war zone," she said. Then with a lighter tone, she added, "And yes, he's not bad looking. I may be old, but I'm not blind."

"I can't wait to meet him."

"Get in line," Nurse Agnes said.

Count me in. I was wide awake now. I looked over at the spunky blonde and then at the wall clock. Ten o'clock. I sighed. I had been asleep for several hours, which meant I would be up half the night. I dreaded the long hospital nights – my older roommate's moans, the squeaky wheelchairs, hushed voices in the lobby outside my room. My hospitalization was going on nine days.

As if Nurse Agnes heard my thoughts, she said, "Looks like Dr. Paterson is getting ready to discharge you. You could be getting out of here in a couple of days."

I contemplated what going home would mean - convalescing, Jim's courtship visits, Mom's Sunday pasta dinners. They were holding my new position at Bamberger's for me. I was grateful it wouldn't start for another six weeks. My cast would be off then. I knew I couldn't get back on a bus. I'd been too traumatized and did not know when, or if I could ever get back on one again. I had money saved and, with Dad's help, would be getting a car. That was something to look forward to, wasn't it?

"You don't look too excited to be getting out of here," Nurse Agnes said, shaking down a fever thermometer.

"Just lost in thought," I said.

She slipped the thermometer under my tongue. "You know, I've been a nurse a long time. Almost thirty-five years."

Unable to speak, I opened my eyes wide to convey *Really?*

"That's right. I was going house to house when I started, seeing sick patients during the Spanish flu epidemic, if that gives you any idea. I should be retiring soon, but I'm not ready yet. I'm a nurse. It's who I am. And I can tell you, I've seen it all. I know people. Sick people. Healthy people. But one thing's for sure - I've never seen anyone as glum as you are right now after they've been told they'll be leaving the hospital. Call it my nurse's intuition."

I closed my eyes. Did it show that much?

"Five minutes up," Nurse Agnes said, taking the thermometer out of my mouth to read it. "See, there it is. No temperature. Now smile."

"I *am* grateful to be going home." I tried to smile. "Guess I'm just tired." How could I tell her what was really on my mind? That the good part of each day was talking with Dr. Paterson and all that would end soon.

What was wrong with me? Dr. Paterson was seven years my senior, no doubt being pursued by many women. According to Nurse Agnes, a line of swooners was already forming. Perhaps there was someone special already in his life. I rolled over onto my good arm, preparing for another restless night.

***

The next day I heard footsteps coming toward my room. I put my book aside and propped against a pillow, an expectant smile spreading across my face. Jim came through the doorway and my heart sank. He was all smiles and eagerness. He leaned over, smelling of nicotine and aftershave, and kissed me hello.

"Thought you might like these," he said, laying a few more comic books on my lap, one with Superman on its cover. "Some of them are pretty old, but I gave you a good mix. My dad was into them, too. I've got a lot more where they came from. Let me know if you run out."

"Thank you." I heard the disappointment in my voice.

Jim pulled the privacy curtain that separated me and my roommate, enclosing us inside it. "So, I hear they're letting you outta here soon." He flopped down in the chair beside my bed.

I forced a smile. "Looks that way. So I won't need any more comic books."

Jim dove straight into talking about his plans for us. I heard words like car rides, movies, Scrabble games. But all I could think about was the conversation we needed to have that was long overdue.

"Jim," I began, cutting him off gently. "We need to talk."

He looked at me, puzzled. "Isn't that what we're doing?"

"Yes. No. I mean, I haven't been totally honest with you. Please listen to me while I've got my nerve up to do this." I took in a shaky breath. "I don't think we should be seeing so much of each other. Things between us have been going too fast. We need to slow it down – whatever this is."

Jim blinked and his eyes moved over my face with thoughtfulness. "I can do that."

I swallowed hard. "I think you should do more than that. I want you to see other people." Jim's stunned pause and the hurt look on his face affected me more than I'd expected. "Please, try to understand."

"I'm not interested in seeing anyone else. Where is this coming from?"

"It's coming from a place of honesty."

Jim reached for my hand. "I'll give you whatever time you need. I'll wait for you."

I shook my head gently. "I don't want you to feel you have to wait for me. After all, we're just friends."

"Friends?" Jim said like it was the foulest word he'd ever heard. He looked hurt and then his gaze cooled. "You want us to be just friends?"

Why was he making this so darn hard? "You're a really great guy."

"I don't like where this is going," he scoffed.

"You deserve more than I can give you. I'm not being fair to you."

"Look, you've been through an ordeal. You're not thinking clearly."

"I've never been clearer," I said. "I've had a lot of time to think."

"Don't do this, Elizabeth." Jim pleaded. "Let me help you."

"You already have. More than you know. You've been a good friend, but I can't hold you back any more. I want you to know--"

"I want *you* to know. Don't you understand?" Jim stood up and paced around my bed. "I'll do whatever it takes. I want you."

Besides Jim's pacing and the low wheeze of my sleeping roommate, the only other sound I could hear came from inside my mind. *Don't stop now.*

"Jim, please don't make this any more difficult than it already is. We need to slow things down."

"Like break up?"

"I need time and space to figure things out - to figure *me* out."

Slouched at the foot of my bed, Jim raked his hand through the top of his hair, mumbling to himself, but his eyes were shouting, *Why are you doing this! Why?*

"I don't like this," he said, piqued. He gathered himself and gripped the foot rail of my bed, steadying his gaze on me. "Seeing you, being with you, it's all I ever think about. Every moment of every day. The bus accident - the thought that I could have lost you - it made me realize how much you mean to me. You want honesty? Well, this is *me* being honest. I care for you. I can't just turn it off. I think . . . I may even be in love with you."

Jim shut his eyes and lowered his face into his hands. I closed my eyes, tears brimming under my lids in the strained silence that followed. *Love? How could I have not seen it?* I had nothing else to say. The sound of a throat being cleared startled me. Dr. Paterson stood in my doorway.

"Excuse me," he said, detecting disquiet, looking from Jim to me. "I can come back later."

"No," Jim moaned, taking a deep breath and straightening his back. He considered me sadly for long seconds, his face red and staring into my eyes. "You can stay. Looks like I'm on my way out." Without another word, he hurried past Dr. Paterson, carelessly bumping into his shoulder, and out of the room.

Dr. Paterson approached my bed with caution. "I've come at a bad time."

I inhaled. "How long were you standing there?" I asked, feeling self-conscious and looking away.

"Not long."

"I'm an awful, terrible person," I said, staring at the uneaten food on my tray. "I hurt him. I didn't want to hurt him. I should have been clearer from the very beginning. I should have never let things get this far."

Dr. Paterson took a seat in the chair. "Life would be a whole lot simpler if everything were as clear in the present as it is in hindsight."

"That was really, really hard," I said. "But I had to be honest with him."

"Sometimes we have to do hard things."

"I thought I'd feel better, but I just feel worse." I put my face in my free hand.

Dr. Paterson gave a low sigh. "Well then, perhaps this will cheer you up a bit. I wanted to give you the good news myself." I glanced over at him. "I'm discharging you tomorrow morning. You can leave here."

In that bewildering and heart breaking instant, I burst into tears. The confused look on Dr. Paterson's face contrasted with the empathy in his eyes. "Well, that wasn't the response I expected."

I swiped at a tear and reached for a tissue from the side table with my good arm, knocking over the box along with a glass of water. Dr. Paterson picked up the box of tissues and handed it to me, then grabbed a towel from the bathroom and threw it over the water spill. He sat back down again, bowed his head, and let me cry it all out.

Tears continued to spill out of me as I tried to speak. "Sorr . . ." I caught myself before finishing the word.

Dr. Paterson grinned, forming slight dimples under his high cheekbones. "No need to say sorry." I smiled slightly, sniffling. "So," Dr. Paterson began, deflecting, "What awaits you at home? What are your plans?"

I blew my nose into a tissue. "I'm going to take it one day at a time I guess." I looked down at Tennessee Williams's play still in my lap. "As for today, I'm going to try and finish this book. The characters in the story are so tragically hopeless. I'm afraid it won't have a happy ending. When I get home tomorrow, I'm looking forward to a home-cooked meal - anything homemade for that matter. Car shopping, driving practice – I'm excited for those things. I'll have more independence. My new position at Bamberger's won't be starting for a few more weeks. My arm should be good by then, right?"

"Yes, it should. You're well on your way to a complete recovery," he assured and stood up. "Remember the exercises I showed you that you can do as soon as you're able." Just in case, he repeated it to me for good measure. "Arm raised straight up in front of you to shoulder height." He demonstrated. "Pause, lower it, and then repeat. Your arm will get stronger with time and exercise."

"Got it."

A brief lull followed, and I didn't want our chatting to end so I said, "And what about yourself? Beyond being an ER doctor, I mean. What are your plans?"

"I appreciate your asking," he said, jotting down something in my chart. "There. Discharge orders are in." He looked at me then. "To answer your question, like you, I'm taking it one day at a time. Soon as I get the chance, I plan to start shopping around for a house of my own. Some place not too far from the hospital. But far enough to get away."

Our conversation moved to small talk until eventually there was only one thing left to say, which I had been privately dreading. "Well, I'm going to leave you to that book of yours." Dr. Paterson turned to leave.

The time had come. "Thank you. For everything you've done for me."

He flashed me a smile and my heart fluttered. "You take care of yourself."

I could put it off no more. "Good-bye then. Even under these circumstances, I'm glad to have met you," I said with the finality of it being unlikely I would ever see him again.

"Likewise. And, um . . . no driving lessons for a little while longer. Promise?" I nodded. "Oh, and by the way." Dr. Paterson turned and faced me from the doorway. "That girl in the play you're reading – what's her name? . . . The one with all those glass figures . . . " he said, trying to remember.

"Laura?"

"Yes. Her. Well, you are not her. Your story can have a happy ending." Once again, he left me awestruck.

Alone with my own thoughts, I knew Dr. Paterson had helped me realize things about myself that I hadn't. I was resilient. I was strong. Not to mention . . . I was alive. And that was something.

***

"Let's get our girl home." Wearing his gray plaid cap and a broad smile, my father arrived early the next day.

A nurse wheeled me down the corridor, a bag of Jim's comic books and my personal belongings in my lap. Nurse Agnes had bid me good-bye earlier and wished me well, declaring that I was a mighty sight better than when I first arrived. I felt as though I were saying good-bye to an old friend. She had shared some of her nursing experiences with me over the course of almost two weeks. She was an impressive and inspiring woman who I would never forget.

"Dr. Paterson isn't in today or he would've wanted to see you off personally," she'd told me. I let her know that he had already come by yesterday. "Glad to hear it," she said. "You're very special to him, you know."

I looked at her with a slight tilt of my head, trying to read her face, to see if it might give something away.

"He could've released you to another doctor's care like the others, but he stayed on your case." She smiled. "I know people. Nurse's intuition."

Passing Nurse Agnes again at the nurse's station on my way out of the hospital, I thought of something I wanted her to pass along to Dr. Paterson. "Nurse Agnes? One more thing," I said to her. I put my foot out to stop my wheelchair ride. "Could you give Dr. Paterson a message for me?"

"Sure, hon. What is it?"

"Tell him, I finished the play and he's right. I'm not Laura."

CHAPTER 8

Amanda

"You could have warned me at least," I say to Jesse as he saunters over to me.

Jesse gives me a stealthy smile. "You were perfect. You sounded honest, unrehearsed."

"Great job in there," Dawn says to Jesse. I give her a frustrated look.

"Was it because I tucked my hair behind my ear? Is that what spurred you on?" I persist.

Jesse throws his head back and laughs. "Of course not. I hope I haven't upset you."

"You used me. Admit it," I say, part-teasing, part-bothered. "Nothing to be upset about really, is there?"

"Let me make it up to you," Jesse says. "I'd like to buy you ladies a drink."

"We have a spa appointment in a half-hour, but thank you."

"Afterward then," Jesse says, undeterred. "Meet me in the executive lounge before tonight's dinner - will you? Please say you'll come."

Dawn opens her mouth, and then closes it again, catching on that something's happening between the two of us.

"Perhaps," I say, opening the buttons to my suit jacket and feeling warm all of a sudden. "We'll see."

"I'll take that as a yes," Jesse says, his confidence unabated.

I catch myself smiling and quickly erase it. "Take it as a 'we'll see.'"

As Dawn and I walk over to the elevators, I can feel Jesse watch us, but I don't want to look back. "Is he still looking in our direction?" I ask Dawn while staring at the elevator door.

Dawn looks surreptitiously over her shoulder. "Yep."

The doors open and we step inside. Dawn turns to face me as soon as they close. "What was that all about?"

I let out a sigh and shake my head. "I'm not sure." I hit the third floor button for the spa. Dawn maintains her questioning look. "Is it possible," I ask her, "to be both intrigued and annoyed with someone at the same time?"

"Sure," Dawn says. "It's called 'smitten'."

***

At six thirty I head toward the elevator that will take me to the executive lounge floor. I feel a little anxious, especially without my wing girl by my side. Dawn is using this time to talk to her fiancé before heading over to dinner, so I am left alone to my own devices.

Feeling refreshed and invigorated after a deep-tissue massage, I tell myself I'm ready to take on whatever I need to. I glance at my reflection in the wall mirror opposite the elevator station. I'm wearing a nude-colored, sleeveless bodice and a miniskirt under a sheer midi-length white appliqué cocktail dress. A white fringe shawl is draped over my arm. The bouncy blow out hairstyle from the afternoon is gone. This evening's look is glossy, poker-straight hair, affecting a more dramatic look.

Riding the elevator, I realize I want to call Nana before it gets too late. Dorothy's last text said everything's fine. Still, I like to hear Nana's voice. I tell myself to be sure to do so before dinner starts.

The elevator doors open. I take a long breath, releasing it slowly. Here goes . . .

Jesse is sitting on a leather sofa when I enter the room, engaging in conversation with some others, a drink in his hand. He abruptly stands up when he sees me, his eyes wandering over me, resting when they reach my eyes. A smile ignites his face. "Amanda, you look beautiful."

"Thank you. Dawn's on the phone with her fiancé. She'll catch up with us at dinner."

"There're a couple of seats over here," Jesse says, pointing to a private area of two blue suede chairs around a small round glass table. "What can I get you to drink?"

Fully aware that I'm on an empty stomach, I opt for red wine. Jesse is drinking scotch by the looks of it.

Socially adept and polished, he navigates our meeting with attention to every detail. He offers me the chair with a view of the outside and makes small introductions of people he knows who are also in the room.

"Thank you for your part in my lecture today," Jesse says. "I couldn't have done it without you."

I chuckle. "Somehow I don't think that's true."

"So, you said your friend's engaged. What about you?"

"Not engaged." I grin because I'm pretty sure he already knows that. But then I give him more. "No significant other." My turn now. "You?"

"Single," he says. With that awkwardness out of the way, we both nod and smile.

From Jesse's body language, he appears interested in everything I have to say. He leans into the table, wanting to learn more.

I swirl the wine in my mouth before letting it slide down, smooth and easy. I tell Jesse that I recently got out of a relationship, that I live and work in Asheville. Jesse tells me his office is in Charlotte, and that he has lived there since he finished Duke Law. His roots though are in Pennsylvania, where he was born and raised.

"You're a good speaker," I say. "You were a natural up there. You managed to engage us in a rather unpleasant topic. No easy feat."

"I've been doing this for over ten years now," Jesse says. "I got into malpractice defense a few years after finishing law school."

I do the math in my head as to Jesse's age, rather than coming out and asking him. Jesse chuckles. "Thirty-eight," he says, reading my mind.

I smile, the wine doing its magic. "Thirty-four." I gaze out the window, the dusk sky's oranges and reds merging with a scattering of light over the city. "What a lovely view."

"Yes, it is," Jesse says, looking only at me.

The way he carries himself, his body language, everything about him emanates skillfulness and control. He does this a lot I think, realizing that I'm no match for his experience. I try to dismiss feeling self-conscious the quickest way I know how. I take another larger-than-usual sip of wine. I fidget with a crystal-beaded bracelet on my wrist and clear my throat. "You know," I say, feeling less nervous, "I'm a bit out of practice with this sort of thing."

Jesse tilts his head archly. "What sort of thing would that be?"

"I was in a relationship for over three years, attending school, and studying all the time...I didn't go out a lot." I take another sip of wine. Comfortable in Jesse's company, I realize I may be telling him more than I should. Too much. Too fast. Jesse's discerning look tells me that he has already picked up on my inexperience, but he coaxes me further.

"Why did you break up?" he asks. His curiosity about me is evident.

I run my fingers around the rim of my wineglass. "It didn't progress. It just stalled. Or rather, died."

Jesse narrows his eyes, studying me, but it does not make me uncomfortable as I would think it would. Strangely, it makes me feel validated. I lean against the chair's back and cross my legs. He gives me room to continue. "It was no one's fault. It just ended. Actually, it was probably over before either one of us wanted to admit." *Why am I telling him all this?* I glance down at my almost-empty glass. *Slow down, Amanda.*

"Let me get you another drink," Jesse says without missing a beat.

Before I can respond, he orders me another. "I think I should have something to eat."

Jesse points over to appetizers spread out on a counter. "I think I will," I say, rising from my chair, stumbling a little. The four-inch heels and wine – not the best combination.

Jesse is up, clutching my arm. "Let me help you," he offers. He guides me over to the assorted spread of starters – smoked salmon and cheeses, bourbon bacon lollipops, caviar. We fill our small plates and return to our little table, Jesse's hand protectively back on my arm.

"So, you were saying..."

"Remind me again," I say with a laugh.

"You were telling me about the breakup in your relationship, coming to terms that it had ended," Jesse says, evidently not ready for that topic to be over.

"There isn't much more to say. I moved out. I looked at apartments before deciding to move into my grandmother's house in Asheville. It's the perfect location, not far from where I work. Which reminds me," I say, veering for a moment. "I want to call and check on her soon." I take another bite of my caviar-topped cracker, washing it down with wine. "My grandmother has a part-time caretaker but is otherwise somewhat independent. Her home...I love her house - a big farm-style house tucked inside the Blue Ridge Mountains."

"Sounds wonderful," Jesse says. "I do business in Asheville and visit it often."

"It's a charming town. I often get lost in those blue-toned mountains. The forest firs, the wildflowers . . . autumn is my favorite time – reds and oranges and yellows." Words are falling from my lips, the wine doing most of the talking now.

Coming out of my reverie, I glance around and notice that the executive lounge has emptied. It's just Jesse and me. "Oh," I say, "dinner must be starting."

"Of course we could just stay here," Jesse says.

I smile, although I consider that he may only be half joking. My phone dings a message and I pull it out of my purse. It's a little past seven.

Dawn
Where are you?

"Excuse me," I say to Jesse.

Me
Coming.

"Dawn's looking for me. Perhaps we can continue our conversation another time."

"I plan on it," Jesse says with assurance. He rises up to assist me.

Riding the elevator up to the top-floor steakhouse alone with Jesse arouses my senses. A bouquet of amber and magnolia, my fragrances, are warmed by his scents of oak and vanilla and whiskey. The hollow hum of the ride melds with our low breathing, our far corner retreat into the tiny space evoking closeness and intimacy. I shift positions and lean on the wall, fully mindful that this is the most pleasant elevator experience I've ever had - and the most exhilarating.

When Jesse and I enter the restaurant, he's besieged by his other lawyer friends who have reserved a seat for him at their table, a teeming room of people coming between us. Dawn catches my eye and waves me over to where she's sitting. The group around our table is some of the same people we met earlier during lunch, a momentary fellowship already in progress.

"So, how did it go?" Dawn asks me as I take the seat she's saved for me. A long exhale is all that comes out of me. I can't seem to find the words. "That good," Dawn says.

"Maybe. Or could just be the wine." I drape my shawl over the back of my chair. "I don't think I'm going to need this."

I glance around the lively room, a chorus of doctors, healthcare workers and lawyers mingling. Jesse is talking with his friend, Matt, his hands clasped in front of him on the table. He turns his head to look my way. From across the room, our eyes lock, and it surprises me at how much I already miss our twosome.

"What's his story?" Dawn asks me.

"Well, he's single for one."

"Good start."

"Lives and works in Charlotte," I say.

"And . . . " Dawn says. "What else? I mean, did you get any sense of whether he's seeing someone? What's his history? An eligible, good-looking guy like that? There has to be more."

"We didn't really go there," I say, realizing all of a sudden that I did go there, telling him about my recent past relationship with Tom and my nominal dating life. Jesse never revealed anything to me about his past, his relationships, or his dating life. It wasn't that he was evasive. He just wasn't as forthcoming as I was. Thinking back on our talk, I remind myself that Jesse is a model of cleverness and practice, easily extracting information about me while he still remains a mystery.

A waiter recites our entrée options for the evening's dinner extravaganza: bourbon steak, chicken piccata, and grilled salmon. I realize that I'm starving. Dawn and I both order the bourbon steak signature dish.

The gregarious, networking Jesse is no longer sitting at his table. He's making his way over to the bar, a terrace that extends past the building's edge so it seems to be floating on air, with a 360-degree view of downtown Nashville. Working the room and occasionally looking my way, he stops every now and then to speak to someone and eventually I lose sight of him. After an appetizer salad, I excuse myself so I can call my nana. Crossing the floor and exiting the room, I feel like I'm being watched, dismissing it as my own imagination.

"Call Nana," I say into my phone. She answers on the first ring. "I didn't wake you, did I?"

"No, no, I was just resting, dear. Watching the news," she says. "How is it down in Florida?"

"Tennessee," I say. "I'm in Nashville. Remember?"

"Oh, that's right. How's it going so far?"

"So far pretty good. I'm glad I came. It's been eye-opening."

"There must be lots of doctors in attendance. Eligible ones, too," she says.

I sigh. "There are all kinds of people here. Doctors, nurses, lawyers, administrators. Keeping my options open."

"Good for you, dear," Nana says.

"Dorothy's been texting me. Told me you beat her at Scrabble again. I'm glad she was able to be with you longer while I'm away."

I look up briefly; Jesse is making his way down the lobby. "Well, I should get back to the dining room now. Call you again tomorrow."

"Love you," Nana says. "Enjoy Florida."

"Tennee-." *Never mind.* Instead, I say, "I love you, too."

I turn in time to see Jesse close by, watching me. He approaches when he sees I'm off the phone.

"I didn't mean to disturb your call," he says.

"Oh. That's okay. My nana," I say, realizing Jesse was near enough to hear me say "I love you" into the phone and thinking somehow that it needed explaining.

Jesse nods. "I want to see you again." It's a statement, not a question.

"Oh?"

"I enjoyed talking with you, but our time was too brief. Can you meet me later?"

"Meet you . . . where?"

"Not here. After dinner. On the rooftop, say around nine-thirty?"

I nod tentatively. "I guess I could."

"So . . . is that a yes?"

I know I want to. "Yes."

We exchange smiles while walking back to the restaurant, turning off in different directions, one last glance at each other before parting ways.

CHAPTER 9

Elizabeth
August 1953

Except for a more conscious and deliberate approach to life, the accident had not changed me. I had not changed me. Physically and mentally, I felt more spirited, but spiritually I was no different than before the accident – unfulfilled.

The most intentioned thing I did was to insist on putting some space between Jim and me, giving us time to reflect without any pressure. My mother, much to my chagrin, told me I should have given it more of a chance. "One day," she said, "in time, you could get there." I didn't think that a person should have to work so hard at being in love with someone. I knew love. I was in love once. It was easy and exciting. I was not in love with Jim.

I'd been keeping myself busy working the cosmetics counter at Bamberger's for almost three months, standing for hours at a time in high-heeled shoes but never complaining. I was content when customers walked away from my counter delighted with their purchase. I provided women with beauty tips to enhance their looks and boost their confidence. I found that aspect of my new job particularly rewarding - that I could make even the smallest amount of difference in someone's life with just a shade of lipstick or a hint of powder.

Peggy, from my high school, was getting married, as were so many during that time. She stood across from me at my counter on one particular day in late summer, soliciting makeup ideas for her big day.

"It's so good to see you again. I'd ask how you're coming along," she said from across the counter, "but from the looks of it, you've recovered beautifully. You look wonderful. Everyone was pulling for you."

"I appreciated all the cards and get well wishes, and thank you for coming to see me in the hospital. It helped me get through it," I told her.

Then we talked about her engagement and upcoming wedding. "I have time tomorrow between one and two. Let me put you down for a one-on-one make-over tutorial."

Peggy came back on the following day right on time. "Thank you so much for doing this." She placed her purse on my counter. "The wedding is only two months away and I'm starting to get the jitters."

"Of course." I laid out several different makeup samples. Peggy took a seat in the chair in front of my counter, ogling everything like a kid does in a candy store. "Okay," I said, going over to her side of the counter. "Are you ready to look glamorous?"

I went straight to work on Peggy's makeover – cleansing, moisturizing, and applying cosmetic shades and colors I chose for her - while she rattled on about her wedding dress and all things wedding. "You know," Peggy said, "you can bring a guest to my wedding, of course." Her bubbly energy matched her springy curls. "A lot of our high school crowd is going to be there."

Except Robbie . . . and few others who lost their lives in the war. "I'll most likely be going alone, but thank you. It will be nice to see everyone."

"It will be a kind of reunion," she said in an exuberantly high-pitched tone. "Don't know if you've heard, but Jim is planning on bringing a woman he met. It's not anyone we know. You won't mind, will you? I mean, you and he have been broken up for a while now, isn't that right?"

I had been putting crème powder on Peggy's face and stopped for a few seconds, the cosmetic sponge frozen in midair between us. *Jim's moving on.* I mused. I wondered how he was doing, and I felt a sense of peace that comes with knowing I had made the right decision.

"I hope I didn't upset you," Peggy said. "I thought you should know."

"No. Not at all. I'm happy for him," I said. "Jim's a terrific guy. Whoever he winds up with will be lucky to have him." I held up a mirror to her face. This was my favorite part – the moment of truth.

"Oh my," Peggy said. "Is this really me? I love what you did to my eyes. I look so..."

She was at a loss for words, so I finished it for her. "Lovely," I said. "Your eyes are very pretty; I just enhanced their prettiness. You're going to be a beautiful bride."

"Thank you. You're a doll." She gave me a hug.

After Peggy left, I was putting away some of the cosmetic samples I had used on her when another customer approached my counter. "I'll be right with you," I said, closing a drawer. I stood up and turned around. A woman around my age with spirally blonde hair and prominent dimples was browsing products through the glass countertop. She looked familiar but I wasn't sure. "May I help you?"

"I was wondering if I could see some blushes and lipsticks," she said. "I left my date over in the men's department, so I have a little time."

"Certainly. Is it for anything special?"

"No. Not yet anyway." She gave me a conspiratorial grin. "But a girl can hope, can't she?"

"Of course she can." I studied her skin tone, the color of her eyes and began pulling out some shades that were right for her fair complexion.

"This is actually only our first date," she disclosed. "I really like him, but I can't tell if he likes me."

"I see. What's your name?"

"Shirley."

"I have something I think you might like, Shirley." I held up a Max Factor Crème Puff. "This will even out your skin tone and give your face a beautiful glow. He won't be able to look away. We can apply a light blush to it later. Let me show you."

Once I was finished, I passed a mirror over to her. "See for yourself."

Something in the reflection caused her to look behind her. "I'm over here," she exclaimed, waving someone over.

Shirley turned back to look at me. "He's coming over now." Her cheeks had blushed pink all by themselves.

A man came up alongside her. "Do you like how this looks?" She looked over at him hopefully.

He stood silently, not responding, then uttered a single word. "Elizabeth?"

My eyes saw what my mind would not let me believe. Standing before me in a navy blue knit shirt was Dr. Paterson.

"Dr. Paterson," I said, slowly trusting my eyes. "I didn't recognize you without . . . without your white..."

"Well, hello," he said, a smile stretching across his face. "I like to take a break from wearing the white coat on my days off. I do have another persona," he quipped. "It's good to see you. You look really well."

Aware that the hairs on my arms now stood up from goosebumps, I collected myself and said, "I'm well. Thanks to you in great part." I managed a smile. "See." I stretched my healed arm out in front of me.

"Impressive," he said.

"Still a little stiff from time-to-time, but stronger every day."

"And the driving. How's that going for you?" He remembered.

"It's good. Really good, in fact. I love our new Ford. It's a family car mostly. Dad drives a truck for work, but on weekends he likes to take the car out." I was getting carried away by my excitement at seeing him again. I forced myself to look back at Shirley – her face a contortion of confusion and suspicion.

"So you two know each other then," she said, stating the obvious.

"I was his patient . . . once."

"Swell." Shirley frowned.

Dr. Paterson's eyes stared at me when I looked into his.

"I remember now . . . " he said to me, turning his back to Shirley. "You told me that you'd be starting a new position at Bamberger's. Well, good for you." His sincere smile touched me.

A look of irritation crossed Shirley's face as she narrowed her eyes. A flashing light seemed to go off inside her head, connecting the dots. "I thought you looked familiar," she gawked, interjecting. "I remember you from the hospital."

So that's where I saw her. She was the spirited blonde nurse who was bent on meeting Dr. Paterson.

"You're that poor woman who was in the terrible bus accident a few months back," she said. "I'm sorry. I didn't recognize you." That she had stressed the words "poor woman" with fake compassion did not escape me. I understood she was competing for attention now.

I was so sick and tired of being painted as the 'poor woman' – the one whose fiancé died overseas, who lost her sister at a young age, who narrowly escaped death in a horrific bus accident.

I placed a coral-shaded lipstick on the counter between us. "I think this will compliment your color tone beautifully. The color of a woman's lipstick says a lot about her. Coral is warm and friendly." I accentuated the word "friendly" as a subtle reminder. "I think it suits you."

Shirley sighed, somewhat mollified.

Dr. Paterson's eyes smiled. I could feel him watching me, both amused and delighted.

"Would you like to try it on?" I heard myself ask.

Shirley slicked it over her lips while my eyes followed Dr. Paterson's strong gaze. Standing that close – only a counter between us – was having an effect on me, a heightened sense of awareness.

Shirley smacked her lips together and glanced up at Dr. Paterson. "Do you like this color on me?"

Dr. Paterson pulled his eyes from me a moment too late. He unbuttoned the single button at the neck of his shirt, and one lackluster word stumbled from his mouth. "Nice."

Not the response Shirley had hoped for. With a begrudging smile, she bore her eyes into mine. "So tell me, what exactly does your lipstick color say about you?"

They both watched me now. I could feel my cheeks heat. "Red. Well, it's . . . adventurous. I'm wearing a rich red by Christian Dior." Dr. Paterson's eyes were on my mouth, and I had to look away. "Would you like to try on the red?" I pretended not to notice the change in Shirley's disposition.

She blotted her lips with a tissue and stood up stiffly. "Perhaps some other time."

"Certainly." I was pretty sure Shirley wasn't going to become a new customer of mine. "Let me know if I can be of help in the future."

Shirley pulled a face. "That won't be necessary." Her voice sounded flustered. "What did you say your name was?"

"Elizabeth." Dr. Paterson answered for me.

Shirley walked off in a huff while Dr. Paterson held back a little. "It really is a nice surprise seeing you again," he said, smiling.

"Same," I said. I could barely believe what had just transpired. I had to pinch myself a few times.

"I hope I get to see you again sometime."

"That would be really nice."

"You coming?" Shirley called after him.

My eyes followed him as he walked off with Shirley, looking back at me over his shoulder once, before vanishing in a crowd of shoppers.

It was only when they were out of sight that I unfroze, feeling shaky all of a sudden until I realized I'd been holding my breath.

***

"Enjoy the rest of your day," the pleasant elevator operator said as he slid open the gold scissor-gate door and let me onto my floor after my shift break.

"Same to you." I smiled back and walked straight over to my counter. That's when I saw him. Dr. Paterson was leaning casually against the counter. His legs were crossed at the ankles, one hand tucked inside his pants pocket. My heart quickened, and once again I had to trust my mind to affirm what my eyes were seeing. He watched me walk over.

"Hello again," he said.

A ripple of sheer pleasure coursed through me. It had been one week to the day since Dr. Paterson had turned up at my counter the first time. I hadn't been able to get him off my mind since. And now, here he was, in the flesh again, looking more dapper than ever. "Hi," I chirruped.

"I offered to help this gentleman," the woman covering for me explained. "But he wished to wait for you when you got back from your break."

"Thank you. I've got it from here." I stepped behind my counter.

"I only wanted the best," Dr. Paterson grinned. "It's my sister's thirtieth birthday on Sunday. I was hoping you could help."

"Thirty is a milestone." I glanced around for any signs of the blonde nurse with him.

"I'm here alone," Dr. Paterson said, as if reading my thoughts, his eyes twinkling.

"I see." I straightened my posture, put on a professional smile, and fumbled with the makeup samples, pulling out our bestsellers. I was glad he couldn't see my knees shaking under the counter. "So, tell me a little about your sister. She has a couple of children, isn't that right?"

"You have a good memory. Two very rambunctious boys." He chuckled.

"Let's start with the color of her hair."

"Brown. Like yours." Dr. Paterson's close scrutiny was making my heart pound.

"Eye color?" I heard myself ask, inviting more gaze from him.

Dr. Paterson looked into my eyes. "Darker than yours. Yours are...I'm not quite sure what color your eyes are," he wondered, not looking away.

"Hazel," I said, feeling his eyes linger. "My eyes are hazel."

I'd gathered a selection of cosmetics for his consideration when he said suddenly, "I'll take them all."

"All? Are you sure?"

"And throw in a face cream, too." Dr. Paterson turned around to see that a woman and her teenage daughter had come up behind him, waiting their turn to speak to me.

He took the bag from my hand. "Elizabeth," he said in a low voice, leaning over the counter, "what time do you get off?"

I was completely caught off guard. "Around six."

"Can you have dinner with me? There's a new diner near here - Tops Diner. Do you know it?" he asked in a hurried, hushed voice.

There go my knees again. "Dinner . . . today?"

"I know its short notice. It's my only day off."

"Yes, I know the place."

"You do? Could you meet me there at say . . . 6:30?" And then, as an afterthought, he asked, "I wouldn't be keeping you from someone . . . a boyfriend perhaps . . . your comic book friend?"

"Jim? No. Moved on. You also have a pretty good memory."

Dr. Paterson chuckled. "So you're free then?"

"Free as in tonight or free as in unattached?"

"Both."

Be still my heart. "I'm not dating anyone, so I guess that makes two yeses."

In the background the mother and daughter argued with one another.

"Great. We can talk more, catch up," Dr. Paterson said.

"I'd like that," I said, living up to my berry red lip color and half believing my luck. I had to be dreaming. I'd know in a few short hours.

CHAPTER 10

Amanda

My stomach is in knots. Ever since Jesse's invitation to meet, I haven't been able to eat much, leaving half my dinner on the plate, when two hours ago I was famished. It is true that I haven't been with anyone in a year, longer if you count the platonic months with Tom in our last year together. If this isn't a romantic liaison like Dawn said, then why does it feel so clandestine?

I start toward the elevators when I hear my name called and turn around. Eddie approaches me with a drink in his hand. "You're not leaving now, are you?" he asks, stopping me in my tracks. "I had hoped to be able to catch up with you."

"Eddie. I'm sorry. I-I've come down with a headache. I'm going to lie down."

"Oh. That's too bad. Do you have something to take for it?" the doctor in him asks. "If not, I--"

"I do." My anxiety is rising and I'm starting to sweat. "I get these from time to time." I put my hand to my forehead and close my eyes to give my excuse more credibility. "A quiet, dark room is what I need right now."

"Of course. Feel better," he says. "By the way, you look lovely this evening."

I step out onto the terrace of the roof, bright lights illuminating the perimeter of an outdoor pool and bar, the Nashville skyline lighting up the night. Feeling a slight chill in the air, I wrap my shawl around my shoulders.

In the haze of dark and light shadows, Jesse appears like a vision. "I was afraid you weren't going to show."

"Sorry. I got a little held up."

Jesse takes my hand in his and guides me over to a private cabana, an ambiance of warm lights, rattan lounge sofas with pillows, and a stonewall fire pit. "I reserved this for us," he says.

"How wonderful," I say, taking in the scene. A glass of red wine sits on a small glass table near the sofa. On the coffee table is a dessert plate of petit fours and chocolate covered strawberries. "I took the liberty of getting you wine, but if there's something else you'd rather have..."

"No, that's fine," I say, thinking Dawn's use of the word 'romantic' might actually be playing out. "Thank you. I'll stick to wine." Standing under the cabana, I do a slow twirl, taking in my surroundings. Jesse has thought of everything; he's the perfect host. I wonder how many times he's done this. His familiarity with presentation and entertaining is very apparent. I'm not sure how I feel about that, but for now, I'm just going to enjoy it.

"Come," he says. "Let's sit and relax for a while."

I sit on the couch cushion closest to my glass of wine. Jesse sits adjacent to me with enough space between us so we can see one another's faces. "I like being with you," Jesse says. "I enjoy talking to you. It's quieter out here, more peaceful."

A mild night breeze drifts in as I settle back against fluffy pillows. "I could get too relaxed," I say, slipping my high-heeled sandals off my feet.

"That's the idea," Jesse says.

"Are you here for the entire convention?"

"No, I go back, day after tomorrow."

This news disheartens me, but I don't let it show. "You mean you won't be around to hear healthcare futurists speak on the role of artificial intelligence and how technology is changing the medical field?" I say with a tinge of incredulity. "Surely you wouldn't want to miss *that*."

"Unfortunately, I do have to be back. It all sounds very interesting, but what I'll miss most of all, frankly, is seeing you. We've only just met. I wish we had more time. I'd like to get to know you better."

My heart soars. *Yes . . . yes!*

I sip the wine to slow my heart; the mellowness pleases and soothes me. "I feel the same," I say. "You're quite an interesting guy, Jesse Taylor."

Jesse peers over his drink. "And how is that?"

"Oh, I don't know. You're confident – perhaps overly so." Jesse grins and nods. "You're playful, yet reserved; outgoing but also traditional."

"You can tell all that?"

"Intuition, I guess. You give me a lot to think about. You're an enigma of sorts."

Jesse gives me a sideways glance, setting his drink down on the trunk in front of us. "I like that it keeps you wondering." He slides back on the sofa, turning full body to face me. "My turn."

I take a breath.

"You are smart . . . you're beautiful . . . you're caring and kind."

I smile. The combination of Jesse's eyes on me and the wine flowing through me induces a cozy feeling. I slip my shawl off my shoulders, laying it over the back of the couch and bring my bare legs under me. "Are you so sure about all that?"

"You phoned to check in on your grandmother, didn't you? That was a big giveaway."

I chuckle. Bringing my glass to my lips, I continue smiling into my drink. I reach for a strawberry and bite into it. Juice trickles down my chin. Before I can grab a napkin, Jesse catches it with his finger. The intimacy of his touch thrills me.

"You're even more charming with strawberry juice running down your chin," he says.

Dabbing at my mouth with the napkin, I fling my head back and chuckle. A sweet talker. I quip back, "You should see me eat powdered donuts."

"I'd love to," Jesse says.

No longer wearing his red power tie, Jesse's shirt has two buttons open at the top. He removes his jacket, laying it across the sofa arm, and rolls up his shirtsleeves.

"Thank you," I say, "for doing all of this. It's really sweet."

In those casual, playful moments between us, we take bites from the chocolate-dipped strawberries, and pass little iced cakes between us, enjoying one another's company. I realize that spending time with him is easy and natural as the space between us gets smaller.

"How is it that we can know so much about each other when we've only just met," I say.

"You said it yourself. Intuition. My instincts are usually pretty good. They have to be in my line of work."

"So what else do your instincts tell you about me?"

"They tell me that you are very able and confident in your vocation, dedicated and fulfilled. Your personal life, though, is less satisfying." Jesse looks into my eyes; seriousness crosses his face. "You're afraid to trust maybe - a little cautious and guarded."

The truth of what Jesse says hits the mark, its intended effect rendering me defenseless. I wasn't expecting that. I take another sip of my drink before placing it on the table beside me and lean against the sofa's back. Feeling vulnerable, I close my eyes. It's been months since Tom and I broke up. Long, lonely months of living with numbing indifference and neglect. Why haven't I been able to feel anything until now? "Am I that transparent?" I say.

Jesse takes my hand in his. "Maybe . . . a little."

I open my eyes and look into his. "I know," I say quietly. "I know."

Jesse's face is close to me now, his eyes gazing into mine. I can see flecks of yellow and brown in the color of his pupils. "Your openness is positively charming." He lifts my chin and gently parts my lips with his, tasting of sugar and strawberries. He kisses me tenderly.

My eyes flutter open. Jesse is watching me, appraising, his eyes saying, *Shall I continue?* I stare back into his, willing mine to convey my desire for more.

Jesse takes me in his arms, gradually lowering me so that I'm lying against his thigh, his eyes never leaving mine.

My heart is racing. "I'm not used to--"

"Shhh," he whispers. He cradles my head in the crook of his elbow; the stubble of his face leaning over mine grazes my lips, which are faintly quivering.

I yearn for his mouth on mine again, even though I'm nervous, my lips opening to receive his. Jesse bypasses them, his lips gliding over the rest of my face, my neck, caressing with his breath. My body shudders, dormant feelings awakening inside of me. I can't remember when I've ever felt this way, when reality is so much better than my dreams.

For a fleeting moment, I recognize I may be crossing into dangerous territory. A man, as enigmatic as I have ever known, a man I could fall for, doing things to me that are making me swoon.

I let myself go, my head falling back, hair splayed over a sofa pillow behind me so that I'm staring up at bright stars piercing the night, twinkling in the openings of the cabana's covering. The only sounds I hear come from our breathing and the faint crackle of the fire.

It's easy for me to lose myself, feeling safe and warm in Jesse's arms, thirty-three stories up in the sky, surrounded by an endless night. Jesse's sample kiss has me longing for more. He looks down at me, considers my parted lips. He wants to, as much as I do. I know he does. But he exhibits control and skill, kissing my chin, the small spot behind my ear lobe, the hollow of my throat, paying attention to every facet, every detail.

I groan and writhe, but he does not give in to my cravings. He endures, tracing his fingers over my eyelids, the bridge of my nose. "You're so beautiful," he says. My eyelids fall. I'm at his mercy. He cradles me in his arm and with the tips of his fingers traces my lips, open and waiting for him. I open my eyes so I can look into his – transfixed and longing. So this is what true desire feels like. It's my last thought before Jesse leans down and closes his mouth climactically over mine.

I inhale him, my mind blotting out the rest of the world.

***

Nestled on the sofa together, my head leans on Jesse's shoulder, my feet elevated on the couch as we continue gazing at the fire in silence, immersed in a trance. I don't want this perfect night to end. Jesse has shown me what I have been missing, what I longed for. I won't ever want to settle for less.

I turn around to face him. In the glow of the fire, I see that his eyes are closed. A fringe of hair has fallen over his forehead. The soft hum of his breathing tells me he's fallen asleep. I watch him for a while, his lips slightly open, his veil of dark lashes. *God, you're gorgeous.*

"Jesse, are you sleeping?" I kiss him gently on the lips. "I hate to leave, but I have to go." I swing my legs off the sofa.

Jesse gets up to join me.

I head to my room in a trance. I realize I have so much to learn about Jesse, so much to discover, but I make a choice not to overthink him. Not now. Not while all I want is to still feel him.

CHAPTER 11

Elizabeth
September 1953

It was a few minutes past six-thirty when I pulled into the parking lot of the diner. *Breathe*, I told myself, *just breathe.*

I walked toward the shiny steel railcar. I was glad I'd worn my favorite Gibson-girl blouse to work that day. I still couldn't believe I was meeting up with Dr. Paterson outside a hospital setting. It had been over four months since I was hospitalized, and yet it seemed a far cry away now.

I stood in the doorway of the crowded, narrow diner with its galley kitchen and row of barstools. Dr. Paterson stood up from his seat at a small booth in back, motioning me over to the table. He waited for me to sit down before returning to his seat. "I'm so glad you could do this on such short notice. I've had to eat alone on far too many occasions in the past few years. I can never seem to get used to it. I appreciate your coming."

"Thank you for asking," I said. "Have you eaten here before?"

"Yes, for a quick breakfast. It's close to the hospital. You?"

"No. It's my first time here."

"You have to come for breakfast sometime. They make the fluffiest butter pancakes I've ever tasted."

"I'm usually a buttered-toast-and-coffee gal, but it would be good to change things up."

"That's right. Live it up a little," he said. "Of course, there are loads of things - food being one of the biggest - that seem to have a heightened appeal for me ever since I got back from South Korea. Anything made from scratch beats quick meals out of a tin, so I may not be the best judge."

The waitress brought over my drink and asked if we needed more time to look over the menu. I picked up the oversized menu, perusing its ham and cheese combo sandwich - the Jim Dandy - the Maverick sirloin sandwich and fries with gravy, the pies and cheesecakes, feeling somewhat overwhelmed. Peeking over the menu at Dr. Paterson, with his casual and convivial manner, his down-to-earth practicality, the way he half-reclined in his seat, offering up friendly suggestions of what I might like to try, I was at once put at ease. Any nervousness I had felt earlier was replaced with a sense of warmth and unpretentiousness, and it was just as it had been during our daily talks in the hospital - totally and honestly familiar.

After we ordered, I picked up where he left off. "Was canned food all there was?"

"No. We had plenty of breakfast bars - good for a nutritional pick-me-up, but not much else. We ate plenty of stew for sustenance, and sometimes we had steak. Tangerines were the best. They grew everywhere there."

"It must have been quite an adjustment coming home."

"A good adjustment," he stressed. "I didn't have time to dwell on it, but I was definitely homesick. When there's no lunchtime or dinnertime and time is irrelevant, it feels good to be able to wear a watch again." Dr. Paterson looked down at his wrist as if to make sure it was still there.

"Considering how shorthanded doctors were, I'm astounded at what you all had to do."

He gave a small nod. "It was tough, but I like to think we kept the number of casualties down. At least that's what I want to believe. It helps me sleep a little better at night."

It was easier talking about the Korean War now that the fighting was over thanks to the recent armistice. We both had experienced so much death in the last couple of years – on a large scale for Dr. Paterson who saw many soldiers die. We were of like minds and spirits, our past traumas uniting us. But no one felt the need to move away from it more than me, even if my memory would not be so forgiving.

"So . . ." I started, wanting to get it out there as quickly as possible. "The blonde nurse you were with last week . . . are you and she . . . ?"

"No. We aren't dating if that's what you're asking."

"I think she really likes you."

"Yes. Well, she's very nice."

There was that half-hearted word again – *nice*.

"I'm really happy to see you again," Dr. Paterson said, changing gears. "You look . . . wonderful . . . and happy." He gave me a simple smile and I flushed.

"Thank you. I'm doing okay. I like my new job. I hope your sister likes what I picked out for her. Tell her to feel free to come see me if she wants," I offered.

"I'll mention it to her. I think she'd like that. Barbara is pretty easy going. She's the quintessential 'you shouldn't have' type."

"You and your sister...are you close?"

"Yes, we are. It's just us two. Her boys grew up so much while I was away. I missed family."

An all-too-familiar pang of loss swooped in and I tried not to let it show, but it was too late. "What was your sister like?" Dr. Paterson asked.

I remained wordless for a few moments. No one had ever asked me that. It seemed like most people were afraid to ask for fear of upsetting me, but I wanted to talk about her - needed to. "Thank you," I said, smiling through little wisps of memories. "She loved paper dolls and jump rope and chewing bubble gum." An image flickered of her hula-hooping on the sidewalk in front of our house. "She was two parts energy and three parts sunshine. When she passed, it was like an eternal light went out in my home. My parents...." I briefly closed my eyes and had to take a breath. Dr. Paterson put his hand over mine, giving me a kind look, encouraging me to go on. "My father can't . . . he never talks about her. My mother . . . she often sits on the edge of my sister's bed, holding Posey's stuffed bear and staring at her pillow, talking to her as though she were still there. Frankly, I do it too sometimes. Occasionally, my mother will strip the bed and wash all the bedding and I wonder if maybe this time she won't make the bed up again, hoping she doesn't. But she does, leaving it exactly the way my sister liked it. It's been almost three years." I feel my eyes fill up. "I miss her terribly."

When the waitress brought over our food order, I realized my hand was still lying under his. "Sorry." I pulled it back and wiped a tear.

He gave me a reminder grin. "No need to ..."

"Say sorry," we finished together and chuckled.

Looking at the food spread out on the table, I was shocked by the quantity. Fries, burgers, bowls of soup, a club sandwich, and salads. "We ordered all this?"

"I'm really hungry. I skipped lunch today. Don't worry. I'll eat whatever you can't finish." He reached for the catsup on the table. "What do your friends, your family, call you?" he asked. "Do they call you Liz?"

"Yes. Liz, mostly. My father calls me Lizzie." And then, as an afterthought, "Occasionally, I've been called Beth, but not so much."

"Do you have a preference?"

"No. All of the above."

"Beth," he said, listening to the sound of it, the "th" coming off his tongue like a tiny ocean breeze. "I like it. Can I call you Beth?"

"Fine with me." I was still whirling.

"My name's Joseph by the way. Friends call me Joe."

Joe. It sounded oddly casual to my ears, but my mind understood its meaning.

It was touching watching him eat, relishing every bite. A thought occurred to me then - how much fuller life would be if we tackled it in the same way – appreciating every moment, no matter how small or insignificant. I loved that moment.

Joe lifted a forkful of gravy-covered fries to his lips. "So, you're happy at your new job?" he said before putting it into his mouth.

"I am. I find it very satisfying, particularly when I can help lift someone's spirits with just a few little makeup tricks." I took another bite of my club sandwich. "This really is quite good," I remarked. "Of course, my profession is not nearly as intense as yours."

"Health and beauty - two counterparts to good living," Joe said in his usual way of making me feel good about myself, never patronizing.

"It's been busy," I added, and then think that a steady flow of customers doesn't equate to an ER doctor's meaning of the word busy. "That is, sales are up." Joe circled his hand around his drink glass, and I couldn't help noticing his long, slender fingers. "Did you always want to be a doctor?"

"I thought about it a lot when I was younger. Anatomy interested me. But I think what solidified it is when I watched my grandfather – my idol - die in front of me. I was nine at the time. We were all sitting around the dining table one Sunday when my grandfather collapsed. Everyone thought he had a heart attack, but he'd choked to death. I believe he might have been saved if someone had known what to do or what to look for."

I immediately thought of my sister, wondering if her life, too, could have been saved if her infection had been caught earlier.

The waitress cleared our plates from the table and Joe asked, "How about dessert?"

"Oh, I don't think I could," I said.

"You've got to try the strawberry cheesecake. We'll share it." He put the order in. "Coffee too?"

"None for me," I said.

"That goes for both of us. I have to get an early start tomorrow."

"What time is it?" I asked, not wanting the evening to end but knowing it had to. My parents might be worrying.

Joe checked his watch. "Eight-twenty."

"Is it really?" The time had flown.

We felt an urgency to say all the things still unsaid as the end of the evening drew closer and time clashed rudely with our enjoyment of it. I asked Joe to be sure to say hello to Nurse Agnes for me. I followed up on how his house hunting had come along and he admitted it hadn't, finding time to do it being a major deterrent. Then Joe said, "I'd like to know something before you leave here tonight, if you don't mind. The scar under your hairline – has it healed well? May I see it?"

I pushed my hair back so he could look at it. He reached over and glided his fingers across the slightly raised scar, still pinkish in color under the foundation I had applied over it. Touching my skin ever so lightly, meeting my eyes - the man now, not the doctor. It aroused a strong emotion in me, a feeling of absolute tenderness that left me speechless. *What was happening to me?*

Joe took his hand away and spoke in a soft voice, his eyes not leaving mine. "It's healing nicely. I'm pleased."

Feeling self-conscious, I first looked away, patting my hair back over the scar, and then to the uneaten cheesecake between us, dazed.

After he paid the tab, we walked out to the parking lot together and he saw me to my car.

"Good night, Beth," he said, enunciating the end part of the name and not the beginning, already making it his own rendition. "I really do enjoy talking with you."

We came together in an embrace, holding each other for what seemed like elongated minutes, our hearts beating against one another in a hug that seemed to say, "Somehow, I feel I've known you all my life." I stood breathless in front of him and felt my cheeks heat.

"I've missed our talks," he said.

"We never seem to run out of things to say, do we? Well, good night . . . Joe."

I turned to go when Joe blurted, "Are you working this Saturday?"

I spun around to face him again. "Saturday? Yes. I start work at ten."

"Can you meet me here again before then? For an early breakfast."

I wanted to. "Saturday morning?"

"I promise you . . . the pancakes are amazing. I really want you to try them."

I looked down at the ground for a moment before lifting my eyes to meet his – bright and expectant. I realized I was seeing him with new eyes. I dropped my gaze. "Okay," slipped easily from my lips.

Night was beginning to fall around us. I watched Joe outside my car window taking bouncy steps to his own car, turning once with a friendly smile and a wave of his hand before he got into his.

Pancakes and promises. What an unexpected day. The day we became Beth and Joe.

CHAPTER 12

Amanda

Today is Jesse's last full day at the convention, and I catch myself looking for him, wondering if we'll get much opportunity to see one another again before he leaves. I missed him at breakfast this morning. Dawn darts a glance behind us.

"He just came in; he's sitting in the far back of the room with some of the others," she whispers.

I can't hide my excitement from her. I smile wide, even as I force myself to look straight ahead, focusing on this morning's lecturer.

Day two's program, hosted by Jesse's legal team has started - the first half focusing on medical malpractice insurance, the second on post-Covid protocols for the medical community. Although Jesse isn't presenting today, he's assisting and supporting colleagues from his firm.

When we break for lunch Jesse walks straight over to me. "Hello there."

"Hey," I say. A flashback from last night rouses inside of me.

"I overslept," Jesse says. He gives me a flirtatious smile. "I had a great time last night."

"Me too."

"What are your plans for later?"

"Dawn and I were thinking of lounging by the pool after this thing is over today. Dinner is still up in the air."

"That's perfect," Jesse says. "A bunch of us were planning to go for a swim. I'll look for you there."

"Okay," I say, wondering how I'll ever get through the afternoon's lecture.

"By the way, I like your hair like that."

I reach up to touch my high ponytail, remembering this morning's rush to get ready. A coy smile breaks out on my face. "It was the best I could come up with."

Matt is hand signaling to Jesse. "See you over at the pool later."

***

After sitting through the afternoon's lectures and glancing at the wall clock periodically, Dawn and I head to the rooftop pool. In my phone call to Nana, I had hinted at having met an attractive lawyer. I knew she would enjoy hearing that.

"I'd like to meet him someday," Nana said.

"It's still too soon for that." I didn't want either of us to get our hopes up.

"That so*meday* can happen in a blink."

"Is Dorothy with you now?" I ask.

"Yes. Doing some cleaning and laundry at the moment. I've got the Scrabble board out for when she's through."

"Nana, you are ruthless."

"I have to keep up my mental acuity, dear."

"Yes, but maybe you should go a little easier on Dorothy. She's never played before you introduced her to the game."

"She's getting better, and a little competition never hurt anyone. You should know I only play to win."

I chuckle. "Don't I ever." Even as young children, Nana never helped me or my cousins win at board games. She used to say that we gained a whole lot more playing fair and learning how to lose. "I'll call you again," I say before hanging up.

We step onto the rooftop, blinking in the bright sunshine. Although it's later in the afternoon, the heat hasn't abated. I slip on my sunglasses when I see him. Jesse springs up out of the pool's water closest to a basketball net, his tanned, muscular back and shoulders releasing the ball into the air, making the shot.

"How about these two lounge chairs?" Dawn asks, making me realize I'm still staring. Jesse hasn't seen me yet, as he's actively involved in a water basketball game.

I peel off my white crochet cover up, unveiling a black, two-piece bathing suit. To compliment her olive complexion, Dawn sports a bright pink tankini.

"Amanda!" Eddie calls my name and Jesse stops in mid-air and looks over my way. For a split second our eyes meet before Eddie, in marble print swim trunk and transition glasses, walks over to me. "I'm glad to see you're feelin' much better."

Dawn gives me a confused look. "Yes, well, fortunately last night's headache is all gone," I say, tipping Dawn off. "This is my friend, Dawn. We're getting ready to lie here in the sun for awhile."

"Howdy do, ma'am. Would it be all right if my friend and I join you ladies?" Eddie waves someone over. He introduces us to another thirty-something man named Ted, a married podiatrist. Dawn and I stretch out on two lounge chairs. Eddie pulls another one over, bringing it to my side; I can feel him eyeing me behind his dark lenses while I apply sunscreen over my under-tanned arms and legs. "SPF 50," he reads, nodding approval.

I sip a mojito and pretend to listen to what Eddie is saying, but behind my dark glasses I'm watching Jesse play a rigorous game of water basketball. A blonde woman leans over the side of the pool to say something to him. Jesse laughs and then resumes playing. *Who is she?*

I'm enjoying the camaraderie of like-minded medical professionals, but in the back of my mind I'm still wondering who the blonde woman is. After a while I say, "I need to go for a dip." I remove my sunglasses and walk over to the pool.

"Wait up," Eddie says, following close behind. His hovering is becoming annoying. I jump in and swim the length of the pool under water, emerging near a decorative boulder. Eddie has lost me, or rather, I lost him. I can see his head a good distance away, bobbing over the water in pursuit of me. I catch myself laughing and dip behind the rock where I can hide, enjoying some alone time. From behind the rock, I take another peek and spot Eddie swimming in my direction.

I duck under the water again, years of breath-control training during my college days on the swim team serving me well. I open my eyes under the water, looking up, when I see Eddie over the top. He is looking all around him and then he spots me and breaks into a smile. I come to the surface and flick back my hair.

"Wow," he says, "how did you get away from me so fast?"

In that instant, a basketball smacks the water between us, and Eddie jumps back to get out of its way. I spin around to see Jesse swimming over to us.

"Sorry 'bout that. It got away from me." Jesse apologizes.

Eddie hands Jesse back the ball.

"Didn't mean to interrupt," Jesse says.

I glare at Jesse. I wish I could believe it was an accident.

"No harm done," Eddie says.

"Really, I'm sorry about that," Jesse says. "Let me buy you a drink."

Where have I heard that before? Jesse must have a cash reserve just for apology drinks.

"Not necessary," Eddie says.

"I insist." Jesse extends his hand to Eddie for a shake. "I'm Jesse, by the way."

"Yes. I remember you," Eddie says, shaking Jesse's hand. "You're the lawyer who spoke yesterday."

"You have to let me buy you a drink," Jesse says. "I won't take no for an answer. In fact, a bunch of us are talking about going over to a beer garden not very far from here later. Say, around 7:30? You and your friends should join us." Jesse looks over at me, gives me a smug smile. "It should be a lot of fun. Less formal than last night's dinner of course. Classic Nashville."

"Well," Eddie says, looking over at me. "How does that sound to you . . . want to go?" He pauses then adds, "This is my friend, Amanda. Have you two met?"

"Yes, we've . . . met," I stammer. I wish Jesse would wipe the grin off his face.

"Well," Eddie says, trying to read my face, waiting for an answer. "What do you say? I'll go if you go."

"I have to check with Dawn, but I don't see why not. We didn't make any plans."

It's extraordinary, really, watching Jesse in action, controlling the entire situation. Not only did he accomplish stopping Eddie in his tracks, but he's winning over the man's friendship. He drapes his arm around Eddie's shoulder.

"Hey, Matt!" He shouts over to his friend, "Meet Eddie. He and his friends will be joining us this evening."

"Great," Matt says, giving him a thumb's up from the other side of the pool.

I picture Jesse in a courtroom, his presence commanding, a spirited defender and adversary. I'm not sure what I'm feeling. Part of me is fascinated; the cautious side of me is apprehensive.

***

Flipping through the arsenal of summer dresses I had packed, it takes me a nanosecond to decide on the more fitted, striped metallic one. My counterattack dress. I dress it down by wearing a pair of cowgirl boots with it. Something inside me is swelling. I felt it emerge the moment I witnessed Jesse's forceful exchange with Eddie. A sense of retaliation and retribution toward Jesse stirs within me now, emboldening me in ways I never thought possible. I'm not sure which makes me warier. The fact that he needed to throw Eddie off course or the blonde woman he was laughing with.

A group is assembling outside in front of the hotel. Eddie gave me his cell phone number so I could text him when I was ready to come down. He said he'd be outside waiting.

"Are we ready?" Dawn asks.

I shoot Eddie a text.

Me

On our way down now.

Eddie

I'm out front with the others.

So now he has my phone number.

When Dawn and I come through the front entrance of the lobby, Eddie steps outside the group to greet us, his hands tucked inside pockets of gray, classic-fit shorts.

"You look terrific," Eddie says.

"Thank you," I say, giving Eddie a hug, my first counterpunch smile over his shoulder at Jesse, who is standing right behind him.

"You, too, ma'am," Eddie says, turning to Dawn, the polite gentleman in him unfailing.

"Back atcha," Dawn says, laughing out loud.

"I don't think we've met," a woman in the group says, coming over to Dawn and me. She's the blonde woman I saw talking to Jesse by the pool earlier. "I'm Sue. I work with Jesse and Matt." I begin to feel foolish. I really do have to let my guard down a bit.

Sue looks around our age, has a short, blunt-cut, blonde bob, and is wearing a pink t-shirt dress with designer sneakers. We easily strike up a conversation with her. Jesse is chatting with Eddie and Tom, his social adeptness on full display.

We stroll onward together toward the brewery. The sun, low in the sky, casts a golden and reddish glow, live music blaring long before we reach the entrance.

Dawn lets out a holler. "They're playing my song!" She sings along to "It's You I've Been Looking For."

Jesse and I glance at one another, our harmonized thoughts stirring with the lyrics. Remembering him, being in his arms, his lips on mine . . . I want to be alone with him again, but my mind tells me that for now I'm safer in a group. I need to sort out my feelings, learn more about who Jesse is while watching him with others.

A cell phone rings and we all look at each other. It's Jesse's. He takes the call, falling behind us as we continue walking. When I glance back, he's immersed in conversation with whoever is on the other end.

The brewery is alive with people – voices raised in conversation to be heard over the live music, sporadic hoots and laughter coming from outside as well as inside. The energy of the crowd moves us toward the moonshine tasting bar on the distillery side – pickle, salty caramel whiskey, butter pecan cream. Some of the guys in our group grab a table that has opened up, adding another to it to make it longer. Beers are airborne, passing through hands and sliding along the tables. The place is in full party mode.

"The salty caramel is to die for," Dawn shouts over the din. Sue and I agree, licking our lips.

I pull my lips from my glass. "Although this butter pecan is a strong contender. What do you think, Sue?"

"I think I'll reserve my decision until after I've tasted them all. How many are we gonna taste exactly?"

We look at the bartender. "Seven," she says.

"Seven lovelies," Dawn says. "Where did I hear that from?"

"Seven is heaven," I say.

"Or could be seven deadly sins," Sue says.

We all laugh. "Cheers to that," Dawn says. We give Sue a high five.

"So how long have you known Jesse and Matt?" I ask Sue.

"Six . . . no, seven years."

"You're friends then," I say, trying to learn more.

"You could say that. Work hard, play harder. It couldn't be truer for us. We're sort of like family."

"That's wonderful," I say, before taking a sip of Sunbeach sample number five.

"Well, they seem like a couple of fun guys," I say.

"Yeah, they are. Matt's the more easy-going one. Jesse is clever as hell, but he can also be intense."

"Intense? In what way?" I ask.

"There's a seriousness about him. He can turn it on like a switch when he needs to. He was a great friend to me during my divorce. I don't know how I would have gotten through one of the worst times of my life without his friendship. I'd like to think I was there for him too, when he needed someone."

My feelers are up. "Why?"

"How's it going over here?" Eddie, who has the worst timing, has stepped between Sue and me wearing a newly purchased cowboy hat. "We ordered a tray of tacos. Come over to the table when you're done."

What did Sue mean when she said she was there for Jesse when he needed someone, too? Now I may never know.

Dawn gives out a hoot. "Did you get a taste of the peach whiskey?"

"Was that number six?" Sue asks.

"Feels more like sixty," Dawn says. "But who's counting?"

Sue says, "This is way more fun than last night's stuffy dinner."

Dawn smiles wide. "Oh . . . we like you, don't we, Amanda?"

I could learn so much from Sue about Jesse, but the inquiring momentum has ended, and I can't get it back.

The bartender pours our seventh tasting of moonshine. Key lime pie. By this time, we all feel fine.

I slide off my barstool, the floor swaying beneath my feet. Dawn, Sue and I are a tangle of giggles and squeals as we make our way over to the table where the men have saved us seats. "Here they come," Eddie announces. He jumps to his feet and waves a bartender over. "Can we get you ladies a beer?" He pulls out the chair next to him. "Amanda, your seat's right over here."

"Well, thank you, Eddie," I say, feeling loopy. "Mighty kind of you." I swipe his cowboy hat off his head and place it on mine, my hair bouncing off my shoulders. "Mind if I borrow this?"

"It's yours," Eddie says, giving me a folksy smile. "Looks way better on you anyway." He tips the front of it down over my eyes. "Yeah. Just like that."

Jesse is at the other end of the table, watchful eyes in a somber face, muscles twitching. The serious side of Jesse. Under my hat, I peer into his eyes for a split second, conveying a strong message. *So what now? You gonna throw a taco at him?*

I lift a mug of beer to my mouth, a beer I can't seem to remember ordering, but here it is, right in front of me. Tacos and pretzels are passed around. Dawn and some of the others are vibing to the music. I push back my chair. "Ladies' room break," I say. Dawn, who usually accompanies me, is ensnared in the song. My legs feel a little less balanced than usual, but my boots make walking less of a challenge.

I exit the ladies' room, heading straight for the outdoors, where a kaleidoscope of stars and string lights ignite the night.

"Do you want to talk about it?" a voice says, coming up behind me. Jesse is standing over me, his head cocked, searching my face.

I look him straight in the eyes. "Did you really have to almost smash him with your ball?"

"I could see he was bothering you."

"It was rather impetuous, don't you think? Whether he was or wasn't bothering me was none of your concern. I could handle it. I *was* handling it."

"I'm sorry. I just...I wanted to get him away from you. It was the quickest way I could think of to stop him."

I give Jesse a disapproving look.

"I know. He didn't deserve that. He's a decent guy. I've even grown rather fond of him." An ironic smile crosses Jesse's face. "You do something to me," Jesse says. "Ever since I met you. It's . . . well, it's making me do crazy things. I'm not gonna lie." He leans down, tilts up my hat and looks steadily into my eyes. "I haven't felt this way in a long, long while. Life has taught me to appreciate moments like this when they happen."

"So, you're saying you appreciate me?"

Jesse's face draws closer as he looks into my eyes. Seconds sneak past, diverging with our time, which has stopped. "I'm saying . . . I want to kiss you this very moment."

My eyes must be telling him I want him to, too, because in a swift move, his mouth claims mine. The warmth of his lips and tongue shatter me. My hat falls to the ground.

Jesse wraps me in his arms and kisses the top of my head. "Amanda . . ." he says, "I want to see you when you get back home, where we can talk more."

"Aren't we talking now?"

"No. I mean *really* talk. I'd like us to get to know each other better." Jesse lifts my hat up off the ground, smooths my hair, and places it back on my head. "They're probably looking for us. We should go back," Jesse whispers.

"Right." *Who are you, Jesse?*

He stays back a little so I can go first.

"Everything all right?" Eddie asks when I return to our table.

"Fine," I say, averting his eyes.

Dawn murmurs in my ear. "You two were gone for a while."

Jesse returns, grabs his beer and chugs it.

Sue looks from him to me, revelation showing on her face. She knows about us. She lifts up her glass of beer and clinks it with mine.

When the night progresses into the harmfully late stage, we all agree it's a good time to walk back to the hotel. The lawyers are flying home tomorrow. The rest of us have day three of lectures to attend in the morning. Dawn, Sue, and I make one last trip to the ladies' room. I lag behind when I notice Jesse standing outside in the spot where we had kissed. I step out into the night air then realize Jesse is on his cell phone, his back to me. "I know, honey," I overhear him say. "I'll be home tomorrow. I miss you too."

I retreat into a dark shadowy area, my mind reeling with questions. I'm frozen with dread, my stomach churning with tacos and whiskey and beer.

"There you are. Ready?" Dawn says over my shoulder. I move without thinking and follow her, my heart pounding in my ears.

"A last-minute tryst with Jesse?"

I link arms with Dawn and walk faster, pushing through a crush of people. "Let's get out of here," I say, fuming.

"You okay?" Dawn asks, keeping pace with me.

"No," my voice quavers. "I'm not okay."

CHAPTER 13

Elizabeth
September 1953

"Shall I order us some more?" Joe asked, finishing his last bite of pancake.

We only had an hour when we met at the diner for an early breakfast on Saturday morning. We didn't want to squander a second of it so we dove into conversation while eating triple-stacked jumbo pancakes heaped with strawberries and whipped cream. It was easy being with Joe, as it always was, his doctor's veneer melting with each one of our get-togethers. Everything about him fascinated me, and I soaked up every word he said, savoring in his brilliant insights and reveling in his casual quips. I was getting to see his less serious side, which I found equally mesmerizing.

"I couldn't eat another bite," I said, looking down at my half-finished portions and pushing off from the table. "I mean, it's delicious, but you can't be serious." I gave him an incredulous look.

"It's hopeless to try and stop me, you know." Amusement covered his face as he persisted, motioning for the waitress. I must have had shock written all over my face. When the waitress came over to our table, he simply asked for the check. I shook my head and he laughed out loud.

"Dr. . . . Joe, I mean." I was still trying to get used to calling him by his first name. "Thank you again for the breakfast invitation. I loved the–"

"Company?" he interjected with an impish grin. He had a hundred different smiles, one more charming than the next.

"I was going to say pancakes."

"Touché."

We hurried to our cars, but not before Joe said, "Let's do this again. I gotta see when I can get off next; things have been really hectic at the hospital. But I'll make it happen."

"Yes, well, I'll need to check my schedule. You know, girls gotta have their lipsticks."

Looking intrigued and amused, Joe pulled me into him. "You're a curious one, Beth." He held me for a brief, tenuous moment and then leaned down so he could look me in the eye. It was serious Joe now. "I want to see you again." He said it with such tenderness, my heart opened up and I beamed a smile. I started to speak when he closed my lips with his, giving me a tentative kiss, a hint of strawberries and coffee and cream passing between us. My eyes closed. He kissed me again with warm, urgent intensity, carrying with it all the emotions he dared himself to feel. My body went limp; my head was spinning. I couldn't remember if I was ever kissed like that before. I should have remembered that.

It was hard when we had to pull ourselves apart. I felt he didn't want to either. When we got into our cars and drove off to work in different directions, my thoughts were a clutter of sensations that I couldn't seem to separate. As I got further away, insulated by distance, emotions of the last few minutes merged uncontrollably with the last few years, and I couldn't stop what was coming. A cascade of pent-up tears rushed out, and I cried until I could hardly see the road anymore. "Joe," I said softly, loosening my grip on the wheel. "Oh . . . Joe."

***

I visited Robbie's gravesite on the following Sunday, laying flowers over his plot as I did on the first anniversary of his death. It was hard to believe it would soon be two years since he had passed. In my dreams I still saw him wearing his uniform, young and zealous. When I was with Robbie, I knew who I was. I knew me. Lately, I didn't recognize myself.

Could I be opening myself up to love again? Robbie was my first experience with love. He was my best friend before he became my lover. He gave me a foundation to love. What I was feeling for Joe was intensely different. It was provocative. This older man both alarmed and thrilled me, and it was as if I didn't trust me anymore, my thoughts mystifying and overwhelming and emotive.

The days in between seeing Joe felt like forever. My moods were up and down. My parents - my mother mostly - took notice. "What's gotten into you? You're not yourself."

I didn't know how to tell her, or even what to tell her. I could try to explain what Joe and I were to one another – friends for now, who were attracted to each other. To my own ears, the word "friends" sounded foolish. Friends didn't make me blush the way Joe did, nor did they make my heart throb and my skin tingle. The hopelessness of my true feelings might not escape my mother's natural instinct. My mother was still adjusting to my breakup with Jim, a decision I knew was right as soon as I made it. No, I couldn't tell her. Not until I knew *what* to tell her.

***

A spread of sausage links and eggs and toast sat on a table between Joe and me one September morning when we were able to schedule another early breakfast rendezvous. I was sipping coffee and glancing out the window of our booth when I noticed it had started drizzling. Considering the unpreparedness of what I was wearing that day – a fitted pink cardigan over a buttoned-up white blouse - I said, "I didn't bring an umbrella with me."

"It's just a sprinkle." Joe looked amused. Then, out of the blue as was his usual, he said, "I'd like to take you to a nice restaurant on Saturday. It's called The Divan Parisien in New York City. Will you join me?"

"Dinner this Saturday?" I placed my coffee cup back in its saucer with a little too much vigor. *Did Joe just ask me out on a date to a fancy restaurant?*

"This will be the first weekend in months that I have off. It doesn't happen very often. Please say you'll join me. If you say no, I'll be left alone with a book for companionship."

I found that somewhat hard to believe, but I didn't want to put it to the test either. "Yes." I smiled into my cup. "I would love to have dinner with you."

"I'll pick you up. Maybe we could do a movie too, if you'd like. *From Here to Eternity* is playing. People at the hospital are talking about it. I haven't been to the movies in . . . well, I don't even remember when. What do you say?"

"Sounds like fun," I said, playing out all the related scenarios that went with Saturday's date. It was only a few days away. Joe would have to meet my parents. Whatever was I going to wear? I needed a new dress!

In the diner parking lot before each of us left for work that morning I anticipated his kiss, remembering and longing for it. A light rain dotted our clothes as we stood near my car. He steadied my face in his hands and guided it upward so I could see his eyes captivated, his lips parting, enticing me until we could no longer wait. When his lips left mine, slowly and unwillingly, he kept his face close, caressing my cheek with his breath until he reached my ear and whispered, "Saturday."

Rain trickled on my face as we both looked up at the deepening murky sky. Joe helped me get into my car for cover a few seconds before the rain poured down, soaking him before he got to his. Slamming his car door shut, he looked out the window at me, wet hair swept over his forehead, laughing and shaking his head. He was adorable. Knowing I didn't have to wonder when we would see each other again thrilled me beyond belief. I blew him a kiss and then drove off.

It was always hard leaving. I felt the familiar parting ache, but the imminence of Saturday cheered me up at once. There was a lot to do in a short amount of time. First and foremost, I needed to have a talk with my parents. I hadn't even told them about Joe yet. And last, but not least, I needed a new dress. I had seen a really pretty red dress on a mannequin in the women's clothing department at Bamberger's - a Jane Derby boat-neck swing dress with a pretty satin sash. It had caught my eye, but I recalled the price was high - nearly $12.00! It was more than I'd ever spent on clothing. My mind was spinning. I'd need shoes too. The Baby Toes heeled shoes in the shoe department came in different colors. Red too, I hoped. In my mind, I was planning everything from my hair to my feet, accessories and all. It was the most fun I'd had in a very long time.

CHAPTER 14

Amanda

"You must have gotten in late. I didn't hear you come in," Nana says. "How was the convention?"

I carry my mug of steaming hot coffee into the sunroom to join her before I have to leave for work. The sun is rising behind a mountain, casting its rays across the peaks and into the valleys. It is my daily oasis of calm before the workday begins.

"It was good," I say, gazing out the window and then at her.

"Well...what else? It certainly sounded like it wasn't all work and meetings," she says.

I can hear the loving expectancy in her voice. I feel so foolish. Why did I have to go and tell her I'd met an attractive lawyer? I should know better. I shrug away, moving closer to the window, and take a sip of my coffee. It burns my tongue. "I met a lot of nice people and we got to do some fun things. The hotel we stayed in was beautiful...some thirty-three stories high." I turn around to look at her again. "The view of Nashville from up there was spectacular."

Nana isn't sidetracked. "Tell me about that exciting new lawyer friend you met. What's he like?"

Frustration rushes out before I can quash it. *Ugh.* "He's not exactly what I would call a friend. He's arrogant and self-serving and . . . who knows what else."

Nana gives me a dubious look. She's probably thinking she's never seen me so emotional and on edge before. Serves me right for letting myself get carried away with Jesse's romantic overtures. I sigh and give Nana a quick account. I owe her that at least. "He seemed nice at first. Until I got to know him a little more. Well, actually, I really don't know him at all."

"Hmmm," Nana says, her face telling me she knows only too well that there's usually a hidden catch in the details, but she lets it go.

Dorothy arrives at the house, and I go over to kiss Nana on the cheek. "Have to go. Love you."

"Love you, too."

I head back to the kitchen where I left my cell phone on the counter by my purse. "Good morning," I say to Dorothy. Her short, plump frame and middle-aged face is capped with a cute graying pixie cut. "Nana is ready for you, and she's quite in her element. She's even got the Scrabble board pulled out for later."

"She's beaten me three times in a row," Dorothy says.

I laugh. "Well, maybe today's the day you'll break her winning streak."

"Or she'll kick my butt again." She grins as she passes me to join Nana in the sunroom.

I check my cell phone messages. Dr. Cullen has left me several. A patient of his, a sixteen-year-old female and two-year post-transplant heart recipient, experienced a high fever and headaches and was rushed to the emergency room last night. She's been admitted to the hospital and Dr. Cullen is in consultation with the cardiothoracic team and wants me in the loop since he's away this week on vacation.

I scroll through my other messages and see one from Jesse. My heart leaps.

Jesse
I'll be in Asheville today for a hospital administrative meeting.
Can we meet? ...I have to see you.

My fingers have a will of their own.

Me

Not sure when I will be done making rounds.
Could be late.

Jesse

I'll wait...what I have to say can't.

Dawn's voice is inside my head. *You need to confront him. At least hear him out.*

Me

I'll try.

I don't know how I feel about seeing Jesse again. My emotions run the gamut from magic to misery. To be honest, I'm more wary of what he'll say than what he hasn't said. I took a chance on someone again. Perhaps that's how the story goes: two people meet...stop. Two fleeting, fabulous days...full stop.

I can make myself forget Jesse if I will it. With the passing of time, when I can no longer still feel him, I'll be fine.

***

Dawn is getting off her hospital shift and comes over to me. "Hey. I was hoping I'd see you. You'll never guess who I saw earlier."

I wait for her to tell me.

"Jesse's here."

"Here...now?"

"Yes. Apparently in a meeting with administration."

"So he's still at the hospital then?"

"I think so . . . I guess he is. He came over and said hello to me, asked if I knew when you'd be in. I told him you might be doing rounds later."

"Yes, well, he's hoping we can get together sometime today. I don't see how that's going to happen with everything on my schedule."

"There's something else," Dawn says. "He heard about the young heart transplant patient in room 320."

I'm getting annoyed. "What about her?"

"He wanted to know how she's doing. He looked troubled or upset or...something. When I asked him how he heard of her, all he said was that her case is well known and that the hospital is a small world."

I swear he's getting on my nerves. "Incredible how word travels. I'm going over to see her now. Her fever and headaches are worrying. The poor girl has been through so much already."

Dawn throws on her shoulder bag. "I'm heading out. Long day. Greg's fixing me dinner."

"He's a keeper," I say.

"I'll be off on Friday. Wedding gown fitting. If you can get away, I'd love your input. My mom and sister are coming. We can do lunch."

"I would if I could. But with Dr. Cullen away on vacation, I don't see how I can. Send me photos, will you, please? I'd love to see your dress."

Dawn gives me a quick hug before starting for the elevator and I head to the nurses' station in the pediatric ward. I ask for the chart on the sixteen-year-old patient of Dr. Cullen's. It's the first time I'll be meeting Lisa who, two years ago, suffered severe end-stage heart failure. For someone so young, transplant was the best option; however, she was too sick to wait for a new heart, so a mechanical pump called a left ventricular assist device was implanted to help preserve her kidneys, lungs and liver. That same night a thirty-two-year-old woman died as a result of a car accident. Her ID card said she wanted to be an organ donor and Lisa woke up with a new chance at life.

I enter room 320. Lisa looks like a typical sixteen-year-old girl – medium-length brown hair streaked with turquoise highlights, wireless AirPods in her ears, eyes closed and preoccupied. She's had two years since she received the new heart, and although rejection is always a risk, it usually occurs within the first year.

I put my hands over her ankles, checking for swelling. Lisa opens her eyes and pulls the AirPods out of her ears.

"Hello," I say. "I'm Amanda. I work with Dr. Cullen." I'm aware that several healthcare workers have already been in to see her over the past two days and I'm just one more whose name she won't remember. "How are you feeling today?" I go over to her side, taking her temperature.

"I feel okay," Lisa says. "Do you think I'll be able to leave here in a few days?"

"Well, we'll see. Your temperature's still a little high."

Lisa's blood tests indicate an infection for which heart transplant recipients are at high risk due to anti-rejection medications suppressing the body's immune system. Hopefully, a heart biopsy won't be needed to rule out rejection. "Any more headaches or achiness?" I ask her.

"It's gotten better. I have to go home by next weekend."

"You sound like a girl with plans," I say.

"Well, yeah. My boyfriend's hoping I can go with him to his parents' summer place in Folly Beach. If I can't make it, it'll really suck."

My instincts tell me Lisa's weekend beach plans may be overly ambitious but instead I tell her we're waiting on more tests.

"I even bought a new bathing suit, a one-piece that covers my scar but has cutouts on the sides. We're going dolphin watching."

I remember what it was like being sixteen, when the only pressing thing on my mind was what I was going to be doing on the weekend, when you're living for two days and not in the moment. An indulgence Lisa appreciates better than most of her peers, when each and every day is a gift to be celebrated.

I press on Lisa's abdomen. "Do you feel any pain in your tummy?"

Lisa shakes her head.

I listen to her heart, for the sound that shows it's functioning normally. No irregular heartbeats or murmurs. "So what's he like?"

She likes that question better than the medical ones which she's no doubt had to answer repeatedly over the last couple of days.

"He's one year younger than me and really cute – although *he* doesn't think so. He likes sci-fi and Mexican food and Minecraft." Lisa looks up at the ceiling, ruminating. "He's kind of a nerd, but he makes me laugh. He gets me. Ya know? I think that matters a lot. He makes my heart flutter." She catches herself. "Figuratively speaking, of course."

I smile. "He sounds very nice."

"He is," Lisa says. "Did I say he was cute?"

"Yeah. You might have mentioned something about that."

Lisa's cell phone dings a new text message. "It's him," she says.

"I'll be back to check on you tomorrow. Rest well for now."

"I can do that," she says.

I make three more stops during my rounds and then go over to the locker to retrieve my purse. "Have a good evening," I say to the nurses at the desk. I start down the corridor leading to the hospital staff's parking lot exit when I see Jesse coming toward me. Wearing a pewter gray suit and an eager smile, he's carrying a large briefcase with him. My breath catches in my throat.

"Amanda," he says.

I wish he didn't have to look so handsome. "Jesse."

"I'm so glad I caught you. Are you heading out?"

"Yes, I am."

"Can we go somewhere to talk?"

"Well, I–"

"I think I know why you've been distant with me. I can explain everything. Give me a chance...please."

"You don't have to," I say. "You don't owe me anything."

"Yes, I do. Have you had dinner?" He's persistent.

"I had a late lunch today. I was just planning on a light supper." The closer to me Jesse stands, the more I remember him - the feeling of being kissed by him. I recap the mantra inside my head. *I can forget. I'll be fine.*

"Let me join you. Pick a place. Any place."

His steady gaze makes me more eager than edgy. "Do you like Thai Tom Yum?"

"Perfect."

I get the feeling no matter what I chose, I'd have gotten the same answer.

We agree on a Thai restaurant on Hendersonville Road, fifteen minutes away by car.

"I need to get my visitor's parking ticket verified," Jesse says. "Should only take me a minute and I'll be right along. Do you want me to follow you or meet you there?"

"You can follow me. I drive a white Honda Civic."

While Jesse leaves to get his visitor ticket stamped, I head outdoors to my car, keys in hand. Daylight is fading. As I approach my car, my cell phone rings inside my purse. It may be Dr. Cullen. I open my purse, reaching inside. Someone suddenly grabs me from behind. I scream and spin around, glimpsing a guy in a hoodie. He yanks on my purse, but I'm not letting go of it. My mind is overtaken with dread and thinking, *No, not my ID cards, my phone...my passwords!* I clench my purse straps tighter, pulling back, screaming with a tremor in my voice. "No!"

"Give it to me, bitch." He hisses, sounding more desperate. "Give it to me!" His fist slams my face and knocks me down, my head hitting the ground hard. Lying there, my purse straps still wrapped around my wrist, he yanks on it while his hood falls back. Eye slits pierce me with darkness before he smashes my arm with his foot and I scream out in pain as he wrestles my purse away, then runs across the lot with it.

"Help!" I cry out. "My purse!"

I'm on the ground, my arm and hands are scraped, and I can taste blood inside my mouth. A man runs over to ask if I'm okay. Another runs in the direction of the man with the hood.

"Come on," the man who came to my aid says. "You need to be looked at. Let me help you into the ER."

"No, no" I say, "I'll be fine. I just need a moment."

He tries to help me to my feet before I lapse into unconsciousness.

CHAPTER 15

Elizabeth
October 1953

Joe pulled up in his splashy sports car at five o'clock on the dot. I watched through the window as he got out, smoothing his dark blue suit jacket and holding a bouquet of fall flowers, colors vibrant and striking against his car's whiteness. He came around and started toward my front door, and I gasped at his appearance, suave and elegant in formal attire.

Glancing in the vanity mirror one last time, I smacked my red painted lips together and stood up, brushing out my full red swing dress.

My parents sat at the kitchen table as nervous as I was - my mother, drumming her fingers and muttering about how she could have made the dress I purchased for much less money and better, and my father, smoking his third cigarette and telling my mother that her tapping was getting on his nerves.

I went to open the door. "You look beautiful," Joe said and gave me a sweet hug.

"Thank you. Come meet my parents."

"It's so very nice to meet you," Joe said, passing the bouquet to my mother. Then he went over and shook my father's hand as he stood up from the table.

"Is that the new Chevy you got out there?" Dad asked him.

"Yes, it is."

"How do you like the Corvette so far?"

"I'm still testing her out." Joe admitted. "Do you prefer Fords to Chevys?"

"No. Depends on the model," Dad said, easing into exchanges about one of his favorite topics. "I've worked on both."

"Perhaps you could take a look at my car's engine for me sometime. I'd like to get your opinion." My eyes danced between my mother and my father, and I was relieved to see they both looked more relaxed, their stiffened shoulders looser now, their smiles emanating from Joe's warmth and pleasantry.

Intermittently, I caught Joe's eyes on me, gleaming with admiration. I left them alone together while I went to retrieve my bolero jacket. I could overhear Joe reassuring my parents that he would take good care of me and get me home at a reasonable hour. He assisted me with putting on my jacket before we said good night to them and walked outside into the chilly autumn air. Opening the passenger side door of his two-seater, Joe said in a voice thick with emotion, his eyes riveted on me, "Beth, I could hardly take my eyes off you in there."

I sidled into the bucket seat and smiled at him. "You look really handsome."

Riding with Joe in his car, all gussied up for an evening out in the city was as natural as it was glamorous, my red dress blending with the luxurious red interior. The enclosed air imbued with scents of leather – so much leather! And spice and my fresh floral perfume. More intoxicating was Joe's nearness, the profile of his handsome face as he focused on the road ahead, a vibrant fall scene rolling past us, excitement surging as we got closer to our destination. I felt like a princess riding in a carriage – a fast one. If this was a dream, I didn't want to wake up.

We were listening to AM radio, enjoying Nat King Cole's *Pretend*, when I saw something out my window that startled me. A young child around two or three was alone, half-waddling, half-running along the sidewalk, screaming and crying hysterically as we passed.

"Joe," I cried. "Did you see that?"

"I saw it." The questioning look on his face mirrored my own.

"What should we do?"

Joe glanced at me and gave a sigh. "I'm gonna turn around. We should check it out."

Joe did an illegal pullover with his car across the street from where the child now stood, crying uncontrollably. We both got out and went over to him, Joe keeping back a little since the child appeared to fear me less. I leaned down. "Hello. What's your name?"

The little boy only sobbed, staring off to the side and then up the span of the sidewalk. "Where's your mommy?" I asked following his gaze until, halfway up the street, I spotted someone lying on the sidewalk near the curb. "Joe!" I yelled, pointing.

Joe raced up the block while I coaxed the child to take my hand. His cries had eased somewhat as we trudged up the sidewalk to the spot where Joe was.

When we reached him, he was removing his suit jacket and folding it to place under a woman's bleeding head, loosening some of the tight clothing around her neck. She was still until her arms began flailing, teeth clenched, her body convulsing violently.

The little boy erupted into tears again, so I moved him gently away from the scene. "Is that your mommy?" I asked, to which he nodded, crying some more. "It's going to be okay." I patted him on the head and then bent down so he could see my face. "Don't cry. We're here to help." Trusting me more, he reached his tiny fingers upward, wanting to be picked up. I lifted him in my arms and held him without a single thought other than to calm him. His tears and sniffles subsided.

Remembering a nursery rhyme I used to sing to Posey when she was little and couldn't fall back to sleep, I started singing softly. A tear ran down my cheek, the lullaby evoking all kinds of memories. Rubbing and patting the young child's back while he was faced away from his mother, whimpering now, I glanced over at the scene, watching Joe tend to the woman. He had rolled her over onto her side and was talking to her. I moved in a little closer so I could hear.

"Your son is here with us. Don't worry," I heard Joe tell her. "I'm a doctor. You've hit your head hard, but you're going to be fine. I believe you may have had a seizure. Have you ever had seizures before?"

"No," the woman murmured, visibly disoriented and scared.

Rocking the exhausted child in my arms and continuing to sing the lullaby, I laid his head on my shoulder.

"Listen, I'm going to stay right here with you until the ambulance arrives," Joe said. He looked over at me apologetically.

I nodded and mouthed the words, "It's okay."

I looked up and down 45th Street. A man had walked out of a café across the way and I moved swiftly in his direction, trying to get his attention. One arm still carried the sleepy child, the other waved him over. "Please, can you help us? We need an ambulance."

The man retreated to the café and a few moments later came outside to tell me a call had been put through. "Thank you," I said, swaying while still holding the young boy in my arms. He felt heavier, his arms hung loose, and he switched his face onto his opposite cheek where it rested again on my shoulder.

The weary child and I returned to Joe, my high-heeled shoes clacking on the sidewalk, and I let him know that an ambulance was on the way.

"Billy," the woman moaned. "I need to see him."

I moved over to the curbside and bent down so she could see her son over my shoulder. She smiled and stretched her arm out to touch my dress. "Oh my," she said, coming out of her daze. "I've met my angel, and she's beautiful."

I glanced over at Joe. He was looking at me, smiling.

I lowered the sleepy child into his mother's arm so he was lying close to her, waiting for the ambulance to arrive. The woman's purse was on the ground not too far from the spot where she'd collapsed, its contents spilled out. I gathered up her things and put them back inside her purse, keeping it near her.

My feet were killing me from my new shoes. Going over to the nearest tree, I leaned against it for some respite, taking in the touching scene before me and seeing it through my heart's eyes - Joe continuing to care for the woman with skill and tenderness. The mother wrapping her arm around her child as they lay huddled together on the pavement. The man from the café coming over to offer any assistance until the ambulance arrived. The sun setting in the sky in a streak of ink blue and violet. I hummed the lullaby tune still in my head.

Hush a bye, don't you cry
Go to sleep little baby
When you wake, you shall have
All the pretty little horses

How I segued to a state of all-encompassing purity, I couldn't tell you. I only knew that my consciousness completely changed, my mind expanding outside the scene, embracing emptiness and love and enormous pleasure. I felt childlike, my senses experiencing firsts in all their innocence, all concurrently. The pain and sorrow and doubt that had followed me with tenacity became nonexistent. And then there was the guilt I seemed to always carry with me . . . from loss, from allowing myself to feel again, for surviving when others hadn't. I felt lighter as I let go of everything that weighed me down, thoughts of purposefulness and awareness and harmony coursing through me. Spiritually, I never felt more alive.

The shriek of sirens pierced through my serenity. Lying on a stretcher, her child and purse intact, the woman was placed in the ambulance while Joe reclaimed his dirty, bloodied suit jacket from the ground and draped it over his arm.

Joe held my arm and steered me back to his car where a few male pedestrians stood admiring it. "Nice car," one of them said, "and a flip top, too. Does she burn rubber?"

"She does," Joe said.

He turned his soiled jacket inside out and placed it over the back of his seat. Settling into his car, Joe sighed, long and hard. "Well, that certainly wasn't planned." He looked at his watch regretfully. "Our dinner reservation was over an hour ago."

"Is the woman going to be okay?" I asked.

"She's where she needs to be now. They'll run some tests and see what's going on with her."

Calm and at peace, I gazed out the window.

Joe looked at me. "Beth? Are you all right? You seem far away."

I leaned back on the seat and observed the sliver of moon low in the sky. It was as if it was smiling at us. I couldn't deny the strong feeling that something in my life had shifted and I would never be the same again. All I could do was nod.

"I promise to make it up to you." He looked me over. "Oh no. Your dress."

I looked down at my dress and saw what he had seen. The hemline was frayed in one spot; a simple mend for my mother. I guessed I must have torn it when I leaned down over the curb or against the tree. Besides the tattered hemline, my dress looked disheveled and unclean, especially where the child had cried and drooled on my shoulder. And my hose had a run in them along the seam.

"Joe," I said, finding my voice and looking him in the eye. "Isn't it wonderful just being alive? I was outside my body back there, or something like it, seeing everything externally."

"What?"

"Just look at me. I've been Cinderella'd!" I threw my head back in laughter, happy tears springing to my eyes.

"Now I'm worried." Joe ran his fingers through his hair. "I need to get some food in you." He moved the car into a parking spot closer to the café and helped me out of my side. "Let's get something to eat here. We can also get washed up."

Stepping outside, I surveyed my rumpled dress again and giggled. Joe looked at me with a concerned eye.

"Oh Joe, Joe, Joe." When we reached the café's doorstep, I turned toward him and impulsively threw my arms around his neck, kissing him on the cheek. Joe drew his head back, looking equal parts pleased and cautious. I snickered. "I'm thinking about how this is going to look to my parents. Can you imagine the looks on their faces?"

"You're delirious." Joe draped a protective arm around my shoulder and led me into the café. "You'll feel better after you eat something."

"I have never felt better in my life." I was giddy with pleasure.

Joe studied me for a while, trying to understand.

"Joe, I don't know how, but I'll try to explain what's happened to me. If only I understood it. But first, I'm going to go to the washroom."

"I don't think I should leave you alone," Joe said, more serious than joking.

"Order me anything you'd like."

"Anything?" Joe asked.

"Anything."

Joe glanced over at me with a raised eyebrow, inciting more laughs from me. "Oh Joe," I said, before working my way toward the restroom, leaving him in a fog of confusion. "I have so much to tell you."

CHAPTER 16

Amanda

I'm lying on a hospital bed, an icepack leaning on the side of my face, curtains drawn around my room. I can hear talking and whispering right outside: *a victim of a mugging...she passed out.*

I lift my head, but it hurts. I turn it to the side. I'm alone in the room. Then I see it on a chair against the wall. My purse.

I want to get up and check inside it, but the curtain pulls open and a nurse I recognize walks in. "Amanda. How are you feeling?"

"A little sore I guess. How long have I been here?"

"Maybe twenty minutes. We could give you pain meds intravenously if you need."

"No. I can take something orally. I think I'm mostly shaken." I raise myself up slowly to a sitting position, hanging my legs over the side of the bed. "My purse...how-?"

"A gentleman who says he knows you. He's still here, talking to the police right now. I'll let them know you're awake."

Is it Jesse? "Can you pass my purse over to me first?"

I rummage inside it. Everything seems to be there - my wallet, my car keys, which must have fallen out of my hand, and even my cell phone. *Oh, thank God.* I put my head in my hands and sigh with great relief.

The nurse returns with Jesse by her side. My head is swelling with questions more than from the injuries. "Jesse."

"How are you doing?" He looks into my face, scowling at what he sees. I reach up to my sore cheek, swollen now.

"Keep the ice pack on it some more," the nurse says. I pick the ice pack up again and notice the scrapes on my hands and some cracked fingernails.

"You had us really worried," Jesse says. "From the looks of it, you put up quite a fight."

"I...I guess I resisted. I was so incensed. I didn't want him to take my purse. It all happened so fast. I would've given him whatever cash he wanted. I just wanted my cell phone, if that makes any sense." I look down at my purse. "How is it that my purse is here with me now?"

"You have him to thank for that," the nurse says, nodding at Jesse. She passes some pain meds for me to take with a glass of water.

"But how?" I ask, playing the scene back in my mind. "Was that you who went running after the attacker?"

"I heard your screams. I was over near the side where he took off running with a woman's purse, so I took off after him. I was able to catch up to him when he tried to jump the barrier. The rest is what you see."

"Oh my god." I remove the ice pack from my cheek for a bit to relieve the stinging of the cold. "You could have gotten hurt." For the first time I notice that Jesse isn't wearing his suit jacket and his shirt looks rumpled.

"I could say the same to you. He could have had a weapon. You didn't know. You could have gotten killed."

I close my eyes, Jesse's words ringing painfully true. "I know. Resisting was a risky thing to do. I realize that now."

"Luckily, he didn't have a weapon on him. None that I saw. The important thing is that you're okay," Jesse says.

"So the guy's been caught?"

"No. He got away. I hit him pretty hard and he dropped your purse, but then he took off. I didn't chase after him; I was too worried about you. I did get your purse though."

"You actually fought him?" I shudder. "I'm so sorry about all this."

"I'm sure the attacker didn't expect to be pursued by a black belt," the nurse chimes in.

"You're a black belt?"

"How well exactly do you two know each other?" the nurse asks, looking from me to Jesse, the irony of it like the big question mark that hangs over us.

Jesse looks at me and nods. "I'm a black belt. Anyway, we think – that is, the police and I - that he was an addict needing money for drugs. Speaking of which, an officer and hospital security guard are right outside. They want to ask you some questions if you're up to it."

"Sure," I say. "But then I have to go."

"Not so fast," the nurse says. "You can leave here, but you can't drive. You hit your head."

I sigh. "Of course."

"I've got you covered," Jesse says.

"You've done so much already. I can call a cab or an Uber."

"I've got this," Jesse says firmly, looking from me to the nurse.

I don't really have much choice. And he did get my purse back for me. "Okay. Thank you. For everything."

***

After giving my account of what happened to the police and hospital security guard, I walk out with Jesse holding my arm. "I really am fine," I say. "I feel bad you have to do this."

"I'm not leaving you. I don't have to be anywhere. And there's no place I'd rather be than with you right now." Jesse opens the passenger door of his car for me, then runs around to the other side and gets in.

I admit I'm grateful. I feel safe and protected for the moment. In the short-term, I can let my guard down.

Jesse drives me to my nana's house and pulls into her semi-circular driveway. "Well, I can see why you like it here," he says. "It's quite nice."

"Thank you again. I'm so grateful for your help and for getting my purse back. You've saved me a lot of aggravation."

"I only wish I had walked out with you. This wouldn't have happened if I had."

"You didn't do anything wrong. You did everything right. Do you have any idea how many times I've walked out of that hospital and through the parking lot alone? Even at night sometimes. It wasn't even really dark out yet."

"That's another thing," Jesse says, his car still running in the driveway. "The cop and I were talking about that. He's seeing more crimes happening right in broad daylight with criminals becoming more desperate and brazen. The mugger may have been watching you. It's very possible he was targeting you . . . as a medical professional. I have a feeling the assailant has done this before. They're bound to catch him."

I look out my window. Nana left the front porch globe light on for me like she does before she retires for the night, especially when she thinks I'll be home late. "I've never been a victim of a crime," I say. "It still doesn't feel real."

"Tomorrow is going to be difficult. Take time for yourself."

"I'll be fine, really. I have so much on my schedule this week and people depending on me. I'll be all right."

Jesse looks at me with an expression of doubt. "You need to go easy on yourself. You've been through a frightening ordeal."

"People need me," I say. "I just have to come up with a story for my nana as to how I got this bruise on my cheek. I can't tell her I was mugged. She's ninety. I don't want to upset her."

"Those bruises are going to need some explaining."

"Are you sure you don't have to be anywhere?"

"I've cleared everything. This isn't exactly how I planned for the evening to go, but I had already freed myself up. I'm just glad I'm able to be here with you."

"So am I," I admit. "We have yet to have that talk you're so intent on having. And I have some questions of my own. I'm ready whenever you are."

"You've been through a lot today," Jesse says. "It can wait. You need to rest."

"Not until I fix you something to eat," I insist. "You must be starving. Why don't you come inside for a while? We can talk there."

I lead Jesse down the long walkway lined with solar-powered lights that leads to the front wraparound porch, letting us in quietly through double front doors. I key in the security alarm code and rest my hand against the front foyer wall, slipping my feet from my shoes.

"Shall I?" Jesse says, reaching down to untie his shoes, the fresh scuff marks a painful insignia of all that has transpired in the last few hours.

"You can leave them on." I lead him through the house and all the way to the back where the kitchen is, turning on a light. I point to a chair around a large chunky wooden table that's central to Nana's country kitchen. Stepping inside the room instantly comforts me; it has remained the same as I always remembered it, although now somewhat out-of-date – the long, rustic carved table where our family often sits, distressed cabinetry, white lace window swags, and fruit and floral kitchen accents. "Please, make yourself comfortable."

"You should rest. We could just order something."

I scrounge around the refrigerator. "I can make us a turkey and cheese sandwich on toasted bread." I pull it out. "How does that sound? But first I have to get out of these clothes. They feel so dirty. By the way, my nana's bedroom is all the way down that hall and she's fast asleep by now."

"Go ahead. I can take it from here."

In the shower, the vigorous hot water drums my body and I imagine it washing off all the nastiness of my mugging, as if it could erase that awful incident somehow. Lifting my face to the spray, I allow myself a much needed cry as the tears flow.

I towel myself dry and put on a long night shirt with shorts, my hair hanging loose, and head back downstairs. *Jesse . . . in my house, in my kitchen, fixing us sandwiches.* Another thing that doesn't feel real.

Jesse has the toasted bread slices laid out. "Mustard or mayonnaise?"

"Mayo."

While Jesse fixes our sandwiches, I pull out a can of vegetable soup and heat it up in a pot.

Nana's kitchen is warm and homey, but it can't compete with the Marriott's rooftop terrace, cuddled on a rattan sofa under the moon and stars. I get another idea.

I set the two turkey club sandwiches on small plates, two glasses of sweet tea, and two bowls of soup on a fruit-and-floral-decorated tray. "Now," I say, "can you carry that upstairs for me while I lead the way? I don't trust my steadiness yet."

We walk down the long hallway on the second floor and through my bedroom to its sliding doors, which I open to reveal a two-seat balcony overlooking the mountains. "You can set it down here," I say, pointing to a white wrought iron table between two cushioned patio chairs. The summer night air is warm and symphonic, a chorus of sounds coming from crickets and bullfrogs and the occasional screech of an owl.

I grab a citrus-scented jar candle from my dresser, lighting up the night with it, and add it to the tray. "How's that for improvising?"

In the glow of the candlelight, Jesse's charming face looks content.

"Eat the soup before it gets cold," I say, giving him a wry smile. "That sounded so much like my mother."

We listen to the concert of the wild as we eat, the candle's perfume mingling with the scents of woodsy pine.

I take a hungry bite of my sandwich. "Ouch." My reverie is short-lived. I gingerly touch my bruised cheek.

"You okay?"

"I think the pain meds are wearing off already." I stand up.

"Perhaps I should go. You need to rest."

"Don't go," I say, surprising myself. "Stay."

Jesse gets up and comes over, tightening his arms around me. "I have so much I want to tell you, so much I need you to hear, but now isn't the right time. You're tired. I can see it in your eyes."

He steers me back into my bedroom. "You should lie down. Let me help you." Jesse pulls down the covers of my four-poster bed.

"Fate, it seems, had other plans for us this evening." I sit down on the side of my bed. "Are you planning on driving back to Charlotte now?"

"I don't know. I may get a room at a hotel. Don't worry about me. I'd like to check in on you tomorrow morning."

"About that...I'm fine I tell you. You'll see."

Jesse gives me a disbelieving look. "No one in your family knows what you've been through. I'm not comfortable with that."

I get up, taking Jesse by the hand. "Come with me," I say, walking him back out into the hallway and stopping at a doorway to one of the guest bedrooms. "This is where you'll stay tonight."

"I couldn't impose," Jesse says.

"It's the least I can do for you after all you've done for me. And this way, you can see for yourself in the morning that I'm totally fine. I get up at six. Dorothy – she's Nana's aid and housekeeper - gets here around eight. I've already cooked up a story for Nana. I won't take no for an answer." The side of my face throbs. I look away from Jesse, so he won't see me wince. "You wouldn't by any chance have any extra clothes with you?"

Jesse lets out a sigh, a sign he's relinquishing any arguments. "I keep extra shirts and things in my car trunk."

I take Jesse back down the flight of eighteen wooden stairs and wait for him in the front entrance while he retrieves a satchel from his trunk, taking care that he doesn't set off the house alarm.

I close my eyes from the pain in my face. Jesse sees it.

"Come on." He gently nudges my back, walking up the stairs behind me and returning me to my room. He helps me into my bed, placing the covers over me. I see him, through half-closed eyes, leaning over me, the expression on his face sincere and heartfelt.

"You don't have to . . ."

"Shhh," he says, tucking me in. "Rest now. I'll be here in the morning."

Those are the most beautiful sounding words.

CHAPTER 17

Elizabeth
October 1953

When I returned from the ladies' room, refreshed and suddenly starving, Joe was seated at a small round table waiting for me and telling me he'd already ordered. A dish of Swedish meatballs and onion rings and fries arrived at our table first. "These are just the appetizers," Joe said, digging in. I loved watching Joe eat - the way he enjoyed food, savoring it. "I hope you're hungry."

"I'm famished."

Joe reached for my hand. "You were amazing with that child."

"You were pretty amazing yourself, Dr. Paterson."

When those plates were taken away, southern-fried chicken came out along with eggplant, pasta, and a toss salad.

My eyes grew wide. "Joe!"

He laughed. "So, what exactly happened to you out there? The suspense is killing me."

"I had left. That is, in my mind. I left my body and entered a boundless, beautiful space. It was all so vivid and freeing, like I was watching a movie. I had no control over it, yet I wasn't scared at all."

I spent the next hour trying to put into words the inexplicable. What I had experienced was difficult to convey, if not impossible. The gratification that came with service and care to others had allowed me to let everything go, fully unburdening myself. It was a magnificent and illuminating feeling that profoundly affected me. A fleeting thought occurred to me that Joe might think me delusional, but instead, he let me talk on, listening attentively, and encouraging more.

I leaned back in my chair, my shoes kicked off under the table, sipping my drink and feeling filled with nourishment and conviviality.

"I believe what you may have experienced was a satori moment."

"A what?" I asked.

"A sudden spiritual enlightenment," Joe said. "Satori – meaning newly awake life. It sounds like it."

"It was much longer than a moment. Or at least it seemed that way. But then how do you measure timelessness?"

"When I was in Korea, I befriended a Japanese-American soldier who served as an interpreter and translator during the war. He asked me once why I became a doctor. I told him it was a calling, a need, not something I could easily explain. He defined it as what the Japanese call a satori moment, when one can see into their true nature, realizing their true potential."

"Tell me more." I was fascinated. I leaned forward and rested my chin on my hand.

"When you are one with your true spirit, only then can you thrive," Joe said. "My version may be a little different from yours, but often, during and after a life-saving surgery, I experience a profound positive energy, leaving me with a sense of total balance and comfort."

"Yes, I think I understand. A holistic awareness transported me today. I believe that. I never experienced anything quite like it before. So . . . I didn't scare you off?"

Joe snickered. "Scare me off? Not a chance. Every minute I spend with you has me yearning for more. You fascinate me." He looked at me for what could have been only a moment, but I never knew a moment could feel so long. "From the way you throw back your head when you laugh to the pout of your lips when you feel unsure or unhappy, you keep pulling me in. I want to know every part of you. I want to get into your mind, your soul."

I looked down at his empty wine glass. He'd only had one so I reasoned it couldn't be the wine talking.

"You already have my heart." I lay my hand over his and interlaced my fingers with his long ones. "The other two are a bit more complicated."

Joe laughed. "I like to be challenged. You should have figured that out about me by now." He winked and motioned for the check. "Come on. What do you say we get out of here?"

The night air was much colder now. Joe wrapped his jacketless arm around me tightly, sharing his body's warmth with mine, the smell of autumn leaves mingling with the scent of his skin. Back in his car, Joe started it, turning up the heat. We sat basking in silence, neither of us wanting the day to end. The spiritual high I felt earlier had left me feeling warm and safe and with heartfelt hope. Being with Joe had the same effect. I was in a place of serenity and honest fulfillment.

"Do you believe in soulmates?" Joe asked. He looked over at me, patiently waiting.

I let the word soulmate ruminate in my mind for a while. From the moment I met Joe, I sensed a strong connection. I didn't realize it at the time, nor did I understand it. I only knew that he stimulated me mentally, physically, and emotionally. When I was with him, I felt whole. When we were apart, it felt like a part of me was missing. "Do you think that's what we are?"

"I know that when I'm not with you I think about you every day. All day. Whenever I'm with you, it revives me. It feels right and good."

I met his gaze, his words touching me. "I feel it too. The first time I felt the connection, when I knew that you understood me, was when you told me near my last day in the hospital that I wasn't the fragile girl in the book who collected miniature glass figurines. I knew you knew me."

"Beth, I'm falling for you."

I didn't speak. I couldn't. My mind was going off again, not in the ethereal sense, but more physically. I instantly flushed.

Joe looked into my eyes. "I think I first felt something for you when I saw you sobbing in the hospital bed after you broke it off with your comic book friend and saying you must be a terrible person. You were so vulnerable and beautiful. You had me right then and there."

I chuckled. "I was a complete mess that day – knocking things over, blubbering into a wad of tissues, and hating myself for what I did. What I had to do."

"I'm glad you did it," Joe said, smiling. He leaned over, his lips caressing my neck, my face, my ear. I lifted my chin, seeking his mouth on mine. He kissed me briefly, and then drew away slowly, provocatively drawing his thumb over my lower lip. Desirous for more, my eyes still closed, I parted my lips, enticing his. He grasped the back of my head, thumbs tracing my jaw, and kissed me again, deeply and amorously. I was in a dreamlike state, Joe putting a climax on an already magnificent day, intensifying all my senses at once - the smell of rich leather blending with spices of Joe's cologne, the warmth of his mouth and the softness of his lips.

When at last we broke our kiss, Joe leaned back his head and sighed. "I guess I have to take you home now, don't I?"

I pouted. "I guess you do."

***

I watched the tiles in the Holland Tunnel whiz past us as Joe drove us out of the city toward home. He walked me to my front door and pulled me into an embrace.

"Stay awhile, won't you?" I asked.

"I might have to," he said. "You may need some help explaining what happened to your dress." We laughed. *Who would ever believe it?*

Fortunately, when we got inside, it was dark, only a night light left on. My parents were in their bedroom so explanations could be put off until morning. Heating some water on the stove for tea, I went to my bedroom and slipped out of my dress to get more comfortable.

I came out wearing a pajama pant set with a bed jacket. We sat cuddled on the rocker on my screened porch under a large afghan, talking away the night, not noticing the time, just being in the present. Breathing in his scent, I curled into his tall body, feeling more complete than I'd ever felt before.

"You know," Joe said, "it's been a little over six months since I returned home from South Korea. Only now, with you, do I feel like I'm truly home."

We locked eyes in the darkness, igniting with intensity, our lips and mouths fusing once more. I couldn't get enough of him and I think he felt the same.

"Joe?" I said craning my neck so I could study his face. "Before you were drafted, was there someone special in your life?"

Joe grinned. "There were a couple of girls I was seeing. On and off."

"A couple?" Suddenly, I wanted to know everything.

"There was no one girl in particular."

"You weren't in any serious relationships?"

"No. I was still searching . . . waiting."

"Waiting?"

"For someone like you."

Joe's sincere eyes penetrated mine and I couldn't help but wonder if when morning came, I would believe all that had transpired in the last twenty-four hours.

It was a little past midnight when Joe left and I flopped down on my bed, exhausted but too dizzy with happiness to fall asleep. I would no doubt dream of Joe tonight, as I had on so many nights. Only now, I was living my dream.

Somehow, I knew it was a day I would remember the rest of my life.

CHAPTER 18

Amanda

My alarm startles me awake. As I start to rise, glimpses of last night come to me in spurts. Jesse . . . here . . . just down the hall. I move slowly, my body and head a tremor of spasms and aches, clashing with my will. I need to shower, to get ready for work. I walk cautiously to my connecting bathroom and reach for the pain pills I left on the vanity. I swallow them down with water, my eyes filling with tears from the pain I feel – throbbing and pulsating pain rendering me helpless. My face stares back at me in the vanity mirror, a shocking revelation of the injuries I sustained. *Oh my god.* A black-and-blue sphere stains my left eye; under it my cheekbone is tri-colored and puffed out, my jaw clenched tight. I put my head in my hand and let out a moan.

I hear a tap on my bedroom door. "You can come in," I say in a weak and unfamiliar voice, shuffling back into my room.

Jesse appears in the doorway, showered and dressed - same slacks, different shirt. He takes one look at me and comes over. Jesse had told me that today would be hard. My face presses lightly against his chest - firm and sturdy, smelling of soap and linen - as his strong arms wrap around me. "Just don't say I told you so," I mumble into his shirt.

"Let's get you back in bed." Jesse practically holds me up. He lays me back down and props two pillows behind my head. "Have you taken anything?"

"Just did," I answer. "Waiting for it to work some magic."

Jesse leans over me. "Can I get you water?"

I shake my head. "No. Thank you." I turn my head to the side and face away from him, feeling ashamed and contrite. "I did a really dumb thing yesterday. I'm paying for it now. I keep reliving it, all the mistakes I made. I wasn't paying attention . . . got distracted with my purse fully open while I dug for my cell phone . . . which was going off by the way. It was the perfect storm. I still can't believe this happened."

"I know," Jesse says, placing his hand over my arm. "But you're safe."

I close my eyes, tears escaping from under the lids. "I'm stronger than I look you know." My eyes flutter open and I face Jesse again, resolute and resilient. "I once fell off my bike skidding down a steep road. Cracked my elbow in two places. I was nine at the time. I cried and then got right back on the bike. The handlebars were all skewed, but I rode it all the way home using my one good arm. My biggest concern was that I didn't want to leave my bike on the side of the street. So, I pushed ahead, tears streaming down my face ...but I made it home."

"Hmmm, after the way you refused to give up your purse yesterday, that doesn't surprise me." Jesse grins and then turns more serious. "You had me worried when they told me you were in the ER."

"Sorry."

"Look," Jesse says, straightening his shoulders. He sits down on the edge of my bed. "Here's how today is going to go. I'm going to leave before your grandmother gets up. I have some calls to make and then I'm going to get breakfast and coffee and bring it back here for us. She'll think I just stopped over. You can tell her you fell, or whatever story you've concocted, and that I came by 'as a concerned friend' since I heard what happened to you." It's Jesse in his element, commanding and assured. He stands with his hand on one of my bedposts. "As long as you understand that you are *not* going anywhere today. And that I plan to stick around awhile."

Jesse doesn't wait for my approval, nor does he give me a chance to argue. He goes to the door. "I'll see you in a couple of hours." And then he's gone.

I stare up at the white canopy over my bed. Jesse has been so caring. My feelings for him are returning, and I want so much to trust him. I can feel it coming - tears pooling in my eyes. The pain from my face and head is subsiding, but there's a new kind of pain. The one inside my heart.

***

It's nine-thirty and I've managed to take a shower and put on shorts and a t-shirt. I slip my feet into flat sandals. Dorothy is downstairs with Nana after I filled her in. Poor thing. When she saw my face and I told her what had happened, she cried. I had to calm her down before she could go back to Nana. I told Nana that I had tripped and fallen on the hospital stairs, but not until after I applied foundation on my face to conceal some of the purplish color. With the exception of a quick morning kiss on her cheek, I kept some distance from her so she couldn't see how bad it really was. It helped, too, that she didn't have her glasses on when I told her.

I called my office and Dr. Cullen, explaining what happened and arranging for coverage in my place. I want to remain hopeful I can return tomorrow, but I can't make any promises, as frustrating as that is for me. I also made sure to tell Dawn, before she heard it from others. It really upset her and she was ready to run over and see me, but I told her about Jesse and that he was coming over.

The outpouring of shock and concern is overwhelming and understandable, but having had to repeat the story of my ordeal several times has desensitized me, especially when it still rings unbelievable - a nightmare I'll wake up from. Except for the physicality of it, when I recap what happened to me, it's as if I'm talking about someone else. I'm not that woman, the victim of an assault. I'm an observer, a witness, looking in, removed and dispassionate. It's easier when I take myself out of the scene.

I start back down the long flight of stairs, taking watchful steps, my heart racing at the prospect of Jesse's return. Nana is settling in her wingback chair in the sunroom while Dorothy cleans up the breakfast dishes in the kitchen. I walk past.

"Such a beautiful day." I join Nana in the sunroom. The pink roses from her ninetieth birthday celebration have begun dropping petals. I try my best to sound chipper and not raise any concern or suspicion. I don't want to worry her. I stare out the window with my arms crossed so she can only see the good side of my face.

"Yes, it is," Nana says. "But I'm more interested in how you're feeling, dear. Did you hit your head when you fell? Have you been checked out?" Nana the nurse will not be sidetracked.

"Yes, I'm a bit sore, but the pain meds are working fine. I'm just giving myself some much-needed self-care today." I have to get past this somehow, put it behind me. If only I could erase it from my memory. I will. I'll push it back, way back, until it fades away.

The doorbell rings and Dorothy goes to answer it.

"I wonder who that could be this early in the morning," Nana says.

I cross my arms tighter and continue to gaze out the window, telling myself to remain calm and collected.

"Amanda, there's someone here to see you," Dorothy calls out.

I make my way to the entrance foyer where Jesse stands. He's wearing khaki shorts, an untucked white polo and canvas sneakers. He holds a bouquet of flowers in his arm, a coffee carryon container is gripped in one hand, and a bag I recognize from one of my favorite café's is clutched in the other.

"Jesse," I say, feigning surprise. "What are you doing here?" I am the absolute worst actress.

Dorothy is standing behind, watching us. "Dorothy," I say, in a low voice, "this is the man who got my purse back for me. Jesse." Jesse gives a polite nod.

"How very nice to meet you," Dorothy says. "I hear you're quite the hero." Dorothy tears up again.

"Perhaps you can take something off Jesse's hands," I say. "Bring it into the kitchen."

Dorothy takes the coffee carry-on and the bag of breakfast treats from his hand, leaving in a tizzy of sniffles.

Jesse meets my eyes and I flash him a soft smile, careful of my sore face. "Hey."

"Hey, yourself," Jesse says, handing me the bouquet of feathery plumes, daisies and lavender. "I thought you could use a little cheering up. I also picked up a couple of things for myself," he says, glancing down at his shorts.

"I can see that," I say. "Thank you for the flowers." I take them from him. "Come. Let me introduce you to my nana."

I take Jesse through the house's large living area and past the kitchen to the back sunroom where Nana spends her morning Zen time, natural light welcoming us in. "Nana, this is a friend of mine. Jesse."

"It's very nice to meet you, ma'am," Jesse says.

Nana takes one look at the bouquet of flowers still in my hand and then back at Jesse. "I don't believe we've met before." She looks at him askance. "How do you two know each other?"

"Well, we met at the healthcare convention last week," Jesse says.

"So, you're a doctor?" Nana asks.

"No, ma'am. A lawyer," Jesse says.

"Oh. You're the arrogant one."

"Nana!" I put my face in my hand. It amazes me the things Nana remembers most.

Jesse laughs out loud. "That would be me."

"Well, now that we've established who you are, why don't you sit down awhile?" Nana says.

Dorothy enters right on cue, avoiding looking any of us in the eye. She places a basket of croissants, mini bagels, and muffins on a table. "I'll bring in your coffees, too," she says, her eyes dropped.

"A person could get lost in this view," Jesse says, looking out at the mountains.

"I lose myself in it every day," Nana says.

Dorothy sets down the coffees Jesse brought and takes the flowers from me. "Let me put these in a vase for you. Is there anything else I can get you?" she asks, looking mostly at Jesse, trying to make our guest feel comfortable.

"No, thank you," Jesse says.

Dorothy has just turned to leave when the doorbell rings again.

"I'm curious as to why there are four cups of coffee here," I say.

"Well, I didn't know which one you would like, so I got Macchiato, Cappuccino, latte, and regular."

This makes me smile. "Any one of those is fine."

"No. You have to choose one."

"I'll take the latte. Unless, of course, you'd rather have that one."

"The latte is yours. Here you go," Jesse says, picking it out. "I would have pegged you for a Macchiato though."

"Why's that?"

"Macchiato's are bolder, stronger." He grins.

I look over at Nana and realize she's watching us. I'm not sure how much of it she hears since her hearing's gotten worse, but from the look on her face she's pleasantly amused. Dorothy enters again with a fruit basket. "This came for you," she says.

"Oh my," I say. Probably from my office. "Just put it in the kitchen for me, please."

"Don't you want to know who it's from?" Nana asks.

"Yeah, well, sure. I'll take the card," I tell Dorothy.

I read the card to myself, realizing that all eyes are on me. "It's from Dr. Cullen," I say. "How very sweet."

"Yes," Nana says, "but isn't he on vacation? How did he hear of your accident?"

"He...well, he happened to check in with me earlier." I stutter. "We had to discuss some of the things going on with our patients, so, of course, I let him know why I wasn't going to be in today." I squirm and reach for my latte, taking a strong gulp.

"Well, that certainly was very nice of him," Nana says, apparently satisfied.

I stare into my cup longer than necessary, then turn to Jesse. "Why don't you let me show you some of the house . . . I want you to see the wine cellar."

Jesse rises on cue. "Hope to see you later," he says to Nana as we exit the room.

I lead Jesse down to the wine cellar, a dark, cool room with built-in wooden racks, a few bottles of wine, dim lighting and two rustic wooden benches. "This used to be filled to the top with all kinds of wine," I say. "It was my grandfather's pastime; he was a wine aficionado. He passed away ten years ago. There are only a few good bottles left, the ones my father and uncle left behind."

Jesse pulls one out. A 2012 Albert Bichot Côte de Nuits from the Burgundy region.

"I'm a fan of pinot noirs," I say. "My grandfather had gotten that bottle for me, saving it for a special occasion. I wanted to open it with him, but we never got the chance."

"I think I would have liked your grandfather," Jesse says. "And your grandmother isn't this feeble-minded, frail little woman I was expecting."

I plop down on one of the benches. "No, she is not." I stare down at my bare feet. A perfectly nice French pedicure in total contrast to my broken fingernails. "Look, I want to apologize for Nana. That's the real reason I brought you down here. She no longer has any filter. She says whatever comes to her mind, no matter how it comes out. I didn't really mean it when I called you arrogant."

Jesse laughs. "Sure you did, and well deserved."

"I was . . .well, at the time I was confused and maybe a little angry with you, if I'm to be completely honest."

"Good," Jesse says. "Honesty is a good place for us to start."

"What do you mean?"

"There are things about myself I want to share with you...it's important to me."

"Why?"

"Because . . . well, *you've* become important to me. And because you'll hear about it sooner or later and I'd rather you hear it from me."

I'm getting a bit scared. "What are you saying?" Now I have to know.

Jesse sits down alongside me on the bench and takes my hand. "I'm saying that you matter to me. I like you a lot."

"You matter to me, too." I lean against his arm, the good side of my face resting on his strong shoulder. Preemptively, I speculate and brood as trepidation of there being another woman in the picture gnaws at me.

I stand all of a sudden and pull him along, burning with curiosity. "Come on."

"Where are we going?"

I need to get this over with. I survived a mugging. I think I can survive whatever it is Jesse has to tell me. "Somewhere more comfortable where we can talk. I want to get to know you."

CHAPTER 19

Elizabeth
November 1953

I was in love. I couldn't deny it. And I was sure Joe was too. It happened in a blink. My life had a vibrancy to it now, a purpose and hope that did not exist before. My parents were enamored of Joe. And during one of our breakfasts, he invited me to come along with him in two weeks for his nephew's birthday party.

"My family will all be there."

Wearing a two-piece dress under a nautical cardigan and in the most casual of settings against a background of seven-year-olds whooshing past and blaring on party horns, I met each one of Joe's family members.

Joe's dad, Richard, came over to stand by him, putting his arm around his son's shoulder affectionately. He crinkled me a smile and the same warm brown eyes as Joe's looked back at me. Joe was broader and taller than his dad, but their mutual love and admiration was unmistakable. "What can I get you two to drink?" he asked, making me feel right at ease.

Joe found his mom sitting in the living room, legs crossed and nursing a glass of punch. When he went over and kissed her on her cheek, her sideways glance was fixated on me. "Mom, I'd like you to meet Beth," Joe said.

"It's so nice to meet you," I said. His mother bent her head with just the right amount of cordiality, her mouth spread into a thin line, and I sensed disapproval in her demeanor. "I'm Joan," she simply said. She continued to study me and I immediately flushed with discomfort. I was relieved when his dad came over with our Cokes.

"Thank you, Richard," I said, more grateful for the interruption than I should have been.

"Dick," he said. "Everyone calls me Dick."

Joan cleared her throat.

"'Cept maybe my wife," Dick said.

Joe's sister, Barbara joined us then. "Please, don't be shy. Help yourself to some food." Barbara's warmth and friendliness was a welcome contrast to Joan's coolness.

Joe stayed at my side most of the day, except when his brother-in-law stole him away for several minutes so he could see Joe's new Corvette. Dick filled in during Joe's absence with pleasant talk and encouragement for me to help myself to more food.

Joan, on the other hand, had plenty of pointed questions. "So, how was it that you met my son again? You were a patient at the hospital, isn't that right? You look so young. When did you graduate high school?" Taking a bite of her pinwheel sandwich, she kept her eyes on me.

I answered each one of her questions with short, tactful answers. "An accident sent me to the hospital. Yes, that's right. I graduated 1949." Clearly, her queries felt more like interrogations and were aimed at one thing. Was I good enough and deserving enough to be with her revered son? The one commonality I tried to stay focused on is that I shared in her obvious admiration for Joe. "Joe is a wonderful doctor," I said, stoking her pride. "You must be so proud of him."

"Joseph" – she was the only one who didn't call him Joe - "was always very studious and disciplined. Even as a child, I never had to push him. He pushed himself."

"Yes, I can see that." I appreciated that Joe was the first in his family to achieve a higher education, but I wanted to be sure to convey to her the trait of Joe's I valued most of all - his kindness. "You've also raised a very compassionate and kind man," I said with grace and aplomb. "The medical field is better for it."

At that moment, Joan seemed satisfied. She placed her small empty plate on the nearby table and folded her hands starchily in her lap, leaving an orbit of frostiness around her.

"The new Chevy sure is pretty to look at," Joe's brother-in-law commented when he and Joe returned to the living room, "I'll give you that. But my gut tells me the new Corvette is a fad. It ain't gonna last. You can tell your Manhattan car dealer friend I said so."

"I would, but I wouldn't want to depress him," Joe said, laughing.

"Joseph," Joan said, "you're looking thinner. You need to keep up your strength with all those hours you've been putting in. Are you eating enough?"

Joe shook his head. "I weigh the same as I have for the past three years."

"I lost ten pounds," Barbara retorted. "Don't I even get a mention?" Her husband reached behind her for a piece of birthday cake. "Oh no, you don't." She gave him a gentle slap on the hand. "That's your second slice. Have another helping of Jell-O salad instead."

Just then, Joe's nephew pretend-galloped through the middle of the living room on the motor scooter we gave him for his birthday. Wearing a cowboy hat and a toy pistol set, he collided with the coffee table.

"Really. You couldn't have gotten him a doctor's kit instead?" Barbara muttered warmly to Joe.

"Settle down, cowboy," Joe said, scooping his nephew up and raising him high in the air. "You need to take that horse back to the corral."

It was entertaining watching and listening to Joe with his family – the exchange of witticisms, the ease of being together, the obvious love and care they had for one another. But beneath my enjoyment at meeting the most important people in Joe's life, one spark of apprehension remained – I was pretty sure Joe's mother didn't like me. I was dismayed and wondered how I could bring it up with Joe, but I didn't want to be that girl who whined or put him in the position of having to defend his mother. I let it go. Perhaps, I hoped, once she got to know me better, she'd change her mind.

***

Mr. Harris - *married* Mr. Harris, the department head - was at my counter one afternoon, his roving eyes behind owl eyeglasses only inches from mine.

His loose throat jowl vibrated as he spoke to me about my upcoming semiannual review.

"I've been watching you . . ." My fingers tightened around a foundation bottle. "...the way you conduct yourself, Elizabeth. It hasn't gone unnoticed. I plan to put in a good word for you." Mr. Harris lay his heavy hand over mine, stilling it. "I can be very influential to your advancement here."

I didn't know which repulsed me more – his stale tobacco breath or the skin of his fingers over mine. I slid my hand out from his grasp and busily returned the bottle to its display shelf. "Why, thank you, Mr. Harris," I said, affecting naivete. "It certainly is nice to feel appreciated for my work here."

Happiness balanced with relief when Joe walked over. I could feel the pasted smile on my face loosen. "Looks like my boyfriend's here. We're having lunch together upstairs."

Mr. Harris's wet-blanket look was priceless.

***

"So . . . what else are you planning on doing on your day off today?" I asked Joe. We were finishing our sandwiches in the wood-paneled restaurant on Bamberger's tenth floor.

"I'm meeting up with a realtor. I'm gonna look at some houses."

"How exciting! Though I'm sure your parents will miss having you home with them again."

"It isn't as if I'm home very much."

"Joe," I started. "I'm glad I got the chance to meet your family. They're so proud of you. It really shows. Your mother -" I needed to get it out there. The more I thought about it, the more worrisome it became. "I don't think she likes me for you."

"My mother enjoys playing matchmaker and has been trying to fix me up with the daughters of her church friends ever since I got back. It gives her a sense of status and she loves the attention she gets from it. It's not personal. Don't pay her any mind."

"Oh. I see." Easier said than done when I could still feel her chilly gaze on me. I lowered my eyes and continued. "Have you met any of those women . . . the one's she picked for you?" I had to know.

Joe propped himself forward and crossed his arms over the table, looking amused. "I've met a couple."

I looked away and slouched in my seat. It wasn't very reassuring to know that the contender in our growing relationship was Joe's mother.

Joe reached over and turned my face with a finger. "Beth . . . look at me." I met his clear gaze and braced myself. "My mother can do all the choosing she wants." He gave me a sincere smile. "I choose you."

I smiled a sigh. "Thank you for meeting me here during my lunch hour. This was nice," I said.

"So . . . who was that man at your counter when I showed up? He walked off so quickly." Apparently, Joe had concerns of his own.

"Oh. That was Mr. Harris. My boss." I checked the clock on the wall. "Speaking of which, I'd better get back to my counter."

We headed toward the elevator, and I decided to ask the question that had been tugging at me. "Did I mention a girlfriend of mine who's getting married in a couple of weeks? I was wondering . . . I mean, I'll understand if you can't get off, but I thought—."

"Yes," Joe said.

"You will?"

"Yes, I'll go with you. That *is* what you're asking me, isn't it?"

I kissed him on his cheek before we got onto the elevator, the operator nodding a hello.

Riding down, Joe said, "I don't think I like him very much."

"Who?" I asked.

"Your boss, Mr. Harris."

I shook my head and sighed. "You're a good judge of character."

***

Peggy made a beautiful bride – from her long-sleeved lace wedding gown to her bouquet of white peonies and a wedding hat with netting. Her church wedding rivaled the stylishness of Jackie Bouvier at last month's high society wedding to John Kennedy. Peggy's reception venue was simple and elegant - a buffet of different foods on a long table that extended the width of the hall. Pork chops and fried chicken, mashed potatoes, and green-bean casserole. Pigs in blankets and deviled eggs too.

Jim had immediately recognized Joe from the hospital. It felt awkward at first, and while they shook hands graciously, I sensed that, were it not for Jim's new girlfriend, who was hanging on his arm, he might have been less magnanimous.

It had been four years since I'd seen some of the high school gang all together. Had it not been for Joe's attendance, it would have been emotionally harder for me. Joe must have seen me silently weeping when some of the guys Robbie used to hang out with gathered for a photo, bantering with one another like they used to in high school. How was it possible that I could be happy and sad at the same time?

Joe's hand was on my back, consoling me with gentle pats and rubs. The most wonderful, kind and sensitive man stood right next to me, right there and then. It was challenging, assimilating our worlds, conceding our pasts. My friends were not Joe's friends, so I understood if he felt like an outsider. At the same time, Joe's mother clearly did not approve of me dating her son. Things were so much easier when the world was ours alone.

I pushed up on my high-heeled toes and kissed Joe on his lips. "Thank you," I said.

"For what?"

"For being here with me." I enunciated the last three words separately to emphasize my meaning.

Attending that wedding together solidified us as a couple. Letting go of the past, living in the present, hopeful for the future. Me in my restored red dress, the two of us wrapped in each other's arms, we slow-danced and shuffled to the record "Till I Waltz Again With You" by Teresa Brewer. It was romantic and elegant and beguiling. In our private space, in our private world, detached from our surroundings, I whispered in Joe's ear, "Don't let this night end."

A new man was in my life now, a man who was choosing me for reasons I had yet to fully understand. It hurt that Joe's mother didn't like me, but I rationalized that some relationships simply needed more time.

CHAPTER 20

Amanda

Jesse and I are sitting on large wooden rocking chairs on the front wraparound porch, our coffees getting cold on a small table between us. The view in front of the house is lovely, albeit some mature beech and oak trees blocking some of the mountain ridges. The air smells of sweet pinesap. I place my cell phone down on the table keeping it close by should my office need to reach me.

A floral delivery van pulls up and I hear myself sigh. "Delivery for Amanda."

"Yes, that's me." Reluctantly, I rise from my rocker. I take the flower arrangement from him and put it down on the porch floor, pulling out the card so I can read it. "These are from my office," I tell Jesse. I poke my head inside the house once more looking for Dorothy. She meets me outside on the front porch.

"Dorothy, I need you to do me a favor. Can you please take these up to my bedroom, but don't let Nana see them. I don't want to stir up more questions."

I slump back into the rocking chair, turning it a little so that I'm facing Jesse. "Phew. News spreads fast. My parents don't even know what happened to me, and I aim to keep it that way. The fewer people who know about this, the better." Jesse watches me, wearing a skeptical look on his face, but says nothing.

A text message dings from my phone and I take a quick look at it, relieved. "Dr. Cullen," I say out loud. I text Dr. Cullen back and return my phone to the table. Turning to Jesse, I explain, "I just received some good news about a patient of ours. She's a two-year heart transplant patient. We were waiting on some test results, and apparently, the ultrasound doesn't show any evidence of rejection going on. So nothing indicates we'll have to biopsy her heart."

"That's great news," Jesse says.

"Yes. Perhaps she'll be able to go to the beach on the weekend with her boyfriend and his family after all."

Jesse remains quiet, visibly solemn. He stands up and walks over by the porch railing, leaning on it.

"Do you know who I'm talking about? Dawn told me you'd asked about her status the other day."

Jesse continues staring out into the trees. "Yes, I do," he says. "She's the girl who has my wife's heart."

The stillness that ensues is anything but noiseless. It pierces and deafens and jolts. Jesse turns to face me, the muscles in his face and neck constricting. "You heard correctly."

My shock is evident. "How –?" I choke out the word.

"Let me start from the beginning." Jesse lowers himself into the rocker and stares down into his lap.

I silence my phone and wait.

"A little over five years ago, I met a girl," Jesse says. "We were intimate. Once. We'd been drinking. Anyway, a couple of months later, she told me she was pregnant with my child. A paternity test confirmed it. After our daughter was born, I felt compelled to do the right thing, so a year later, on our daughter's first birthday, I married her mother. We were trying to make a go of it, becoming a family unit. One evening two years ago, my wife was returning with our daughter from visiting her sister in Raleigh. It was during rush hour. She was traveling westbound on Interstate 40 when she was rear-ended, causing her car to swerve and strike a truck in the right lane."

Jesse pauses, his eyes glazing over as he looks at me. "Thing is...that's not what killed her." He shakes his head. I reach over and take his hand in mine, urging him to go on. "My wife . . . Sarah, had some minor injuries, but she was okay. She was so overwrought with our young daughter crying in the back seat that she quickly unbuckled herself and jumped out of the car to check on Emma. That's when an oncoming car veered into her."

I blink at Jessie in horror. "Oh . . . my."

"She was still alive but had suffered severe head trauma. She never got to unbuckle our daughter out of her car seat. Emma was almost two-and-a-half at the time."

I sense that Jesse is holding back tears. Nothing in my wildest imagination could have prepared me for this. I try to hold it together. For me. For him. "Emma . . . she's okay then?" I ask.

"Yes, thank God. Although most probably she has some traumatic memory of what she saw. Even as young as she was, I can't assume she doesn't remember anything, even if she can't put it into words. She has occasional nightmares - wakes up screaming for reasons she can't explain."

"So...you're a father." I feel like I am saying this to myself mostly.

"I'm Emma's dad."

Understanding dawned and I said, "I'm so sorry. I overheard you talking on your cell phone that night at the brewery." My mind flashes back to the day. "Emma is the person you needed to get home to, isn't she?"

"Emma had woken up crying. My mother put her on the phone so I could reassure her I was going to be home soon. Talking to me calms her down."

Jesse releases my hand, swipes the sweat from his brow. "Sarah's driver's license indicated she wished to be an organ donor. I never knew. It's not something you talk about when you're young, when that day seems so far away. It was the most harrowing day of my life. One minute, I learned my wife was brain dead and that my daughter was unscathed, and the next, as Sarah's husband, they wanted my thoughts on donating her organs."

Jesse's forehead falls into his hands while he pauses, and I'm not sure if he can go on. He lowers his hands onto his lap then pulls in a breath before he resumes. "I was told about the teenage girl who was in end-stage heart failure. Somehow, I didn't feel like I should be the one to consent to it. I was her husband for a year and a half. I eventually learned who the dying girl was who'd be receiving Sarah's heart and that it was a perfect match."

"How did you find out? I mean . . ."

"I have friends on the inside." Jesse inhales deeply, letting it out in one extended sigh, the exhalation of long held emotions and anguish. He looks over at me. "Sarah's untimely death saved the lives of several people, who received her heart, liver, and kidneys."

I realize my jaw is hanging open. I force my mouth closed and fix my hands on my knees.

"In the first few months," Jesse says, "I was bent on following the young girl's progress. When I heard she may have relapsed . . . well, it was like losing Sarah again. I don't know how to explain it. But then the last few years of my life have been anything but typical or foreseeable."

Jesse pauses, eyes on his hands, the only sound coming from the creaking of the chair as it rocks. I say nothing, waiting for him to decompress from the misery he's just relived. In a matter of a few minutes, I've learned that not only is Jesse a widower and a father of a four-year old girl, but that his deceased wife's heart is in one of my patients. It's a lot to absorb.

I cross my arms and lean back, turning my gaze to a blue jay, a timely distraction, watching it slip furtively through the low branches closest to the porch. I realize Jesse has no idea what I'm thinking as I dig around for the right words.

I turn toward him then, not exactly sure what I'm going to say. I begin, "I'm so sorry for what you've been through. The way you've dealt with all this says so much about who you are. It sounds like you're doing the best you can. I know this wasn't easy, sharing it with me, reliving it all." I stare back at the blue jay - the epitome of bravery, posing fearlessly on a thin branch.

"You deserve to know. I want you to know everything."

"You haven't told me anything about yourself though. Those are things that happened to you, very hard, tragic things. But you are not those things. I want to know *you*. The man you are...the son, the brother, the successful lawyer, the single father...the husband, however short it was."

"I married Sarah out of a sense of duty. I cared for her, but I didn't marry her out of love. I married the mother of my daughter. There were problems in our marriage. We were anxious and uneasy around each other most of the time. We were both unhappy. We differed on just about everything, except how much we loved Emma. We were like two ships passing in the night. That's how our marriage endured. It took me eighteen months of therapy not to feel guilty about what happened."

"It wasn't your fault, what happened. Why would you feel guilty?"

"Because I could have loved her more . . . because if I had been with them, this might never have happened. Sarah was from Raleigh so she drove back and forth there often while I was at work. Still, I had my own guilt to contend with."

Jesse leans his head back and sighs softly, rocking himself.

"Do you have any pictures of Emma you can show me?" I ask, deflecting. It seems to work because Jesse's face lights up as he pulls out his phone and swipes through some of the photos he has on it. "This one's pretty recent, taken last month at the beach in Kitty Hawk where my parents' summer house is." He passes his phone to me. "That's my girl."

A small face squinting under a floral beach hat and carrying a pail and shovel looks back at me. "She's adorable," I say. "Who's with Emma now while you're here with me?"

"Emma's with my mom. My parents live twenty minutes from me."

"I'd like to meet Emma someday. When I don't look like I do right now."

"I would love that," Jesse says.

***

We are standing on the front porch again after lunch; Jesse is saying good-bye. He's filled me in a little on his growing up in Hummelstown, Pennsylvania, before his family moved to Charlotte and began spending summers on the Outer Banks. Now he wraps his arms around me, hugging me. "You need to lie down and rest," he says. "I'd like to call you later . . . check in on you again if that's okay."

"Of course you may," I say, nestling my head in his neck. I hated to see him go, but I felt exhausted and needed to rest.

"One more thing," Jesse says. He pulls his phone out of his shorts pocket and scrolls through it. "I think you should tell your parents what happened. I know you'd rather tell as few people as possible, but I'm afraid the news is already out there." Jesse passes me his phone. "I just saw this in the local news section."

I take his phone in my hand, squinting at the screen and scanning the words – victim of an early evening assault . . . mugging victim knocked to the ground. And then I see it. My name. It jumps out at me, intrusive and startling. My legs feel unsteady. "No," I say, reading on as it identifies Jesse as trying to stop the attacker. I grab onto the porch banister and hand Jesse back his phone, scrunching my face in anguish.

"I'm sorry," he says.

I lean my forehead down on his chest. When all I want to do is push it down and move past it, the publicized news of my mugging attack distresses me more than I ever imagined it could. "Looks like I need to make a few more phone calls," I say, my voice muffled in his chest.

Jesse lifts my chin, so I look into his eyes. "You have to call your parents before they read about it or hear about it from someone else. And then, turn your phone off. You hear me?"

"Yeah. I hear you."

Jesse kisses my forehead. "Promise me you'll lie down and rest."

I stare down, trying to grasp it all, my preference for privacy gone now.

"Promise me." His voice is firm on this point.

I give a nod.

"It'll pass. We just have to weather the news storm for a few days. The important thing is that you're okay. It could have been so much worse."

"I know," I say. "I hate that it brings it all up again, when all I want to do is forget." I lean against the porch column and rub my forehead.

"I know how you feel. I had to live through the news about what happened to Sarah for months."

"How did you get through it?" I ask. "I don't mean to compare what you went through with this, but . . ."

"No. It's an honest question. And I won't lie to you – it took a lot of work. I had to acknowledge what I was feeling first – all the sadness and grief. Anger was the hardest for me to let go of. In time, I realized I didn't want to just endure; I had to overcome it somehow. I focused on positivity and hope again. Good friends, the support of family, my little Emma...they helped me get through it."

"Thank you," I say, my voice tired. "I'm so grateful for how you have already helped me, for our friendship."

"I'm here for you," Jesse says. "Just let me in."

I kiss Jesse lightly on his lips before he turns to leave. I watch while he gets in his car and drives away, willing myself to go back inside the house. Then I remember that my phone is still on the table where I left it between the rocking chairs. I pick it up and see that I've missed over a dozen phone calls and text messages, even from people I don't normally talk to.

Oh my god.

I reenter the house and schlep up the flight of stairs toward my bedroom, bracing myself for a difficult conversation with my parents, the anonymity of my experience no longer possible.

CHAPTER 21

Elizabeth
December 1953

The holidays approached with a deluge of activities and crazy work hours, making it challenging for Joe and me to find time for each other. I tried figuring out what to get Joe for Christmas, something he would enjoy. I picked up two books – *Fahrenheit 451* by Ray Bradbury and Agatha Christie's newest release, *A Pocket Full of Rye*. I also bought him a shirt I liked at Bamberger's – a light gray polo knit, and a pack of solid white handkerchiefs I'd have my mother embroider them with Joe's initials.

On a Sunday in the middle of December, Joe came over to my house for a homemade pasta-and-meatballs dinner. My mother and I were in the kitchen cooking and setting the table. I could overhear Joe and my dad in the living room talking.

"My car dealer in New York wants to know what first-time buyers think of Chevy's new car," Joe said. "I haven't gotten back to him yet. Frankly, I'm a little disappointed in its Blue Flame Six engine's performance. Your opinion would mean a lot to me."

"Come on. Let's take a look," Dad said, grabbing his coat and heading outside with Joe.

It was a mild winter so far; little snow had fallen. When dinner was ready, I called them inside. Joe loved my mother's pastas, made from scratch, with freshly grated parmesan cheese. He said he'd never tasted anything like it. My mother said he was welcome to have dinner with us every Sunday if he had off. Dad was somewhat quiet and introspective through most of dinner. He excused himself, and I felt his touch on my back as he passed me, retreating to his favorite chair in the living room to rest.

After clearing the table, I took Joe's hand and led him into the living room to show him the red paper carnations I'd made to decorate our tabletop tree. Under the coffee table where the tree was displayed, were Joe's and my parents' wrapped presents topped off with the extra red carnations. Joe caught his name on one of the gift-wrapped books I got for him.

"That one's for me? Let me guess. You got me a box of cigars," he teased.

I tapped him on the hand and feigned surprise. "How did you know?"

We chuckled a little too loudly, rousing my dad from his nap for a few seconds. Hushing one another behind giggles about to break out, we snuck past him out of the living room and returned to the kitchen for dessert and coffee, the low hum of Dad's breathing telling me his nap had recommenced. My mother slipped past us, joining him in the living room.

Joe had brought over the game Kalah and while we sipped coffee and nibbled on dates and cookies, he taught me how to play, the object being to capture the most seeds. He beat me three games in a row, even though he tried to help me win the last round.

"Let's do it again," I said. "And don't help me this time. When I win, I want it to be completely earned."

"Okay. No mercy."

By the fifth round, I had my first legitimate win. Spurred by competition with a worthy opponent, I had to resist taking out the Scrabble board next. Joe looked like he was getting tired.

We moved into the living room; my parents had retired to bed. Cuddled on the couch together, we were gazing at the tree when Joe began to doze. I didn't want to disturb him. With our hectic schedules, I wouldn't see him again until Christmas, so I appreciated his nearness even in his sleeping moments. I rested my head on his arm, feeling content.

Twenty minutes had passed when Joe woke abruptly, alarmingly, his eyes looking around and flashing bewilderment.

"It's okay. You were just napping." I hugged his arm.

Joe gave a loud sigh and then cupped his forehead in his hand.

"I didn't want to disturb you," I said. "You looked so tired."

He gazed up at me, glassy-eyed and looking embarrassed. "I-I didn't sleep well last night."

"Joe, it's okay." I looked into his eyes. He was somewhere else, and I couldn't seem to bring him back. "What is it?" I sensed him drifting away into a distant, unreachable place. Suddenly, I was desperate to know. "Talk to me."

He ran his hand down his face and squeezed his eyes shut. When he opened them again, he wouldn't look at me, only stared straight ahead.

"On one of my earlier days in Korea, after stifling heat and two consecutive days of surgery without rest, I needed to take a break. I said so to one of the senior surgeons and he pointed to an area inside the tent where I could rest. And then he said something I will never forget. 'Just remember, while you're napping, men are dying, waiting for you to get up.'"

"Oh, Joe." We sat in silence for a while. Then I kissed him on his cheek. "Are you able to talk about it?"

He looked at me and shook his head, but his eyes were telling me something else. "It's hard. It's so very hard," he said in a low voice. Tears glossed over his eyes. "I asked the surgeon in charge when my shift would be over and he said, 'could be days from now.' I hadn't showered or slept. I was scared. Not for me. For those I couldn't help. Men were dying everywhere . . . screaming for help. They were all so young. Many of them younger than me." Joe looked at me then. "I never asked about shifts again. I still see everything in my sleep - the wounded men covered in bloodied white sheets on metal tables, the dark brown tents, the dusty dirt roads under my feet." He leaned his elbows on his knees and glanced back at the Christmas tree, memories washing over him.

"It was Christmas time . . . songs were playing on an old phonograph and they were serving some kind of pudding, small tokens of home. I remember it was freezing cold. I could hear artillery shells all around us, the choppers coming in. A private orderly came for me and led me to the five-gallon bucket to wash my hands so I could prepare for surgery. They were bringing someone in as he said, 'you physicians are our hope - our heroes.' A young man with a gaping chest wound was brought through the tent, and I said, "No. The men fighting on the front lines . . . the helicopter pilots pulling the wounded soldiers from the battlefields...those are the heroes."

A tear rolled from Joe's eye, and I lay my hand on his cheek. "I think...maybe...there were lots of heroes."

Joe took a deep, cleansing breath. "I'm sorry for going on about this."

I put my stop hand out. "No need to say . . ."

"I didn't mean to bring you down. I shouldn't have done that. I don't know how to stop it."

"The bad dreams?"

"Yes. I've always been in control of my emotions, focused and driven. I don't know how to handle weakness."

"Do you see this as a weakness? I see it as being human."

"I can do better. I should do better. I'm a doctor. The way I had to shelter my heart so I could do my job . . . it was so hard."

I turned so I was facing him. "You don't have to suffer in silence, Joe. It's because of who you are as a person that makes you such a compassionate and conscientious doctor. I want you to be able to talk to me. Always. That's what we do - you and me. It's who we are." Even as I said it, I knew I would never be able to fully comprehend what it was like for him, being hurled into a frontline mobile hospital of a war zone mere hours after graduating medical school, but I had to try.

"Joe, did you have to go through some kind of training for what you had to do there? I mean, I know you finished medical school, but it's not really the same thing, is it?"

Joe shook his head. "I had no training in combat medicine. Being besieged with casualties was my training. By the time my service was nearing the end, I was performing artery transplants, trying to save limbs. I . . . I learned a lot during that time. We all did. That much I can say. Soldiers who might not have been able to walk, walked."

"That's something to be proud of, Joe."

"I feel like I can talk with you about most things. But this . . . it's so hard . . . I'm afraid to go too deep."

"I know. But if we can't share our deepest feelings with one another, then what good is that?"

Joe stared into my eyes. "I've already said too much. I don't think I'm ready."

"Okay. But when you are, you don't have to feel like you need to protect me from hard truths. I want to know you. I want to understand you and all that you've been through. I wouldn't like it if you couldn't share yourself with me. You don't have to struggle alone."

"It's just war nerves. Time will heal."

Joe's willingness to expose some of his deepest struggles and stressful memories with me was proof of his trust. It warmed my heart and I reached up to hug him, kissing him tenderly on his lips. When I started to pull away, he gripped my shoulders, his lips coveting mine with fervor and passion. He kissed me long and hard, releasing a storm of pent-up feelings. I knew this kiss was different somehow, deeper in raw honesty and trust, its meaning undeniable.

"And that," I said breathless and dizzy, "is the emotion I love the most."

CHAPTER 22

Amanda

Jesse
Already missing you.
How are you feeling today?

Me
Improving. Thanks.
Miss you too.

Jesse
How did the call go with your parents?

Me
It was hard. I wanted to cry, but I didn't
I'm the girl on the bicycle – pushing ahead.
Worst part is, Mom calls and texts me nonstop now.

Jesse
Your grandmother know anything yet?

Me
No, but she's still asking questions.
I'd hate to have to tell her what really happened.

Jesse
Well, she can see that you're okay.
That should put her at ease.
Did you go to work today?

Me
Part-time. Made a few rounds.

Jesse
How did you feel about walking out to your car?

Jesse
Amanda...?

Me
I was never left alone.
Security has been beefed up.

Jesse
Good. Taking Emma to Kitty Hawk this weekend.
Wish you could come.

Me
If this were any other time, I would love to.
Think I should use this weekend to rest up some more.
Next week is going to be a busy one for me.
Have a bit of catching up to do.

Jesse
I understand.
I'll be thinking about you.
I never stop thinking about you.

What I haven't told Jesse in his calls or texts is that I've been having terrifying flashbacks and nightmares and that I'm not eating or sleeping well. I wonder if the man who attacked me has ever been caught. If not, have there been other victims since me? Could he still be lurking near the hospital? When I close my eyes, I can still hear him yelling. I ask myself what I would have done if he had been armed. Would I have given in immediately? Or would I have been killed perhaps? Victim – that's me now. It would be harder to believe if the ramifications weren't so real. I tell myself the unending questions and nightmares are temporary, that given time, it will fade naturally.

***

"I don't know how I would've gotten through those first twenty-four hours were it not for Jesse."

Dawn and I are sitting on the deck off the sunroom on a late Saturday afternoon, surrounded by a mountain oasis and drinking sweet tea. Nana is taking her usual nap. Dawn is the only person I'm willing to see besides Jesse, who's spending the weekend with his daughter and family in Kitty Hawk. "He really has been wonderful."

"It's impressive how he pursued the attacker to get back your purse for you. He's the talk of the hospital now," Dawn says.

"It's made these past few days a lot less hectic for me since nothing was taken. I am so grateful." I pour more sweet tea from the pitcher into Dawn's half-empty glass, filling it to the top. "He asks how I'm doing all the time. I tell him I'm coming along. I don't tell him about the nightmares I've been having. My experience pales in comparison to what he's been through. I haven't shared too much about him with Nana or my parents either. I'm still not sure about us."

"His is an incredible story. It pretty much explains why he had this mysterious aura about him."

"I'm getting to know him," I say, hugging an outdoor pillow.

"And?"

"And, I like what I see so far," I say, showing restraint.

"Hmmm," Dawn says. "If I wasn't your best friend, I wouldn't know any better, but...I saw you two together. Remember? You two couldn't take your eyes off each other."

"Well yeah, I do find Jesse attractive."

Dawn gives me a side grin. "Okay. I get it. You're still in protective mode. Suit yourself. I have a feeling Jesse will bring you around."

"I'm getting there." I take a sip of my tea.

Dawn chuckles. "Well then, brace yourself for a wild ride because he's really into you. It's plain to see."

I shake my head and laugh. Dawn is as entertaining as usual. "Thank you," I say.

"For what?" Dawn asks.

"For getting my mind off things I'd rather forget." I lean forward. "Now, pass your phone over to me so I can see the pictures of you in your bridal gown. I cannot believe your wedding is in three months."

***

I turn from side to side in front of my free-standing floor mirror trying on a sleeveless blue-floral sundress. I had purchased the dress sometime in early June. It's now the end of July and it feels looser, the pleats billowing out more as I get ready for my date with Jesse.

I pinch my waist and run my hand over my stomach, the thinness surprising me. I walk to my bathroom and stand on the scale. Since my mugging sixteen days ago, I have lost a total of eight pounds I didn't need to lose. I try on two more dresses, settling on a yellow buttoned casual shirt dress. Straight and knee-length with cuffed short sleeves – it hugs my curves and is more flattering. And - it happens to go well with my turquoise nail polish. A gold beaded choker and cuff bracelet finish off the look.

I'm excited for my date with Jesse tonight. I want to impress him with how well I'm doing, a picture of health, since the last time he saw me quite battered and bruised.

Behind a smokescreen of guarded feelings, I know I'm falling for Jesse and it scares me. Dawn sees right through it; I wonder if Jesse knows it, too.

I need to go deep if I want to be honest with him, deeper if I am honest with myself. It is hard being vulnerable with my heart. But Jesse left himself vulnerable too, when he shared some very intimate, difficult things with me. Things that endear him to me more.

Jesse is at my front door ringing the doorbell. Dorothy, who is still at the house, invites him in while I snatch my woven summer handbag from my chair and start down the flight of stairs.

His eyes brighten as he looks up from the foyer landing. He smiles, watching me, happy in the moment. He's casually dressed in a light-blue button-down shirt with the sleeves rolled up to his elbows, dark blue jeans and leather loafers without socks. "You look terrific." He greets me at the bottom of the stairs and kisses me on the cheek.

"Told you I'm all better," I say.

Dorothy is beaming from ear to ear before she catches herself staring. We follow her into the living area where Nana is sitting, her cane leaning against the stone fireplace.

"How do you do, ma'am," Jesse greets her.

"Nice to see you again," Nana says. "How handsome you two look." She turns to me. "Be sure to bring an umbrella along. I hear thunderstorms are in the forecast for tonight."

"Yes, I will," I say, going over to kiss her on her cheek. "Love you."

Jesse and I walk outside together toward his car. It's going to rain soon; I can smell it in the air. A mix of dark clouds threatens the sky, and the little sunlight that's left is descending behind surreal silhouettes of mountain peaks in the fog. He opens my door and I slide into the front passenger seat. Jesse gets behind the wheel and starts the engine, turning toward me before he drives us to the downtown restaurant.

"I'm so happy to see you. I've missed you an awful lot." He lays his hand on my shoulder. "You sure you're feeling okay?"

"I am. I've put it all behind me now." I do not tell him that my subconscious hasn't been able to let it go. "How was the weekend at the beach with your daughter and family?" I deflect. "Hope you got to spend some quality time with Emma."

"We had a really nice weekend," Jesse says, pulling out of the driveway toward the street. "Good weather all around. Emma loves it there."

"Do you get to the beach a lot?" I ask.

"I try to get down there whenever I can get away. One of my sister's and her family are vacationing there this week. We all take turns."

"Who's watching Emma now?"

"She's with my parents today and tomorrow. I don't know what I'd do without them. On weekdays, I have a sitter help out until I get off from work. My sister, who also lives in Charlotte, helps me out a lot, too. She has two kids of her own, so Emma loves going over there."

"It must not be easy, but it sounds to me like you are managing well."

"Well, if watching *Moana* over a dozen times and playing Calico Critters with her counts as managing, then I'm that guy." Jesse laughs. "It helps that I grew up with sisters. She's becoming a real chatterbox." Jesse turns into Biltmore Avenue and starts looking for a place to park.

I picture him with his young daughter, a strong, confident dad raising a strong, confident girl. My dad was much the same. Unlike my mother, the vocal micromanager, Dad was quiet and unassuming, but his resolve was steady and reliable. I always knew where he stood. He was dependable.

"You know," I say, "your influence on Emma is greater than you realize. My dad was the calm in the storm of my growing up and making all kinds of mistakes. He helped me find my way. Mom would scream and yell. Dad would say things like 'Want to talk about it?' or 'If you come away from this having learned something, then all's not lost.' Mom was the disciplinarian; Dad was the teacher. He had a way of turning everything into a teachable moment."

As I think on it, I was lucky to have two hero men in my life – my dad and my grandfather, which might explain my high expectations. But I don't tell Jesse that.

"I appreciate hearing this," Jesse says, finding a spot on North Lexington and pulling his car into it. Sometimes, I feel like I'm muddling along and that Emma's missing out."

Jesse gets out of the car, goes over to the parking meter, and then helps me out of my side. The familiar Bohemian vibe hits me in an instant, a lively fanfare of music and art.

"It's been a while since I was in this area," Jesse says. The mellow jazz sound from a saxophone floats through the street.

We stroll along the sidewalk, Jesse and I glancing at the downtown shops and restaurants, an eclectic, bustling pageant of activities, stopping to observe a living statue of a man holding an umbrella and posing as if he's blowing in the wind. "However does he keep that pose?" I say, fascinated. Jesse reaches into his pants pocket and pulls out some bills, throwing them into the busker's tips pail. When we come to the front entrance of our restaurant, Jesse opens the door, allowing me to go first.

"Jesse Taylor," he says, turning to the hostess.

She checks her reservation book. "Right this way." The hostess takes us through an intimate dining room and seats us at a corner table, a clear bud vase holding yellow buttercups and a floating candle in a cocktail glass at its center.

Jesse pulls out my chair for me and I sidle into it, then he takes his seat across from me. I look into his eyes, eager to resume our conversation and emphasize my point. "Emma is lucky she has you," I say.

"I feel like I'm the lucky one," he says.

"You have each other. That's what counts."

Jesse smiles, looks from the buttercups on our table to my yellow dress. "I was noticing the color yellow, which seems to be dominant here. What is it they say, that yellow is the color of sunshine and positivity? How appropriate."

A young waiter comes over to take our drink order. An Appalachian Sour for me, a Gin Manhattan for Jesse. "You look beautiful in yellow - your dark hair, your dark lashes . . .." Jesse leans in, the warm glow of the candle dancing in his mirror eyes, reverie forming on his lips. "I really missed you."

"I missed you, too," I say.

Our drinks arrive and I must remind myself to sip mine slowly since I haven't had much to eat all day.

Jesse holds up his glass. "What should we toast to?"

I bring mine up. "Here's to staying positive."

"And to getting to know one another better."

We clink our glasses and take sips from them, my lips puckering.

"Too sour? I can get you a different drink," Jesse says.

"No, it's rather delicious." I take another sip and lick my lips.

Lightness spun with blissfulness flows through me and I feel the sway of letting everything go. When the night is over I'll think back on this, remembering how we sat across from each other in a long silence, where language seemed intrusive and pointless, and I was transformed, feeling safe and more whole than I've ever felt before.

CHAPTER 23

Elizabeth
Christmas Eve 1953

Standing on the corner of Halsey Street after a frenzied work shift on Christmas Eve, I buttoned up my wool coat to the top against the frosty air. Patches of soiled snow from a previous day were scattered around, and the clouds loomed heavy with more to come, perhaps only moments away. I wished it would just get on with it, pretty everything up again with sparkling whiteness in time for Christmas. It was cold enough for snow.

I could hear the Cathedral Basilica of the Sacred Heart's newly installed church bells ringing once again, a sound that I loved whenever I heard it. I looked in its direction, the ornate French Gothic twin towers on the city's highest peak piercing the sky overhead.

This would be Joe's and my first Christmas together, and finding love again was the greatest gift I could have ever hoped for. My heart leaped with joy when I spotted the little white sports car with the black canvas top driving down Market Street. Joe picked me up because he had something planned for us, but wouldn't say what.

We drove past the Adams Theater and out of the city for thirty minutes. We sat quietly during the ride, listening to Christmas songs playing on the car's radio. The car slowed in a suburban neighborhood lined with a canopy of sturdy oak trees, their bare, gnarly branches reaching across one another; fallen brown leaves mixed with patches of hardened snow were scattered along the trees' bases. Joe pulled into a driveway of a big, red-brick house landscaped with shrubs freshly dusted with snow. A gentleman stood under a covered porch at its front entrance.

"Joe, where are we?"

"We're in a town called Summit," Joe said. "I want to get your opinion of a house I'm considering buying."

Joe introduced us and the realtor promptly led us through a mahogany front door with rectangular panels, the two on top in glass. We stood in a central front hall that was as big as my kitchen at home. I peeled off my winter gloves, stuffing them into my coat pocket, and swiped my wet hair from the snowy mist, back from my forehead.

"It's even bigger than it looked from outside," I said.

Joe grabbed my hand. "Come see the living room." The room was tastefully furnished by its present owners, an elderly couple who had fittingly stepped out. A real pine tree decorated with colorful bubble lights stood near a big picture window, but the focal point was the stone fireplace and elegant mantel adorned with Christmas porcelains.

"Oh, Joe," was all I could say.

I could have stayed there longer, admiring the layout, but Joe's enthusiasm for me to see everything required quicker strides. He navigated the house as though he'd lived there all his life, the realtor following us a few feet behind, wordlessly, since Joe was doing the work for him. Together, we traipsed through each room of the two-story center hall colonial, its four bedrooms, formal dining room, and home office where Joe appeared most animated. Every now and then I noticed that, while I was surveying each of the rooms, Joe was more intent on watching me and my reactions. Finally, he said, "Well, what do you think?"

"I think it's wonderful."

"Come," he said, going to the back of the house, toward a cozy kitchen – soft yellows, white eyelet curtains on a window above the sink, a Dutch boy and girl salt and pepper shaker set and various knickknacks lining the sill. He steered me over to the sliding glass door, a picturesque area with a deck that backed up to a private wooded area, a tranquil space where one could connect with nature. It had gotten dark outside, so he turned on a floodlight so we could see the backyard. Snow flurries sprayed the air with speckling whiteness. It is then that I gave him my longest, most satisfying sigh. "This is the crème de la crème. You have to buy it," I hastened, and then had to laugh at myself for having gotten so caught up in it all. "I mean . . ." I pulled back a little. "If you can, that is. It looks expensive. Are you sure you can afford it?"

Joe broke out laughing.

"I think that's an important question," I said in my defense.

"Beth," Joe said, turning serious, "I already bought it. It's mine. Well, it will be." He dropped to one knee and held out a small velvet trinket box. "And yours, if you'll have me."

I had to lean against the wall to steady myself, my mind reeling.

"Beth," he said slowly, giving me time to grasp what was happening. "Will you marry me?"

It took a few bewildered seconds before my brain told my mouth what to say. *Yes, yes! I will marry you.* I was crying so much I didn't remember if I actually said *yes* out loud, but Joe said that, somewhere in all the noise, I did.

He stood up, reaching for my trembling left hand, and slid a two-carat solitaire emerald-cut diamond ring with diamond baguettes on either side onto my finger. I held it up to my eyes. Under the ceiling light the stone on my engagement ring sparkled. I threw my arms around his neck and kissed him wherever my lips landed - his neck, his chin, his face. Joe lifted me up so that my feet dangled, covering my mouth with his. When he lowered me to the floor, we were still kissing, his hands clasped around my head, his thumbs brushing my cheeks, moist with salty tears.

"I had no idea. I mean, we never talked about it."

"I know how you make me feel whenever I'm with you. I know that I hate being apart, not seeing you for days on end. I want you to be my wife. I want to be able to come home to you. I want a life with you. I've spent a lot of time in my solitary years at medical school, and then in South Korea - years when I could only dream of someone like you. And now, I've found you. I've never wanted anything more. I love you."

"I love you, too," I said.

I threw back my head, breathless and ecstatic. "I can't wait to tell my parents."

"Actually," Joe said, "they already know. I asked for your father's permission, and he gave me his blessing."

"When was that?"

"The last time I was at your house. We had stepped outside to look at my car's engine. Remember that?"

"Yes, I remember. So, they've known for two weeks?" I shook my head. "Well, that would explain the conspiratorial whispers and grins."

We came together again, wrapped in each other's arms, two hearts beating as one.

Coming out of our private reverie I looked around, remembering we weren't alone. "Joe, where did the realtor go?"

"He's waiting for us out front. He only came as a favor to me." Joe winked.

Leaning on his shoulder, my lips gliding over his neck, I murmured, "I love you so much."

"I love you, too," he said, kissing the top of my head.

I glanced back to a cumulative winter wonderland happening outside since the clouds had opened. "Look. Snow's coming down fast now," I said.

Joe unlocked the glass door and slid it open. We stepped out onto the deck which was blanketed in snow and I tilted my face upward so I could feel the falling flakes melt on my skin. Joe caught me as my heeled shoes began to slip, and I burrowed my pink-cheeked face inside his coat as he held onto me. "Don't worry. I've got you," he said, my heart melting at his words. "Merry Christmas."

That this would become the first in an annual Christmas tradition lasting nearly forty years in that house, the house where we would raise our family, I could not have begun to fathom. With a full heart, my one cheek leaning on his coat and gazing up at the sky, I said, "Merry first Christmas, my darling."

CHAPTER 24

Amanda

When we exit the restaurant, it's steamy outside, the sky darkened and drizzling rain. A humid waft carries the smell of hearth-baked bread from a nearby bakery. Jesse wants us to go for a stroll to a nearby dessert bar, the creative foodie scene tempting us with more options. He tells me to wait by the restaurant's front entrance under the covering while he goes to retrieve the umbrella I left in the car.

Even though the sky is threatening heavier rain, the clamor from people on the street has not abated. Then, without warning, it all comes back to me in a blaze, relentless flashbacks charging me. I glance over my shoulder and clutch my purse under my arm. There's no one behind, yet the sensation of being pounced on is strong, spiking fear in me. I lean against the restaurant wall's exterior and instantly seize up; small, staccato breaths exacerbate my panic. I try to call out for Jesse, but my voice is choked.

He comes toward me opening my umbrella, takes one look at me gasping for breath, and drops the umbrella at his feet. "Amanda!" He takes me in his hands, a swift assessment revealed in his alarmed expression.

I'm rooted in the spot where I'm standing, immovable and locked. Only my heart is racing.

Jesse's eyes are steadied on mine as he talks me through. "Take a deep breath, nice and easy. That's it. Exhale ...long and slow."

I feel myself calming, lightheadedness easing. "Oh Jesse." I collapse in his arms.

"Come on. I'll take you back to the car."

I hold up my hand, inhale a deep satisfying breath, feel my lungs expand. "No . . . no. The night is still young. I'm okay now. Honest. I don't want to go home yet."

"Are you sure?"

"Yes, I'm sure. You're here with me now. I'll be fine."

We walk down the block in pensive silence while Jesse holds the umbrella over us, his other arm wrapped around my waist as the rain picks up.

Sitting inside the bar, Jesse pulls the green-and-white-striped straw from his pineapple mojito, swirling it, and then takes a swallow from the glass. He sets it down on a table and leans forward with his elbows on his knees. "So, are we going to talk about what happened to you out there?"

Nursing my drink in my lap, I lean back on the couch and cross my legs. "I'm sorry you had to see that."

Jesse has a discerning yet compassionate look in his eyes. "You had a full-blown panic attack back there."

"I-I guess I did. I tried to talk myself out of it but it got away from me. I've never felt that before." Jesse quietly waits for me to continue. "It was intense. I've experienced snapshots and flashbacks of my attack, and yes, even nightmares, but that was definitely different. I guess my standing there, alone and exposed, stirred up the memories. I don't know how else to explain it."

"You did. And it's not hard to understand," Jesse says.

"I know what you're thinking." I won't say it, but Jesse does.

"PTSD doesn't usually go away on its own. All the signs point to it," he says. He takes my hand in his. "You were the victim of a crime. It's not something you can easily get over."

"It's just so frustrating. I thought I was stronger."

"Whoa," Jesse defends. "Hold on there. This has nothing to do with strength. It has to do with reconciling what occurred. It was a traumatizing thing that happened to you."

"I thought I could handle it. I thought I *was* handling it." I take a sip of the mojito, tasting mint and pineapple. "I'm not coping very well."

"I hope you'll talk to someone who can help. Dealing with this head-on will make you stronger than before it ever happened. I can say this from my own experience. You don't have to do this alone. I bottled up all kinds of emotions when my wife was killed. It was eating me alive until I went for counseling. You should look into therapy that focuses on trauma."

Therapy? Really? "I thought it would be easier if I tried to forget what happened. I just want to feel normal again." I bow my head and stare down at my drink, resigned. "Guess you can't rush normal."

"I'm sorry you have to go through this. I don't need to tell you it can be hard. It takes courage and patience to go down that path. You have to be willing to accept support."

Maybe therapy would help. "I'm going to call a colleague of mine, a therapist who specializes in cognitive therapy."

"Good for you."

"It's horrible," I say, feeling the need to vent. "Sometimes I just want to scream. I want to move past it, get as far away from it as I can, but it follows me everywhere I go. I may never stop looking over my shoulder, but I want to think I'll return to some sense of safety again one day. I have to believe that."

"You will." Jesse pats my hand. "It's gonna take time. But you won't be alone."

I take another sip of my drink and bite into the pineapple wedge, pondering Jesse's words - *you won't be alone.* What exactly did he mean by that? Words can have so many meanings. I want to believe Jesse is speaking of himself, that he intends on becoming an integral part of my life, but the over-thinker in me has been wrong before. I caution myself to get out of my head.

"Thank you," I say with a deeper sense of gratitude. I squeeze his hand. "Thank you for telling me what I didn't want to hear, but needed to."

A tray of churros is on the table in front of us, a crock of warm, smooth chocolate on the side. "Now," I say, grateful for the diversion, "are we going to try these or not?"

Feeling exhilarated on mojitos and cinnamon sugar, we leave the dessert bar and confront the slanting rain outside, my compact umbrella barely keeping us dry. We navigate puddles to avoid getting splashed. Wipers swipe swiftly across Jesse's car windshield as he drives us to Nana's house.

Sitting in his car in Nana's driveway, we wait for the deluge of rain to subside. "You're going to spend the night," I tell Jesse. "I won't let you drive home in this weather. I'm not ready for this night to end. Are you?"

"*End* – that word should be forbidden," he says. "I much prefer the word *begin.*" Jesse smiles with the brightness of hope and expectation. He leans over and kisses me on the mouth, our breaths hinting of mint leaves.

The rain is relentless. He turns off the engine and grabs his satchel of extra clothes and toiletries from the back seat, and we take off for the front porch. A sharp crack of lightning followed by a loud boom of thunder detonates in the distance. I involuntarily scream, and Jesse takes my hand and pulls me along with him. We soar over the few steps until we're under cover of the porch roof. When we reach the top of the stairs, Jesse drops his satchel and we fall into each other's arms, drenched and laughing like a couple of kids, the scent of summer rain hanging thickly in the air.

I let us in and we take off our shoes near the front door. "Go right on up," I say quietly. "You know where you can change. I'm going to check on Nana before I head up there."

"Mind if I shower before I change into drier clothes?" Jesse asks.

"Of course not. Make yourself comfortable."

I peek in on Nana, sleeping soundly in her bedroom, an open book still lying on her chest, glasses slid down her nose. Apparently neither the thunder nor my scream woke her. I mark her place in the book she was reading – *Where the Crawdads Sing* - and place it next to her Bible on the nightstand along with her eyeglasses.

I start up the stairs when a quick glance at Jesse's and my wet shoes in the front hall stops me. As much as I like what it implies, I realize how it will look to Nana if she sees it. I take Jesse's shoes with me up the stairs to dry on the second floor landing.

In my bedroom, I slip out of my dress and go over to my bathroom mirror and shake out my hair. The clamminess of my skin sends shivers all over me before I step into a warm shower.

I'm dressed in silky blue pajamas when Jesse taps on my bedroom door. "Come in." Standing just inside my doorway, he's wearing gray drawstring knit pants and a white cotton t-shirt. "Much better," I say. "Is Emma staying over at your mom's?"

"She's spending this weekend with her aunt and cousins. It's very helpful having them close by."

We retreat to the sunroom, dark and shadowy at this time of night, a warm glow coming from the string of solar bulbs my Uncle Joe hung outside over the adjoining deck right before Nana's ninetieth birthday celebration. Rain still pours down heavily.

"I can turn on the ceiling fan light if you'd like."

"No. I like it just like this." Jesse opens his arms, enclosing me in them, and kisses me on the forehead. "It's perfect," he says, sotto voce. We sink into an upholstered sofa that should be at the end of its lifespan but is still in fair condition since it's hardly been used in the last ten years. Jesse snuggles me to him, our eyes doing most of the connecting.

We stay like that, cuddled on the sunken couch, and gaze out the windows, lightning branching over mountains in the blackened sky, both eerie and serene. I want to believe that Jesse could be mine; he's everything I ever wanted. Being with him gives me hope. The scariest words I'm afraid to say bubble up inside of me. *I think I could be falling in love.* All the self-doubt, the painful suspicions, the guardedness seem so far away now. But am I ready for complete vulnerability?

We soon fall easily into a rhythm of conversation.

"Tell me about your childhood. I bet you were a real live wire growing up, Jesse Taylor."

"Have you been talking to my parents?"

"A calculated guess."

"So maybe they had to make a few more trips to the ER with me than with my sisters. And . . . perhaps a few too many meetings in the principal's office. I couldn't sit still in school, but put a ball in my hand and let me run with it . . . that's where I was in my element. Once school let out, I was outdoors playing until dark. I played every sport that's out there. My high school coaches would agree that while I may not have been the fastest or tallest player, I scored high in mental resilience. I liked winning . . . a lot . . . and I never gave up."

An innate quality that no doubt helped him overcome the tragedy in his life, I am sure. It explains so much of what I'm learning about him.

"In my high school, I started a breakfast club." Jesse's eyes flicker with mirth.

"For what purpose?" I ask.

Jesse chuckles. "I wish I could say it was to put our heads together and solve pressing issues going on in school at the time, but it wasn't. It was designed to socialize and shorten the school day. We'd meet at Angie's coffee shop and exchange creative excuses as to why we were getting to school late and missing homeroom, writing notes, and forging our parents' signatures. These breakfasts often ran into first period. It started with two or three of us, then word spread, and it grew to about eight or nine. Boys . . . girls. It got out of control. This went on for a couple of weeks, but in Hummelstown, where everyone knows you, it didn't take long before Principal Cunningham paid us a surprise visit and handed out after-school detentions."

Jesse describes some of his legendary childhood antics, that run the gamut from benign to boisterous, and I catch myself laughing and shaking my head. I knew daring guys like him in my middle and high-school years, the ones who often challenged the staff or stirred up controversy. I was the quintessential opposite – studious and dependable, outwardly nonplussed, inwardly intrigued. I wonder if Jesse and I would've been friends back then or if I would've had a crush on him. I'm guessing not, since we definitely belonged to different clubs.

"How did your parents handle you?" I ask.

"I got an ass-whooping from Dad on more than one occasion. Playing football and basketball kept me out of trouble for the most part. My last transgression – the one that got me in the most trouble – was during the student council election season. I was an athlete first, but politics interested me too. During assembly, this poor guy who was running for vice president and giving his school election speech was getting ridiculed by some of the students. Things went further downhill when they started hitting him with spitballs on stage. That's when he threw his hands up in the air and walked off, quitting on the spot. Something motivated me to run up on stage and announce my candidacy to fill in the vacancy. I managed to grab the students' attention and held their interest. Next thing I knew they were clapping and cheering and whistling. I won't lie . . . it felt pretty good."

"Doesn't surprise me," I say. "You were in your natural habitat."

"Then the student council liaison spoke up and told me I needed to go through a process if I wanted to run for vice president. He asked me why I didn't go through the system, and I answered, 'Because the system sucks.'"

"Tell me you didn't say that."

"What do you think?"

I turn to look up at him, disbelieving, the bristle of his short, sculpted beard grazing my nose. "What happened next?"

"The students gave me a standing ovation. Principal Cunningham gave me a five-day school suspension."

"You were incorrigible."

He kisses the bridge of my nose. "I had some growing up to do."

"So, you were resilient, competitive and rebellious. When did you get serious and apply yourself so you could get into college?"

"High SAT scores that contradicted my grades helped a lot. And I got into college with a basketball scholarship, playing all four years."

"Talent, smarts and luck," I muse. "I, on the other hand, took the straight and narrow. We were both able to reach our goals. We just took different paths to get there."

"You were undoubtedly much more disciplined than I was," Jesse says.

"So, when did your interest in law come into play?"

"Unlike you – you probably knew what you wanted to do pretty early on – for me it wasn't like that. I didn't know until much later, when I realized that the two things I cared about most were honest competition and fairness. Law made sense to me. It had rules. It had two sides – winners and losers. I realized I'd been playing that game all my life."

I wonder if Jesse ever thinks about us that way. In the game of love, does he think we'd make a winning team? *Get out of your head, Amanda. Just feel his arms around you, holding you close to him, safe and warm.* The rain still drums outside.

"How about you? I'm going to go out on a limb here and say that you were a stellar student."

I don't answer him - only sigh in acquiescence. I don't want to tell him how hard I was on myself if I even got a B, pressures I put on myself without any help from anyone else.

I can hear the smile in Jesse's voice. "Thought so." He crosses his arms over my midriff in a snug cuddle. "Tell me, what's the worst thing you've ever done?"

"The worst? Well . . . I . . . it's something I still feel bad about." Jesse says nothing, giving me room. "When I was in middle school, a girl in my honors math class was often made fun of by a few of the so-called "popular" girls. In the girls' room one day, clustered near a sink and passing around a cigarette, these same girls were talking about her and being typically mean. I tried to ignore them but when I went over to wash my hands, one of them lured me into joining them. "You have classes with her, don't you?" the popular girl asked me. I simply nodded. But it wasn't enough. They wanted more. They wanted me to agree with them and join in the meanness. I knew they were testing me. I had to make a choice. Go along or risk their harsh criticisms too. I'm not proud of the choice I made."

"There's a lot to navigate in middle school," Jesse says.

"Worst part is, those girls left the girls' room before me and as I got ready to leave too, the girl we ridiculed came out of one of the bathroom stalls. She had been in there all along and heard everything. I'll never forget the sadness and hurt in her eyes. Eventually, I apologized to her and in time we even became friends. She continued to be in many of my classes throughout high school. Still, I've never been able to forget it."

"We've all done things we're ashamed of," Jesse says.

"Somehow, I don't think you would have made that choice if you were in my position."

"No, maybe not. Which might explain the fist fights I got into."

I shudder and then smother a yawn. I love how it feels being enfolded in Jesse's arms, my eyes closing as I drift off to sleep.

I feel a gentle nudge. Jesse whispers, "Come on. Let me help you up the stairs."

I wish he didn't have to wake me. But I know we have to move to the bedrooms. Morning is just a few hours away.

In front of my bedroom door, I plant a kiss on Jesse's lips. "Good night."

"Sleep well," Jesse says.

I fall into my bed hoping to resume sleeping, but restlessness and anxiety creep back in. I toss. I turn. I reach into my nightstand drawer for a sleep-aid pill, opening the cap. I can't stop thinking about Jesse, just down the hall, the way it feels when he holds me. Safe and belonging. *Take a good look at yourself, Amanda. What are you afraid of? Why do you resist? What do you really want?*

I put the cap back on the bottle of pills and return it to its drawer. Swinging my legs off the bed, I take preliminary steps to what awaits me down at the end of the hall, where my heart wants me to be, where Jesse sleeps.

I crack open the door to the room he occupies. He looks like he's already asleep and I start to leave when he lifts his head from the pillow. Up on his elbow, he watches me enter the room, a soft pool of light coming from the hallway behind. I look into his eyes with longing. He throws back the covers and slides over. I slip easily into the space he's made for me right next to him, in the irresistible, loving nook of his body.

CHAPTER 25

Elizabeth
January to March 1954

The weeks that followed were equal parts delightful and feverish. We talked about a June wedding at the earliest, a ceremony in St. Joseph's Roman Catholic Church where my family attended, with a reception party afterwards. Joan saw it as an affront to her family's Protestant heritage and that was just the beginning of her list of grievances. That Joe would pick an Italian Catholic girl to marry was as disagreeable as it could get for her. After all, there were many suitable young women from her church lining up to meet her doctor son. That's when I realized that trying to get Joe's mother to like me had nothing to do with me at all. It began with my birth, which was entirely out of my control.

Joe gave little credence to his mother's disparagements. "My mother needs something to do. What would you say if we put her in charge of the floral arrangements?" It was a brilliant idea, a distraction from her countless displeasures.

"You have such a great eye for embellishments and décor," I told her. "We could really use your help."

"Joe," I said to him at the end of one long and tiring day. "What do you want?"

Joe looked at me curiously and then kissed me on the forehead. "I want you."

"Yes, but what do you want for our wedding? What do you envision?"

Joe half-smiled. "I see you, my beautiful bride. That's what I envision."

"And?"

"That's all. That's everything."

"I've been thinking. We don't have to have a big wedding and all that goes with having a big affair." I definitely wasn't going to score any points with Joan - not as if I could - but I pressed on. "I realize you have a bigger family than I do, more cousins. And your mother's church friends. Honestly though, I envisioned my wedding day in a more intimate setting. Of course, I'll do whatever you want. But a spring or summer wedding is still months away."

Joe pulled me to him. "That's why I love you so much. We always seem to want the same things. I would've married you yesterday."

In that moment, we realized what we both wanted. Despite pressures from Joe's mother, we felt lighter and energized. The onus of a big, more elaborate wedding fell away, leaving just us. To my future mother-in-law's chagrin, she had to trim down her guest list by more than half. But going small meant we could marry sooner - weeks instead of months from now.

If someone had told me months ago that I would become Dr. Paterson's wife, or that I would be given the gift of love again, I wouldn't have believed it. I was in love with Joe, deeply and passionately, and I wanted our life together to begin as soon as possible. Our wedding date was set for Friday evening, the fifth of March in 1954.

My mother got to work on my wedding dress, a simple white, tea-length dress with a ballerina skirt and high-collar bodice with small fabric buttons down the back. I wore a short veil over pinned-up hair and carried a bouquet of creamy-white roses. Joe and I married in a small chapel with twenty of our closest friends and family, which included Nurse Agnes and her husband. Inside her wedding card was a note that read, *I knew he was taken with you even before he realized it – like I said, I know people. Congratulations you two lovebirds!*

To a clattering of applause followed by clinking of glasses, Joe and I walked hand-in-hand through the front entrance of the Italian restaurant where our private dinner party was held. White-clothed tables and glowing centerpiece candles inserted through pink hydrangea rings (my mother-in-law's touch), evoked a romantic, warm atmosphere, and wine and food flowed continuously. Little organza favor bags filled with candy-coated almonds and tied with gold ribbon sat at each place setting. From appetizers of breads and assorted cheeses and olives to bowtie pasta, the abundance of food delighted everyone. Even Joan grudgingly came around.

Before the skirt steak entrée was brought out, my father gave a toast invigorated by wine and wooziness. His speech was a sentimental mix of sobbing and getting choked up with fatherly love. I went over and hugged him. Then I went over and embraced my mother.

When I turned around, Joe stood up from the table. He looked at me from across the room until we locked eyes, and then he began to speak. "When I first met you, Beth . . . you were like a bird with a broken wing, hurting and unable to fly. I wanted so much to help you, to heal you so you could fly again, and be the beautiful woman you were meant to be. And fly you did. Out of my sight, but never out of my mind. And then, as chance would have it, I saw you again, as beautiful and as engaging as ever, your wings spread and fluffed. You were flying high. I knew then that wherever the wind carried you, I wanted to be right by your side, going through life with you. Today, you've made me the happiest man alive. I've never flown so high. I love you."

The room had fallen silent. I think I may have heard my mother crying. Joe came around from behind the table as I rushed into his arms, tears running down my cheeks, and I kissed him, giving him everything from my heart and soul. "I love you so much."

We cut the two-tiered cannoli cake with the bride-and-groom cake topper and then plotted our departure. While everyone was finishing dessert and drinking coffee and sambuca, Joe and I slipped out the back door to our waiting car, giggling and laughing, and drove away to our new house. Our wedding day was perfect. It was Joe's and my *everything*.

Nearing our destination, words and laughter waning, an unspoken excitement moved in as we contemplated our wedding night, minutes away. I leaned back, my white dress splayed over red leather, and slipped out of my heels. I thought that if there was one day in my life that I could be stuck in, this would be it.

Joe reached over and slipped his hand under the skirt of my dress, tracing his fingers over thigh-high stockings, his strokes slow and deliberate. Agonizing minutes still ahead of us, the mere touch of Joe's hand gliding over my thigh was arousing me and making me tremble for what was to come.

Joe and I walked up to the front entrance of our new house, our path illuminated by the smoky light of a lamppost. Unlocking the door, he pushed it open, then turned and scooped me up into his arms, carrying me over its threshold. When he continued to carry me up the flight of stairs, I clasped my fingers around his neck, my one heel slipping out of its white stiletto, pleading with giddiness for him to let me walk.

He didn't set me down until we came to the foot of our bed. I kicked off my shoes and stood in my nylon feet in front of him, my eyes roving upward to his six foot height. Transfixed and lightheaded on wine and love, I reached up and unknotted Joe's silk tie, our eyes never leaving each other. Joe turned me around and undid the small buttons on the back of my dress, one tantalizing button at a time until it fell off in a puddle of tulle and satin. He was methodically unbuttoning the front and cuffs of his dress shirt when I faced him again. I reached up, gliding my hands over his firm shoulders, and slid them down the inside of his shirt, taking it off.

Joe moved me to the bed and sat me on it as he unclipped the garters. Slowly and with the lightest of touch, he slid my hosiery down one leg, then the other, the feeling of his fingers gliding over my skin making me shiver. I giggled nervously, feeling shy all of a sudden.

I retreated to the bathroom to put on a silky white nightgown and let my hair down. When I returned to the dimly lit bedroom, Joe was fully undressed, eagerly waiting. "My beautiful, beautiful Beth." He patted the bed. "Come."

I slid next to him as he turned toward me. His bare, sturdy chest rippled in the soft light, and my eyes fell to his full manhood, captivated. A gulp caught in my throat as the beauty of his bare body kindled me. I had never been with a man before. Not like this. Joe understood this; my instructor and my learner, wanting to know what pleased me. He ran his fingers through my hair, tumbling loose over my shoulders before burying his face in its floral scent. His hands moved gracefully over my breasts, my body, teasing with his fingers over my gown's sheerness as he circled and fondled, seeking hints of my pleasure. At last, he slid his hands under my negligée and lifted it up over my head, its silkiness clashing with the brushing of his nakedness against my skin.

"I love you," he said, kissing my eyelids delicately and enfolding me in his strong arms, the caresses of his lips and fingers sending shudders throughout my body.

He lay me down and I closed my eyes. Lips quivering, I parted my thighs, preparing for him to enter me. The sensation of mouth and tongue surprised me, feelings of confusion mingling with sheer ecstasy. "Joe," I moaned.

My back arched and Joe wove my fingers with his above my head as he gradually eased inside of me. He was totally tuned in to me, to what I was feeling, to our sensual rhythm. He made love to me slowly, gently, pain mingling with pleasure, blanketing me in the warmth of exquisite discovery and desire, making me feel totally and completely loved. Up until our wedding night, I had only imagined what our lovemaking would be like, but this was beyond anything my mind could dream up. It was the most beautiful thing I had ever known. I loved this man.

My husband. My soulmate.

CHAPTER 26

Amanda

My eyes flutter open; a club chair and ottoman coming into my peripheral view in the early morning's sliver of light. I roll my body over onto my side. The soft whirr of Jesse's breathing tells me he's still asleep in the bed. I don't want to wake him. I want to watch him. My eyes follow his long, sculpted right arm bent at the elbow and raised above his head where it rests on the pillow. A small arrow tattoo is etched on the inside of his wrist. His suntanned face in repose transfixes me - his closed eyelids under well-marked brows, precise facial hair lines near his cheekbones, short on the sides with a patch on a strong jawline that form a circle with his clean trim mustache. The comforter inadequately covers him, having slid down to his waistline, exposing one of his sturdy legs. I follow it to the foot of my bed where I see my panties and slip them back on. Other pieces of my sleepwear are strewn on the floor.

The golden color of the room tells me morning has fully dawned. I draw over Jesse's chest with my fingers, gliding over muscles and smooth skin and caressing soft blonde hairs, excerpts from last night rousing me again. Jesse's bare chest rises slightly with his breathing and he opens his eyes hesitantly.

"Good morning," I say softly. I trail little kisses inside his neck

He turns to face me, his mouth stretching across his face in a smile.

"How was your sleep?" I ask.

"Slept like a baby. You?"

"Same."

Jesse closes his eyes again, beaming.

"I wish we could stay here like this all day," I say, kissing the corner of his mouth.

"If you keep it up," he says, opening his eyes to gaze at me, "I may be incapable of ever leaving."

I shake my hair back and meet his eyes. "I need to go downstairs soon to check on Nana. Dorothy's off on weekends."

Jesse sits up. "That's my cue."

"Sorry," I say biting on my lower lip. "I don't know what to..."

"No need to explain," Jesse says. "I understand."

"But first," I say, "I've been meaning to ask you about the arrow tattoo."

"This?" he says, turning up his wrist to look at it with me. "I got this a year ago, a promise I made to myself that from that day on I'd be forward looking. I couldn't change what happened. I had to move forward...for my sake and for Emma's."

I lift his hand in mine and kiss the tattooed spot inside his wrist.

Jesse tousles the top of my hair. "I should get my things together. I'll text you when I'm on the road."

I pout. "Thank you for understanding."

"Thank you for last night," Jesse says, his eyes twinkling warmly.

I kiss Jesse on his lips and walk back to my bedroom so he can get himself ready to leave and I can wash up in my own bathroom.

***

Dressed in straight jeans and wearing a casual loose-fit T-shirt, I head down the flight of stairs and into the kitchen, making a beeline for the coffee pot. To my surprise, Nana is already sitting at the table, her walking cane leaned up against it. Wearing a button-down housedress and slippers, she butters a slice of toast.

"Nana," I say, rubbing my eyes. "You're up early."

"Last night's thunder kept me up most of the night," she says. "How was your evening?"

"Umm, good," I say, glancing nervously behind me, hearing the sound of Jesse's footsteps coming down the flight of stairs.

"Well, you'll have to tell me all about it," Nana says. "It's been quite some time since I got over that way."

"You're not just having toast for breakfast, are you? I can make us some eggs."

"That would be nice. But you must invite your friend to stay and join us." I start to stutter. Nana gives me a knowing smile. "Hurry now, before he gets away."

Jesse is heading out the front door when I make my way into the foyer. "Jesse," I say, motioning him to come back inside. He gives me a questioning look. "Nana has invited you to stay for breakfast. Would you like to come in and say hi?"

Jesse chuckles and smiles. "Well...all right then." He sets his satchel down by the front door and walks back with me into the kitchen.

"Good morning, ma'am," he says, walking over to greet Nana. "How nice of you to extend me an invitation." He's as suave and as natural as ever.

"It's nice to see you again," Nana says with a smile. "Amanda was about to fix us some eggs. I hope you'll join us."

"I'd love nothing else, but you must allow me the honor of cooking breakfast for you two fine ladies. Cooking eggs is kinda my thing."

Nana and I look at one another. "Help yourself," I say. This should be fun to watch. "Let me know what you need and I'll pull it out for you."

I get out the cast iron skillet, a carton of eggs, butter, olive oil, and different seasonings. I set the table with three plates, utensils, and coffee mugs, the kitchen table sparkling in the sunlight coming through the windows.

Jesse is in front of the stove, frying up over-easy eggs and conversing with Nana about last night's storm and the imposing arena of the surrounding mountains. "Don't think I've ever seen a more exciting rainstorm than the one I saw here last night," he says. "It was awesome."

"Anyone who appreciates nature is okay in my book." Nana gives me a wink.

A gold hair clip has loosened in the back of Nana's coiffed hair. I unclip it, and comb strands of brilliant white hair that's fallen loose with my fingers, bringing them together into a coil and clipping them again.

Jesse's ready for me to pass him the plates. One by one, he lifts perfectly cooked oval-shaped fried eggs from the pan and slides them onto each plate.

I pour coffee into our mugs and pull out a carton of orange juice from the refrigerator, and place it on the table along with three juice glasses.

"Downtown Asheville is quite lively," Jesse says to Nana. "Do you have any special seasoning or sauce you'd like to have with your eggs?"

"Worcestershire. Amanda knows where it is," Nana says, turning toward me. "And I'll have a biscuit with mine, too, honey. There should be some in the bread bin."

Jesse pulls out the chair in front of his plate and sits down. "Asheville keeps on evolving in quirky ways. And there certainly isn't a shortage of great places to eat. No wonder they call it a foodtopia." He surveys the items on the table. "You wouldn't by any chance have any hot sauce, would you?"

I pull out a bottle of hot sauce from the refrigerator door along with the Worcestershire, placing them on the table while Jesse continues to engage Nana in conversation.

"I imagine it's as entertaining as it's ever been," Nana says. "Although I haven't been there in...I don't know when. I don't get out very much anymore."

"I've got toast coming, too," I say, pulling out four slices that popped up from the toaster and setting them on a plate at the table. I take my seat across from Jesse.

"Well," Jesse says, dipping a piece of toast into his egg yolk, "we'll have to do something about that, won't we?"

"Something about what?" I ask, confused and feeling a little like an outsider in this conversation.

"Your grandmother was saying she doesn't get out much."

"Oh. Yes, well, there's the logistics and all," I say. "Usually, Mom and Dad, or my Uncle Joe, help out when Nana needs to go somewhere. That's assuming we can even coax her to go out."

"Well, I'm here. I can help. How about a car ride with us after breakfast?"

"Jesse, don't you have to get back to your daughter?" I ask.

"Emma's at my sister's until Sunday, enjoying playing with cousins. It's all been arranged."

"You have a daughter?" Nana asks.

"Yes, I do. Emma. She's four."

"How lovely," Nana says, looking at me with curiosity. I haven't shared too much about Jesse with her yet. We'll have to have a conversation later.

Jesse looks right at Nana. "I'm in the mood for a scenic ride. How 'bout it?"

"Oh my goodness," she says, shooing him. "It's too much of a bother. I don't move quite as well as I used to."

"It's no bother, ma'am. We could take a ride downtown if you'd like, and if you're so inclined, we could stop and relax a bit in Pack Square."

Did Jesse actually just invite Nana to go on an outing? He's in his element, social and charming.

"There were these bronze statues of livestock the last time I was there," Nana says, lighting up. "What were they now? Whimsical animals suggesting a long trip down from the mountains to the marketplace as I recall."

"A mother pig and piglet," I fill in for her, "and turkeys. Still there. And a whole other array of bronze statues and sculptures. The Confederate ones are almost all removed now."

"Yes, I read about the civil war monument demolition," Nana says. "Much has changed, I suppose. Joe and I would visit the Veteran's Memorial and just sit there for a while."

"Well, what do you say then?" Jesse asks. "You can come see for yourself. It's turning into a nice day for a car ride." He looks from me to Nana. "You won't even have to get out of the car if you don't want to."

I look at Nana. Weirdly, she's not refusing to go. In fact, I almost think she wants to go.

I turn to look at Jesse, his collaborator now. "Nana has a portable wheelchair-like scooter we can use," I say.

Nana looks from me to Jesse. "No. You two go on without me. I would only be in the way." Her argument is politely unconvincing, especially to someone as astute as Jesse.

"Ma'am," Jesse says, rising from the table. "It's settled. We're all going on a little outing." He stops at a framed 8 x 10 photo of Nana's house hanging on the kitchen wall. "When was this picture taken?" he asks.

"Nineteen ninety-seven," Nana says, her eyes dropping with melancholy. "The year my husband and I bought this house."

"It's a fine picture of a very fine house and place," Jesse says. He collects our plates and takes them over to the sink.

I help clear off the rest of the table and join him by the sink, but he bumps me out of the way. "I've got this," he says, in his typical manner of making you believe that he does indeed have everything under control. "I'll take care of the dishes while you help your grandmother get ready. And, when you get a second," he says, smiling effectually, "show me where her mobile scooter is. I'd like to have a look at it."

Nana reaches for her cane, steadying herself while she gets up out of her chair. She loops her other arm in mine, and we walk in the direction of her bedroom. "My, he's rather persuasive, isn't he?" Nana says loud enough for Jesse to hear, her clear hazel eyes alert and amused. "By any chance does he play Scrabble?"

***

Holding onto the porch banister with one hand while Jesse holds onto her other arm, Nana takes each of the six steps down one worrying step at a time. Her mobile wheelchair waits for her at the bottom where Jesse has set it up so she doesn't have to walk the winding pathway to the driveway. I follow behind, carefully stepping over dwindling rivulets of rainwater from last night's downpour.

"Sure you wouldn't rather sit up front?" Jesse asks Nana. "The view's better from there."

"No. I want to sit in the back. I insist."

Jesse helps Nana into the back seat of the car, then folds up her chair and fits it inside his trunk for later use.

"Don't you look nice," Jesse says to Nana before he closes her door. She's dressed in a pink-paisley knit top over brown slacks, her lips shiny with light-pink gloss. She leans against the back seat, her trusty cane lying between her and Emma's car seat, and gazes out the window through her eyeglasses.

By 10:50, we're heading out. "Is there anywhere in particular you want to go?" Jesse asks us.

"You're the driver," Nana says.

I nod. "Yep. This is your rodeo."

"All right then." Donning sunglasses, Jesse drives us through the downtown area, cruising past an eclectic backdrop of restaurants and bakeries, breweries and chocolatiers, where the composite sights of homelessness and performers and children come together. Panhandlers, a juggler on a street corner, children frolicking in the splash fountain, musicians setting up equipment, bronze statues and murals, and art museums and studios.

"Oh!" Nana exclaims. "I feel like I've been away a million years and then some."

Then Jesse takes us to the Blue Ridge scenic loop, a lovely drive through a section of the Pisgah National Forest, with splendid gardens and waterfalls and rolling hillsides spread with a rainbow of wildflowers and panoramic mountain views. Nana's been quiet. We come through another tunnel and I turn my head around to check on her. Looking wistful, she cries softly. "So many memories. When Joe and I first took this route many years ago, it was in the fall - we fell in love with it."

A half hour later, I glance at my watch. "Are you hungry for lunch, Nana?" She's on a consistent schedule. When she doesn't answer, I turn around to see that she's dozed off. I watch her momentarily, slumped in the back seat, her frail form, head dangling forward, shoulders sagging, the humility of old age in contrast with an inner resolve.

"Everything okay?" Jesse asks.

"She's just nodded off," I say, looking over at him. "The drive must have knocked her out."

"Do you think she enjoyed it some?" Jesse asks.

"I think she liked it a lot. Thank you so much for doing this. It was really sweet of you."

"You two are very close, aren't you?"

"We've always shared a special bond. She would tell you she sees a lot of herself in me. I suppose it's true." I tuck a strand of my hair behind an ear and roll my eyes. "I would have to say we definitely share a natural fortitude for getting through difficult things."

Jesse places his hand on my thigh. "I can see that," he says. "Apparently, you both felt a pull toward nursing careers. Are there other nurses in your family?"

"Nope. Just me and Nana."

"When did you think you wanted to become a nurse practitioner?" Jesse exits out of the Blue Ridge scenic loop, driving us toward home.

"You know, I don't even remember a time when I didn't want to help people, so it must have taken root pretty early on. My grandparents were definitely an inspiration. Nana was so supportive of me, something she didn't have when she aspired to be a nurse."

"I'll never forget when I was around twelve - my sister would have been around sixteen then. My parents were away on a vacation cruise, and my sister was at a teenager's summer-long sleepaway camp somewhere in Pennsylvania. So I got to spend one week alone with my grandparents in their house right here in Asheville. They were retired by then. At first, I didn't want to go, but it turned into an extraordinary remembrance for me. Of course, they doted on me every chance they got, which made it all the better."

"I bet it did," Jesse chuckles.

"One afternoon, I was sitting out on the front porch stringing beads for a bracelet I was making when a stray cat came along. It was shaking its head and zig-zagging over the front yard, and I could tell it was in some kind of distress. I called out for my grandparents. Nana came running out first, saw what I was seeing and took careful steps toward the cat. It was struggling. I don't know why, but it upset me and I started crying.

"Crying isn't going to help this poor creature," Nana said. "Pull yourself together and go get your Grampa."

When I came back outside with Grampa, Nana was holding the cat firmly between her hands while it continued shaking its head. "He's got something stuck in his mouth," she said. Together, they assessed what was going on, Nana holding the cat securely, Grampa opening its jaw. Apparently, it got a fishing lure hooked through its tongue somehow."

"Dang." Jesse's eyes are wide. "How did that happen?"

"We think it probably tried to eat it," Nana says, waking up. I turn my head around, and catch her smile. "He must have thought it was a bug or something."

"So what happened next?"

"Grampa ran to his garage and came back with a snipping tool and ether," I said. "I was frozen in place, watching the two of them. What a team they were." I glance back at Nana. "Grampa gave the cat ether until he passed out. Nana laid the cat on the grass, the two of them crouching over him while Grampa snipped the barb off the hook so he could pull it through the cat's tongue without causing any tearing."

"Wow," Jesse says. "That cat sure fell upon the right house."

"A short time later, the cat stumbled around for a while until it could stand and then dashed off." I let out a sigh. "That tells you everything you need to know about my grandparents."

"I forgot that time," Nana says to me. "But that's why I have you to fill in all those missing memories for me."

**

We order take-out chicken and waffles for lunch and eat together in the sunroom, Jesse viewing and commenting on some of the photos and memorabilia on Nana's lace-covered table and the burgeoning plants and fragrant lemon tree over in the corner.

"Joe bought that lemon tree fifteen years ago when it was only a foot tall," Nana says. Her eyes gaze around the room in a nostalgic sweep. "Now look at it. It's been making lemons for the past eight or so years."

After lunch, I help Nana to her bedroom so she can take her usual midafternoon nap. When I return, Jesse is already straightening up.

"Nana's thoroughly exhausted. She said to be sure and thank you for an unexpectedly pleasant day. She also said...and I'm quoting . . . 'that one there is quite a catch.'"

Jesse gives me a modest grin and takes me by my shoulders. "It gets harder and harder leaving you, but I'm afraid I have to get going."

"I know," I say, looking into his eyes. "You have a two-hour drive ahead of you and there's a little girl who needs her daddy. I had a wonderful time." I plant a kiss on Jesse's lips. He pulls me in tight. "Funny, isn't it," I say, my head lying against his chest, "that two of the most important people in our lives happen to be ninety and four years of age – an interesting dichotomy, yet each relies upon us."

Jesse lifts my chin with his finger and covers my mouth with his, a long, lavish kiss that will need to sustain us until we see one another again.

CHAPTER 27

Elizabeth
August 1954

I had wed a couple of months before my twenty-second birthday, just shy of spinster territory in those days.

"You saved me," I said to Joe, only half-joking for he truly was my knight in shining armor. Joe, however, saw it a little differently. He told me I was the missing piece of him. He loved my resiliency and endless curiosity. I loved how he challenged me to be the person I wanted to be.

The early fifties were not a favorable time for women who desired anything other than housewifery. I enjoyed working, being productive outside the house and using my people skills. Joe must have realized that because, in his pragmatic style, he told me while I didn't have to work anymore, he wouldn't discourage me if it's what I wanted.

Nineteen fifty-four was a year filled with national potential and progress. You could feel it everywhere. Life, it seemed, was getting bigger, faster and louder – cars, engines, rock and roll music. On the medical side of things, polio inoculations were starting and cigarette smoke was acknowledged as a link to cancer. I only smoked a little in high school, but I never really liked it enough to want to spend money on cigarettes. Joe smoked while he was in the service, but had since quit.

We settled into married life easily, as though it were the most natural thing in the world. Most of the time we were in sync, but we were equally appreciative of the times when we weren't. One such time came sooner than we expected.

The Atlantic hurricane season of 1954 was among the worst in a long while. Hurricane Carol had developed near the Bahamas, and came through New Jersey at the end of August, causing downed power lines and damage to boardwalks. The worst of its impact was felt in the New England area and the National Guard and American Red Cross had to be deployed. Besides the death toll, hundreds more were injured. Doctors and nurses were needed to provide disaster-relief medicine to the overwhelmed hospitals in those areas. Since the Korean War, Joe had been assisting the Red Cross on an as-needed basis and now was called on to do so again. Surgeons trained in trauma medicine were especially needed.

"Joe," I said as he was packing a suitcase for himself. "Let me come with you. I can be of help somehow. I can use my vacation days at work."

"It's demanding and stressful work. We'll hardly see one another."

"Joe," I implored, "I can help with the children. You know I have a knack for it. Remember when you helped the woman on the side of the road and I took care of her son until help arrived?"

"We could be gone for two or three days. I won't know until I get there. It's probably best if you stay here."

"Please say yes." I wasn't ready to quit.

Joe stopped what he was doing and put his hands firmly on my shoulders. "I have a feeling you're not going to let this go."

Looking up at him, I shook my head. He pushed back a strand of my hair and kissed the scar on my hairline. "Are you saying you wouldn't rather stay home watching shows on our new television set while eating bonbons?"

Somehow, I knew Joe didn't expect me to answer that. He saw a fire in me to help and be around people and I couldn't very well do that if I stayed home all day long.

"I won't be a bother. I promise. You won't even see me."

Joe kissed me again on the forehead. "I always want to see you. It just may not be possible." He gave a long sigh. "All right then. Start packing. We'll need to get on the road as soon as possible."

***

An emergency disaster-relief site was situated among the havoc and destruction caused by Hurricane Carol as many families sought food and shelter, their homes unlivable since the storm made landfall. I put myself to work helping distribute clean drinking water and meals that were dropped off from warehouses, feeling the distress of the homeless disaster victims at a very basic level. Joe was still at the hospital dealing with the more traumatic injuries – broken bones, head injuries and concussions, lacerations, and chest pain.

Children were dispersed among the havoc, looking lost and disoriented. I went over to a little girl who was crying. "Are you hungry?" I asked. The children soon became my most vital effort, where I thought my talents could be put to greatest use.

I looked around for a spot where they could sit down and eat properly. A door that had been ripped off its hinges in the storm became our makeshift table, and I summoned several children over to it. I then passed around bowls of rice and beans. I engaged them in anything other than the aftermath of the storm's wreckage while their parents rummaged desperately through water-logged ruins for anything they could salvage.

It felt heartwarming to be able to help in any way I could, but it was the disaster relief nurses who filled me with awe. I watched them, clearly the first responders, their roles at the forefront, and I wished I could do more - make a real difference like them. I had missed my opportunity to go for nursing. I watched them assessing for illnesses and stress or hypertension, administering tetanus shots, and lending a shoulder to lean on. One nurse's head was bowed in consultation with a female hurricane victim. I overheard her say, "Don't think about everything all at once. Only tackle one day at a time."

"But I don't even know where to start." The woman sobbed.

The nurse patted her on the back. "That's why we're here - to take some of those things off your shoulders for now."

"How do I begin to rebuild my life? I've lost everything."

"I know things seem terrible right now, but that will change. You are safe and alive," the nurse reminded her. "And that is something."

Joe and I retired to our hotel room late at night, completely exhausted. Lying in bed snuggled in Joe's arms I thought about the emotional strain of this one crushing day, and how Joe had experienced multiple days like it and worse in the war in Korea. It gave me a whole new perspective on what his last few years must have been like - a young doctor, just out of medical school, being thrown into a war zone like that, where so much was expected of him.

"Beth? Honey, are you still awake?"

I had been so deep in thought, remembering the nurses at the forefront today and thinking how much I admired them and that I wanted to do what they do. "Yes. I'm awake. I can't seem to quiet the thoughts in my head. It's been quite a day. You'll probably be asleep within minutes."

"I wish that were true," Joe said. "But that's not usually how it works."

I turned to face him. "What do you mean?"

"Never mind. Close your eyes. You need your sleep."

"Are you saying you can't fall asleep?"

"I'm saying that I don't want to fall asleep. There's a difference."

I came up on my elbow so I could see his face. "Is it because of the night terrors? Is that it?" He sighed and kissed my forehead. I wanted him to open up and talk to me. "More bad dreams?"

Joe stared up at the ceiling. "Last night I dreamt I was back there, inside the dark brown tent. I couldn't find my scalpel. I looked everywhere for it, but it was too dark, and I couldn't see anything except the white sheets. Men were crying out and I was crashing into the metal tables, frantically looking for my scalpel."

I lowered his eyelids, kissing them softly. *My poor, poor husband.* Many nights he would talk in his sleep, waking me. Most times, he didn't realize it, and I didn't have the heart to tell him. I learned not to wake him abruptly, giving him time to navigate through the confusion. One time, he bolted upright in bed, his eyes wide open, sweating and breathing rapidly. It scared me. I tried to console him, but he was unresponsive, looking anxious and on high alert, and I realized he was back there, across the world in those brown hospital tents. I spoke softly to him, easing him back down. The next morning, he didn't remember it at all. I knew then that my loved one's suffering in his sleep was my new reality and that I needed to do whatever I could to help him through it.

"Honey," I said, hugging him and giving him butterfly kisses on his face and neck. "I have this go-to scene that helps me when I want to escape a dark place. It's on a mountaintop overlooking fields of flowers and streams. You need to create your own escape scene." I kissed the bridge of his nose and smiled. "Or, you can borrow mine."

"I like that you're here with me. I'm glad you came," Joe said.

"Me, too."

Joe rolled himself over onto his side and leaned in to kiss me, his hand moving down the contour of my figure. He watched me closely, his fingers masterfully caressing all the right spots on my body. Then he whispered in my ear. "Let's escape together."

**

Back at home, Joe and I were on our back deck one beautiful, crisp Sunday morning drinking coffee. Besides being my favorite day of the week because Joe usually didn't have to work, it was my favorite time of the day. We'd made love in the early dawn, falling back to sleep again in each other's arms for another two hours before rising. I would stay in my lounge dress for most of the day and Joe would whip us up some pancakes, his one tried-and-true recipe which included nutmeg and vanilla and some kind of fruit.

Two deer had emerged from the woods behind our house and were lolling in our yard. I stood up slowly from my chair and moved closer to the railing to watch them. I stayed like that for quite a while, immersed in what I called my Zen satori. Joe came up behind me and wrapped his arms around my waist.

"Penny for your thoughts," he said.

"Which ones?" I asked. "The forever-in-the-background ones or the newer ones that keep pushing forward?"

"Hmmm. Sounds like there's a lot going on inside that head of yours," he said.

"I was thinking how much I love you, how happy you make me." I leaned my head back against his chest.

Joe kissed the top of my shoulder, tightening his squeeze. "Let me guess, that was your forever-in-the-background thought. What about those pushier thoughts you mentioned? You're up to something. I can see it in your eyes."

"Since you know me so well, then you should be able to read my mind," I teased. "What am I thinking?"

Joe spun me around so that he could face me.

"You're thinking...we haven't really had a honeymoon yet. Where should we go?"

I laughed.

"Am I at least warm?"

"No. But it's a nice idea."

Joe stared at me, squinting. "Are you going to keep me guessing?"

"So," I said taking on a more serious tone. "What would you say if I told you that I'm thinking about resigning from my job at the department store?"

"Really? Fine. Whatever you—"

"My heart is calling me in a different direction. I like how it makes me feel when I'm helping others, but I know I can do more."

"Do more? How?"

"I want to become a nurse."

Joe took two long blinks before speaking. "I didn't see that coming."

"I know you didn't. I can't seem to shake the feeling. My bus accident deterred my dream of going for nurse's training. I was planning to apply before it happened. I think I could be a good nurse."

"Yes, but the nurses I know - all of them in fact - were single when they went through training. They couldn't be married to study nursing. That would be your biggest hurdle."

"I know, but there must be some way. I've already been reading some of your medical textbooks. It's fascinating. You could help me, couldn't you?"

Joe ran his fingers through his hair. "I could look into it, but—"

"I didn't know I would still feel this way."

"Still . . ."

"I can't explain it, but from the time I got to know Nurse Agnes, and then watching the disaster relief nurses in action, it makes me want to be more like them. I know I have it in me to do what they do. I just keep feeling the pull." I bit my lip and briefly closed my eyes. "When you found your calling to become a doctor, was it obvious to you at the time? Did you ever question it?"

"I can't expound on 'the calling'. All I can say is that I only had one plan. To become a doctor. For me, there was no Plan B." Joe took my hand in his and kissed my fingers. "What I would say to you is that you should just keep on reading and learning and see where it goes. I guess . . . I mean . . . if you still think this is what you want, we'll figure a way."

"I don't mean to be difficult," I said. Joe kissed the inside of my wrist. "You could have had your pick of wives. Your mom wanted you to marry her girlfriend's daughter." Joe kissed the inside of my elbow. "But instead, you got stuck with me." He kissed the inside of my neck. "I'm sorry if I'm not a 'bonbon' wife." Joe burst out laughing. "Now I've gone and done it. I finally pushed you over the edge."

In between surges of laughter, Joe returned to planting kisses, this time all over my face. "This is way more fun," he said, pulling me into him.

"Joe, I'm being serious." I frowned.

"And that's why I love you so much. I never liked easy or predictable. You should know that."

"I only know that I love you," I said. "You are the kindest, most understanding—" Joe kissed me on the lips. "Husband," I said when he unsealed my lips.

"Now, about that honeymoon..."

Joe kissed my lips gently again, and as he started to pull away, I reached up and held his face firmly between my hands, not letting him go. I gazed into his warm, expressive eyes. "This is our honeymoon," I said and then kissed him, hard.

My feet left the ground, Joe lifting me up, our mouths still kissing, slow and long, until we found ourselves inside our house, my lounge dress being lifted over my head, our bodies tumbling to the kitchen floor. We never made it to our bedroom.

CHAPTER 28

Amanda

The days are whisking past and if I were paying attention, I would have noticed summer winding down. Labor Day weekend is coming up and Jesse's making plans for us that include Emma. I find myself looking forward to it. It's an audition of sorts if Jesse and I want to take our relationship to the next level.

It's easy being the fun aunt who spoils her niece and nephew with gifts on their birthdays or holidays, and then gets to go home, leaving the disciplining to others. But I feel a certain level of anxiety in the prospect of a relationship with Emma. Nana's wise counsel that I need to just be myself and not try so hard is rational. She assures me that everything will fall naturally into place. "Children have an innate ability to sense genuineness when they see it," she says.

I'm taking Friday off to drive seven hours to the beach town of Kitty Hawk, joining Jesse, Emma, and his parents for the Labor Day weekend. Since Dorothy will be off on the weekend, my parents offered to stay with Nana, partaking in her quiet, indoor mountainous retreat . . . but only after I answered the deluge of rapid-fire questions from my mother. "Who is Jesse? How did you two meet? Is it getting serious? What does he do for a living? When am I going to meet him?"

I go over to Nana, who's seated at the kitchen table, and hold up two sundresses. "Which one?" I ask. "I can't decide."

"Might be easier if I could see them both on you," Nana says, and then laughs out loud.

"What?" I ask.

"I just had a memory trigger. Did I ever tell you the conundrum I faced when your mother was deciding what dress to wear for a school homecoming dance?"

"I don't think I've heard that one."

Nana's eyes grow distant with memories. "Both grandmothers got on the case. My mother, of course, went right to her sewing machine and created a pretty pink shift dress with a V-neck, I recall. Caroline loved it. That is, until my mother-in-law took her shopping at Saks where she saw a flashy party dress with flared sleeves that she fell in love with."

"So, of course, Mom wore the dress from Saks, right?"

"Yes and no. I insisted she wear both - one for the dance in the gymnasium, the other for the town parade that followed the next day. There are pictures of both, so each grandmother thought she only wore theirs." Nana shakes her head. "The things I did for peace."

"I barely remember my great-grandmothers. I was too young when they passed away."

"Your mother was the only granddaughter of each so they loved spoiling her."

"Well, that explains a lot." I snicker. "You must have had your hands full when mom was a teenager, when the domineering princess personality started to take hold."

"You and your mom had stalwart fathers, which helped. Your mother was a daddy's girl through and through. When your Grampa came home after a life-saving surgery and Caroline would storm him with her teenage gripes he used to say, 'Not now, Caroline.' He'd pour himself a glass of wine and retreat to his study. After a while, he'd tell her to come in and close the door behind her. I wasn't privy to those conversations. I only know that when Caroline came out of the sanctorum, she was a little bit wiser and a lot more reticent."

"So, Mom didn't have Grampa wrapped around her little finger then?"

Nana laughs. "Only when he allowed it." She studies the yellow floral print dress and points to it. "That one highlights your almond brown eyes and lovely tan. You should wear that one."

***

My bags are packed and parked by the front door. Walking over to the brewed pot of coffee I had set on a timer, I see that Nana has gotten herself up. Wearing a powder blue robe and leaning heavily on her cane for balance, she takes wobbly baby steps through the kitchen toward the sunroom as she makes her way over to her favorite chair. I watch her. Some days she doesn't need her cane, except for security, but today she relies heavily on it, and her breathing seems more labored than usual.

"Morning, Nana. Can I get you something? A glass of water or orange juice perhaps? I still have some time before I have to leave."

"No. Thank you, dear."

I take my coffee mug and join her in the sunroom. "Not even a bite to eat this morning?"

"I felt a bit queasy and didn't sleep well last night. I just need to sit down and relax a bit. I always rest better here in my chair."

"Did you get any sleep at all?"

Nana breathes heavily as she settles into her chair, which conforms cozily to her body after so many years' use. "A little," she says. "I couldn't seem to get comfortable."

I help lift up her feet, notice some swelling in her ankles, and place them on the ottoman in front of her chair. She's wearing the warm, quilted, beige slippers I gave her last Christmas, easily able to slip in and out of them from where she leaves them on the floor by her bedside.

I bring a padded accent chair closer so that I'm sitting directly across from her. "Do you feel nauseous?"

"Feeling's passed now," she says, closing her eyes briefly.

An alarm goes off inside my medically trained head that tells me something more may be going on with Nana. Everything is suspect in a ninety-year-old. I know Nana. It's not what she's telling me that worries me.

It's what she isn't telling me. She would rather suffer in silence than stop me from my beach getaway. I look over my mug while I sip coffee, studying her surreptitiously - her hair unkempt, skin pallid, shadowy eyes. "How does your head feel?" I wonder if she may have symptoms of lightheadedness or dizziness.

"My head is fine."

"Any feeling of indigestion?"

"Now, now, Nurse Amanda," Nana says, "before you start checking off your list of heart symptoms, let me make it easier for you. No, I'm not in any immediate danger, and yes, I took my pills this morning."

"Well, speaking from one nurse to another," I say, "You won't mind then if I take your blood pressure." I can be just as stubborn as her. I get up to retrieve the blood pressure monitor.

Nana calls after me. "Weren't you supposed to have left for the beach by now?"

I find the blood pressure kit in Nana's bathroom, her pill box organizer still left open on a tray.

Nana is fast asleep when I return to her. I'm not able to lift up her robe's sleeve enough to put the pressure cuff on without disturbing her so I decide to let her rest, and call my mother instead.

My mother picks up on the first ring. "Are you and Dad on your way over?" They're coming from Raleigh, a four-hour drive.

"We should be there in a couple more hours," Mom says, conferring with Dad, who's driving. GPS indicates ETA is 11:30. Why?"

"Just wondering," I say. "I'm a little worried about Nana. She's sleeping in her chair now, but she doesn't look well. I wanted to take her blood pressure, but I didn't want to disturb her. She didn't sleep well last night."

"Do you mean to tell me you're still home? When did you plan on starting out for the Outer Banks?"

"I had hoped to leave an hour ago," I say, "but Nana looked so weak this morning, and she won't eat anything."

"Did she take her pills?"

"She says she did."

"Let her sleep then. I'll call you when we're there and give you an update."

"I'm leaving the blood pressure monitor on the table next to her in the sunroom. When she wakes up, I want to get a reading."

"All right. We'll check it out. You go. We'll be there as soon as we can. Dad noticed some water damage where the deck is attached to the house when we were there last for Nana's party. He wants to look it over more carefully. Says decay may be starting."

"Yes, well, I could give you a whole list of things in this house that need looking at," I say. "But I don't have time to get into it right now. Better be on my way. I'll be in touch."

"Drive carefully."

***

The sun is beginning its descent over the sound when I pull my car into the spot saved for me at Jesse's parents' split-level vacation home. Jesse comes over and wraps me up in a big hug. "So glad you could make it," he says. "Run into too much traffic?"

"A little on 64," I say. "I had to stop once for gas."

"I wish you had let me pick you up," Jesse says.

"It didn't make sense for you to have to do that. It would have added an extra two hours to the trip."

"Well, you're here," Jesse says. "That's all that matters." He kisses my lips. "I missed you."

"I missed you, too."

"Did you eat anything on your way over?"

"Some pretzels and a peach."

"Come on then," Jesse says. "Dinner's waiting inside. Let me show you to your bedroom where you can wash up first."

Jesse grabs my luggage from the trunk and leads the way, past an outdoor shower stall and picnic table. I follow him inside, where his mother is tossing a large salad at the kitchen counter. She's a tall, stately woman - taller than me by at least two inches even in her flats. She wears her gray-blend hair in a short bob, a silver streak framing her face. She lets go of the wooden salad fork and spoon and steps around the island. "So nice to meet you," she says, smiling cordially, her eyes crinkling at the sides. "I'm Cheryl."

"Thank you so much for having me," I say. "It's such a pretty spot, encircled by both the ocean and the sound." I can tell that Cheryl smiles with her eyes a lot.

"Yes, we love it here. You'll have to tell us all about Asheville. I haven't been over that way in quite some time, not since I visited the Biltmore estate years ago."

"There'll be plenty of time for you ladies to chat," Jesse says, putting a guiding hand on my back and wheeling my luggage behind him. "I'm gonna take Amanda up to her room so she can get settled in."

Jesse moves me quickly through the house and into the living room where his dad and Emma are, his dad sitting on a recliner, a book turned down on the chair arm, reading glasses lowered on his nose so that he can view the television over them. Emma is kneeling near the coffee table in Disney *Frozen* pajamas, drawing paper and crayons spread out. "Dad...Emma, this is Amanda," Jesse says.

Jesse's dad stands up, removes his glasses, and extends me his hand. "Welcome, I'm Bob," he says.

Emma swipes a paper from the table and bounds from the floor. She dashes over to us and hands me her colored drawing, then clings shyly to Jesse's leg. "Why, thank you," I say, making out two stick figures, one taller than the other, a house proportionately too small, and an overpowering sun with a smiley face, its yellow rays squiggling in all directions. "Did you make this yourself?"

Emma nods. I lean down so that I am almost level with her. "Is this one you?" I venture, pointing to the small stick figure in the drawing. She nods again, still clutching Jesse's leg and smiles coyly, her blonde hair tied up in an adorable messy double bun. "And this one?" I ask, pointing to the tall figure.

"Daddy," she says.

"Of course. I can see that."

"I'm going to take Amanda upstairs now," Jesse tells Emma. "She'll be back down for dinner."

Emma returns to her drawing table while Jesse and I start up the stairs. "This one's yours," he says when we reach the top landing. He pushes open the door to my room and rolls my luggage inside it - a blue coastal quilt on a king sized bed, white nightstand and six-drawer dresser, a wide rustic pallet shelf on the wall decked with charming coastal décor.

"How lovely!" I say, sitting on the edge of the bed and kicking off my slip-ons.

Jesse lays my luggage down on a low table and comes over to sit next to me. He covers my lips with his, pressing tenderly. "I'm going to leave you now," he says, unconvincingly. "Come downstairs for dinner when you're ready."

***

After dinner, I help clear the table. The buttered noodles in front of Emma are only half eaten; her head slumped over in sleepiness. Jesse lifts her out of her booster seat, Emma's head snuggles in the crook of his neck as he carries her up the staircase to bed. "This is late for her," Cheryl explains. "It's way past her bedtime."

"I'm sorry if I held up dinner," I say, collecting dinner plates from the table and bringing them over to the sink. "I had some pressing things to take care of at home."

"Oh, it was no problem at all, and Emma ate at five. She was too excited to meet you to be put to bed at her usual time."

"She's a sweetheart. I look forward to spending more time with her tomorrow."

Jesse returns. "She's fast asleep already," he says, and then turns to me. "How about going for a walk?"

"Just as soon as I finish up here."

"You go right ahead." Cheryl urges. "I've got this."

I sense she wants nothing more than to see her son happy. It must be hard to watch your child suffer.

The night is warm and inviting, and I admit I long to be alone with Jesse. He looks me over, eyeing the calf-length boho summer dress I'd changed into for dinner. "You might need to bring along a light jacket or sweater," he says. "It gets pretty windy."

Jesse and I walk the quarter mile to the beach holding hands, our matching desires in the silence powerful and palpable. When we get to the end of the boardwalk to the beach, we kick off our sandals where we leave them so our feet can touch the sand. The waves and wind have picked up velocity. Locking our hands together again, we sprint to the water's edge, the waves crashing against our ankles.

I turn my face toward the night sky with its sprinkling of faint stars and a smoky half-moon. Jesse wraps his arms around me and draws me close, his eyes gleaming in the faint moonlight. He leans down to kiss me, pulling slowly from my mouth, his lips roving down my chin, the length of my neck, the little hollow of my throat, my head falling further back. A rolling wave coupled with Jesse's erotic kisses knocks me off balance. I totter backward and Jesse catches me, lifting me up into his arms.

Still holding me, he moves us deeper into the ocean. He plants another kiss on my mouth and takes another further step in. I pull from his lips, turning my head to the side; Jesse is almost knee deep in the ocean, my flowing dress sweeping the water.

I gasp and let out a squeal. "Oh no. Don't drop me!" Jesse throws his head back and laughs. "Jesse," I say, clutching onto his neck with both hands, "don't you dare!"

"I won't drop you," he says, laughing. "You can trust me. But first you have to say the words I want to hear."

"What words?" His eyes sparkle with mischief.

He releases his hold on me, then quickly catches me, lifting me up higher as the waves rush under me by only a foot. I let out a scream. "I'm waiting," he teases.

"I'm going to get you for this," I say between gritted teeth.

Jesse shakes his head. "Nope. Those aren't the words."

"Umm...don't drop me...*please*? Those words?"

Jesse laughs. "Better."

"You're awesome...and amazing," I rattle on, going in a flattering direction. The peak of a wave rocks us, Jesse steadying his feet in the sandy bottom.

"Getting warmer," he says, laughing some more, his husky voice stirring me.

I feel the words *I love you* rise up and threaten to burst out of me, but I fight the urge, forcing them back in. Jesse flips me up higher and I scream out, "I trust you!" He catches me and carries me onto shore. When my toes hit the sand at the shoreline, I turn to gaze at him. "So I got it right then?"

"*Do* you trust me?" he asks, meeting my gaze.

I realize that I do. "Yes, I trust you."

"Then those words were absolutely perfect," he says.

Walking barefoot along the surf, the ocean's bioluminescence extending far and wide, we fall into an easy rhythm, holding hands and swinging arms, the spontaneity of the day as exhilarating as I have ever known. My damp dress wraps around my legs, my hair blowing wildly in the wind. I'm floating - carefree and happy. We don't say anything, the repetitive whooshing sound of the ocean waves transfixing us. Anyone watching us would think we were lovers in a picture perfect scene, but neither of us has spoken of love. Those three tiny words simply hover, waiting for the right moment, a moment as imaginable as it is bewildering.

***

Late at night, Jesse and I tiptoe up the staircase of the house. Bypassing my bedroom, Jesse leads me to the rooftop deck that faces the faintly glowing ocean. It's furnished with four Adirondack chairs and a princess play tent for Emma in the corner.

"I have something for you," I say to Jesse, thinking this may be a good time to give it to him. But then, when is it ever a good time to pass on a letter from the girl who received your wife's heart? I go back to my room and pull a sealed white envelope from my purse.

"Can I get you something to drink?" Jesse asks when I return to the deck. "Wine perhaps?"

"No thanks." I hand the envelope to Jesse. It bears no name or any indication as to who it's from. Jesse gives me a perplexed look.

"Let's sit first," I say. We slump into the chairs as I try to figure out how to start what I'm about to say. "The heart transplant recipient . . . you know who she is. During her last doctor's office visit, she left this letter that she wished to be passed on to her heart donor.

Jesse looks down at the white envelope and falls silent, the only sound coming from the rolling rush of ocean waves in the distance.

"I haven't read it, nor do I have any idea what it says. I'm just passing it on." I really hope it doesn't upset Jesse too much.

Jesse takes in a long, deep breath.

I give him an encouraging smile. "I can tell you, Jesse, only that she's doing well. We have reason to be optimistic."

He slides the envelope into his shorts pocket. "I'll read it later, after I've poured myself a drink."

I extend my arm so it reaches him in his chair and clasp his hand in mine. Moonlight shimmers over the black ocean and for the next several minutes, we sit in the peaceful hush of night, staring out into the ocean wordlessly, alone with our own thoughts. A gentle breeze tingles me and I can still smell the salt on us. After a while, Jesse turns his gaze toward me, ready to talk but steering away from the envelope's content.

"Any word on Nana?" he asks.

"Blood pressure is a little higher than usual, but my mother says she's been sleeping peacefully. She's being treated for hypertension, and I always worry she could suffer a heart attack. Silent heart attacks typically go unnoticed."

"Wouldn't she be able to recognize the symptoms herself being that she was a nurse and all?"

"It's not the knowing that concerns me," I say. "It's the telling that worries me. Nana is not always forthright when it comes to her health. She has taken on a resigned attitude."

"Ninety is a good run," Jesse says.

"I don't know what I'll do when she's gone." I tear up. "She's been my anchor all my life, keeping me grounded, helping me love myself more and shaping me into the woman I am."

"For which I am humbly grateful," Jesse says, kissing my hand. "And how have you been doing?"

I'd like to deflect, but I know Jesse won't allow it. "Me?"

"Yes...you. Any more panic attacks?" He locks his fingers with mine.

"Safety still remains an illusion, especially when I'm in crowded places and feel like I can hardly breathe. Therapy is coming along, but I'm still a work in progress."

"Aren't we all," Jesse says, more an assertion than a question. He puts his hand on my knee. "Give it time. And don't be so hard on yourself."

"I'm trying."

"I've been thinking. I want to show you some black belt defense techniques . . . when you're ready, of course."

I shudder. "Self-defense moves? I hope I never—"

"Hopefully you won't ever need to use them, but it won't hurt to know how."

I tighten my arms around me and lean back, my eyelids heavy all of a sudden.

"Come on," Jesse says, putting his hand under my arm and helping me up, "let me help you to your room."

Jesse pushes open the door and flicks on a switch; a low light comes from the nightstand lamp.

"I'm going to get out of this dress."

"I'll leave," Jesse says, moving toward the door.

I place my hand on his arm. "Don't go."

I pull a long nightshirt from my luggage and lay it across the bed. I turn around and lift my dress up over my head, braless and trembling, and do a quick change. Jesse walks over and draws down the covers for me and I collapse onto the mattress. His eyes gaze into mine, wanting, but he kisses me on the forehead instead and whispers, "Good night."

I reach for his arm. "Stay with me. Just until I fall asleep."

Jesse moves unhurriedly, lifting his shirt up over his head and tossing it aside. The broad contour of his bare chest in the soft light catches my breath. I breathe out slowly. He covers me with the quilt and then lies down on top of it next to me. Leaning on his elbow, he glides his other hand along my arm, the feel of his touch on my skin giving me shivers. He rolls me gently onto my side, his fingers kneading my neck and shoulders with gentle rubs. A soft sigh escapes my lips.

"Close your eyes now. I'm here with you."

CHAPTER 29

Elizabeth
October 1954

We had planned to have dinner with my parents on Sunday, my mother enticing us with her notable baked lasagna meal, which had quickly become one of Joe's favorite dishes. Joe and I lived only twenty minutes from my parents, but a cold front had moved in as we listened to reports about a strong hurricane moving up the coast from the Carolina's.

"Mom," I said into the kitchen phone. "I don't think we're going to make it today, but Joe says we'll take a raincheck."

"I understand. The weather's not looking too good," Mom said. "How come you sound so tired?"

"Do I? I don't know. I woke up feeling a bit poorly. If you do make lasagna, can you save us some?" Normally, my mouth would water at the mention of it, but talking about food was making me queasy.

"Of course. What will you do then for dinner tonight?" Mom was always curious to know if we were eating well.

I winced ahead of telling her. "Leftover tuna casserole." I heard her gasp on the other end of the line. A tuna casserole was blasphemy to an Italian mother. "It's a Betty Crocker favorite," I tried.

"Since you're no longer working, I would think you could come up with something better than tuna casserole. Have I taught you nothing?" Her voice was lighthearted and serious at the same time.

"I'll make him a chicken scallop dinner tomorrow to make up for it. It's the least I can do after I shocked him with my aspiration to become a nurse." Oh God. The inside-my-head voice didn't just say that out loud, did it?

"What? Elizabeth, you can't be serious." I could see her throwing her hands up in the air. "Why on earth would you want to be a nurse? It's hard work. Besides, you don't really need to work. You're married to a doctor for Pete's sake."

"Well, apparently you and all the nursing schools are in agreement. They don't take married women, so there's that."

"Well, good. That's the most sensible thing I've heard yet. Elizabeth, just be happy."

I frowned. "I *am* happy. I'm very happy." *Why would the fact that I'd like to be a nurse mean that I wasn't happy? Mothers!*

"Well, you oughta be." It was no use. She'd never understand. I wasn't even sure I did.

What I didn't tell my mother before we hung up was that while I had officially resigned from working, I now spent my increased spare time reading Joe's medical textbooks. Conversations between Joe and me where I raised medical questions had become commonplace as I wanted to learn everything I could. *Can a seizure cause a person to have dangerous gaps in breathing? Is there a time window for CPR?* Joe would consider me as he looked up from his newspaper or from across our kitchen table, willing to engage.

I walked into the living room where Joe was listening intently to weather updates on the radio. After killing hundreds of people in Haiti and then striking the border of North and South Carolina, Hurricane Hazel had gained strength over the Gulf Stream and was headed for New Jersey, bringing strong wind gusts.

"We need to get out the candles," Joe remarked. "We could lose power."

An unwell feeling came over me again, my head and stomach vying for which felt sicker. Joe went to find candles while I retreated to the bathroom, feeling nauseous and having no appetite. That's when the power got knocked out.

"Beth?" Joe called out.

"I'm in here," I called from the bathroom.

The wave of nausea passed as quickly as it came on, but I still felt a general malaise. I nearly gagged at the thought of another day of tuna casserole.

Joe stood in the hall holding a candle so I could see my way through the darkened house.

"I'm going to lie down," I said. "Steer me to the couch." I could hear the intense wind howling, whipping branches and stripping leaves, followed by the sudden onset of wind-driven rain pelting the grounds outside.

Joe set the candle down and covered me with one of my mother's knitted throws. "What other symptoms do you have?"

In the dark room I closed my heavy eyelids. "Tired mostly," I mumbled.

"The National Guard is mobilizing in the Carolinas," Joe said, sitting on the edge of the couch, news of the pending hurricane still emitting from our kitchen radio. "President Eisenhower is declaring it a major disaster."

"The Red Cross must be on high alert," I said.

Joe gave a low sigh. "Probably already deploying."

"Are you thinking what I'm thinking?" The disaster storm of two months ago was still fresh in my mind.

I don't know if he ever answered me because I dozed off and slept half the day away.

***

Hazel had brought massive destruction to parts of the Carolinas. New Jersey experienced power outages and flooding. Once the coast was clear, Joe was prepared to head down to the Carolinas to work with the Red Cross again.

"I don't think you should come this time." Joe advised. "You aren't feeling well."

"I'm fine now." I reassured him. Joe felt my head and seemed satisfied that it didn't feel warm. "I could be very useful." He looked at me sensibly; saw the pleading in my eyes. "So, it's a go?"

He acquiesced, under one condition. If I felt too weak or tired, I was to rest at the downtown hotel he had booked for us. I agreed, even though I knew it would take a lot for me to stay away.

***

We arrived in the Carolinas a few days after the storm had made impact there, devastating scenes in the hardest-hit areas unfolding in shocking ways – splintered wood, roof shingles and debris everywhere, sinks and toilets ripped out, glass from blown out windows, sturdy black oaks bent or toppled over, houses gutted, many non-existent. Some houses no longer had their second floors, the first floors open and filled with sand. Gone were the boardwalk and the hotels nearest the water. We swung past the hospital where boats were stacked up in front as if by design.

"I have no words," I said.

"I do," Joe said. "It looks like a war zone."

Joe drove me to the Moose Lodge in Wilmington where the Red Cross had set up a support shelter. No shortage of areas needed assistance - people who'd lost everything, children in need of care, others still trying to find loved ones. I put myself right to work, aiding in anything my talents could be used for.

The disaster relief nurses were there checking for wound infections, internal bleeding, or any signs of illness from the contaminated waters, as well as providing emotional support. Joe went over to the hospital to assist with the more critically injured.

In between doling out food and clean water and directing people to safe sleeping places the Red Cross had set up, I felt bouts of queasiness and a general unwell feeling come on me again, but I pushed it away. Folks were disoriented and in utter distress, some walking around aimlessly with no plan of how to move forward yet. It was heart wrenching, my discomforts slight in comparison.

Before I knew it, the arduous day turned into night. A very young girl was crying for her doll. Her family had evacuated safely, but somehow her doll got separated from her in the disorienting and frenzied days. Her mother was exhausted and incapable of pacifying her child.

"Let me try," I offered. The mother nodded wearily, grateful for any assistance. I crouched down to her level and asked, "What's your doll's name?"

"Sal-ly," she said through cry heaves.

"Did you say Sally?" I put my hand to my mouth in feigned surprise. "Did you know that there are other dolls and toys that have gone missing too? I heard they are in a safe place being looked after by a doll named Sally." The little girl stopped crying and looked at me interestedly. "That's right," I said. "Sally has a very important job to do. She's taking care of all the other lost dolls. And do you know what Sally would want you to do? She would want you to be brave just like her and help take care of your mommy and daddy." The young girl's cries subsided, and putting her thumb in her mouth, she snuggled up to her mother on a cot, unable to fight off her much-needed sleep any longer.

"Thank you," the mother said as I pushed up off the floor.

I must have stood up too fast because dizziness swooped in like a tidal wave and I sought some place to sit down. When was the last time I had something to eat? I was trying to make it over to an open cot when my vision grayed out, right before I passed out.

When I came to, my feet were elevated on a pillow and a nurse was taking my blood pressure. "How are you feeling?" she asked.

I started to lift my head.

"You mustn't get up yet," she stressed.

I was lying on a cot - the one I never made it to.

"Your husband is on his way over," the nurse reassured. "He's not far. You fainted on us."

"I'll be fine," I said. "I don't want to trouble anyone."

She rambled off a succession of questions at me. When's the last time I ate or drank anything? Had I been feeling ill or had any other symptoms? Had I ever fainted before?

"Beth," Joe said, coming up behind her. "Honey, what happened?"

The nurse answered for me. "She passed out cold. Pressure was 80 over 50. It's come up a little since."

Joe wanted to see for himself, checking my pulse and heart rate. Someone brought over a cool cloth and placed it over my forehead. "Could we have some water brought over please?" he asked.

"I feel fine," I said to anyone who was listening. "Can I sit up now?"

"Nice and slow," Joe said, helping me.

I took the glass of water and sipped it.

The nurse took Joe aside, conferring a distance away from me so that I couldn't hear them. "I'll take it from here," Joe said, returning to me. "Do you have any of those salt crackers with you?" he asked.

"Yes, in my purse."

"Good. Come on, let's get something to eat and head over to the hotel."

After a diet of crackers and fruit bars, I felt both revitalized and foolish.

"Well, your color's coming back," Joe said. He was sitting across from me on a chair in our hotel room.

"I'm sorry. I may have been feeling a little squeamish still, but it comes and goes. You're not mad?"

"No. Not mad." He had a mysterious look on his face, like someone challenged to secrecy.

"What were you and the nurse talking about?" I asked. "I know you were talking about me." It made me anxious.

"We exchanged some notes. I don't want us to get ahead of ourselves, but, it's quite possible you could be pregnant. Have you missed your period?"

"I might be a little late." Could it be? "It's not always regular."

"It may still be too early, but when we get home, we'll make an appointment."

"Oh, Joe, I'm so happy. I don't even care if I don't feel well."

Joe came over to sit alongside me on the bed and kissed me on the temple. "We have to wait and see. In the meantime, you need to get plenty of rest. My orders." Joe was making every effort to contain himself, keeping his voice calm and unemotional, but his glistening brown eyes gave him away.

I tucked my face inside the crook of his neck and felt tears forming in my own eyes, a million thoughts going through my mind. Everything I wanted for myself came down now to one aspiration. I might be having a baby.

We hugged each other, crying and laughing.

CHAPTER 30

Amanda

I open my eyes, disoriented in the first waking moments. A small face lit with blue-gray eyes is standing at my bedside watching me. I lift myself up onto my elbows.

"Emma. Good morning," I say.

She shows me the doll she's holding, a baby doll with blonde locks like hers. Emma's face is so close to mine I can see a sprinkling of faint freckles on her petite nose. The area below her lips and chin resembles Jesse's. I sit fully up, swinging my legs over the side and give her a gentle hug. Emma holds out her doll for me to hug too, which I do. I reach for my phone; the time says 7:15.

"Is your daddy up?" I ask.

Emma shakes her head.

"I see." Fully awake now and feeling energized after an untroubled sleep, I head over to the bathroom to quickly wash up, and throw on a pair of pajama shorts to go under my nightshirt. Emma waits for me. The smell of bacon wafts up the stairs. In the hallway, Emma's bedroom door is ajar.

She takes my hand and brings me into her room. At first, I don't see him and then Emma points upward to the top of a twin-sized bunk bed where Jesse is sleeping, his long, muscular limbs hanging over parts of the rail guards. I whisper, "Is that where Daddy slept?" I realize that he did and it makes me feel bad. I would have been fine sleeping in the top bunk.

"Let's not wake him," I say, carefully stepping over scattered toys on the floor to get to the door. A framed picture on a white dresser catches my eye. I lean down to look at it. It's a photo of Emma as a toddler being held by her mother, a pictorial vestige of a woman she won't even remember. I feel a rush of empathy for Emma, and it cloaks me in sadness. Also lying on the dresser is the opened letter from the heart recipient to Jesse, the words beckoning me to read them.

To my donor,
I don't know you, and yet in some way I feel I do . . .
You are the man who lost his wife in a tragic accident.
You are the man who consented to donating her heart.
You are the man who helped another person live.

My 10½" scar reminds me what organ donation means. I'm so grateful for the chance to live my life when it could have ended.

In all the time since I got my new heart, I'm making memories. I celebrated two birthdays, I'm applying to college next year, and I've met someone I really like. I might even love him. I didn't know that was something I could ever have. I didn't know it would be worth all I went through to live. Love truly is worth fighting for.

I hope in some small way this helps you cope and brings you peace.

I know you. You are the person who I pray for every day.

Thank you for giving me the gift of a second chance life.

Lisa

Emma tugs at my arm. The other is placed over my heart. I blink back tears and glance up to see Jesse still asleep.

"Come on," I say to Emma, rebounding. "I have something for you."

I retrieve from my luggage the small gift I'd bought and walk with her out onto the deck, into a tranquil morning already brightly lit by the sun. Together we climb into her play tent where Emma opens the pink unicorn purse I got her and takes out the play makeup inside and I help her get ready for a princess party.

An hour or so later, Jesse finds us on the deck, still playing inside her tent. He sets a tray containing two mugs of coffee, a cup of juice, and a bowl of berries onto the table. "Princess Emma and Princess Amanda need to come out and have their breakfast," he says. Emma pokes her head outside the tent. Jesse lifts her up with one arm, taking my hand and pulling me up with his other. He gives Emma a kiss and puts her down, handing her sippy cup to her.

"Good morning," he says to me, smiling. He hands me a mug filled with hot coffee. "Light with one Splenda," he says. "I remembered. Looks like you've been up a while. How did you sleep?"

"Really well, thank you," I say with a meaningful smile. "But I wish I could say the same for you. You didn't tell me I had taken your bedroom and you were sleeping in a twin bunk bed."

Jesse gives me a wave of his hand. "It's fine. Besides, I fell asleep next to you for most of the night. I only went into the bunk bed very early in the morning."

We sink into the chairs, sipping our coffees, Jesse filling me and Emma in on his plans for the day.

After a breakfast of bacon and eggs that Jesse's dad cooked, Jesse and I get into our bathing suits, the weather outside looking favorable for a beach day. Emma sits in a little rocker in her room as Jesse kneels and applies sunscreen to her exposed skin. It's touching, watching him care for his daughter, sharing a moment of tenderness and love. He plants a kiss on the tip of her nose.

"Okay," he says, "stand up now and turn around so I can do your back." Jesse snatches up some of Emma's beach toys, a pair of her sunglasses, and a sun hat, throwing them into a beach bag.

"Can I help with anything?" I ask, following him down the hall.

"I think I've got it all," he says. "The towels are downstairs."

Wearing a sheer white cover over my white bikini, my beach bag on one arm and holding Emma's small hand in the other, I make my way down the stairs. Jesse's at the bottom landing, watching us, a stack of towels under his arm, his smile emanating appreciation and gratitude. Emma runs ahead of us as Jesse scoops me into an impulsive kiss.

***

Emma is already digging and playing in the sand near where Jesse and I laid our towels. I kick off my flip-flops and sink my bare feet in the sand. Fine grain is interspersed with tiny bits of coarseness. I look around at a pristine beach with blue-green water. Brown pelicans soar overhead then duck under the lapping waves. A sailboat rides the ocean breeze, going nowhere in particular.

I lift my chiffon swimsuit cover over my head, the warmth of the sun already baking my skin. It won't be long before I'll have to go in the water to cool off. I sense Jesse watching me behind his dark lenses, the corners of his lips upturned in a smile. I lower myself onto the towel while Jesse grabs a juice box for Emma from the small cooler he brought along. He leans over and passes it to her, his hair, lightened to a summer blonde, making a flattering contrast to his tanned skin. With Emma's head bent near her father's, the likeness of their hair color is striking and for a fleeting moment I wonder what a child of ours would look like with my darker hair. I've been having thoughts like this, my desire to have a child deepening and growing stronger. Seeing Jesse with his daughter evokes all kinds of feelings in me – kindling and stimulating urges I thought I had repressed. It isn't that I never wanted to have a child. I like kids. I didn't want to have a child with the person I was with. Between graduate school and my past ambivalent relationship, the years continued to pile on. *I'm turning into Vinny's girlfriend. Only it's me now, my foot that's stomping, my biological clock that's ticking.*

I pull a bottle of sunscreen from my beach bag, and spread it liberally on my legs, arms, and chest. It's the end of summer and I have a fairly good tan base, but I easily burn if I'm not careful. Jesse watches me, mesmerized.

"You know you're turning me on," he says. He takes the bottle from me, applying lotion on places I can't reach when my phone dings. He is rubbing my shoulders, my back, his hands doing more than smoothing on ointment, putting me in a trance. My phone dings again and reluctantly I reach into my beach bag for it where I keep it protected. Cupping my hand over it to block out the sun, I read the text and cringe. *Oh no.*

"Is it about Nana?" Jesse asks, his fingers massaging the nape of my neck.

"What? Oh, umm, this isn't about her. It's something else," I say.

Jesse picks up on my uneasiness and stops what he's doing. "Everything all right?"

"Yes," I say, rotating so he can see my face. "It's just a message from Eddie." *Who always did have the worst timing.*

"Eddie?" Jesse lowers his sunglasses so he can look at me over them, his brows drawn together. "From the Nashville convention? That Eddie?"

"The same one," I grunt.

Jesse's eyes search mine before he puts his sunglasses back over his eyes. He lowers himself down on the blanket, clasping his hands behind his head, an illusion of casualness, except for the smile that's hardened on his face. "I'd almost forgotten about him." Jesse expels a breath. "So, he's been texting you, has he?"

I inhale sharply. "On occasion." I can't see Jesse's eyes under the dark shades, but his jaw tenses and tightens. "Friendship texts," I quickly add. "Just to keep in touch."

"Really?" Jesse says. "So, what did he say exactly in his text?"

I sigh. "He says he's going to be in Atlanta next week and wants to know if we can meet somewhere in between for a drink."

Jesse pushes his sunglasses up on top of his head and narrows his gaze at me. "And what will you say?"

The way he asks makes me frown. "I'll tell him I can't, of course. I don't know. I'll make up some excuse."

"So that's it," Jesse says. "You'll make up some excuse? Is that the best you can do?"

"Well, what would you have me say then?" I ask, recognizing derision in his voice. "Please tell me."

"How about no?" Jesse's voice sounds brash and puts me on edge. "No, I can't meet up with you because I'm seeing someone."

I'm feeling defensive. I shouldn't though.

"I don't have feelings for anyone but you. This is the first time he asked to meet me. He's never asked that before. It's just been a hello or how-was-your-day thing with him. Don't you trust me?"

"It's him and his texting I don't trust. You need to tell him about us. And then delete him from your contacts," he says, forcing it out.

Jesse's strong reaction alarms me. My eyes narrow. "Do you know how unreasonable you sound? I've only known you for two months. I have friends and acquaintances, people in my life who came before you and during you. I can't just delete everyone from my phone who's not you. I wouldn't ask you to." The words rush out, but they're out there now, rain gushing through the sunshine. I gaze out over the ocean, a pelican plunging into it head first. A chance look at Jesse again meets with a grimace of disapproval. I feel a strong surge of heat and reach for a water bottle, the mood instantly changed.

Jesse seems about to say something when Emma comes over and pulls on his hand. "Daddy, take me in the water." Jesse gives me a sidelong glance as he stands up, the warmth in his eyes cooled, replaced by distrust.

Taking a drink of water, I watch as Jesse strolls toward the ocean, holding onto Emma's hand, his tanned body towering over her fair, dainty one. I want to smile and cry all at once. Emma stops and turns around, running back to our blanket. "Manda, you come, too," she says, pulling my hand. It is the first time Emma has called me by my name. It touches me and I feel a sting of tears.

I look up and meet Jesse's eyes. I want to think I see understanding in them, reconciliation, but it's not there.

The three of us meander in the ocean's shore, Jesse and I holding Emma's hands, lifting her up over rolling waves, a respite from the escalating tension. We wade and cool ourselves in the water; we build things in the sand; we watch the amazing, huge pelicans winging over waves; we look for seashells and snack on chips, and cotton candy grapes. For a while, we can forget. Most of the exchanges between me and Jesse are connected to Emma, the buffer between us. *Emma, be careful you don't get sand in Amanda's hair. Would Daddy like some more grapes, too?* Jesse passes me a few grapes, and our fingers touch, our eyes meeting briefly. He is focused and gracious enough, but underneath it all I sense a temporary truce, the matter of Eddie's text messaging not yet over.

"Are we all ready for lunch? It's later than I thought," Jesse says.

After showering in the outside shower at Jesse's house and changing, we work together wordlessly, packing up a picnic lunch for ourselves – chicken salad sandwiches, grilled cheese for Emma, macaroni salad, watermelon bites, and sparkling strawberry lemonade. Jesse's parents are out grocery shopping for tonight's barbecue. I wrap up the sandwiches and pass them to Jesse to put in our cooler, my hand brushing against his, our eyes saying everything we can't, a much needed talk on hold for now.

We picnic at the Kitty Hawk Park, Emma taking only a few bites out of her sandwich before she runs toward the playground. Ribbons of sunlight come through branches of the tree that shades us; a smooth wind caresses my face and my hair. "This is really nice," I say.

"We've been having some great weather." Jesse is affable, but the reserve is still there. "I'm glad you could be here to enjoy it."

With my heart in my throat I ask, "Are you?" I give him an opening, wondering if his position has softened a little, hoping it has.

"Of course, I am." A generic response that gives nothing away. "And Emma really likes you."

Jesse's answer, while it pleases me to hear, leaves me deflated. *And what about you, Jesse? What about you?*

Emma needs help getting into a swing. Jesse has just taken another bite out of a second sandwich when he starts to get up from the bench.

"Stay and finish," I say. "I'll go over and help her." I lift Emma into the swing, pushing her while reciting the *Five Little Monkeys* nursery rhyme. Some older children are running and chasing each other in the background, others swinging high in bigger kids' swings. When Emma wants to get down, I lift her out of the seat and place her on the ground. An older boy's voice, deep and angry, startles me. "Give it to me!" he shouts, whizzing past and chasing another boy.

My body starts to shake and I begin to sweat, pressure building in my chest as I feel my heart pounding. Realizing I'm having another panic attack, I try talking myself out of it.

Emma! Where's Emma? I spin my head around and see her running toward the bigger swings where older kids swing fast and high, oblivious to her. I'm frozen. I open my mouth to yell for Jesse but I can't catch my breath. He's walking in another direction, toward the trash cans. *Breathe, Amanda. Just breathe.* My therapist said that when a panic attack happens sometimes you just have to let it run its course. My vision closes in and I feel dizzy. *Focus on something else. Focus on Emma.*

I refocus and breathe slowly, my feet moving, rushing to swoop up Emma right before a big kid's foot almost makes contact with her head.

Jesse's there in a flash. I'm on the ground with my eyes shut tight, clutching Emma to my chest. He squats down and wraps both arms around us. "It's okay. It's okay."

I breathe in and out, in and out, waiting for the lightheadedness to clear.

"Daddy, why is Manda crying?" Emma says. And then, "Manda has a boo-boo."

Jesse lifts up my arm. "Goddamn," he says. My elbow is scraped and bleeding.

I open my teary eyes and look into Emma's worried ones. "These are happy tears," I say, giving her a small squeeze.

"Come on, lean on me," Jesse says. "I've got you."

"I can walk," I say.

"You're hurt."

Emma runs ahead of us while Jesse wraps a protective arm around me. "I'm so sorry." It rushes out of him.

"You didn't do anything." I blow on my injured elbow.

Jesse sets me down on a nearby bench and places his hand on my shoulder. "I shouldn't have come down so hard on you earlier. It's just that I can't bear the thought of someone else showing an interest in you. I have faith in you and in how you'll handle this thing with Eddie...I do. It's not you. This is about me. It's my own issue, something I know I have to work on."

"I don't like fighting with you," I say, in a release of emotions. "I hate it. I get that you're passionate. The coolness though...that hurt the most. I was lonely in my last relationship. Detached. I don't ever want to feel that way again."

Jesse cups my face in his hands. "I'm so sorry," he says again, stroking my cheek. "You didn't deserve that." Jess sits down alongside me, does a quick scan, and spots Emma kneeling at the picnic table eating watermelon. "I didn't tell you everything." Jesse starts to say.

I look into his eyes, confused and questioning.

"My wife was having an affair. I didn't know it when she was alive. Maybe I had a few suspicions. I found out later - little things that added up – the secret outings and unexplained absences, her old boyfriend sitting in back of the church sobbing. It didn't occur to me that she never asked me to go along on her visits to her sister's house in Raleigh. I was too busy at the firm to even notice, but I later found out she often went back there to see a former boyfriend. I also learned she was with him before she headed home with Emma in the car on the day of the accident. Apparently, our one-night stand had occurred during one of their breakups, but she never got over him. Our getting married started on pretty weak foundation. I know we were destined for a split-up, but I was faithful to her while we were married. That kind of dishonesty...well, it did something to me."

"I'm so sorry," I say, looking into his eyes, the warmth and calm returning. "It explains a lot. I guess we're both bringing our past hurts with us. It's hard to let it go. I had gotten so used to disinterest that your strong reaction put me off a little."

"So . . . what I'm hearing then is that I need to go easier on you, show less passion." It's playful Jesse again.

I catch his implied meaning and laugh. "Don't you do any such thing."

"I couldn't even if I wanted to," Jesse says. "It's what you do to me."

The dappled sunlight on his face makes me want to kiss him. I give him a peck on his cheek.

He looks down at my elbow scrape. "Does it hurt?" he asks.

"Stings a little."

"Come on. Let me take care of that for you."

Jesse rounds up Emma and grabs the cooler.

"Emma," he says on our way to the car, "What does Daddy always tell you about running in front of other kids when they're swinging? You can get very hurt." Jesse puts the cooler in the trunk and comes back to my side of the car with a first aid kit. "Promise me you won't do that again," he says to Emma. Jesse crouches outside my door and cleans my wound, then applies ointment on it.

"I'm sorry," Emma says, watching Jesse bandage my elbow from the back seat.

"Good thing Amanda was there," he says, smiling at me with his eyes. "She saved you from getting really hurt."

"Manda saved me?" Emma says.

"Yes," Jesse says. "She saved you." Jesse looks me in the eyes. "You might say she's saving us both."

CHAPTER 31

Elizabeth
June 1955

With the exception of occasional morning sickness in the first couple of months, my pregnancy continued without incident. Along with being an attentive and loving husband, Joe was thrilled at the prospect of becoming a father. This new dimension to our marriage transcended all of its parts, deepening our love for one another.

We were sitting on a glider on our back deck one evening in early June trying to get in the last few minutes of daylight before nightfall when I experienced my first strong contraction. Joe's arm draped over my shoulder as we rocked rhythmically, my head leaning on his chest.

"Oh," I cried, putting a hand to my belly. I had a disturbing sleep the night before, feeling slight cramps and heaviness. "I think it's time. That was sharper than what I felt last night."

Joe placed his hand on my hard belly and felt the baby move, strong and vigorous. "He's an active one and right on schedule."

"He could be a she," I reminded him.

"Are you ready to become a mother?"

"Too late for that now," I said, before another tightening thumped me. I sat up straighter, putting my hand on my lower back, pain radiating from there. My suitcase was already packed. All Joe had to do was grab it. I'd been ready for this moment for a long time it seemed, longer than the nine months of gestation. From as far back as I could remember - perhaps when my little sister was born or maybe even earlier - I knew motherhood was an integral part of my blueprint and that I'd want to be an eager participant in the essence of creation.

Joe was looking at his watch. "Did you just feel another contraction?"

"Yes!" I cried through another stronger, longer one.

"They're coming quickly. Come on. Let's get you into the car." He helped me up. "Just remember, keep breathing."

My doctor, who was also Joe's colleague, met us in the delivery room. Even though fathers weren't allowed in delivery rooms, Joe was an exception.

I was in active labor as soon as we arrived. I felt the sensation of pushing; the pressure against my spine alarming me. "The baby's coming!"

"Her labor appears to be moving very rapidly," I heard the doctor say to Joe and an attending nurse.

"Breathe, honey, breathe," Joe said, leaning his face down where I could see him, and touching my cheek.

I bawled, I screamed, the urge to push overpowering, but unproductive. "I can't," I cried. "I can't do it."

"Squeeze my hand," Joe said. "Squeeze as hard as you can."

I squeezed and pushed with as much force as I could, my head bursting with concentration, achieving the same unsatisfactory result.

Joe stepped aside briskly and conversed with my doctor. I heard "change in baby's heartbeat," and "fetal distress."

"No!" I screeched. "Something's wrong. Joe!"

Joe came back to me quickly. "You're doing great, honey," he said, wiping my forehead with a cool, wet cloth. "The cord is wrapped around the baby's neck. We're going to perform a C-section."

My heart sank. "Oh no...no, no." From Joe's medical books, I knew cesareans were rare, performed only in emergency situations. Panic rose in me exponentially. I let out a guttural scream derived from a place of fear mixed with intense pain before a mask was placed over my mouth and nose.

Joe gave my doctor the go-ahead. "You're going to go to sleep now, Beth. I love you."

I shook my head. Tried to speak. "Noooo," I moaned inside my head before I fell into oblivion.

***

A soft breeze blew my way. A hint of new-baby smell. The sound of soft crying and fussing. My eyelids fluttered open.

"Honey. We're over here."

I followed his voice, my vision still fuzzy, but I could make Joe out, pensive and tranquil. He was seated in a chair close to my hospital bed, holding our swaddled infant in his arms.

"Say hello to our daughter," he said, standing up slowly.

I couldn't believe I was looking at my daughter. "A ...girl? Is she okay?"

"She's perfect." Joe leaned down and kissed my forehead, our newborn daughter crying mildly between us. "How do you feel?"

I nodded, reaching for her. Joe gently placed her on my bosom; her cries subsided long enough for me to see the blue of her eyes. "Hello...Caroline." I looked from my daughter to Joe. He was smiling. Hearing me say her name for the first time was surreal. We had discussed names for boys and girls; Caroline was Joe's grandmother's name – one we'd both agreed on.

Caroline's cries became stronger, more persistent, and I prepared to nurse her.

In that tender moment when I first held my newborn child, the haziness and distortion of time melted away. I rejoiced in the present, the precious force of life embracing me in pure joy. It was an indescribable feeling of unimaginable love the first time I held baby Caroline. In the blink of an eye, my own wants and desires became secondary.

Watching us, watching me breastfeed, Joe smiled from ear to ear. "You have never looked more beautiful to me than you do right now. I didn't think it was possible to love you more." He leaned over and kissed our foreheads. "My girls . . . I'm on cloud nine."

"She's beautiful, isn't she?" I said to Joe.

Joe sat on the edge of the bed, outwardly mesmerized. "Yes, she is. Like her mother."

"I think...I think maybe she has your nose."

CHAPTER 32

Amanda

Emma is asleep in the car when we get back to the house. Jesse carries her inside and up the stairs to her bedroom for a late nap. Jesse's parents are in the living room watching television. I go over and join them.

"What happened to your elbow?" his mother asks, noticing the bandage.

"Oh. It's nothing, really," I say.

"She pushed Emma out of the way of a flying swing," Jesse says, coming down the stairs. "I think we can all use some margaritas." He looks at me. "How about it?"

"Sure," I say.

"Mom? Dad?"

"Well, since you're making them," his dad says.

Jesse and I later retreat to the upstairs deck with our Margarita drinks, where we can look out at the ocean and bask in each other's company. "I'm going to barbecue steak tonight," Jesse says, lowering himself into his chair. "Maybe throw on some kabobs and clams too. How does that sound?"

"It sounds wonderful. I'll be hungry by then." I take a sip of my drink, tasting salt and tequila. "Mmm, this is just what the doctor ordered."

"And after dinner," Jesse says, "I'm taking you out on a date."

"Really? Where to?"

"A beachside bar and grill where they have live music."

"I'm in," I say, leaning my head back on the chair, feeling rested. In the distant sky, I spot a hang glider.

Jesse sees where my eyes are focused. "Have you ever gone hang gliding?"

"Oh, no," I say. "I've had enough excitement for one weekend. Don't even think about it. I could have another panic attack up there."

Jesse reaches for my hand, holding it in his. "Okay, we'll drop it for now," he assures me, and then winks. "But maybe not forever." He changes gears. "Have you checked on Nana? How's she doing?"

"Mom says she's not in any imminent danger, but I can hear the gravity of what she isn't saying. We all see it. Nana's health is worsening. I don't know how much longer we'll have her with us."

"I'm sorry," Jesse says. "I'm real glad I have the chance to get to know her. What will you do then? Where will you go?"

"Well, I haven't really given it a lot of thought. I suppose I should." I stare out at the ocean. "Nana's house will be part of her estate so of course, I'll have to move out eventually. I'm not sure what will happen to it. My mother and uncle wanted Nana to sell years ago - thought it was way too much house for her. The repairs and upgrades will cost a fortune since not much has been done to it in the last ten or fifteen years. It has to be over seventy years old now." I take another sip of my drink and look down sadly, feeling drowsy. "It's a shame really. I love that house. There are so many memories in it. It could be beautiful again."

"It's a great house," Jesse says, "with a great piece of property in a great location. It'll sell easily."

"I've been saving up my money. I can afford to buy myself a small house not too far from where I work. I could do that now if I had to. In my mind, that's as far as I've gotten."

Jesse squeezes my hand. "That's good enough for now."

"I know that time is going to come," I say with a sigh. "I just pray it's still a ways off."

I close my eyes, feeling relaxed and drained, the margarita's intended effect working like a charm.

***

I wake up in the top deck's Adirondack chair, my empty margarita glass still sitting on the table next to me. Jesse isn't in his chair but I can guess where he is. The sweet smell of barbecue smoke fills the air. I make my way down to the kitchen and offer my assistance. Then I play a game of Hungry Hungry Hippos with Emma while Jesse grills the meat.

"Would you like me to set the table?" I ask Cheryl.

"No, I'll take care of it. You and Emma keep playing."

I've been enjoying getting to know Jesse's parents a little more. Witnessing what a solid couple they are, supportive and loving, I better understand what Jesse meant when he said his family helped him get through his tragedy.

Jesse's mom helps out with Emma a lot, but I can see that Jesse is very hands on with her. He does not pass off his responsibilities where Emma is concerned to his mother, taking on the position that he is her father and whatever he says, goes.

Nightfall comes quickly. Emma's already fast asleep in her lower bunk. Jesse and I had tucked her in, Jesse showing me the routine – her baby doll and favorite blanket must be with her, a white noise machine gets turned on, and of course, her *Elsa* night light.

Wearing my yellow floral-print tiered sundress - Nana's pick - I add a seashell choker to accent the sweetheart neckline. My highlighted brown hair is blown out full and playful, and a pair of long, gold shell earrings move with me. I make my way down the stairs to join Jesse for our date night. He's waiting in the living room with his parents, dressed casually in cargo shorts and a classy-looking maroon polo shirt. He rises from the sofa, his eyes dancing, and lets out a soft whistle.

"Have a good time," Jesse's parents chime in together, obviously pleased to see Jesse so happy. We bid them good-night and head out the door.

We stroll quietly on the waterfront. The beam from a lighthouse stretches into the air, repeatedly lighting up the dark ocean as we mosey in the direction of the beachside bar.

From across our table of oysters and drinks, Jesse stares at me, fully mellow, while we listen to an acoustic rock band playing in the background. I can see affection in his eyes. He reaches across the table to hold my hand. I feel it coming - the words "I love you." My heart races.

In a conflicted instant, his face covers over in restraint and the words evaporate between us. "I'm up for partnership," he says in a self-conscious rush.

I'm somewhat dazed but manage to say, "That's wonderful," ever aware that Jesse has opted for less vulnerability. "This is something you really want, isn't it?"

"It's something I know I'm suited for."

"Yes," I say. "I think you're right."

"These last few years...well...it took so much from me. Tragedy defined me for so long, I let go of things that were important to me before it happened. But that can't be my whole story. I won't let it be."

"Of course not," I say.

"I'm just getting back on track. Remembering who I am . . . who I was. I had this whole big plan once," Jesse says, ruminating. "I'm back now . . . making plans again."

It makes me wonder - did you plan on me? I wish I could've said that out loud. "Good for you, Jesse," I say, turning my gaze back to the ocean.

When I look at him again, he has a faraway look, like his thoughts have taken him somewhere else.

The band starts playing "Brown Eyed Girl" and Jesse stands up, reaching for my hand. "Let's dance."

We sway to the music, Jesse's face buried in my hair. The other couples on the small dance floor easily fall away. "You smell so good," Jesse whispers in my ear, the closeness of our bodies stirring us both. When the song ends, we return to our table and Jesse looks at my half-finished drink. He wants to be alone with me, as I do with him. I pick up my drink and swallow the rest.

Afterwards, Jesse pays the tab, and we walk outside. He reaches over to kiss me, urgent and longing. I put my finger between his lips and mine, slowing him down, his eyes lingering with intensity as I brush my lips over his lightly, teasing him.

We stroll towards a dock with several boats tied up, our mood contemplative and eager. Hearing the sound of melodic water, the smell of saltiness, we walk a footpath lit with solar lights until we come to a big sailboat. "This is my family's boat," he says. "I'm gonna take her out tomorrow. Weather looks good for moderate winds." He climbs into it and then offers me his hand. I step onto the wooden deck, my heart beating wildly in my chest. Jesse pulls me along as we stoop down into the cabin below; a light gives off a warm, burnished glow. I take in a small sturdy table, a marine-upholstered bench seat, and a navy blue stars-patterned quilt on a berth meant for two. Crouched and leaning, Jesse turns on a fan that's mounted on the berth wall.

The bed beckons us, the mood unbroken. We sit silently on its edge, our shoulders pressed together, the fan's breeze blowing on our backs. The boat rocks us gently as waves slap against the hull.

He turns to look at me and cups my face in his hands. The soft, light caresses of his lips on mine sends tingles throughout my body. Then his kiss changes, deepening with desire, and I lose myself in him as we fall onto an array of puffed and padded stars.

CHAPTER 33

Elizabeth
Present

I'm certainly no stranger to treading my own path, knowing when to be patient and when to forge on. I had to put my desire to become a nurse on hold for years. I waited until my children were older and the requirements less rigid. The biggest block for me was that in the fifties no nursing school would accept a married woman and especially one who became pregnant. With the exception of Joe, I received plenty discouragement back then.

One day while my mother-in-law was visiting us – she often came unannounced - she saw medical textbooks strewn around our living room. From the kitchen, I overheard her talking to Joe. "Why are all these books out? It looks as if you're still in medical school."

"Elizabeth's reading those," Joe said.

"Whatever for?"

"She has hopes of becoming a nurse one day."

"Honestly," Joan huffed. "She's a wife and a mother. You'd think that would be enough."

And that's how it was. Fortunately, my husband was more encouraging. Ours was a marriage of equals in its truest sense.

By 1967, when Caroline was twelve and Joseph was nine, the eligibility restrictions had eased somewhat for admission to nurse's training, and I entered a program at a technical school. I remember how excited I was. I felt like a schoolgirl. I loved learning as much as I needed to do something meaningful. I'd never really forgot my dream of becoming a nurse. I just had to shelve it for a while.

My mother couldn't understand why I'd want to take on something like that, but she eventually came around when she realized I wasn't letting it go. Joan, on the other hand, saw my dream as selfish and foolhardy. How a selfless profession such as nursing could be construed as selfish I could never understand, but then that was the enigma that was Joan. I still called her Joan, even though Joe's dad lovingly became Pop after we married, which is what Joe called him. Once, early in our marriage, I called her Mom, trying it out, and she sharply replied, "Joan will suffice." Further attempts at any closeness with her were put on ice so I resigned myself to a coolly polite relationship with her. She was, after all, the woman who brought the man I was madly in love with into the world, which automatically gave her carte blanche. When it came to my children, though, that's where I drew the line, so our distressing relationship persisted.

Once, on a Sunday afternoon we were dressed and ready to go out for dinner to celebrate Joe's promotion to Chief of Surgery. Joe's parents and mine were joining us. Caroline was around thirteen at the time. When she walked down the stairs in a mini dress with tall white boots I questioned her as to where the dress came from. Her answer came in two words. "Grandma Joan." It was a skimpy halter-top dress. "You're going right back upstairs and taking that off," I said.

A quarrel ensued - typical during that time - and Joe came over to see what the commotion was all about. "Listen to your mother," he said. "Go change into something more appropriate."

"You always agree with her!" Caroline shouted.

"When she's right, I do."

"I hate you," Caroline shouted, turning to me. "Grandma Joan would let me wear it!"

Joan usurped my authority and overstepped her boundaries on more than one occasion. Later in the evening, I took her aside and told her that while I appreciated her buying gifts for our children, anything questionable needed to come through us first.

"All the girls are dressing that way," Joan said. "It's the new look. If you weren't so distracted with all your medical books, you'd know Caroline's taste in style has changed. Your daughter's growing up."

"And that, Joan," I said, "is it right there. Caroline's *my* daughter. You will check with me first."

I received my diploma from the nursing program in 1969. I never regretted that decision. I loved my family and my home, but I was also happiest when I was helping people. Housework could not fulfill me the way nursing could.

For graduation, Joe presented me with a box of bonbons, which had become our inside joke, and a note that said, "Still my bonbon wife." Privately, I think Joe thought I would give up on nursing eventually. But when he saw my resolve, he was supportive.

I've witnessed countless medical innovations over my twenty-five years as a nurse. When I started, there were few, if any, disposables and everything had to be sterilized and reused. When my first amputation patient died of internal bleeding, I was wrecked. I may not have gotten through it without Joe's comfort and counsel. Eventually, it deepened my sense of empathy, and the technical and human aspect of my profession motivated me to become an acute care nurse in my later years.

A year after Joe and I both retired from our medical professions and my mother, who was living with us at the time passed away, we returned to Asheville, North Carolina, a place we'd visited with our children when they were young. Its natural, long-range mountain beauty and serenity was forever embedded in our memories. Looking for a potential home, we drove up to a big, southern-style, white farmhouse at an elevation of 2500 feet. Shrouded in a blue haze, it had a front wrap-around porch, and a back deck with a view of the Blue Ridge Mountains in every direction. We knew we'd found our next home, our final spot. The farmhouse sat on two acres of land, most of it undeveloped forest. Joe and I decided to buy it then and there.

When we first moved in, it was like a second honeymoon. I rushed to the back of the house, to the deck and open porch with a stunning landscape of mountains morphing into a blue-like ocean, and my heart soared. I realized that in my mind and in my dreams, this was my escape scene. It was picture-perfect. Joe had opened a special bottle of wine for the occasion and brought my glass to me, unfolding his plans to make it a sunroom with glass walls and ceiling that we could enjoy year round. We spent hours together in that room, lazy days talking and sharing and looking forward to more special moments to celebrate. If we weren't in the back room, we'd sit out front, two old-timers rocking on the porch together, a reprieve from our many years' service in the medical community. We very much enjoyed mountain living in our twilight years. It had become a part of us.

My thoughts take me back to a beloved memory.

We'd gone out for a drive and had stopped to stretch our legs and take in the scenery. "Beth, look. Over there." Joe pointed in the direction of an open field. "He's a beauty." He passed the binoculars to me. "Do you see him?"

I could certainly hear him. We were half a mile away, but the bugle calls that cut through the fall air were loud and unmistakable. "Yes. I see him now." The rutting bull elk's sound alternated between a low growl and an intense high pitch scream.

"He's huge," I said. "I think he's wearing one of those GPS collars." Peering through the binocular's lens, I scanned the area that surrounded the elk. A harem of cows was just beyond. And then, another elk with an equally tall and impressive set of antlers approached the first bull. "Joe. There's two now!"

"Let me see."

I passed the binoculars back over to him.

"Would you look at that . . . I think we're about to see a fight between them," Joe said.

I looked across the mountains, fall colors blazing. Above a ridge, a dark cloud had gathered. "Looks like a storm may be coming."

Joe pulled the binoculars from his eyes and looked up at the sky. "Doesn't look too imminent."

Bugling . . . bugling . . . bugling . . . crack!

"They're at it! We're in for a spectacular show," Joe said.

The last time I had seen Joe this excited was the day he was given the keys to our newly purchased mountain house.

A cacophony of elk grunts and screams and crashes pierced the air.

"Pass it over . . . pass it over. My eyes aren't so good anymore," I said.

"Better than mine," Joe said, passing the binoculars over to me.

"Oh dear . . . oh my goodness."

"What's happening?" Joe asked.

"They're pushing each other around with their antlers. Oh no! One of them just flipped the other to the ground."

The binoculars flew between us as we witnessed a most amazing outdoor entertainment and we forgot to look at the sky where layers of heavy black clouds loomed over us.

"Beth, it looks like it's going to pour any second."

"I can't leave now," I said. "I have to know what happens." The dark clouds cast far-reaching shadows down the mountains. I was unable to pull my eyes away from the scene of the elks fighting for dominance. "Some of the cows have run off," I said. "Do you think it's because a storm's coming?"

"Not sure."

"It looks like the two elks are going to fight to the death." I winced. "Does it always have to end that way?"

"No, it doesn't," Joe said.

"I sure hope not." A boom of thunder startled me.

"We need to go." Joe clutched my arm. "Now."

"But Joe—"

"We might *just* make it to our car in time."

We walked as speedily as two seventy-something-year-olds could, across a field and up a hill. I glanced behind me. I couldn't help myself. I felt like I'd walked out on a thrilling movie.

"Beth, be careful. I don't need you falling," Joe said, grabbing my hand.

Another clap of thunder detonated the sky charging with heavy black clouds. I could see our car at the end of the trail. We let go of our hands so we could go faster and our walking changed to a sprint. *I think we're going to make it.*

At the same moment as we reached our car, rain gushed down. I screamed, and we flung ourselves into the car, drenched. Still squealing, I looked over at Joe. He was sopping wet. It reminded me of a much earlier day, a lifetime ago, when he walked me out to my car after we'd dined and he made it to his a little too late. He had looked so adorable with his wet hair swept over his forehead. Only it was silver now.

"Look at the two of us! We're soaking wet." I started to laugh. Joe's eyeglasses were fogged and I could see his scalp through separated wet strands matted to his head.

"You think this is funny, do ya?" He swiped streaks of rain from his eyes and pushed up the heat, looking irritated.

Unable to stop my fit of hysterics, I leaned over, laughing so hard, I was crying. I gasped for air and clutched my stomach. "I'm sorry," I said between bursts of infectious laughter.

A smile creased Joe's eyes, and then he chuckled. "All right, all right, maybe it's a little funny. We almost made it. We could have if you hadn't lingered so long."

"Me? I seem to recall someone saying something about the storm not looking too imminent."

He snickered. "I was distracted."

"Now we'll never know what happened," I said.

Joe leaned back in his seat and reached over to stroke my wet hair. "Your willfulness never changes."

"How do you think it ended?"

"Probably a stalemate," Joe said.

"Then it was all for nothing."

"What do you mean?"

"Leave it to males to continue fighting one another only to find out the cows have all run off."

Joe shook his head. "That reminds me of a funny thing Groucho Marx once said: 'I could dance with you 'til the cows come home. Better still, I'll dance with the cows 'til you come home.'" Our laughter rippled through the car.

There are so many memories in this place. We bought our house twenty-five years ago and it became a special gathering site where many important family occasions were celebrated – birthdays, graduations, engagements. When my Joe passed away ten years ago, I knew I could never leave. Even when his cancer got bad, I kept him home and took care of him along with a hospice nurse who would relieve me from time to time. Joe had spent numerous hours inside a hospital and I vowed I wouldn't let him die there. I still feel his presence.

And now . . . developers are interested in buying up land in Asheville to put in condos and townhouse units, setting their sights on mine. Life is fraught with having to make hard decisions. I think about that as I ponder my latest quandary. The builders are anxious to get an answer from me, but I won't be rushed. No amount of money could sway me to sell it to them if I had my way. But I know that my way is not my children's way. They see a house in need of work, land that needs tending.

Of all the tough decisions I've had to make in my life - some I've long forgotten, some I'm still living with - like not telling my children about the unsolicited lucrative offer already made on my house and property - this one is way up there on the most heart-wrenching, agonizing list. When they hear of the generous offer, they'll be relentless.

When I'm gone, I won't be able to protect my house any longer, so why should it matter to me what happens to it? Perhaps it's my old age and increased sentimentality. Perhaps it's because my home here on the mountain was to be Joe's and my legacy, to go on for our family for generations. Or, perhaps it's because Joe's ashes are interred near the exceptionally tall Carolina Hemlock tree we both loved, where I also want my ashes to be buried.

I sighed. *Oh Joe. How I wish you were here. I never imagined I'd have to decide this alone.*

CHAPTER 34

Amanda

From marshes and dunes and beautiful beaches to mountains rising on the horizon, I continue my westerly drive, the various blues over the mountains letting me know I'm almost home. I enjoy the beach, but my heart warms at the sight of the forested, mountainous landscape with its peaks and valleys, the allure of the delicate blue fog that is Asheville. My temporary home. I can't stop the tears rising up in my eyes and trickling down my cheeks.

A final day of sailing with Jesse and his family and a visit to the Wright Brothers National Memorial concluded my weekend in Kitty Hawk. Jesse is returning to his home in Charlotte so Emma can start preschool.

My long drive home has allowed me to ponder all the feelings I had while there. The perceptions . . . and the concerns. When I'm with Jesse, my heart is in overdrive, my head taking a back seat. I've been going over the weekend in my mind, analyzing scene after scene, dissecting his words. *It's my issue . . . the last few years took so much from me . . . I allowed my tragedy to define me . . .* While the weekend was enjoyable and Jesse showed me a good time, it was subduing. Our passions fall in perfect step with one another, but the open-ended question of love is still unanswered.

My heart aches for the man I've fallen in love with, who I give myself to more passionately than anyone I've ever known. The driven lawyer with unfinished visions, whose experiences have forever changed him. I see him – standing confidently at the brass wheel of his sailboat on the open water, the wind in his hair, piloting and guiding - a truer side to the man who's still healing and grappling with a tragedy that thrust him into single parenthood. He's back at the helm of his life, recollecting his goals, chasing his partnership dreams, balancing work and raising a daughter. I have to ask myself, *Where do I fit into all of it? Am I feeling love more than he is?*

Jesse had said, *I let go of the things that were important to me . . . I'm trying to get back to who I was.* Who Jesse was before I came into the picture doesn't bolster my confidence, when all I want to do is look forward.

From open salty ocean air and hot sand to conifers and laurels outlining my trail, the earthy scents of mineral rock and pinesap meet me in the driveway to Nana's house. After retrieving the mail, I walk along the pathway to the front door pulling my suitcase behind me. Sweet yellow clover and mountain mints tickle my nostrils.

When I enter the house, I can hear the blare of Nana's television. My parents left early in the morning and have already gotten home. I shuffle through the envelopes. Most are addressed to me, but there are two for Nana – one from Woodsedge Builders, the other from some law office. Probably junk mail. I leave hers on the kitchen counter and go over to her room to look in on her. She's asleep. I lower the volume on her TV and start to walk out when she calls my name.

"Amanda?"

"I didn't mean to wake you."

"I've been sleeping on and off all day. How was your weekend?" she asks in a soft voice.

I sit down on the foot of her bed. "It was very nice. Plenty of good weather. But tell me . . . how are you feeling?"

"Oh, just dandy," she says, shooing the question away. "So . . . how did it go with meeting Jesse's family?"

"Emma's a real cutie. And Jesse's parents couldn't have been more hospitable. They seemed happy for Jesse."

"Well, why wouldn't they be? He introduced them to a nice girl."

I smile. "You're not the least bit partial now, are you?"

"That's a very big hurdle to get over. But from the sound of it, it went well. Better than the first time I met your grandfather's parents."

"Grampa's parents? What happened?"

"My future mother-in-law hated me. That's what happened."

"She hated you?"

"I was of the wrong nationality and religious affiliation."

"Yes, I think I heard about that. Maybe it was from Mom. That must have seriously been hard." I've been learning a lot of little family secrets since I moved in with Nana. "So when did she come around?"

Nana laughs. "Who said she did? Joe was her golden child. I don't think anyone could have measured up. Her resentment gradually dwindled of course, but she remained a force to be reckoned with. Anyway, that was a long time ago. Tell me more about Jesse's family."

"It was touching, watching Jesse with his young daughter, a side of him I hadn't seen before. He's a good father. And a good son, from what I can tell."

Nana folds her hands over her midriff and gives me her old-soul smile that lets me know what she's thinking without having to say it. *Jesse would make a good husband.*

I return her smile; that's all for now. "How about a cup of tea?" I ask, deflecting.

"That would be lovely, but let's have it out on the deck."

***

Nana and I sip tea together in our private reveries. I feel as though I'm looking into a Monet painting, a mountainous landscape glossed by smoky blues and glowing green watercolors.

"I missed this," I say, suddenly realizing I had vocalized my internal thoughts. A warm, light breeze tingles my skin.

"You feel it too, don't you?" Nana says, needing no explanation. "I've often seen it in your eyes – that look that says 'I'm home.'"

"The mountains humble me. Ever since my visits here with you and Grampa so many years ago, I've felt a strong connection to this place. I didn't know it then, couldn't describe it really. But no matter what earth-shattering problem I was facing, it embraced me. I felt it even as a young girl. It still renews me."

"I like to think we're on the edge of heaven's stairway," Nana says. "I won't have too far to go from here." Nana lets out a heavy sigh. "Not too long either I suspect. I'm coming down the pike."

"Nana, you don't –."

"Honey." She gives me a thoughtful wink. "I've already gone through the last toll booth."

I look over at her, feeling the truth of her sentiments, and my shoulders slump. Her face is a portrait of composure and wistfulness emanating from the mindfulness that hers was a life well-lived.

"You and I have seen many people at the end stage of their lives," Nana says. "I've made my peace with dying a long time ago. My heart is weak and getting weaker. I know we've talked about this before, but I must be clear. I want to go as naturally as possible, with no prolongation or heroic interventions of any kind."

My eyes moisten and I reach over to touch her frail, arthritic hand, feeling the veins and soft wrinkles underneath mine. "I'll see to it you get all the care and comfort you need. And I'll be respectful of your wishes. You don't have to worry."

"I'm not worried, honey. All I need is for you to just help me through it."

Nana has shared many of her experiences as a nurse with me over the years, and as there often are, certain patients leave their indelible mark on us. One woman whose family wouldn't let her die is one that I know resonates with Nana. It was in the mid-seventies and Nana said a terminally ill, elderly woman had to be resuscitated numerous times because her family members couldn't say goodbye, despite her eyes pleading with them to let her go. Late one night, after her family had gone, the woman spoke to Nana of her husband who had passed away over ten years ago. "I've kept him waiting long enough," she said. Nana still remembers the smile on that woman's face in her final moments when she said, "He's waiting for me on the other side. I must be on my way." Then she closed her eyes.

"I brought you home a treat," I say, needing to change the subject and indulging her sweet tooth. "Chocolate and maple fudge."

"A little taste from heaven." Nana quips. Her sense of humor and taste are intact. "Now tell me something, dear. How have you been feeling?" Nana completely changes course, seemingly bent on getting some serious things off her chest.

"I'm fine. Why do you ask?"

"I know what happened to you. I know how you got those bruises a few months back."

I say nothing, only look at her, a cooling cup of tea clutched and forgotten in my hand. Of course Mom would tell her.

"I sensed something more had happened to you, that it wasn't just a fall. I asked your mother if she knew anything, and I made her tell me."

"I didn't think you needed to worry. I still don't. As you can see, the bruises have all healed."

"Yes, by the grace of God. But how are you dealing with what happened mentally?"

"I wish I could just forget . . . I'm treating it though. I've been going to therapy."

Nana sighs. "Good girl. Too many think they can do it alone. Did I ever tell you that your Grampa suffered from PTSD? Of course, they didn't call it that back then. Trauma was invisible in those days; war veterans were told they were shell-shocked. He struggled for years with what he saw and had to do in Korea. He had many disturbing and sleepless nights, nights when I'd find him walking in his sleep and had to steer him back to bed."

"I didn't know."

"He put up a good front. He'd tell me he was handling it and not to worry. His symptoms didn't start until months after he got back home."

"Grampa always seemed so in control of his emotions."

"Traumatic memories intruded on him many nights. For him, the forgotten ones were not so forgotten. The brain remembers."

"Yes. It does. I can never walk alone," I say. "At least not without having to look over my shoulder a hundred times. My attacker took that away from me."

Nana shakes her head sadly. "Poor dear. It's going to take some time."

"When you were in that awful bus accident when you were younger, you told me once that you couldn't get on a bus afterward. When did it change?"

Nana looks down into her lap. "It didn't," she says quietly.

"It didn't get better?"

"Oh, the nightmares eventually stopped. But the way I coped was by avoiding bus rides."

"Surely you've been on a bus since?"

"Very seldom. And, I drove your mother and uncle to and from school when they were young as much as possible so they wouldn't have to ride the school bus. But walking on foot . . . that's different. It can't be avoided so easily." Nana regards me carefully. "Don't look so discouraged. Today, there are more coping tools that start with recognizing trauma for what it is."

"I still can't believe that in all these years you wouldn't get back on a bus again." I am dismayed.

"I understand that buses are a safe way to travel statistically speaking, but I preferred being the driver in my own car. I did only what I could do. In my day, trauma got swept under the rug." I sigh. "Chin up. You are stronger than you know."

I pat Nana on her leg. I will miss this woman when she's gone. I wonder if she knows how much of an inspiration she's been for me and how she's shaped my life - never judging, always listening, continually encouraging.

"So . . . how are things going with you and Jesse?" says the woman with a one-track mind.

"You really are trying to cover a lot today, aren't you?"

Nana grins. "He seems sweet on you."

"We enjoy one another, and we're having fun." Flashes of us on the bed inside his family's sailboat cabin make me blush. "He's affectionate and caring. He's also a doting father who wants the best for his daughter."

"Nothing wrong with that."

"I remember he told me that he married Emma's mother because he felt like it was the right thing to do. He did it for Emma, not for love. I've been asking myself if he's looking for the right partner to be a mother to his daughter. She's his whole world. I admit it's crossed my mind." Baring my soul has never felt so important.

"Why can't he have both?"

"He can. But...which came first? Is it wrong for me to want him to want me for me?"

Nana slumps a little in her chair. "You're over-thinking."

"Maybe. But it's complicated. Jesse's complicated. He has jealousy and distrust issues he needs to work on; his former wife had been unfaithful to him. So there's also that."

Nana clucks her tongue. "Good heavens. I don't know about all that. I only know what I see. And I trust what my eyes are telling me."

"Besides being a single dad, Jesse's very focused on his career. He wants to make partner at his firm. His life was put on hold for a few years and now it seems like he is bent on catching up. Nothing is going to get in the way of his goals again if he can help it. Not promises. Not sacrifices. Not even love."

Nana remains silent. She's opened a floodgate and my feelings pour out.

"On the ride here, all I could think about was how much I've given up. I may never have a child of my own. I could love Jesse's daughter. That wouldn't be hard to do. I'm thirty-four. Time is not on my side."

"You two need to have a conversation," Nana says. "Communication is key. Your grandfather and I always talked things through. Even when we disagreed or argued, we never went to bed angry with one another."

I take a sip of the tea I'd almost forgotten was there, cold now. *It's easier when the words "I take you to be my lawfully wedded wife, to have and to hold . . ." aren't just notions.* I thought all I needed was to feel desire again, but I realize I need more. Desire and passion isn't a problem for Jesse and me. But love is.

I look steadily at Nana. "He hasn't told me he loves me." It hurts to say it out loud. "All reasons for having a discussion should start there. That ought to be the starting point."

I think Nana's mind must be spinning from all she's heard in the last few minutes, but her face reveals nothing. Her bridled expression is not unsympathetic. It comes from a place of experience in having heard it all.

"What are you going to do?" she asks.

"There's nothing to do but wait and see."

She nods and gives me a sage smile. "A popular song from my time comes to mind. Que Sera, Sera. Whatever will be, will be."

"Exactly. Now," I say, standing up, "how about some of that maple fudge I brought back for you? It's your favorite." I start to go. "Oh. Two pieces of mail came for you. I left them on the kitchen counter. One's from some builder, the other from a law office. Do you want me to bring them to you?"

Nana's eyelids close for a couple of long seconds, and I could swear I hear her grumble before she opens them again and stares out over the mountains. "No. They can wait. I'll open 'em when I'm good and ready."

CHAPTER 35

Amanda

It's a beautiful early autumn day as I drive myself over to Jesse's house in Charlotte, a hint of changing leaves twinkling in a golden sun. I haven't been to his house yet, the house he bought for his new family nearly four years ago.

I wish I could shake the nagging feeling that something's going on with Nana. It would seem plausible that it would have something to do with her health, but then why did she become observably distressed and agitated when I mentioned the two pieces of mail addressed to her? What isn't she telling me? Or anyone else for that matter. I'm afraid to say anything to my mother. Not because she couldn't get to the bottom of what's been on Nana's mind these days, because she *could*, with unrelenting persistence. If Nana has something to share with us, she'll do it when she's ready.

I pull into a cul-de-sac and up to Jesse's four-bedroom brick ranch. Emma is riding her tricycle up and down the driveway. When I start to park alongside the curb in front of his house, Jesse scoots Emma over and waves me into the driveway. I already missed him but seeing him as he comes over to greet me, makes my heart leap.

Wearing a sweater over jeans, he takes me in his arms even before I've had a chance to get fully out of the car, swathing me in his fleece and heady oak scent, triggering tantalizing flashbacks below the deck of his family's sailboat a few weeks ago. His mouth on mine takes my breath away, and I wrap my arms around his neck, steadying myself before I kiss him back just as hard. He closes the car door behind me and considers me for a moment, dressed sportily in skinny jeans and cowgirl boots. My hair hangs loose over my shoulders, and he brings his hand up to move a lock that's fallen into my eyes. "I missed you."

"Missed you, too."

Emma pedals over to us.

"Hello, Emma. I hear you like preschool." I bend down to give her a hug and then remember the items I brought with me, still in my car.

"I brought cookies," I say, retrieving them. "Hope it's all right." Then I pass a pink-wrapped box to Emma. "This one's for you."

"Emma has something for you, too," Jesse says. "Isn't that right, Emma?"

Once inside the house, Emma runs over to me with her latest crayon drawing - a beach scene with not two, but three stick figures, one with long brown hair. "Oh, Emma," I say, holding it to my chest. "I will treasure this. Thank you so much."

Jesse lets Emma open up my gift to her - a pair of cute cowgirl boots identical to mine. She's delighted and spends the next several minutes attempting to swap out her sneakers for them, insisting she can do it all by herself.

"Thank you," Jesse says. "You didn't have to do that."

"I know." I glance over at the kitchen. "What smells so good?"

"I'm making chili. It's a special recipe of mine."

"Smells wonderful. Perfectly cooked eggs...now chili. You're full of surprises."

Jesse lifts the lid off the pot of chili to stir it as I gaze out the kitchen window. The cute little swing set and fenced-in yard is an eerily idyllic contradiction to the tragedy that befell Jesse's family. That I'm standing in Jesse's deceased wife's kitchen does not elude my thoughts, and I have to force myself to shake off the feeling.

After an afternoon of board games and Jesse's home cooked meal, evening sneaks up on us. Jesse puts Emma to bed then pours us each another glass of wine while we sit on the sofa in front of the fireplace and gaze at the fire.

"I got great news this week," Jesse says. He smiles in that unique way that he does, eyebrow cocked, his mouth tilting upward on one side. "My name's getting moved over to the partnership column."

"Congratulations. I know how much you wanted it and how hard you worked toward it."

"Thank you. I have."

"So, how will things change for you exactly?"

"Well, I'll be putting in more hours, especially in the first few years. There's definitely more responsibility required of a managing partner. There's even some talk of a satellite office in the coming months. Exciting times for the firm."

"A satellite office . . . where?"

"Not sure where, and it's still a way's off. There's a whole lot of things to think about. More childcare for Emma being among them."

A storm of cautioning breaks out in my head, where it has been swelling. I take a slow sip of my drink to buy some time to process the news, wondering again what's to become of us. I should just be happy for him, but there are too many relationship hurdles that I find worrisome.

I can't seem to pull my eyes from the flames, the blue in them hypnotic, but I also don't want him to see my face. I'm not good at hiding my true feelings as my mind plays out all the scenarios if Jesse and I are going to continue seeing one another. Jesse may want me to move in with him, or maybe we'll just see each other on occasional weekends mostly. Neither is good.

Finally, I risk him seeing my face, putting words to the question in my heart. "What about us?"

"Hey." He reaches for me, laying his hand over my shoulder. "Don't look so worried. This isn't going to change anything for us. This is a great opportunity. Ever since I started at the firm, I vowed I'd make partner before I turned forty. I've had to push that goal back somewhat, but I worked hard to catch up and prove myself. I'm securely on that path now. And . . . it doesn't hurt that I'll make a whole lot more money."

Jesse rubs my shoulder and leans forward, his eyes drawing me in. "We have a good thing going. I'm not gonna mess that up. We'll just keep going on as we have been."

My face closes, falling back to the flames, his last words ringing as painfully loud and clear as a warning bell. A déjà vu moment grips me as the past and present coincide unkindly. I've been here before. A place I don't want to be ever again.

I give myself a good talking-to. *Is this what I want for me? To just go on? Did he mean it the way it sounded? Or did it sound exactly the way he meant it? Am I to believe that Jesse, the most skillful talker I've ever known, misspoke?*

I face Jesse and brave the question. "What are we to each other?" I need to know how much of him he's willing to give me. I love our passion, but is it all just sexual love, nothing deeper?

Jesse looks into my eyes, thoughtfully gauging his answer. He reaches for my hand, kissing it softly, testing the waters. "You know you're very special to me."

Like a punch in the gut, it lands hard. I pull my hand back and sink into myself. His answer is just the right amount of encouragement without commitment. He will not be thrown off his game. Any qualms that his words may have been an accident have been settled. I understand that Jesse's answer was purposeful, chosen carefully, and it shatters my heart. Those are not the words I wanted to hear. I want us to go deeper. I love Jesse and I need him to love me back.

Jesse looks into my eyes, and my emotions give me away. "Amanda, this is a time for celebrating, not lamenting."

I lean back against the sofa and close my eyes, willing myself not to tear up. *I am stronger than I look.*

The sound of my silence unsettles him. He feels a change in my composure and reaches up to stroke my cheek. "Please be happy for me."

I look into his eyes and feel an immediate pang of sorrow for him. He's right. Jesse's loveless marriage . . . his dreams and goals thwarted in the most shocking way . . . this moment belongs to him. It's his time. We are not in the same place. It hurts to come to terms with that. Jesse is in the now when all I want is the forever.

My throat gets thick, but I'm not going to rain on his parade or say anything that will ruin this moment for him. I will celebrate him. And then . . . even though my heart is breaking, I will do what I have to do. For me. I won't repeat history. I won't compromise. Not when I've come this far. I deserve more. I deserve the promise of love.

I take a breath and regroup. Then, I raise my glass. "Let's toast."

Jesse lifts up his glass.

"Here's to reaching milestones and to new journeys." I catch a crackle of emotion in my voice and hope Jesse hasn't noticed. *Don't fall apart.* We clink our glasses together and I drink the rest of my wine in one swig.

Jesse doesn't completely trust my abrupt shift in mood, eyeing me still with some suspicion. He gives me a ghost of a smile. I keep my lips sealed, afraid that if I open them to say something, I'll cry. Instead, I kiss him convincingly on the mouth.

When we fall onto the couch together, my mind whirling with wine and unrequited love, I tell my heart to be still. Just this one last time.

***

By seven in the morning, I've quietly dressed and tiptoed into the kitchen. I place the note I wrote to Jesse on the counter and head out into the frosty air and to my car. I back out of his driveway, lips quivering, tremulous hands gripping the steering wheel, and begin to drive away.

One quick look in the rearview mirror sends daggers through my heart as Jesse emerges from his front door, running to the edge of his yard barefoot and bare-chested, his face flashing bewilderment as he looks up the street, before he disappears from my view.

Putting Jesse in the rearview mirror like that crushes me. I couldn't face him this morning, knowing what I needed to do. I didn't want him to see me break down; I'm already falling apart. Tears flow freely as I imagine him going back inside and reading the short note I left for him, the most painful thing I've ever put to writing, parting words jostling around in my mind still.

Dear Jesse,

You've got to live your best life for you, so that one day, if the stars align, you'll be ready to open your heart.

Thank you for showing me love's possibilities.

I will remember you always.

Love, Amanda

CHAPTER 36

Amanda

Nana is lying in bed in her room watching television when I enter. "I didn't expect you home so early," she says.

I drop down alongside her on the bed and stare up at the ceiling. "I made a hard choice today."

"Oh?"

I thought I'd cried out my tears in the two-hour drive home but more spring to my eyes. I can't keep them at bay.

"Oh, Amanda, you're upset. What happened?" Nana looks over at me with alarm.

"I let Jesse go." I weep.

I glance at my phone messages and reread Jesse's last text to me. "I never wanted to hurt you." He sent it over an hour ago.

"You broke it off with him?"

"I helped him save face."

"Forgive an old woman, but what exactly does that mean? Did you have a fight or something?" Nana asks, trying to understand.

"No. I heard him use words like . . . 'focus on my career' and 'you have to understand where I've been and where I want to go.' In other words, our timing and expectations are not aligned. I got it mostly right this time. Great guy. Awful timing."

Nana shakes her head. "I don't know. I'm not really on board with this 'timing' thing. It sounds like an excuse to me. Is there ever an ideal time for two people to fall in love?"

"It is when one of you is still dealing with the past and the other is looking to the future."

Nana reaches for my hand and squeezes it. "Call me stubborn, but I'm of the old thinking that love transcends all bounds."

"Gotta love your positivity, Nana. Truth is Jesse's got a lot going on – raising a young daughter, a big promotion requiring more commitment, the fulfillment of his career goals. I would understand it if he can't take on anything else, if he can't take on me."

"Has he said that?" Nana asks.

"No. He doesn't have to."

Thoughts of Jesse flood my head. I have to resist every urge to call him, but it would be awkward to do so now, especially since I ignored his last text. But what would I even say? Nothing has changed. And now, the man of many words has gone silent. I've put him off his game. More likely, he's conceded defeat to the realities that our wants differ.

We may not have been able to go the long distance, but I want to believe there's a reason Jesse came into my life. I don't want to go back to who I was *before* him. Maybe that's all he was meant to be for me.

My cell phone rings. I wipe my eyes and sit up straight, staring with trepidation into my phone's screen.

"Is that Jesse?" Nana's tone is hopeful.

I'm still staring. "No. It's not. It's from the Police Department."

***

A female police officer steers me through the station house until we reach a small back room. I've had to consciously tell myself to remember to breathe ever since I received her unexpected phone call to come in.

She points to one of two chairs at the small rectangular table, the only furnishings in a windowless room. She remains standing. "I'm Detective Schonely. Before we start, can I get you some water?"

"No. Thanks."

"Thank you for coming over right away. We asked you here so you could view a photo array in connection with the crime committed on you," she says.

"Okay." My voice sounds small.

"The perpetrator may or may not be pictured, so don't assume that we know who the perpetrator is. Just focus on the photo array. It's important that you not ask for guidance about making any identification."

My heart is racing as I realize I'm being compelled to return to that awful day, a day as intrusive as any I've ever known, eroding my false sense of security forever. I'm going to be sick. "Excuse me," I say, slowing her down, slowing my heart down. "I think I could use some water after all."

The detective calls for someone outside the room to bring me over some water and then picks up right where she left off.

"Individuals presented in the photo array may not appear exactly as on the day of the incident. Features such as head and facial hair are subject to change, and the true complexion of a person may be lighter or darker than shown in the photograph. Regardless of whether or not you do ID one, know that the investigation will continue. Do you have any questions before we start?"

"No," I say, my voice just above a whisper.

Detective Schonely takes the adjacent chair and passes the first photo in front of me. I shake my head and take a swallow of water. One by one she shows me a photo, putting her initials on the back of each afterward, until we get to the sixth. It stops me cold. Dark, dull slits of eyes, spiky hair on top. I stare at it for a long time - the face of my torment. I don't know what I'm feeling. Anger? Sorrow? Numbness. "It's him," I say.

"I need to show you the rest," the detective informs me, noting my recognition and setting that photo aside. Overhead, a fluorescent light hums as I continue viewing the remaining headshots, shaking my head at each.

"What's your level of confidence in picking out photo number six?" Detective Schonely asks me once we've been through all the photos.

I study number six, trying to be as unemotional as I can. "While I was on the ground he pried my purse straps from my wrist. His face was close to mine and I saw right into his eyes. I couldn't see the whites in them. They were just . . . black. I'm certain this is him."

Detective Schonely has me sign the back of the photo I identified and thanks me for my cooperation. She's just seen me back out into the hallway when a man in handcuffs at the end of the hall turns himself around, our eyes making eye contact long enough to make me shudder. He looks down, shuffling his feet, as another officer urges him on. Detective Schonely quickly steers me back into the room, looking irate. "I'm sorry," she says. "Wait here a little longer." Although she doesn't say so, I get the feeling I wasn't supposed to see him – my attacker, handcuffed and already in custody. When the coast is clear she guides me out, apologizing for the inadvertent encounter, and thanking me once more.

I get into my car and drop my head onto the steering wheel, taking purposeful breaths. I did not have a panic attack in the station, not even when I glimpsed the wretched-looking man who accosted me down the hall in handcuffs. I pushed ahead, choosing control, just as I've been doing each and every morning when I wake up, when I have to tell myself that my attacker won't be able to hurt me anymore, willing myself to get out of bed and not to feel powerless. Bad things happen sometimes, but even though I still dread walking past the place where it occurred, I can take responsible steps to be more vigilant and cautious, increasing my situational awareness.

Before I realize what I'm doing, I pull out my cell phone and scroll to the number of the person I want to share this with the most. Jesse would be so proud of me. Since he chased my attacker down, he will undoubtedly be asked to ID him as well. I should let him know. But of course, I can't. For one thing, Detective Schonely said not to discuss this case with anyone else, especially someone who might also be called as a witness. Just as I felt my strained shoulders lift a little knowing the man who assaulted me has been caught, they seem to droop again with the burden of sadness.

I can't call Jesse. I made my choice. I have to stand by that now.

I do not hit send.

CHAPTER 37

Amanda

It's a crisp, moonless night near the end of October. A black sky saturated with hundreds of stars is brightly visible over the mountains. Dawn is spending the night since we're going hiking tomorrow morning through the Rough Ridge to the summit where we can enjoy spectacular fall colors and views of Grandfather Mountain. Dorothy, who has now transitioned to full time, will be staying with Nana.

I leave Dawn and Nana talking in the sunroom to get on a call with Dr. Cullen regarding one of our patients. When I return, their robust conversation seems to come to a rapid halt.

"Don't let me interrupt," I say. "What were you two talking about?"

Dawn answers quickly. "Constellations and the Milky Way. Look. Out over there."

Nana falls in step. "Yes, it's such a stellar night." She's been having fewer good days, physically speaking, but Nana is more energized than I've seen her in a while.

I look from one to the other, questioning. While it's truly a very beautiful night, the sky lavished with stars, I can't help thinking they weren't solely stargazing in the time I was away. Their excitement is somewhat contrived and hyped, but I go along.

"Nana, are you warm enough with that blanket?"

"I'm fine but I think I'm going to retire to bed now. Should be a nice day for tomorrow's hike."

"Yes. No rain in the forecast at least."

Nana reaches for her cane. "Ah. But you know what they say . . . the weather can change as fast as a hummingbird's heartbeat. Especially where you're going."

"Don't worry. We'll be wearing layers of clothing."

"Well, good night to you both."

I return to Dawn after helping Nana into bed. "So, what would you like to do now?"

Dawn's answer is unexpected. "Could you take me on a tour of the house? I feel like there are so many hidden gems here."

"Well, sure," I say. "I'll show you around if you'd like."

We start down the stairs to the full basement, the bottom few wooden steps sagging, past a gigantic storage room with shelves. "Much of what was stored down here has either been donated or distributed among family members. My mother has most of the Christmas stuff. This other room here," I say, entering an open space. "It used to be a workout room."

When we come to the wine cellar, Dawn moves her head up and down the shelf racks. "Wow! How many bottles can this hold?"

"I think it's around five hundred."

"Now *that's* a hobby I could get into!"

I take Dawn out to the three-car garage. "Nana doesn't own a car any more, not since she stopped driving a few years back, but one of these garages houses an antique car. It belonged to my Grampa."

"What kind of car?" Dawn asks, openly interested.

"A Corvette - the first year they were made."

"Seriously?"

"It's been years since I've seen it. It's been kept under protective cover for my cousin, Joey, my grandfather's namesake and only grandson, but it's really pretty - white with red leather interior. There aren't very many around."

I take Dawn over the grounds in the back of the house, a secluded yard with a fire pit and six Adirondack chairs.

"How far back does the property go?" Dawn asks.

"Two acres I think. The woods take up half of it." I rub my arms from the chill in the air. "Come on. Let's go back inside so I can show you the second floor. You haven't seen the upstairs rooms."

We traipse back inside and up the flight of stairs to the master bedroom. "This was Nana and Grampa's room." I open the door to reveal a queen bed dressed in a patchwork quilt that seems to get lost in the room's large open space, a hope chest, two flower-patterned armchairs, a cherry-wood secretary desk with a hutch, and a wood burning fireplace. "My Grampa used to complain that the queen bed was too big, said he couldn't feel his wife next to him. That should tell you all you need to know about their relationship."

"Did I ever tell you how my grandparents met? My grandfather was in a MASH unit in South Korea. He was drafted right out of his surgical internship. A couple of months after he returned home, he met my nana. She'd been in a terrible bus accident when leaving work one day and was rushed to the hospital where my grandfather was the new surgeon there. And...well...the rest is history."

"Wow. Hallmark, eat your heart out," Dawn says walking over to the vast fireplace. "When was the last time this was used?"

"Has to be over ten years. When Grampa passed away."

I hesitate at the next closed door and experience an abrupt wave of sadness. It's the bedroom Jesse last occupied. I haven't opened it since. I turn the knob, my heart skipping a beat as remorse sweeps over me in a crushing wave. "Just another bedroom." I have to shake off an immediately depressed feeling. *Chin up. This is supposed to be a fun girlfriend weekend.*

I hastily close the door to that room and open another. "My cousin, Joey, stayed in this room for a number of years when he attended the University of North Carolina at Asheville. Joey's the youngest grandchild."

"This room has a balcony in it like yours," Dawn says.

"Yes, it has the same wonderful view. Joey's in Florida now, finishing up his residency. Sorry. I'm sidetracking," I say. "It's hard not to. Whenever I'm in a room or particular space in this house a memory flashes in front of me."

"I completely get it," Dawn says. "There's so much history, and there's a lot of character in this house."

"It needs some work - and painting. My dad says that it's due for a lot of repairs."

Dawn shakes her head. "It surely doesn't take away from the house's charm."

"No, it doesn't. My grandfather took a lot of pride in his home. It wasn't just about the structure, although he took great care to enhance and maintain it. It was the memories and the love inside the walls that mattered most to him and Nana.

Which brings us to this room over here," I say, opening another bedroom door. "My grandfather called it his sanctuary. It was used as a home office and library."

"Ah, the 'man cave,'" Dawn says. "Every house needs to have one."

Two walls displaying full shelves of books and an old leather executive chair tucked under a mahogany desk are the room's focal points. Dawn goes over to the bronze star medal inside a shadow box on the wall, reading the meritorious citation next to it.

"I haven't been in this room in quite a while," I say, joining her. "It moves me every time." I read along with Dawn.

For outstanding professional ability in consistently carrying out his duties in an exemplary manner.

Working under the most difficult conditions, and at a time when there was an unduly high influx of patients, Captain Joseph Michael Paterson of the United States Army, displayed great surgical skill and resolve. His tireless devotion to duty resulted in the saving of many lives and contributed immeasurably to the success achieved by his hospital in accomplishing its mission.

"I have chills," Dawn says.

"I know. I get goosebumps every time I read it, too. He's so missed. My grandfather was Chief Surgeon for some fifteen years before he and Nana retired and moved here. Nana says they lived very comfortably and were blessed. She wouldn't give up nursing though."

"You are your grandmother's granddaughter."

I take that as a compliment. "Yeah, I guess I am." I lead Dawn to the top of the stairs. "Come on," I say. "Are you hungry?"

Downstairs in the kitchen, I pull out some crackers and cheese, hummus, pretzels, and grapes.

"We're going to need our energy for tomorrow. We should be packed and ready to head out the door as soon as Dorothy gets here in the morning. I've always wanted to hike the Rough Ridge in the fall. Just never seemed to make time for it."

"Hey," Dawn says. "I'm excited to do this. And, maybe it'll help me drop another pound or two before my wedding."

I want to say this is a good distraction for me, but then that would bring up Jesse. It surprises me that Dawn hasn't brought him up herself. I know she knows me better than anyone and can see right through me, to the part of me still aching for him. I've been in a funk and she's helping me through it, encouraging me forward. At least that's what I'm calling it. Depressed would be too unendurable.

Perhaps she privately hopes I'll date her cousin, who she's partnered with me in her wedding party. Or maybe she's just sensitive to Jesse being a tender topic and this is her way of helping me take my mind off him. The hike was her idea after all.

"I've studied the hiking map," I say. "There will be some challenges along the way, but the trail we are going on is well-marked and moderate in terms of difficulty. Nothing you and I can't handle."

At around 10:00 p.m., Dawn and I sit on the carpeted floor of my bedroom with our backs against my bed, sipping wine and gazing at the starry night outside the open balcony doors. "Feeling sleepy yet?" I ask Dawn.

"A little," she says. "I'm thinking about the pull factor. You know . . . those things that pull us into a place, unbeknownst to us when it happens. I understand your tie with this house. Of course there are the memories. But it's more than that. It's such a beautiful location. Asheville has that pull factor."

"Do you think you might move to Asheville someday?"

"I'm thinking about it."

"How cool that would be!"

Dawn stands up and sets her wine glass on my nightstand. "We need to get a good night's sleep. After all the times we talked about doing this, it's finally gonna' happen."

I close the balcony door and pull the drapes across. I can't think of anything more inspirational and restorative than a hike to do me some good. "Fingers crossed," I say. "The weather looks perfect. Tomorrow should be amazing."

"Yes . . .," Dawn says. "It will be that."

CHAPTER 38

Amanda

Dawn and I meander through a tunnel of rhododendrons and twisted birch trees, our hiking shoes clomping over well-worn dirt trails, the panoramic mountain views majestic and stunning. If we stand still, we can almost hear the soft whisper of shedding leaves, or the burble of a nearby waterfall. We come to a clearing and I look back to see how far we've gone. "Nana's house, I believe, is somewhere over in that direction," I say, pointing. I can see hikers coming up behind us. We've encountered many so far. Apparently, it's a great day for a hike.

"I think you're right," Dawn says, studying the map.

We rest on a large rock that overlooks a waterfall, relishing the sweet, fresh autumn air that smells of earth and pinesap and crushed foliage. Some of the other hikers amble past us, crunching over a carpet of dry leaves mixed with twigs and pine needles. They throw us a wave. I look over at Dawn, staring out at the landscape, pensive and preoccupied. She's become uncharacteristically quiet in the last few minutes, no doubt totally mesmerized. Nature does that. I pull my thermos of water out of my backpack, take a long cool drink, emulating the cascade flowing over rocks in front of me. Up here in the mountains, I can escape life's turmoil and leave my worries behind.

Dawn glances at her cell phone. "Cell service has been going in and out, but it looks like we aren't getting any now."

"Nope. Probably off the communication grid now."

Dawn stands up and adjusts her backpack. "Ready to move on?"

I check the trail map. We've gone over a mile so far. "We could rest here a while longer if you'd like. We don't have far to go. There's no rush."

"I wanna keep moving," Dawn says, looking restless.

"Okay," I say, buoying myself up. "Let's do it."

After we cross a boardwalk where we see our first spacious vista, the terrain changes. It's rockier and more uneven, with wildflowers and berry bushes scattered everywhere. Climbing over rocks, the change in elevation happens quickly, the air becoming thinner and noticeably cooler.

Dawn and I stop to look skyward. A backdrop of dramatic cliffs beyond the endpoint lookout is only feet away. There's a dusting of snow under our feet now, but the blue sky stretches endlessly above. I take in a deep breath. Euphoria sweeps me, my emotions spilling out. "Oh, Dawn. I feel like we could reach up and almost touch the sky."

Dawn doesn't say anything. She limps over to a rock and sits on it, rubbing her ankle.

"Hey. You okay?"

"Not sure. I think I hurt my ankle. Twisted it or something."

"Oh no."

"You may have to continue without me."

"No. Let's take a look at it. Does it feel swollen?"

"Not sure. I think I just need to rest here a bit."

"You came this far. If I have to carry you up there, I will," I jest. And then, "I'll wait with you."

"Go!" The nervous tone in Dawn's voice startles me. "You have to go," she says, calmer. "I'll be right here. I just need to rest some."

"Okay. But I'm coming right back for you."

I trudge farther uphill, my heart beating faster. Reaching the top, I stop at a rock and stare out ahead at the wondrous scene. Magnificent mountains nearly five thousand feet high draped in rich autumn colors under a vast skyscape. In hypnotizing moments like this, I feel like everything will turn out all right.

"You sure have gone to great heights to ignore me."

I gasp. I know that voice. My eyes dart toward Jesse who walks over to me, a penetrating expression of seriousness on his face.

I gulp in a breath, exhaling in one word. "Jesse."

My legs buckle under me as I begin to lose balance.

Jesse reaches for my arms and helps me find my footing. He holds my gaze, and I can't look away no matter how hard I try. A puff of wind loops around us as I stammer out, "I . . . I felt as though we had reached an impasse."

"Of course, you would. And I don't blame you when all I ever did was talk about myself, *my* goals for *my* future." Jesse brushes aside the hair that's blown into my face, and I exhale a breath I didn't know I was holding.

"These past few weeks without you made me realize that when I had good news to share with you, it was only because of how much you mean to me, that I want it to be about us, not just me. It hurt like hell when you left."

"I'm sorry. It was never my intent to hurt you." I look down for a second and pull off my backpack, which feels heavy all of a sudden, dropping it at my feet with a thud. "You have to understand . . . I hated that I had wasted so much time with a man I didn't really love. I would have hated it even more if I wasted time loving a man who didn't love me back."

Jesse reaches for my hand, his eyes never leaving mine. "You deserve to be loved . . . in all the ways a man loves a woman." He wraps his arms around me and hugs me to him, my body falling limp. "I know I have issues to work on, but I'm not going to let my emotional baggage hold me down. I let it define me for too long. Loving you has freed me."

I can't keep the tears from falling.

"Do you trust me?" he asks over my shoulder. I'm looking out at a brilliant vista, my eyes following an eagle as it soars over high bluffs and dramatic cliffs.

I close my eyes. "I trust you."

He pulls back and lifts up my chin to kiss me. I look into his tender eyes, see the familiar want and need in them. But there's something else. Words are forming on his lips; his voice thickens with emotion. "The sixteen-year-old girl who received a new heart told me love is worth fighting for. She clings to it and cherishes it because it's something she didn't know she could ever have. I have love . . . I'm in love. I could never forgive myself if I let you walk out of my life without fighting for you, without letting you know how much I love you. I'd rather do life with you than without you. I love you." He folds me into his arms, no longer speaking, no longer needing to, the resounding words *I love you* floating around me in the boundless space.

I don't remember when I've ever been happier in my life. "I love you, too."

The expression in Jesse's eyes takes on a euphoric look that must mirror my own. He's smiling at me in that inimitable way that I love. "Amanda . . . will you spend the rest of your life with me?"

He reaches into his pocket and pulls something out of it, then sinks to one knee.

"Jesse?"

"Complete my life and make it whole. Marry me."

I cover my face, my shaky hands doing little to muffle my cries. When I lower my hands my mind has finally understood, I blurt out the words. "Yes! I *will* marry you."

Jesse pulls the glove off my left hand so he can slide a round solitaire diamond ring onto my finger and then takes me in his arms, squeezing me so tight I think he may never let go. I don't ever want him to let me go again.

Catching the tear rolling down my cheek with his finger, he speaks into my ear. "When I first saw you in Nashville – I think I knew then that my life was going to change forever. I'm going to make this work for us . . . whatever it takes. Do you hear me? I haven't figured out all the details yet, but I will. And you'll be at the center of each and every one of them. I don't want to live without you. I want to do whatever I do with you. I want to spend my life with you."

I nod even as logistical questions swirl in my head, the power of Jesse's words overriding them. "I want that, too." I throw my arms around his neck, our mouths crashing together.

Jesse pulls me away so he can look me in the eye. "One more thing." His eyes are shining. "There's a strong chance that my firm's new satellite office could be in Asheville."

"Really? How did that happen?"

"I'm the new managing partner, am I not?"

I can barely wrap myself around everything that's happening. "Of course, you are." I kiss him. "I can't wait to tell Nana and Emma!"

Jesse grins. "Well . . . about that . . ."

"What? They already know?" I throw my head back in surprise and swat him on the arm.

Over Jesse's shoulder, I see Dawn coming up the mountain. Seems as though I'm the only one who didn't know. I have so many questions for her! I laugh a little as she makes her way over to us with an easy gait, her ankle magically healed.

Dawn's face has one big smile of relief on it. "Well?" She lets her backpack drop by her foot, eyes blazing. "What did she say?"

Jesse runs over to a nearby boulder and climbs it. Standing tall, he looks out into the expansive vista, his arms raised, and hollers in as loud a voice as he can, "She said yes!"

"Thank heavens," Dawn says.

Applause erupts from some of the other hikers at the summit. Squealing, I go over to Dawn and give her a great big hug. *My bestie.*

CHAPTER 39

Elizabeth
Present

"Dorothy, today is a very special day and I'm going to need your help." I greet her in the front hall. "My daughter and son-in-law will be over later. They're bringing some starters and hors d'oeuvres, but I need you to go down into the cellar for the wine. Jesse reminded me of a bottle down there that my husband bought for Amanda to be opened on a special occasion."

"What's the special occasion?" Dorothy walks with me toward the kitchen.

"Jesse's asking Amanda for her hand in marriage today."

Dorothy drops her purse on the counter and clasps her hands together. "Oh, how wonderful! I'm so happy for them."

"Amanda has no idea. She thought they were broken up for good. Amanda went hiking with her girlfriend. It's all been worked out. He plans to surprise her when she reaches the summit."

"How will I know which bottle of wine to bring up?"

"You'll know. There aren't so many down there anymore. It will say Albert Bichot on it. It was bottled in 2012."

Dorothy heads down to the wine cellar while I make my way into the sunroom. My cane leans against a table where I left it. Funny how I don't seem to need it this morning.

There's an abundance of sunshine today, the sun already warming up the room as I sink into my chair. The year 2012. Memories come in a solemn flash.

"Elizabeth . . . Elizabeth."

A tap on my arm stirred me awake and I blinked rapidly.

"What is it?" I looked into the eyes of Clara, Joe's hospice nurse.

"It won't be long now," she said.

I darted a look at Joe, his droopy lips, his pale body lying motionless in the bed. The rattle of his broken breaths told me the time had come. I didn't think I had any tears left, but they came sure as a sudden downpour of rain, burning my puffy eyes and falling down my cheeks.

I rose up from the chair where I'd dozed as Clara left me alone with Joe. Our children and grandchildren had all said their good-byes, but I'd been fighting it.

I lay down beside him and spoke into his ear, hoping he could still hear me. "Joe, my life was so much fuller because of you. I don't know how I'm going to go on without you." I choked down a sob. "I love you."

I took his cool, purplish hand in mine. "I know I'm going to have to let you go soon. I'll try not to keep you waiting too long."

I kissed his cheek. For fifty-eight years, I'd kissed this man, and I knew that my last would be as memorable as the first. "I will love you forever . . . 'til the cows come home."

Joe took one last breath, and then he slipped away.

I wipe at the tears forming in my eyes from ten long years ago.

It's been hard for me to make such an important decision without him, but if Joe were here, I'd like to think he would have agreed with me. Jesse set me up with an estate lawyer he knows, and we met at my house when Amanda was at work to discuss my estate planning wishes. The papers have been drawn and signed – an updated detailed will, a living trust, and a letter of instruction. It's good. It's right.

Joe and I acquired a nice fortune in our lifetime, investing wisely and living frugally. My children have also done very well for themselves. So I decided to leave everything I have to my four grandchildren. Upon my death, three of them will receive a sizable monetary inheritance. For

Amanda, I am bequeathing her the house and the land, as her sole and separate property, to do with as she pleases. It was the one safeguard that made any sense to me. Of all my children and grandchildren, she's the one who will fight to keep it, perhaps even restore it. She loves it here as much as I do. I can't predict what the future holds. I can only live in the here and now. But at least I know my house in the mountain will have a worthy defender. And Jessie is no slouch either. He'll make a strong ally.

"Is this the one?" Dorothy held out a bottle of wine.

I look it over. Twenty twelve, the year Joe passed away. "Yes. That's the very one."

Dorothy shuffles off to the dining room to pull out the elegant wine glasses, silverware and small plates.

My heart is filled with joy for Amanda. Later, I'll raise my glass to her and Jesse, to love and to hope and to the cycle of life.

I'm forever aware of how blessed I am that love happened twice in my lifetime. I reach for my favorite framed picture of Joe on my table. Wearing a leather jacket and leaning against his new white sports car, one hand resting on the car, the other inside his pocket, ankles casually crossed, his lips closed in a gentle smile. I look closer at his hand. How I loved his hands . . . healing hands . . . elegant fingers. His father had taken that picture a few months after his return from the service. I study his face. I can see heartache behind the veil of his younger-older eyes. I also see fortitude and resilience and compassion. The love he left behind perseveres. My ailing heart is filled with him. From my window, I stare at the imposing tree where his ashes are buried. *Until we are together again.*

I place his photo back on the table and settle deeper in my chair. There's nothing left for me to do. Except wait. I could do that. I've been doing that all my life. Waiting for another day, a sign of hope, a new beginning. Waiting for love, for wisdom from experience, for the next thing to come – whatever it may be. I've gotten a lot of practice at waiting.

I feel myself float back in time, losing myself in mountainous silhouettes of changing blues, my thoughts drifting on a thread of memory.

Joe and I are dancing to Teresa Brewer's "Till I Waltz Again With You," my head resting on his chest. I look into his eyes. "What if your mother never likes me? What if there are too many obstacles that we can't overcome? What if—"

Joe seals my lips with a kiss and then he looks into my eyes. "The only question you should be asking yourself is whether we are enough. You and I. Are we enough?"

"Yes. Of course, we are. You're enough."

"And you're enough for me."

He twirls me around and then bends me over and kisses me. And then he says, "I love you, Beth."

It was more than enough. It was the whole shebang.

ABOUT THE AUTHOR

Lucille's first novel, *Like Wine*, was a tribute to her mother and getting it into print before she passed was her goal. She considers *Elizabeth's Mountain* to be her true debut novel. When she was young, walking into a bookstore, with its new book smells and feels, was more exciting to her than a candy shop. She has lived most of her life in northern New Jersey and now lives in South Carolina with her husband, close to her two daughters and grandchildren. Lucille loves stories that lift her up and gratify her and where she can take a little of the characters inside of her and sometimes see herself in them.

NOTE FROM LUCILLE GUARINO

Word-of-mouth is crucial for any author to succeed. If you enjoyed *Elizabeth's Mountain*, please leave a review online—anywhere you are able. Even if it's just a sentence or two. It would make all the difference and would be very much appreciated.

Thanks!
Lucille Guarino

We hope you enjoyed reading this title from:

BLACK ROSE
writing™

www.blackrosewriting.com

Subscribe to our mailing list – *The Rosevine* – and receive **FREE** books, daily deals, and stay current with news about upcoming releases and our hottest authors.
Scan the QR code below to sign up.

Already a subscriber? Please accept a sincere thank you for being a fan of Black Rose Writing authors.

View other Black Rose Writing titles at www.blackrosewriting.com/books and use promo code **PRINT** to receive a **20% discount** when purchasing.

Made in United States
Orlando, FL
06 August 2024